Praise for *The Jackal's Share* by Chris Morgan Jones

"The novel is as much Raymond Chandler as John le Carré; as much *The Big Sleep* as *The Spy Who Came in from the Cold*. . . . Chris Morgan Jones has more than equaled his powerful debut and in Ben Webster has created a flawed (of course), likeable central character. I look forward to getting to know him better." —*The Observer* (London)

"With a British appreciation for understatement, Jones elegantly executes the basic elements of the conventional thriller. Take one lone-wolf agent and set him on the trail of an enigmatic big shot with sketchy business associates. Throw in some swanky locales, a few well-placed corpses, and brewing trouble in our hero's marriage. Wrap it all up with a couple of truly tense cliffhangers, and the result is what the great but apologetic thriller writer Graham Greene famously downplayed as 'an entertainment.' . . . Terrific news for fans of first-class thrillers."
—Maureen Corrigan, NPR.com

"Comparisons with Le Carré have bedevilled Jones from the outset. But he does invite them, and never more so than in this elegant novel about the dark, amoral charisma of the superrich. . . . Murky, mesmerising stuff." —*The Guardian* (London)

"Ambivalent as ever about the ethics of the superrich and his part in solving their problems, Webster proves to be the ethically troubled anti-Bond. A more-than-worthy sequel with deft, complex, and believable plotting, tense, gut-wrenching action, and classy literary writing."
—*Kirkus Reviews* (starred review)

"A surprising plot and deceptively simple prose distinguish Jones's exceptional thriller, his second after his impressive debut, 2012's *The Silent Oligarch*." —*Publishers Weekly* (starred review)

D066086-4

PENGUIN BOOKS

THE JACKAL'S SHARE

For over a decade Chris Morgan Jones worked for Kroll, the world's largest investigations company, where he specialized in Russian matters and international disputes. He lives in London with his wife and two children. *The Jackal's Share* is his second novel.

THE JACKAL'S SHARE

CHRIS MORGAN JONES

PENGUIN BOOKS

PENGUIN BOOKS
Published by the Penguin Group
Penguin Group (USA) LLC
375 Hudson Street
New York, New York 10014

USA | Canada | UK | Ireland | Australia | New Zealand | India | South Africa | China
penguin.com
A Penguin Random House Company

First published in the United States of America by The Penguin Press,
a member of Penguin Group (USA) Inc., 2013
Published in Penguin Books 2014

Copyright © 2013 by Christopher Morgan Jones.
Penguin supports copyright. Copyright fuels creativity, encourages diverse voices,
promotes free speech, and creates a vibrant culture. Thank you for buying an authorized
edition of this book and for complying with copyright laws by not reproducing, scanning,
or distributing any part of it in any form without permission. You are supporting writers
and allowing Penguin to continue to publish books for every reader.

THE LIBRARY OF CONGRESS HAS CATALOGED THE HARDCOVER
EDITION AS FOLLOWS:

Morgan Jones, Chris, 1971–
The jackal's share / Chris Morgan Jones.
pages cm
ISBN 978-1-59420-535-4 (hc.)
ISBN 978-0-14-312445-0 (pbk.)
1. Art dealers—England—Fiction. 2. Murder victims—Iran—Fiction.
3. Murder—Investigation—Fiction. I. Title.
PR6113.O7483J33 2013
823'.92—dc23
201203951

Printed in the United States of America
1   3   5   7   9   10   8   6   4   2

DESIGNED BY AMANDA DEWEY

This is a work of fiction. Names, characters, places, and incidents either are the product of
the author's imagination or are used fictitiously, and any resemblance to actual persons,
living or dead, businesses, companies, events, or locales is entirely coincidental.

For David and Carolyn

"If you do not understand a man,
you cannot crush him.
And if you do understand him,
very probably you will not."

G. K. Chesterton

PART

ONE

1.

FOR SOMEBODY SO ELEGANT, in such harmony with the world, Darius Qazai wasn't difficult to spot. In a slow, stately progress he made his way through the church, shaking hands, stooping to offer his condolences, every word heartfelt, every gesture correct, until one by one the congregation settled and Qazai, his face set between solemnity and quiet grief, took his seat in the first pew. It was an immaculate performance and Webster, watching closely from the back, wondered whether it was sincere or merely smooth, and whether he really welcomed the opportunity to find out. In the still air around them Bach softly rose and fell.

A somber rumble as everyone stood, then a pair of hymns: "The King of Love My Shepherd Is," "Thine Be the Glory." Webster sang serviceably now, if a little low, but the church was full and his uneven bass lost inside the swell of sound; above the multitude soared the pure, clear chords of the choir, and beside him he could just make out Hammer's reedy tenor. He sang, paying little heed to the familiar words, and as he looked about him at the inclined heads, dappled with evening light from the stained glass, wondered who all the disparate mourners were. Near Qazai stood the dead man's clients, glossed with the unmistakable sheen of the truly rich: light tans, pristine shirt collars, distant gazes, discreet black hats on the women's heads; across the aisle, the dead man's family, his widow, his two teenage sons, all in black; and the rest—an irregular group of English, Americans and Iranians in tweed jackets and patterned shawls and corduroy suits, a little unpressed—these, Webster guessed, were antiques people. There must have been three hundred mourners altogether.

The priest said some words, another hymn was sung, and the time came for the first address. As Qazai crossed to the pulpit and climbed its dozen wooden steps Webster noticed how fluently he moved and how carefully his expression suggested respect, as if to calm any fears that his presence might overwhelm the occasion. Standing ten feet above the nave he paused for a long time, his arms locked on the lectern, drawing his audience in, his hair and beard pure white and cropped short, his eyes sky blue and alight with confidence. Webster had seen that light before, in those who had achieved everything they had set out to achieve, who were satisfied that they had few, if any, peers. In another it might have looked like arrogance but in Qazai it sat easily as fact.

He spoke only when he sensed that he had everyone, and when he did his voice, though deep, carried effortlessly to the last pew, where Webster crossed his hands over his order of service and listened.

"'In death's dark vale I fear no ill, with thee, dear Lord, beside me.'" A moment's pause. "Stirring words. In death's dark vale."

He took a long breath, as if to steady himself.

"Cyrus Mehr was a great man. A great man and a great Iranian. A man of courage, honor, and fine sensibility. A man who has left behind him a legacy that will outlive us all. I am honored to have known him." Qazai continued in this vein for a little while, full of fine words, before turning down the rhetoric and sketching his relationship with his friend. They had met at a sale of pre-Islamic art over twenty years earlier, at the tail end of that foul war between Iran and Iraq, and had talked about "the twin perils of war and ideology" that then endangered the most precious artifacts of ancient Persia. "A mutually beneficial professional bond" had resulted, by which Qazai seemed to mean that Mehr, through his dealership, had sourced antiques for him throughout the Middle East, so that over time the two men had grown closer, dealer and client had become friends, and when Qazai had set up his foundation Mehr had been the natural choice to be its head. For a decade now, under his courageous leadership, the Qazai Foundation for the Preservation of Persian Art had been a source of hope for all those who would see truth and beauty triumph over violence and oppression.

Webster was half impressed, half wary. For all its sentimentality and the odd moment of bombast, this was an elegant speech, as effortless and steady as the man's promenade through the church half an hour earlier. But Qazai had the statesman's assumption of authority, and to Webster looked like his least favorite kind of client—the kind that wholly believes what he says.

"Cyrus Mehr, then," Qazai went on, "was a great man. A man of principles in a world that has eroded them. A man who stood for something." He paused. "Something important." Looking around the church and up at the vaulted ceiling, as if drawing inspiration from the gods, he took another long breath, and when he spoke again there was a new intensity in his face.

"It has been two months since my friend Cyrus was murdered. Since he was brutally taken in the country of his birth, which, despite everything, he continued to love. As many here still love it. As I still love it. And still we do not know who killed him; still we do not know why it was done. The Iranian government will not tell us, though I believe they know only too well, for they have long ago forgotten the value of a human life.

"They say that he was smuggling, that he was murdered by his criminal friends. This, everyone here knows, is nonsense. Cyrus was a defender of beauty, and of truth, and in today's Iran, to defend those things will get you killed. A land of ancient poetry has been destroyed, and its rulers become mere peddlers of terror, and hatred, and above all fear.

"But I will tell you this, friends of Cyrus, friends of mine." He paused once more, and in that moment the zeal in his eyes seemed to glow through the mask. "Cyrus Mehr did not die in vain. Cyrus Mehr stood for something, and his life meant something. Something beautiful, and true, and, yes, worth dying for. For Cyrus, the vale of death will not be dark."

Qazai bowed his head for a second, and when he looked up again Webster thought he could make out a tear glistening in his eye. If this was all performance, he was some performer.

OUTSIDE, London was warm and bright with evening sun and the noise of Trafalgar Square an assault after the peace of the church. Webster and Hammer were among the last to emerge into the crowd gathered on the great broad steps and stood to one side, awaiting their instructions, while Qazai moved smoothly from group to group like the host at a party.

"What do you think?" said Hammer.

"Like I said. You can have him."

"Tell me you're not intrigued."

Webster squinted against the low sun. "That was quite a speech."

Hammer smiled. "If he didn't have an ego he wouldn't be a great man."

"I don't trust great men," said Webster as a small, precise-looking figure broke away from a cluster of people and walked toward them. He was slight, and so pale that the sun seemed to shine through him. He shook Webster's hand, exchanged nods with him and turned to Hammer.

"Mr. Hammer? Yves Senechal. Mr. Qazai's personal representative." His accent was softly French, his voice scratchy, insubstantial.

"Delighted, Mr. Senechal. Ben's told me a lot about you."

"Gentlemen," said Senechal, "the car is around the corner. Mr. Qazai sends his apologies—he cannot break away. He will join us shortly."

And with that Senechal turned and headed north, toward Charing Cross Road, at no great speed and with a curious, weightless walk.

Hammer leaned in to Webster and whispered, mischief on his face: "So this is your spooky friend."

2.

A s a boy Webster had been a chorister, until his voice had broken, and he still felt the pull of the church's rituals even if its teachings had long ago lost their hold. Some of the stories had stayed with him, the narratives shaky but the mood—the sunlit, rock-like clarity of both Testaments— still clear, and with little effort he could recall how they had once made him feel: pained, guilty, compassionate, at one with sinners everywhere. When he was twelve he had been asked to serve on Good Friday, a great honor, and following the priest in his procession from one Station of the Cross to the next he had had to pinch the soft flesh on his upper arm to hold back the tears.

There were twenty-five years now between him and that devout, per- haps better incarnation. A full ten years, even, since he had left Russia, all traces of his faith trodden out, and in that time he had built, with his wife Elsa, a happy, blessed life that he gave thanks for every day. The thanks were undirected now, but he gave them nonetheless, and until this year had rarely stopped to wonder where he meant them to go. But ever since Lock's funeral, scenes from distant childhood had been breaking in on his thoughts and causing him to wonder whether they were a message or an indulgence; whether they were trying to tell him something or merely offer some obscure comfort to his subconscious.

Lock had died just before Christmas; the funeral, which Webster had attended discreetly, had been held on Christmas Eve; and for the rest of winter and all of the spring his death had occupied Webster without let-up. The Germans had wanted him back for further questioning, and then to give evidence to the inquest—whose predictable verdict, finally, was that Lock had been murdered in Berlin by sinister forces (*finsteren Mächte* in German) who had meant to assassinate his client, Konstantin Malin. The report hadn't said so, of course, but Webster knew that one of the few clear conclusions to be made from the whole episode was that without his meddling Lock would be alive.

So perhaps it wasn't surprising if his mind was searching around for solace. Let it; he couldn't control it. But for himself, he didn't want to be soothed. All he wanted was to work, concentrate, be a good father—and let time and fate decide whether he was doing the right thing.

Three days before Mehr's memorial service, then, on a dark, wet afternoon in early May that was more like winter than the end of spring, Webster had found himself in a boardroom by St. Paul's delivering findings to a firm of private equity investors. Through the glass that covered one side of the building he could see a few tourists scattered over the cathedral steps, the freshly cleaned stone of the facade shining in the rain, the great dome above, and across the river, the dull brown of Bankside tower cutting across the gray line of the Sydenham Hills ten miles beyond. It was a grand view, even in the half-light, and a grand backdrop for two young men in suits, one of them taking notes, the other playing with a hand press (which, he had explained, was part of the therapy for a boxing injury). They seemed as keen to be there as he was.

Four weeks earlier they had given him a routine piece of work: to find out whether there was anything about a man called Richard Clifford that might embarrass them when they came to sell his fashion business on the Stock Exchange. It was due to list the following month, and because the market was quiet, and the company prominent, the world, Webster had been told, would be watching.

Clifford's reputation was good, his visible profile, in the accepted phrase, spotless: no scandal, no litigation, no bankruptcies. But a particularly voluble former client had mentioned "that business in the newspapers"—lightheartedly almost, joking that such things would be viewed rather more seriously now—and when pressed had tightened up, saying it had been a long time ago and that was all he was prepared to say. After a day in the library, Webster's researcher had found two articles, both from the late 1980s, that set out with typical clarity how the *News of the World* had caught Clifford in a sting operation handing over money in exchange for sex with an underage prostitute. A picture showed him bearded and young, all of thirty-one, shielding his face from the photographer he had found on his doorstep one morning.

"You're kidding," said the man with the injured hand, leaning forward on the table between them, his shoulders massive under a shirt that seemed too small for him. He had a taut, blockish face framed with thinning fair hair and set in the constant frown of the important man. His colleague, making notes, merely shook his head and exhaled slowly.

"I'm not," said Webster.

"How could he have kept that quiet?"

"He was charged with procuring but it never went to court."

"Why not?"

"I don't know. I suspect his lawyer claimed it was entrapment and the CPS got nervous."

"Bullshit."

Webster raised an eyebrow.

"He can't have known she was underage."

"He knew." From the wallet of documents in front of him Webster picked a large, folded piece of paper and slid it across the table. "They printed the advertisement they used."

The boxer opened the article, studied it for perhaps ten seconds, and as he passed it to his friend stared at Webster for a long moment as if that might force him to stop this nonsense and finally tell the truth. There was sweat on his brow and the frown had turned from grave to incredulous. Webster knew what he was thinking: there goes my fucking deal.

"Is that your only source? The *News of the World*?"

Webster nodded.

"Well it's not surprising it never went to court, is it?"

"The *News of the World* didn't make things up. Not like that. Not then."

"Of course not."

"They had more lawyers than any other newspaper in London. I talked to the journalist. There were two, one died. It was part of a series of stings. They advertised in a Dutch contact magazine and reeled them in. Clifford's was the first letter they received."

"For fuck's sake. Are you making this up?" He shook his head, took his phone from his pocket and left the room.

For a moment Webster and the boxer's colleague looked at each other.

"How bad is this?" said the colleague, finally.

"What he did or what it means?" Webster was losing patience.

"You know."

"It means your man used to be repugnant. He may still be. And if I know, others know."

The client nodded once and sighed. "Christ." He wrote something in his notebook. "Who else?"

"The journalist. She's retired. Her editor, if he remembers. And then you tell me. Circulation was about three million at the time."

The boxer came back into the room, finishing his call, and stood at one end of the conference table.

"No . . . no. I'll tell him . . . Fuck, I don't know." He hung up and looked at Webster. "Have you written this down?"

His colleague stopped writing. Webster sighed. "This," he took a thin document from the plastic wallet in front of him, "is a draft report. Of all the things I made up."

"Take it home. Shred it. And if this appears in the fucking papers I'll know how it got there."

Webster stared at him. "Excuse me?"

He held Webster's eye. "You're loving this. Do you have any idea how much work we've done?"

Webster gathered his papers and stood up.

"You'll have my bill in the morning. If I were you I'd think seriously about quietly retiring Mr. Clifford. At the very least."

He made to leave, but the boxer blocked his way, standing at the end of the table by the door.

"Two years," he said. "Two years of my time, his time. Half this office has worked on this."

Webster studied him for a moment; there was sweat along his hairline and his neck was tight against his collar. He was giving another of his deliberate stares, and tilting his head forward slightly, presumably for menace.

"Perhaps you should have come to me earlier," Webster said.

The boxer put his good hand on Webster's chest. Webster left it there and looked him in the eye, wondering for a moment what would happen if he were to bring his head down hard on that stubby, flattened nose.

"I'm leaving now."

"If this deal doesn't go through, you don't get paid."

"If I don't get paid, you break our contract, and I tell everyone about the company you keep. Now take your hand off, and move."

"You'd do that, wouldn't you?"

"If it was up to me I'd have done it already."

The boxer finally stepped back a full pace and Webster passed him, nodding to his colleague and thanking him politely for his time.

A FINE, cold spring rain fell as Webster walked back to Ikertu through old streets toward the Inner Temple, where warm squares of light glowed in the dusk. This whole block of London, half a square mile to the west of the City, was given over to the service of clients. The lawyers had been here for hundreds of years, and after them had come accountants and advisers and consultants of every stripe. And a certain sort of detective, Webster thought.

In the rooms all around him lawsuits were being compiled, audits made, presentations pored over, efficiencies mooted, debts rationalized, strategies dreamed up by a legion of associates and directors and partners, all recording their hours, some their minutes, all billing at a healthy rate. It was its own world with its own etiquette, rituals, dress, but Webster, in his tenth year of this, still struggled to feel like he belonged. When he sent out a bill to a client and saw that they were paying thousands of pounds a day for him, he wondered first how it could be so much, then how any client could possibly afford to pay, then what possible value his work might have. He didn't doubt himself; he knew that he was good at what he did. Rather, he watched the hours being worked and noted and charged and found it hard to believe that any of them were contributing much to the well-being of the world.

There was a message for him from the office. Waiting at Ikertu was a new client who had dropped in unannounced, asked to speak to Hammer, and in his absence said that he was happy to wait for Webster's return. The ones who didn't make appointments were usually flakes, and Webster found himself hoping that it wouldn't take long.

His first thought, on seeing the strange figure across the Ikertu lobby, was that he must have been raised in the dark—forced, perhaps, in an unlit shed, and not yet colored in. He was rigidly monochrome: black hair, precisely parted against the palest skin; a white shirt framed by a black tie and suit; black socks, black shoes and beside him a briefcase, also black, which had folded over it a dark-gray macintosh. He read a newspaper at arm's length and sat so still that he might have been set from a mold. An hour had passed since he had called but he seemed unconcerned, as if time, like color, was something worldly that he scorned.

Sensing that someone was approaching he looked up and stood. He was a head shorter than Webster, insubstantial inside his well-cut clothes, and gave a strange, confusing impression of lifelessness competing with great energy. Webster couldn't tell how old he was: forty, perhaps, or fifty.

"Ben Webster," said Webster. "Sorry to have kept you. I had a meeting."

The man's hand was cool as Webster shook it, but dry, the bony grip weak. He held Webster's for a moment and smiled an empty smile. Up close his skin was like wax, tight against his cheekbones and faintly translucent, and his eyes were a deep petrol gray, the fine red lines in the whites the only color in his face. But what was most striking as he talked were his teeth, which were little and sharp like a badger's and discolored almost to blackness.

"Delighted, Mr. Webster." The voice was thin and slightly hoarse. He reached into his jacket pocket, pulled out a wallet and drew from it a business card which he handed to Webster. On the thick cream card were the words *Yves Senechal. Avocat à la Cour, Paris.* No address, no telephone number. Webster had not expected him to be a lawyer. Lawyers tended to try harder to make a first impression benign.

"Mr. Hammer, he is not here?"

"I'm afraid not. Did you have an appointment?"

"I prefer to see you as I find you. You are his partner?"

"I'm his associate."

Senechal thought for a moment, the smile gone.

"Very well. Can we talk in private?"

Webster nodded and led him down a dark corridor past several closed doors to a meeting room, Senechal following with a slow, light step. When Ikertu had taken this office, a floor in a tall glass-lined box, Hammer had named each of these rooms after his favorite fictional detectives: Marlowe, Maigret, Beck. This, the largest of them all, was the Wolfe room. Through the window that made up one wall it looked west across Lincoln's Inn, today a dull green square in the spring gloom.

Senechal declined coffee, took a glass of water, sipped it almost imperceptibly through his thin lips and began. He sat upright, tucked in close to the table, perfectly still.

"I am not here on my own behalf. I have a client who needs your assistance, perhaps."

Webster let him go on.

"He is a very significant man." He spoke slowly, his accent heavily French, and his eyes never left Webster's. "Very significant."

Webster waited again, struggling to maintain Senechal's gaze and finding his ghostly face difficult to address. There was something unfinished about it.

"Before I begin," said Senechal, showing no signs of losing his self-possession, "can I ask you who you are? What is your career? I like to know who people are."

So do I, thought Webster, but let it go. "I've worked here for six years, more or less. Before that for a large American company doing much the same thing."

"You have always done this work?"

"I used to be a journalist. In Russia."

Senechal nodded. "So you know about lies. That is good." He looked at Webster for a moment, as if assessing him dispassionately. "Why did you move companies?"

"Why did I come here? For the chance to work with Ike. With Mr. Hammer."

Another nod, and a pause.

"My client, he has a problem with his reputation," Senechal said at last. "We believe that someone has said things that are unjust about him."

Webster thought he knew what that meant. Some powerful man who had grown accustomed to his lawyers smoothing out every problem had been refused a visa or a loan and was experiencing an unfamiliar sense of powerlessness. He sat back in his chair and crossed his arms. "You'd like us to find out who?"

"Later, perhaps. No. That is not it." Senechal shook his head once, an exact movement. "He would like you to investigate himself. To discover that which can be discovered."

"And then?"

"And then, if there are lies, you can correct them."

"If they're lies."

"They are lies." Senechal's meager lips pressed tight in a line.

Webster thought for a moment. "We don't often do that sort of work." He paused, watching his guest. "How bad is it?"

"Excuse me?"

"The damage. To your client."

"It is an irritant."

"Because this is expensive work."

"I know," said Senechal, with another unexpressive smile.

"Who is your client?"

"I cannot say."

"I can't help you until you do."

Senechal reached down for his briefcase and put it on the table. He took a key from a ticket pocket inside his jacket, unlocked the single clasp and from within drew out two or three pages of paper bound in a Perspex folder. Sliding the briefcase to one side he placed the document neatly in front of him.

"This," he said, "is an agreement I wish you to sign. It commits you to make a proposal in general terms. You will tell us how you work and how much it will cost. If we are satisfied I will reveal my client's identity to you and we can decide the specific things. Between times you will not tell anyone of this conversation."

Webster smiled. "I'm afraid we don't work like that."

Senechal shifted forward in his chair and leaned his elbows carefully on the table.

"This matter is sensitive. Very sensitive. If we do not like the way you work, my client must have protection."

"Everything you say in this room is confidential. As is the fact that you're here. But I'm afraid I won't sign anything until I know who you work for."

Senechal's eyes registered a moment's confusion, as if he found something illogical. "This is a lucrative project. For a significant client."

"I won't make commitments to a man I don't know."

Senechal breathed in sharply, rubbed his chin, made to say something and after some internal calculation thought better of it. Fixing his gaze on Webster and letting him know by it what a foolish decision he had just made, he stood up. "Very well. We can go elsewhere. Thank you for your time."

Webster nodded and at that moment realized what had been troubling him: Senechal's eyes did not belong in his face. Somewhere deep inside them, behind the gray irises, there was a fervor, all too alive, that his pallid body struggled to contain.

He saw his peculiar visitor to the elevators, thanked him, and without anxiety filed him among Ikertu's discarded clients, a motley group of suspicious husbands, miserly bankers and sinister fantasists whose cases were too slippery or too preposterous to take. The client who was too grand to be identified was a rare subclass that would usually have piqued his interest, but some strong instinct told him that he had been right not to compromise—that whatever conflicting forces drove this odd, unpalatable man they were not worth closer acquaintance.

Senechal, though, was too ghostly not to haunt him, and he wasn't surprised when he returned. Two days later an envelope had arrived at Ikertu's offices, of the finest cream paper, addressed to Webster in looping black ink. It had been delivered by hand. The lettering was bold, just short of elaborate, and on the flap was embossed a capital Q. Inside was an invitation to Mehr's memorial service and a note, in the same hand, on a small sheet of paper with another Q at its head:

> *Dear Mr. Webster,*
>
> *I would be honored if you and Mr. Hammer would join me at this important service. We will have time to talk afterward. I may need to call upon your assistance.*
>
> *Yours sincerely,*
> *Darius Qazai*

Looking back, Webster thought that this had been a fitting introduction—grand, proper, apparently frank but in the end thoroughly calculated—but at the beginning he was intrigued, as anyone would be. Qazai had never been a target, nor a client, but if the rich lists were to be believed, it was only a matter of time before he became one or the other. And if this was Senechal's master, he might become both.

3.

AFTER THE SERVICE SENECHAL'S DRIVER took them west across town through Knightsbridge and Kensington, the sun now low ahead of them and London, all red brick and cream stucco, lit up with spring light. The trees of Hyde Park were newly in leaf. Hammer talked, as he always did, quizzing Senechal about his business, his acquaintances in Paris, his views on colonial corruption, Camus, football. Senechal's replies were courteous, brief and unsatisfying. Webster watched the city glide past and listened to Hammer show off his range.

The car eventually stopped outside a restaurant on an otherwise residential street in Olympia. *Lavash*, it was called: *Iranian cuisine, Berian our specialty*. It was early still, and they were the first people in the place. Senechal was clearly known here, and the manager ushered them through the cramped restaurant to a private room that gave onto a courtyard at the back of the building. The simple decoration did its best to conjure Iran. Two of the walls were hung with a gold fabric, a third with a dozen photographs of Iranian landscapes: a fortress in the mountains, a palace on a lake, shepherds' huts on green foothills. Opposite, through the French doors, a band of light touched the roofs of the houses beyond.

Drinks were brought, with olives and flat bread, and the three men sat,

Senechal unhurriedly typing e-mails on his BlackBerry, Hammer—finally
out of questions—stirring his Scotch and soda, and Webster wondering
silently whether a glass of white wine was likely to do much to encourage
Senechal to open up. He eventually broke the silence.

"So it was Qazai."

Senechal tapped a few last keys and put down his phone. He looked no
more human than he had under the bright office lights of Cursitor Street,
and his black teeth showed as he talked.

"Yes. It was Qazai."

"When I looked you up after our meeting I found no mention of him."

"Good. That is as it should be. I am Mr. Qazai's personal lawyer. I never
engage with his public affairs."

A moment's silence, broken by Hammer. "Who else do you represent,
Mr. Senechal?"

"That is not relevant here. But most of my time I dedicate to Mr. Qazai
and his family."

Hammer nodded. "The faithful retainer. Could you tell us a little
about him? While we're waiting."

"You have done some research, I imagine," said Senechal. Not an objection, just a statement of fact.

"Only so much."

Senechal paused a moment, looking at Hammer and making a
decision.

"I will start with his business, then I will talk about him and finally his
family." He said it with the air of a man who leaves nothing unorganized.

Senechal gave them a well-rehearsed account, beginning with some
figures that were clearly intended to impress. Tabriz Asset Management
was one of the largest asset management companies in the world. Its headquarters were in London but a large office in Dubai, run by Qazai's son
Timur, looked after its many clients and investments in the Middle East. Altogether it looked after some sixty-three billion dollars of clients' money,
investing it in debt, properties, currencies, public companies, private
companies—anywhere it believed it could make money. And it made
money. In the previous decade it had made a return, on average, of twelve

percent a year: a million dollars invested in 2000 was now worth three. Hammer said that he wished he'd had a million dollars back then, and Senechal ignored the pleasantry as completely as if it made no sense to him at all. Hammer sat back and let their stand-in host continue his eulogy uninterrupted.

Tabriz was not a company, it was an institution. It had been built by the vision and fortitude of one man, and if they took the job they would soon discover how great Darius Qazai truly was. In 1978, still young, he and his family, alongside so many of his countrymen, had been forced to flee to London from Iran; and with his father, a senior banker and confidant of the Shah, he had set up the first Tabriz company. Poor health had seen the father retire not long afterward, but Qazai was unstoppable. He had invested heavily in property in the eighties and emerging markets in the nineties, had made a fortune in both and today could be said to be the most successful Iranian businessman in the world.

His success had been others' good fortune, too. He was a generous and enlightened philanthropist who funded educational projects throughout the Middle East, favoring those that helped women to raise their families out of poverty. Schools in Palestine, Yemen and Oman bore his name. And he was perhaps the world's most serious collector of Persian art, his foundation the leading authority on pre-Islamic and Islamic art from the region.

Senechal was certainly a loyal evangelist for his client. Most of this Webster had found out for himself in the last day or two but hearing it delivered coherently—and not without an odd vehemence, even passion— Qazai's life story was impressive. He was not wholly self-made, since his family had been rich before the revolution and wealthy enough afterward, but his achievements were his and his talents clear. One of the articles that Webster had read had put it simply: "a canny investor and a brilliant salesman, not least in selling himself." His clients loved him, if Senechal and the newspapers were to be believed, and his commitment to education seemed genuine. For Webster, schooled in the ways of Russia, where it was almost impossible to be a billionaire without stealing something from someone, all this seemed strange, refreshing and unlikely.

Senechal had more, but before he could move on to his master's family,

Qazai himself arrived, immediately supplying all the color that his lawyer seemed to drain from the room. As everyone stood, he made for Hammer, took his hand and shook it vigorously, his other hand on Hammer's elbow, his face smiling and earnest.

"Mr. Hammer. It is a great honor to meet a leader in his field. A great honor." For once, though he wouldn't have disagreed with Qazai's judgment, Hammer seemed off balance, and despite himself Webster smiled.

"I have read about your exploits with pleasure," Hammer said. "If I was not doing what I do I should want your job."

Qazai moved around the table to Webster. "You must be Mr. Webster. A Russian expert, if I am not mistaken. Of some distinction, I understand. I must thank you for seeing Mr. Senechal, and apologize for the clumsy introduction we tried to make. I have got used to guarding my personal affairs more closely than perhaps is necessary." Webster was wary of the flattery, but had to concede this was elegant. "Gentlemen, many thanks to you both for coming all this way. I appreciate it greatly. Please, sit, sit."

Qazai sat down at the head of the table with his back to the window, smiled at Hammer and Webster in turn, took an olive and chewed. He seemed as invincible in this small room as he had in church, but what Webster saw for the first time was his health. He glowed. According to the articles Webster had read he was sixty-one, but he moved and talked with the force of a much younger man; his cheeks were taut beneath the beard, his eyes glitteringly clear, and he held himself as an athlete might, as if every muscle was only for the moment in repose.

Webster had the sense, without understanding quite why, that Qazai was not a private man. His life was lived in view, and he liked it there. You had to read his face carefully to detect the faintest signs of what might be within: in the eyes and the lines around them you could see experience—hard-won, guarded—and a watchfulness that suggested he was slow to trust.

"Gentlemen, you will like this place. I have been coming here once a week for the last twenty-five years. It is nothing fancy, but trust me, the fancy places get it wrong. This is real Iranian food." He took another olive and smiled benignly. Like a king condescending to visit his people, thought Webster, saying nothing.

Qazai, continuing to beam at his guests, shook out his napkin, and the others did the same. Hammer took his and, as he always did, tucked it into his shirt collar, a New York habit that he insisted was merely practical but clearly gave him pleasure; Senechal, for his part, carefully unfolded his and smoothed it out precisely on his lap. Waiters came and poured water.

"That was a beautiful service," said Hammer.

"Wasn't it? More so for being so sad. Thank you for indulging me. I had thought that we could come on here together but there were people to talk to. I was moved that so many came."

Hammer gave a respectful nod in acknowledgment.

"How do you think he died?" said Webster, sensing that Hammer was shooting him a look for his directness.

"Like a hero. Or like a dog. You take your pick." Qazai held Webster's eye for a moment. "Mr. Webster, even the simplest things in Iran are difficult. Insanely difficult. They were hard before but now they are impossible. The Arab Spring is not a term I like. My people are not Arabs. But we are all caged together by these, these little men. These vicious little men." He sighed and shook his head. "You were a journalist, I think?" Webster held his eye and nodded. "In Iran this simple thing—to find something out, to tell people about it—cannot be done. Journalists there are stooges of the state, or scared, or in prison." He paused to allow the weight of his words to be felt. "So you see how impossible it is to investigate anything. Honestly speaking, to know what happened to Cyrus . . . You understand Russia. Iran has its similarities. You understand that some things will never be known in such places. I fear that this will be one of them."

"Would you like to know?"

Qazai's lips pressed together, his eyes lost their shine and for a moment Webster thought his composure was about to slip; but he caught himself, and his smile reappeared. "When we are done with this first piece of work, Mr. Webster, perhaps then I will send you to Isfahan to find out." The smile stayed on his lips.

Two waiters came in bearing trays of food: small plates of smoked egg-plant and spinach in yogurt; three bowls together, one containing walnut halves, one smoked fish, one unshelled broad beans; a basket of the thinnest flatbread; and a huge plate of radishes, spring onions, deep red tomatoes, bushy green bunches of coriander, tarragon and mint. Qazai passed the bread to Hammer and signaled that everyone should help themselves, while Webster watched him, marveling at the deep shine of the man.

"Now, gentlemen. To why I called you here. I will not insult you again by insisting what we say in this room is confidential. It is delicate. It goes to the heart of my affairs." Qazai took sea salt from a small glass bowl, ground it between his fingertips onto his plate and rolled a radish slowly over it.

"I have been working for some time—quietly, you understand—to sell my business. Or some of my business. I plan to retire from the day-to-day and leave my son in charge. One day his reputation will eclipse mine, but he needs room. He is ready to move past his father. It is time. And I want to take some money out, for this and that." He turned from Hammer to Web-ster and back again, diligently dividing his attention, underscoring his words with slow, deliberate gestures. "Now, for my investors to be happy I need a buyer with a name as powerful as my own, and up until two weeks ago I thought I'd found one. A fund manager in the U.S. You would know the name. A perfect fit. Talented people. They wanted emerging markets exposure, we have much the same risk profile—perfect."

He paused to check that his audience was keeping pace; Hammer nod-ded for him to go on.

"The sale was agreed, we were due to announce it, and at the eleventh hour they called it off. Wouldn't tell me why." He put the radish in his mouth, chewed deliberately, and swallowed, frowning now at the thought of this reversal like a child who had been refused its way. "Yves and I," he gestured to Senechal, "could not get them to tell us. I called and called. And then finally their legal counsel tells us that—what did he say, Yves?"

"That you did not pass the test." Senechal let the words slip from his mouth with distaste.

"Ridiculous. That I didn't pass the test, and that they were sorry. He wouldn't elaborate. When I asked him was this final, could I do anything, all he said was that I might talk to you."

"Who was he?" said Hammer.

"Can we come to that in a moment?" Qazai took another radish and dredged it in salt. "Now, what does this suggest to you, Mr. Hammer?"

"That you failed the due diligence."

"Exactly. I failed the due diligence. They ran the rule over me, and they think they have found something." Arms wide he appealed to Hammer and Webster in turn. "Preposterous."

"Have you any idea what that might be?" Webster asked.

"None at all, gentlemen. That's what I want you to find out."

"What they think they know?" asked Hammer.

"Whatever nonsense they think they know. Then I want you to tell everybody that it is nonsense."

Webster asked the next question. "Is this for your pride, or to complete the sale?"

Qazai smiled, a different smile with steel in it, and scratched at the beard along his jawbone. "For my honor, Mr. Webster." Webster held his eye, something stern in it now, and gave the merest nod.

"Why don't you just sell to someone else?"

"Because they may find the same thing."

Hammer interposed. "You know we only do this when we're fairly sure we won't find anything?"

As he turned to Hammer Qazai's brow relaxed. "I am confident you will find nothing to trouble you."

Hammer sat back in his chair. "We need their report," he said finally. "Have you asked for it?"

"I have not seen it." Qazai looked to Senechal.

"We asked for any documents that might help. They gave us nothing."

"We'll get a copy," said Hammer. "If we decide to take you on we'll need to investigate that problem, whatever it is, and we'll need to investigate you. I can't say that this little piece of you is OK until I know that the rest of you is OK." He stopped to check that Qazai had understood.

"OK." He went on. "You'll give us full access—to files, colleagues, yourself. Perhaps even your family. We'll ask a lot of questions, and we'll poke around. Then we'll write a report. What's in the report is entirely up to us; where it goes is up to you. Tell us to destroy it and we'll destroy it. The whole thing will cost a lot of money and you'll have to pay us up front because otherwise no one will believe that we're telling the truth."

Qazai laughed. "You've done this before."

"Not often. We turn most people down."

"Excellent. I do not like ambiguity."

"Neither do I. Questions?"

"No. I don't think so." He looked down the table at Senechal. "Yves?"

Senechal, Webster realized, hadn't yet eaten anything. Throughout the conversation he had been sitting perfectly still at the end of the table, his hands in his lap, moving only to take the occasional sip of his wine. "Who will do the work?"

"If we take it on, Ben."

"This is not a Russian matter."

Hammer smiled. "It might be. You never know." He turned to Qazai. "He's the best I have. Whatever's ailing you, he'll figure it out."

Qazai gave a single deep nod and looked at Senechal. "Are you happy?"

"I think so."

"Yves is never sure if he is happy." Another smile, bold and reassuring, to contrast with his lawyer's empty expression. "When will you decide?"

"Give us a week."

"A week it is. And if you say no, who else might we consider?"

Hammer smiled. "Mr. Qazai, I can with a clear conscience tell you that no one else could do this work. Everyone else is too small to take it on or too big and ugly to be believed."

"And people believe you?"

"They appear to."

Qazai nodded slowly, looking down at the table, considering something new. "So you and Mr. Webster, you are whiter than white? For you to judge my reputation yours must be spotless, no?" He turned to Webster; though smiling, he had a certain challenge in his eyes.

"We don't judge it," said Webster. "We report it."

Qazai thought for a moment. "But to be good at your job you must lie from time to time?"

Hammer answered for him. "You're confusing two things. We don't lie about what we find."

"But you might lie to find it?"

Hammer's smile became a little fixed. "We will be very happy to lie on your behalf. With your permission."

Qazai laughed, beamed at Hammer and raised his glass.

THE NEXT MORNING, in the hope that air and water might bring some order to them, Webster woke early and took his thoughts to the bathing pond on Hampstead Heath. Long before six the sun was already full over the city but a northerly wind blew, and as he cycled uphill along the quiet streets it froze his hands until they were raw and locked on the handlebars. He passed milkmen crawling from house to house, dogs being walked, mini-cabs waiting for their passengers, until abruptly the houses ran out, the roads turned into tracks and he was on the heath, nature's stronghold in the north, extravagantly free and green this morning, the freshly opened leaves of the oaks and beeches calming the gusting wind and dulling the noise of London below.

To swim here through the winter you had to start in late summer and allow your body to adapt as the water gradually chilled, fooling it into accepting the unnatural cold. Webster had been coming here for years and knew its reserved rhythms. Even in May it was truly icy; by August, perhaps July, it would warm a little, and the summer swimmers would come— until October, when the temperature would drop and the pool would empty once again. There were no casual cold swimmers. Today there were a half-dozen people at most, and no one paid any attention to anyone else.

The water, as it always did, seemed to strip him of himself. In the changing room he shed his clothes, and as he dived into the still green-black the rest of him was sheared away. The cold left no space for thought. He swam lengths, dutifully, taking oxygen deep into his lungs, refreshing his

blood, but the swimming was not why he came here: the water alone, that
first dive, took all his clashing thoughts from him, and when they came
back they were different. They had shape; they had order. They fit together.

He swam briskly from end to end, a mechanical crawl, his mind empty
of everything except strains of organ music and images of the day before.
Qazai in the pulpit; Senechal sitting rigid, not touching his food; Qazai's
set smile, with its hint of what, exactly? Superiority. Or menace.

Hammer had liked Qazai, that was clear. When Webster had first met
Ike Hammer, he had thought that two things governed him: logic, and
a love of games. Games and battles. He lived on his own, and when he
wasn't working or running over the heath he was reading—countless books
of military history and game theory, accounts of political contests and
corporate disputes, biographies of generals, statesmen and revolutionaries.
The book he made reference to most often was *Napoleon's Military Cam-
paigns*, a volume eight inches thick that he loved so much he kept two copies, one in his office, one in his study at home. But if he had a favorite
subject it was boxing, the purest contest of all. He had no television in his
house, but would watch film of old fights on his computer, and if you drew
him out could talk entertainingly for hours about the relative merits of his
four favorites: Muhammad Ali, Jack Johnson, Sugar Ray Robinson and Joe
Louis. Robinson always came out on top: "Brains will outfox power every
time," he would say, in what might have been a summary of his personal
creed. One of the few times Webster had seen him lose his temper was when
a colleague had suggested that to fight for the pleasure of others was
barbaric.

For all this, and it had taken Webster some time to realize it, Hammer
was not a cold man. He liked people, and more than anything he liked to
talk to them, energetically and at length, so that when he discreetly grilled
a client as he had Qazai and Senechal the night before, he wasn't just
mining them for information, he was enjoying himself. Before founding
Ikertu he had been a journalist, and a good one. His writing, which Webster had made the effort over the years to track down, had great range,
moving from political scandal through corporate corruption to straight

war-reporting during a spell in Afghanistan. But it had great compassion too. During his first few months with the company Webster had thought that Ike enjoyed a good fight for fighting's sake and had found his zeal ghoulish, but he realized now that in conflict he found not just intellectual satisfaction (because conflict was always complex and always changing) but also the opportunity to see human beings at their best and their worst. More than anything he had become used to observing life when it was exaggerated, heightened in some way, and was impatient, as a result, with the mundane. This, Webster had come to believe, was why he lived alone.

Hammer's enthusiasm for people was catholic, and refused to discriminate between rich and poor, young and old, men and women. It also tended to be instant: he was all curiosity, and for a man who had made his life's work the discovery and keeping of secrets, strangely open. Webster was wholly different. Ever since his time in Russia he had been wary of the powerful. Unlike Hammer he was no logician, and had never stopped to analyze his condition, but he simply felt that people who sought wealth and influence beyond a decent norm were not to be trusted—that there was no honest motive for being an oligarch or a billionaire. The best were vainglorious, the worst vicious, and all, as far as he could see, in a world where most still had nothing, had much more than they could ever justify.

But Qazai was an interesting case. His fortune was innocuous, his reputation honorable, his politics sound. He gave to charity, helped preserve an ancient, delicate culture, railed publicly against a sinister and repugnant regime; Webster couldn't hope to emulate the good that he had done, certainly not while he himself continued in this compromised job. He was even courteous—a little fond of himself, perhaps, but on the available evidence, with reason. And yet Webster sensed, with no strong grounds but great conviction, that Qazai was somehow not right.

He struggled as he swam to assemble his case. The uneasy register of Mehr's memorial; the theatrics of the meeting; Qazai's quick charm; cold, rigid Senechal, a man for hiding secrets if ever he had seen one, and for resenting them, too, perhaps. And the story—the sale of the company, the affront to the great man's honor—was it plausible? Perhaps, but he had a feeling that a man like Qazai wouldn't come to a lowly detective agency to restore his formidable dignity.

On the fortieth length he began to tire and his thoughts defaulted to Richard Lock, as they often did in this place: it was here that he tried to make sense of what had happened in Berlin half a year before. Lock had been a lawyer, paid to hide money and assets, claiming them as his own so that his powerful Russian client could continue to steal unobserved. Webster had been paid to reveal those lies, not by someone who wanted to see them corrected but by someone who wanted the liar exposed, for his own, less than noble ends. He and Lock had both been middlemen. They had both been manipulated. And the deepest source of Webster's shame was that though he repented Lock's murder his anger lay in having been made a fool. It would never sit easily with him, and when he looked now at Qazai he saw, behind the charm and the polish, someone bent on deceiving him once more.

THE HOUSE WAS STILL ASLEEP when he returned. He showered, shaved and took Elsa a cup of tea, sliding into bed beside her; barely awake, she worked her back into his embrace. The room was cool and dark, but through an open window the wind, softly flapping a blind, let in an occasional flash of morning light.

"Jesus, your hands are cold." Her voice was laden with sleep.

"They're not. You're just warm."

They lay there for a minute or two, breathing in time.

"No one up?"

"No. Just us."

Elsa grunted. "Good swim?"

"All right. Quiet."

"What time did you get up?"

"About six."

"It was earlier than that."

Webster didn't say anything.

"What's the matter?"

"Nothing's the matter."

"Ben. Come on."

"It's fine."

She turned onto her other side, facing him, and propped her head on her hand.

"I'm going to tell Ike I won't do it."

She didn't reply.

"He'll make a better job of it in any case."

After a minute of silence she said, "I think he's trying to help you."

"How would that be?" He regretted the irritation in his voice.

"By getting you out of a rut."

"I don't see how this'll help."

Elsa was quiet again. She had the psychotherapist's knack of creating silence for her patient to fill.

"I just don't trust him," he said. "Not Ike, although he's being too clever by half. The client." He moved onto his back. "He's not a good man. And he wants us to say he is."

A pause. "I don't think that's it." He turned his head to look at her, and she went on. "Part of you was impressed by him. And that was confusing. You've got used to seeing the rich as the enemy. They're all corrupt." He looked away. "That's dangerous. It lessens you. It's an irrational fear."

"It's not a fear. It's an observation."

"All right, what about this one? He's charming, he gives his money away, he makes a good speech. What if he's OK? He's not an oligarch. He didn't have to steal anything. He just invests money." She paused. "But that doesn't fit, does it?"

"He makes a fortune doing nothing useful. I don't particularly like that. And I don't like the idea of being paid to give him a new lick of paint. I'm surprised Ike does. It's not what we do."

Elsa sat up in bed, reached for her tea and took a sip. She looked down at him but he didn't meet her eye.

"Poor Ike," she said. "One day he's going to lose patience. Do you ever worry about that? I do." He looked at her. "I don't know how long it can go on. You resent your clients. It's a strange form of self-loathing. If you're not careful it'll spread so you won't trust anyone."

Webster sighed. There were times when he would have preferred to be left alone with his delusions, but she was right. Five minutes into a new day, only half awake, without the benefit of cold and exercise, and she was effortlessly right.

4.

THE OFFICES OF TABRIZ ASSET MANAGEMENT filled four floors at the top of an unexceptional modern tower, clad in pristine white panels and dark glass, that rose high above Liverpool Street Station. Hammer and Webster exchanged their names for plastic passes and took the elevator to the twenty-sixth floor.

The doors opened on a grand lobby of polished wood and gray marble. Vast windows looked west across the city to St. Paul's on one side, and on the other toward a scrappier, lower London that spread east for miles over the flat plain of the Thames. Ahead, three young women in identical dark suits sat behind a long, gently curved counter, on either end of which lilies and irises in bold displays did little to soften the strict, corporate space. Hammer, genial as always, told the first receptionist that they were a little early for a meeting with Darius Qazai and at her invitation found a seat, reaching for a copy of the company's latest report to investors as he sat. Webster stood by the glass with his hands in his pockets and let his eyes wander over the view. From this height he could see the ancient plan of the city, though plan was a poor word for it: it was a twisted mess of old streets, high and narrow, set with squat Edwardian boxes and ugly postmodern towers and half-a-dozen piercing little church spires, all brightly lit by the noon sun.

"It's an odd business," he said, turning and sitting by Hammer on one of the low chrome and leather chairs.

"What is?" said Hammer, not looking up.

"This. Making money by making money."

Hammer raised his eyebrows half an inch. "They make a lot of it. He wasn't kidding."

"Not least because it's so new."

Hammer, frowning and shaking his head in friendly irritation, closed the report and put it back on the coffee table in front of them. "What's new?"

"This industry. Investing other people's money. It's been around what, a hundred years? If that? There's a reason no one trusts them."

Hammer looked at him and smiled. "Why you don't trust them."

"I'm not the only one."

Neither said anything for a moment. Webster reached across Hammer for the Tabriz newsletter and started leafing through it.

"Are you going to tell me what it is?" said Hammer at last.

"What?"

"The reason."

Webster thought for a moment. "All right. If someone you didn't know said to you, give me a hundred pounds and in a year's time I'll give you back a hundred and ten, you'd tell them to piss off."

"I might."

"It's not a natural relationship."

Hammer thrummed his fingers on his knee. "If they'd done it a thousand times for other people I might be tempted."

"But you still wouldn't have earned it. That's the other problem."

"You want to opt out of the pension scheme?"

Webster smiled. "Not just yet."

For a minute he skimmed the pages in his hands, failing to concentrate. It was full of unfamiliar words and phrases that might have meant something in another context: asset classes, alpha, multiples, net asset value, uncorrelated returns. He pinched his eyes closed and gave his head a small shake.

"Do I take it," said Hammer, "that you have taken against our client?"

Webster breathed in deeply and rubbed his chin. "I'm just not sure why you don't give the job to someone else. Julia could do it."

"Yes she could. Perfectly well. But she'd treat him like a client, and you won't."

Webster waited for him to explain.

"He's buying a little chunk of the brand," said Hammer. "A piece of my name. I want to make sure he deserves it. You were made to persecute your clients. Now's your chance."

Webster nodded, and thought for a moment. He was still suspicious of Ike's logic. Like many of his ideas it had a neatness and a symmetry that he admired but didn't wholly trust. One's client should not be one's subject. It was too circular. Clients paid money and expected a result, and without doubt Qazai thought he was buying a crisp, neatly bound report that would somehow perfume the air before him. He might smile and agree now, but in time he would no more expect Ikertu to contradict his version than he would his chef refuse to cook. A deal had been done, funds transferred, and value was due. Webster knew clients like this, and it was usually a long time since anyone in their pay had dared to cross them.

"Do you really think he hasn't seen the Americans' report?"

"That," said Hammer, sitting forward, his leg jigging, "is an interesting question. Either he has and it's nonsense or he's very sure he has no skeletons. What did you make of it?"

"Bland. It looked like the only juicy bit was down to luck. Like they'd stumbled across it."

"I agree. Who d'you think wrote it?"

Webster shrugged. "It's American English. I don't know. Not GIC, unless the house style's changed a lot since I was there. And the name wouldn't fit in the blanks. My money's on Columbus. It's about their level."

Hammer grunted in agreement, and was about to say something more when the receptionist approached them to say that Mr. Qazai was ready now, and would they like to come through.

Qazai's office, one story down, was entirely lined with glass on its two internal walls and gave out onto the trading floor, where perhaps a hundred people sat before pair after pair of computer screens; most were men, their jackets off and their ties loosened, and not one looked up as Hammer and Webster passed. An air of studiousness filled the long, low room.

"Gentlemen," Qazai said, standing as they were shown through the door. "Thank you, Kirsten. Would you arrange for some tea? Most kind." As Qazai shook their hands Webster nodded at Senechal, who was sitting with a phone pressed to his ear at a coffee table across from Qazai's desk, and scanned the room. It was an elegant, functional space. All the furniture was steel and glass and leather; on Qazai's desk was a svelte laptop, a single pile of papers and a speakerphone; and on the coffee table a fine ceramic bowl, intricately patterned in blue and green and ochre, provided the only color in sight.

That and Qazai, who looked fit and cordial and beaming, and who wore a bright scarlet tie as if to emphasize the point. "So. Please, sit, sit. Yves will not be a moment."

Hammer sat on the edge of his chair, looking around and nodding slowly. "You like to be close to the action," he said with approval.

"This is an information business, Mr. Hammer, like yours. I like to know what is going on."

"Will you miss it? If you step aside."

Qazai raised his eyebrows and nodded, a rueful acknowledgment. "I surely will. I surely will. There are things I want to do—with my foundation, mainly—but yes, it will be hard to give up the idea that somehow I am at the center of things. That is how I feel here. I should imagine you feel the same."

"We like to be just off-center," said Hammer.

Senechal finished his call, apparently without speaking, and by way of greeting exchanged nods with Hammer and Webster. Hammer, an assiduous shaker of hands, made no attempt to go further this time.

"So, gentlemen," said Qazai. "I understand that you have a contract for me."

Hammer nodded, and Webster passed him a document. "That's not all we have."

He handed both to Qazai, who thumbed through the first three or four pages, and turned to Hammer, his expression surprised and a little puzzled. "How did you get this?"

"I made some calls."

"I'm impressed."

In fact, Ike had made one call. He had simply phoned Qazai's buyers, asked to speak to the chief legal officer, and during the small talk with which he liked to begin every conversation established that they had in common a Stanford education and at least three acquaintances. After that, it had just been a matter of persuasion: he had explained that Ikertu's work was in the Americans' interest; that he was happy for the document to be redacted so that its creators, and any sources it might name, were not revealed; that the fact of its existence would of course be kept confidential; and, finally, that this was probably altogether neater and more friendly than the other three or four ways that he could lay his hands on the thing, none of which bound him in a debt of gratitude that they both knew he would respect. The lawyer had thought for a moment and hung up saying that he would see what he could do, and twenty minutes later a fax—a great rarity these days—had arrived in the Ikertu mail room. It appeared to be the whole report, minus the first few pages identifying the client and the reasons for the work, but otherwise complete. The whole operation, if one could call it that, had been typical of Ike: direct, charming, and not without a certain suggestion of threat.

"I wanted to know what we were up against," said Hammer.

"And?"

"Most of it's unremarkable. Not a great job, but adequate. The fun comes on the last page."

Qazai nodded, bidding Hammer to go on.

"Ben."

So this was to be his role. Hammer would be nice to Qazai; Webster would accuse him.

"They think you're a smuggler." He hoped to see in the reaction some confirmation that Qazai already knew what the report said, but his only response was to look up and narrow his eyes a little.

"A smuggler?"

"Yes."

"What do I smuggle?"

"Specifically? A stone relief from the eighth century B.C."

"The Sargon relief?"

"You know it?"

"Of course I know it. It's one of the great masterpieces of Assyrian art. Of art full stop. Everyone knows it." He gave a single, abrupt laugh, throwing his head back. "They think that was me? I wish they were right." Smiling, his brow raised, he looked at Senechal for confirmation of the sheer absurdity of the accusation; Senechal nodded once, gravely, in response.

"So you know it was looted?"

"From the National Museum in Baghdad. Of course. It is probably the most important piece still missing."

Webster watched him carefully but could see no hint of a lie.

"Do you know a man called Zia Shokhor?"

Qazai shook his head. "Yves. Do we know a Shokhor?"

"Not that I am aware, sir."

"He's an Iraqi," said Webster. "Lives in Dubai. The report says that some time in the spring of 2003, just after the invasion, he arranged for the relief to be taken by truck through Kuwait and then by sea to Dubai, where it sat for a week in the free trade zone. Then it went to Geneva on a private plane, and into the hands of a Swiss dealer, whose name we don't have."

"And he sells it to me?"

"No. Not exactly. He sells it to Cyrus Mehr, who sells it to you."

Qazai raised an eyebrow and crossed his arms, the levity gone from his face. "Naturally."

"Apparently you ordered it," said Hammer.

"Excuse me?"

"The theory goes," said Webster, "that no thief would choose to steal something that distinctive if it wasn't already sold. Especially when it weighs half a ton."

"Where did they get this nonsense?"

"The report doesn't say. Those parts have been redacted. But my guess is it's taken from the U.S. Army investigation into the looting. There's a lot of detail in there, and the only name missing is the Swiss dealer's. Maybe it comes from him."

Qazai sat back in his chair, took a deep breath through his nose and shook his head.

"And you don't know who he is?"

"Not yet," said Webster.

THE PHONE COULD NEVER do justice to Fletcher Constance, but even over a weak line there seemed to be a great deal of him and Webster, as always, had to adjust himself, as if stepping back to take in the tremendous whole.

"Benedict!" His voice was seldom less than a roar, his full Boston vowels unsoftened by thirty years away from home. "Where the hell have you been?"

"Lying low. You?"

"Me? In Dubai, as usual. I don't know how I stand it. Can't remember the last time I saw Beirut. My housekeeper thinks I'm dead. Ha." A single, staccato laugh. "Sometimes I'm not sure I'm not. In this shiny mausoleum."

"You wouldn't be anywhere else."

Constance sighed a long, bass sigh. "Ben, when was the last time you were here?"

"God. Three years ago."

"With Ike?"

"That's right."

"Three years ago. That was an innocent time, wasn't it? That was fun. They were still building then. Towers going up easy as you'd set ten pins. Now they're up and empty, and one day someone'll come along with a big ball and bang, down they'll all come, but I'll tell you this, Ben my boy, fuck me if the money isn't coming back. Unbelievable. Is that why you're calling?"

Webster laughed. "Not exactly."

One of the many pleasures and difficulties of dealing with Constance was providing him with an audience. He couldn't survive without one. Most of his ranting he did in writing, on his blog, but there was nothing so rewarding for both parties as being railed at in person, when his height and breadth, his creased linen suits and extravagant neckwear (sometimes a blooming cravat), his antique beard and the solid boom of that rhythmic voice made a total, compelling performance, with a great deal of the old American showman about it.

Fletcher Constance was an unlikely banker, by trade, and a controversialist in every ounce of his nature. He had arrived in the Gulf in 1986, working for an American bank and leaving when, in his words, "I realized that my colleagues were halfwits trying to patronize their betters, and I was probably the worst of them all." This was disingenuous, of course, not least because he had been taken on by one of his clients and for a fruitful five years or so had found and made deals on his behalf. The two had fallen out around the turn of the century and now Constance—wealthy, unencumbered with either debts or family—did little but rage against the world, or at least that large part of it that he found venal, shallow, unjust or corrupt.

He occasionally did this in print, for the *Wall Street Journal* and *Forbes* magazine, but most of his impressive output found the world through his blog—cheerily called "The Gulf Apart"—in the form of a daily sermon on the region's commercial excesses. Recent posts had included a diatribe against the management of an underperforming construction company, bold predictions about the number of Gulf businesses that would default on their debt within the coming year, and an analysis of United Arab Emirates politics that had compared the relationship between Dubai and Abu Dhabi to that between "a hooker and her john." What made him so valuable was that he was no crank, that when his enthusiasms didn't get in the way he was usually right, and that for all his noise and bluster he knew everybody—everybody, from sheikhs to ex-pats—and a little under half of them liked him. For as long as Webster could remember, Constance had been trying to leave Dubai to retire to Beirut, to a beautiful 1930s house in the hills whose picture he would produce at the smallest opportunity.

Ike knew him best. They had become friends when Hammer had spent time as a journalist in Kuwait after the first Gulf War, and now if Constance liked the story or the cause he would help Ikertu with what he knew or could find out. His was the most effortless cover: no one ever believed that someone so relentlessly loud could possibly have been a spy.

"So when are you coming out?" said Constance.

"Next week."

"Get out of town. Well, that is good news. Need a place to stay?"

Webster could hear him drawing energetically on a cigarette. "I think I may be someone's guest. We'll see."

"Just say the word."

"I shall." Webster paused. "I wanted to run a name past you. It may not be your patch."

"I love a name. Tell me."

"Darius Qazai."

Constance gave a great chuckle. "Darius Qazai? The Iranian Knight? Ah, my friend, you spoil me. There is no greater fraud in the Gulf. You may have contenders in London but here, in his quiet, oh-so-elegant way, he is without peer."

A rational voice told him to be wary of Constance's obsessions. "Really? You hardly write about him."

"That, it grieves me to say, is because he is litigious, and I am, how shall we say, light on facts. If I had the facts I'd print 'em, and if he wasn't so fucking keen to take all my savings I'd print any old shit. As it is we are at something of a stalemate. Tell me you're about to break it. What's he done?"

"Maybe nothing. Maybe receiving stolen goods. Maybe ordering them to be stolen."

"No." Constance made the single syllable last. "What? From where?"

"Half a ton of ancient Assyrian relief. From Baghdad."

Constance gave a triumphant laugh. "Ha! He's a looter! A fucking looter. Why are rich men always so fucking greedy? They think they can own the world." He laughed again. "Grasping little bastard."

Webster did his best to calm him down. "We don't know it yet."

"Of course. Innocent until, and all that. You're a better man than I, Ben. Who wants us to prove it?"

Webster had thought about this. Tell Constance and heaven knows how he might react; fail to tell him and his reaction would be all too predictable if the truth came out, as one day it surely would.

"He does."

"Who does?"

"Qazai."

"Qazai is your client?"

"He's our client."

Constance was quiet for a moment. Webster thought he could hear him scratching his beard. When he spoke again his tone was cool, the words clipped.

"So that superfine mind of Ike's has come undone. I must say I'm surprised. So how does it work? Which poor unfortunate is Qazai fucking?"

"Himself."

"Neat trick. Could you tell me what you mean?"

Webster explained, both the circumstances of the case and Hammer's supple thinking about it. He tried not to sound apologetic.

"So your job is to demonstrate that he's OK."

"That he didn't go looting. And that he's basically OK. If he didn't and he is."

"And he pays you?"

"He's paid us."

The line went quiet for a moment.

"So he pays me to do my worst?"

"Exactly."

Constance let out a vast laugh, so loud and close that Webster involuntarily moved the phone away from his ear.

"That," he said, "is wondrous. I was wrong about Ike. He's still a genius." He paused for a moment. "Your sources will be protected, I take it."

"Not a word."

"Good, good. Then let me tell you about Darius Qazai."

Constance set off. Because he was a showman he didn't think to ask what Ikertu already knew, and much of what he said Webster had heard, but to hear it from a professional contrarian was refreshing. Slowly he moved to the point: Qazai was a fraud because he wanted the respect of the establishment but would take money from anyone. Constance was convinced that behind the pure white facade of Tabriz, Qazai was investing on behalf of people whose money was far from clean.

"Like who?" asked Webster.

"Well, I hear various things. Some Russian money, some African. All dirty. But these are rumors, and much as I like them I can't support them."

With his free hand Webster shut his eyes and pinched the bridge of his nose. They were straying from the matter in hand. "None of this has much to do with art, sadly."

"Ah, but it might. When we're done." He sniffed, and Webster could hear the click and snap of a lighter as he lit another cigarette. "What do you want me to do?" he said, audibly blowing out smoke.

Webster told him about the Americans' report, about Shokhor, about the unknown Swiss dealer. "I want to know about Shokhor. Anything you can find. Where he lives, what he does. If you know someone who knows him that would be fantastic."

"You want to talk to him?"

"Next week, yes. See what you can do with the shipment as well. I'd love to know who it went to in Switzerland."

"Ben, I am on my way." He laughed again. "I can't believe you're paying me to do this."

TWO WEEKS AFTER QAZAI had signed his letter of instruction and agreed all terms—money up front in stages, his full cooperation throughout, access to all documents, Ikertu to explore wherever it liked—Webster called a meeting of his team in his office.

Hammer was there: they had finally agreed between them that he would deal with Qazai while Webster did the work, a neat arrangement that suited them both and might or might not endure. The contract with the client was no less shrewd. Ikertu would investigate the art smuggling allegations and report what it found. It would also run the rule over Qazai himself, and if it found other reasons to believe that he was less than impeccable it would meet its obligation to say so. Senechal hadn't liked it but Qazai, to Webster's satisfaction, had overruled him.

Hammer sat at the small table; to his right Rachel Dobbs; opposite him Dieter Klein. Dobbs, six feet tall in her low heels, a little drawn today, as most days, and Hammer's favorite member of staff, was Ikertu's most experienced researcher. Twenty years before, she had joined Ikertu as its third employee and was now the longest-serving bar Hammer himself, who adored her for her doggedness, her inspired ability to connect the apparently unconnected and her rigid sense of privacy. Here, in this most curious of offices, no one knew anything about her, beyond the fact that she was married (she wore a ring) and lived in the countryside near Leighton Buzzard (it had said so on her CV, and the company still paid for her season ticket). She was not a sociable person: she never attended the Christmas party, never drank with her colleagues, never talked to them about anything but work. At her interview with Hammer she had warned him about this, and he had loved her for it ever since. Occasionally, in meetings like this one, Webster would look at her thin face, the slight nose and the pressed mouth, the withdrawn eyes, imagine the different lives she might be leading away from this place and conclude that whatever one she actually lived she might be the most contented person he knew. She felt no need to share any part of herself, and if she was quiet it seemed to be less from shyness than from reserve.

Klein, on the other hand, was desperate to communicate his enthusiasm and terrified of making a mistake, particularly in front of Hammer. A serious young man, a graduate of the University of Hanover and business school in France, he had been in the job for almost a year and was still finding it difficult to relax. Webster liked him—he spoke countless languages, wrote well in all of them, understood complicated things quickly—but Hammer wasn't sure, because he saw Klein as unworldly and unformed. "He treats every case like a dissertation," he had once said to Webster, and that was harsh but true enough. For his part, Klein, wanting nothing more than to impress Hammer, as everyone did, and sensitive enough to see his doubts, was always on the brink of nervousness in his company, and today looked more than usually callow behind his serious glasses and blond beard. He was also slightly in awe of Dobbs.

Webster's office was messier than it had been for some time. Documents in scrappy piles covered the desk, and on the walls hung overlapping sheets of flipboard paper on which he was slowly drawing a chart of the world with Darius Qazai at its center.

For now they were considering basics: Qazai, the sculpture, and connections between the two. Hammer raised his eyebrows and looked expectantly around the table. "So. What have we got?"

Dobbs slowly and deliberately opened up the folder placed squarely on the table in front of her and began to speak at a measured pace. She didn't refer to the document once, didn't even look down, but kept her palm flat on the first page as if drawing out the information.

"Every detail checks out, but it hasn't got me very far. Shokhor is an Iraqi by birth but lives in Dubai. He has a company called Calyx that has a single-page website and claims to be in the textile business. The ship that's meant to have transported the relief is called the *Veronese* and it does a regular circuit of the Gulf. The container was unloaded at Dubai and after that I can't find any record of it. I spoke to a friend who put me in touch with an old customs investigator. He knows Calyx, and Shokhor, but claimed not to know what he's bringing in because no one looks. On the manifest the consignment was listed as cotton clothing. I haven't found anything to say it wasn't."

"Is that as far as it goes?"

"He's trying to find out what happened to it. He probably can't. And singling out a private flight to Switzerland from Dubai around that time? I checked. There are at least three or four a day."

For the time being she was done. Webster smiled his approval.

"Any more?"

"One thing. I've done some work on Qazai's companies as well. Tabriz is his big one. Dozens of funds, regulated in London, everything gold-plated. But he has another fund that invests his own money. It's called Shiraz. Shiraz Holding AG."

Webster nodded. Qazai had told him as much.

"Shiraz barely features anywhere. It's based in Switzerland, unregu-
lated—it can invest in whatever it wants. No one knows what it's doing.
Very low profile. But I found a claim in the high court from an investor
trying to get his money back."

Webster looked puzzled. "I thought it was all Qazai's money."

"Apparently not."

"Who was it?"

"Some Swiss fund. It looks like another family office. The claim doesn't
give much away. They invested twenty-five million dollars in 2007 and
wanted it back earlier this year. Qazai told them they couldn't have it, that
the fund was gated."

"This year?" said Hammer.

Dobbs nodded.

Webster looked at Hammer. "He told us he needed cash."

"He did," said Hammer. "Do we know what happened?"

"They settled last month," Dobbs said.

"Interesting," said Hammer, with a slow, exaggerated nod to no one in
particular. "Interesting."

Dobbs, finished, closed her folder, and Webster thanked her.

"Dieter?"

While Dobbs had been talking Dieter had been surreptitiously going
through his own notes, getting himself prepared. With a glance at Hammer
he looked down at them again and began.

"Shokhor is not a prominent man. There is very little on him. There is
almost nothing in the media." He looked up. "I can go through the articles
if you would like."

"Are they interesting?" asked Hammer.

"Not really."

"Let's get to the interesting stuff."

Dieter, abashed, turned his attention back to his notes.

"I have found two things. One is an article in the *Paris Match* that had
a picture of Ava Qazai, the daughter, at the same party as a Yusuf Shokhor,
who appears to be Shokhor's son. They were photographed together. They
seemed to know each other quite well."

Hammer pushed his lip out. "Anything else?"

"Well. I found no links between Shokhor and Cyrus Mehr, the dead man. But one of his old companies—Shokhor's old companies—I found it in the Cyprus corporate registry. It was struck off in 2001, but I thought I recognized its office address. And when I checked it was the same as a Tabriz company. Tabriz Investments Cyprus Limited. That was dissolved in 2003, but for four years they were in the same office building."

"The same floor?" asked Hammer.

"It didn't specify the floor."

Hammer tapped out a tattoo on the table with his fingers. "Satisfactory. Definitely satisfactory."

Behind his beard Dieter blushed and Webster, pleased, brought the meeting to an end.

He and Hammer stayed behind. Outside the sun was shining hard on Lincoln's Inn and through the trees he could just make out groups of people eating their lunch on the grass.

"Well?" said Hammer.

"Why are you so hard on Dieter?"

"That's not hard. You're too easy."

"I'm not sure he enjoys it."

"He's not meant to. But he'll be better for it." Hammer finished shading in a long spiral, like a spring, that he had been drawing in his notebook. "When are you seeing Qazai?"

"Tomorrow."

"What have you got?"

"I've been trying to find the Swiss dealer. After the first Gulf War there was a guy in Zurich who was rumored to have returned some valuable piece to the Iraqis after it somehow came his way. There's lots of chat about it on various blogs. I thought I might have a word with him."

"Go and see him."

"I might. I'm going to Dubai first. Visit Fletcher. See if Shokhor will grant us an audience."

Hammer threw his head back and gave a deep groan. "Oh God. Fletcher?"

"You love Fletcher."

"I love Fletcher like a brother, but the two of you should not be left alone with this case."

"And I'm trying to find out how Mehr died."

"I thought we knew how he died."

"We know what the Iranian news agency said. Not much more."

"Is it relevant?"

"Possibly not. Qazai gets accused of looting. So does Mehr, and dies for it. All in the space of a month. You tell me."

5.

O N THE LOW TABLE in front of Webster the sweetmeats were beginning to pile up. When he had arrived at Qazai's house he had been given tea and with it squares of nougat on flowered plates and almond biscuits flavored with rosewater. He and Qazai had been talking for half an hour now and three new deliveries had been made: a glass jug of orange juice and two small glasses, some fat dates, and a tray of baklava, the neat rolls of pastry shining with honey. Qazai's housekeeper offered him more tea but he declined. He had thought at first that Qazai wanted to be interviewed at home because it was discreet, but now he wondered whether it was to make him feel at once intimate and uncomfortable. This was emphatically not a place of work.

The house stood on Mount Street, in Mayfair, and had grandeur but no charm. It was narrow for its five stories, slightly wrong in its proportions, consummately built. It looked like a hospital for the rich.

Inside, its Edwardian arrogance had been tamed. All but obscuring the dark mahogany paneling a dozen Persian carpets hung from the high ceiling while another, vast, covered the flagstones in the hall with flowering buds and arabesques. Two gauze blinds let in a soft, yellow light from the brilliant spring day, setting the reds and ochres of the walls aglow. The house was silent; the rugs seemed to absorb all sound.

Webster had been shown by the butler into the first room on the left, a large sitting room—also paneled, also hung with rugs, lit with the same warm light—where three deep sofas sat in relaxed fashion around a coffee table heavy with thick art books, many showing the stamp of the Qazai Foundation. The rugs had made some space for two paintings: one, over the stone fireplace, was of a Persian general in battle; the other, the only concession to Europe in sight, was a Dutch street scene, three houses face-on and beyond them, just visible through an open door, two children playing in a sunlit yard. A vase of towering lilies in each corner gave off a strong, sweet scent.

The butler had explained that Qazai would be a few minutes and left Webster studying the contents of a glass display case that dominated one of the long walls. All manner of artifacts were there: pages of ancient Korans, their edges brown and eaten with age; a flask of brilliant-blue glass; a long, thin lacquer box, two lovers in an orchard painted on its side; a pottery lion, turquoise in color, its eyes and mouth worn to shallow impressions; and a dagger, the blade bright and glisteningly sharp, the hilt wrought in gilt with inscriptions in Arabic.

Qazai had kept him waiting just long enough to remind him who was the client, but not long enough to be rude. To Webster's relief he was alone; Senechal was not playing chaperone it seemed. Qazai wore a double-breasted suit of fine navy wool with a faint chalk stripe, a white shirt and a tie of the darkest green, and was as polished and urbane as he had been after Mehr's memorial service. He had asked after Hammer, after Ikertu, after Webster's family, and before ushering him toward one of the sofas had talked him through the various pieces in the cabinet. Which was the most valuable, he had wanted to know, and seemed pleased when Webster, understanding the game, correctly chose the least showy of them all, a fragment of the Koran aged to feathery thinness by its passage from the Arabian peninsula over almost fourteen hundred years.

Webster began by asking about his past, about the history of his companies, and about his investors—for context, he had explained, so that he might understand the significance of his findings, but it was more to put

Qazai at his ease, perhaps off his guard. Qazai had nodded and told him to ask whatever he liked. Webster began with questions about his father, the founding of the business, its financing, its first clients. Every answer was pristine, complete and convincing, worked to a shine through repeated telling and so smooth that when Senechal had finally joined them Webster had barely resented the intrusion. Qazai was clearly quite capable of looking after himself.

He had talked about his art—the collection, the foundation, his friendship with Mehr—and about his family, and very particularly about Timur, his son, the imminent heir to this great estate. Webster, sinking back into the great sofa, took notes awkwardly on his knee. Try as he might he couldn't disrupt Qazai's rhythm. There were no inconsistencies to explore, no grit of any kind.

Qazai didn't mind talking about himself like this. It was clear, in fact, that he had talked about himself a great deal, if the seamlessness of his narrative was any clue. As episode moved easily into episode, Senechal, having no reason to interject, simply sat tapping at his BlackBerry, making notes or typing e-mails, unnaturally upright on his sofa, half an ear on his master, whose account of himself was at once self-effacing and egotistical. Behind every story of his father's canniness or Timur's brilliance lay Qazai's influence: without his father or his staff or his son he would have been nothing, but though he never said as much he left the strong impression that they might have been a great deal less without him.

He had a tendency to bring his homeland into everything. Iran never faded from the story. After over thirty years its steep descent into terror was a fresh insult that he was still struggling to accept. He talked about Mehr again, and the horror of his death, about the rigged election, the spring protests and the shame he had felt when he had not been there to take part. Time and again, Webster had to bring him back to the subject of his own life.

In this he was not like other rich men Webster had met. His passions seemed more powerful than his drive to make money and he was almost reluctant to discuss his success. His mission, as he called it, would not be complete until Iran was free again and he could be said to have contributed to its release. But Webster noticed that for all these fine words he said little about what form that contribution might take.

In fact, there were too many fine words altogether. Qazai was not evasive, quite; his answers were full; his whole account of himself seemed to have substance, and was delivered with conviction bordering on intensity; everything he said had a certain grace. But Webster began to sense that this version of Qazai, complete in its way, was only one of several that he would never have the chance to meet. He imagined them lined up in a mirror-lined closet off the sumptuous Qazai bedroom, somewhere above: this one for memorial services, that for charming investors, another for convincing Ikertu that he was a good man. Webster wondered how many there were, and whether Qazai himself could now tell one from another.

He was expansive about his son. Timur was the really talented one, he insisted, and under his guidance the company would become something altogether more exciting. Sometimes he regretted his own triumphs because they would always obscure Timur's true abilities, no matter how much he achieved. It was for this reason, among others, that he was stepping away. Now was the time, after his apprenticeship in Dubai, to give his son the space to work freely.

"How old are your children, Mr. Webster?" he said, his legs crossed, a glass of orange juice in his hand, wholly comfortable.

"They're young. Five and three."

"Ah, how I envy you that. There is no greater delight. Do you have a son?"

"A girl and a boy."

"Then we are the same. Do you have ambitions for him?"

"No. I have no idea." Nor for her, Webster thought.

Qazai raised his eyebrows the merest touch, in concern more than surprise. He gave a slight nod, as if to himself. "I wanted Timur to have nothing to do with money. To be a writer, or a politician. A historian. It is difficult to be a rich man sometimes, if you love your children. If you leave them everything, it makes them weak. If you leave them nothing, it makes them resentful. I have tried hard not to spoil them." There was a plainness about the way he said this that was new.

"Perhaps every father has the same problem," said Webster. "If it isn't money it's something else."

Qazai thought. "You are right," he said, "very right. But money makes it worse. A poor man can bequeath his love, pure and simple."

"And his poverty."

Qazai looked at Webster for a moment with apparent appreciation and then laughed. "Mr. Webster, you are wasted as an investigator. Tell me, is your father still alive?"

Webster didn't want to tell this man about his family but he answered nevertheless. "Yes, he is."

"What does he do?"

"He's retired. He was a psychiatrist."

"A good man?"

"A very good man."

Qazai nodded, as if that was what he had expected to hear. "Does he approve of what you do?"

There seemed a pointedness in the way the question was asked, so slight that he wondered immediately whether he had imagined it. Qazai waited for him to respond.

"He's not the sort to judge."

"It can be hard to live up to a good father," said Qazai.

"Better to have the opportunity."

"Even when we fail." Qazai held Webster's eye for a second longer than was comfortable, his features firmly set. "As we must."

He drained the last of his orange juice, and his face relaxed into a smile. "I will introduce you to Ava later. She is keen to meet you. I thought you might like to ask her some questions."

Webster, thrown a little by this odd exchange, muttered that that would be his pleasure, though for the life of him he didn't know what questions those would be.

"Now," said Qazai, putting his glass down and clasping his hands together. "What else do you have for me?"

Webster smiled back, without warmth. "Some specifics, I'm afraid. The Sargon relief. Mr. Shokhor. Some questions about Mr. Mehr, if you don't mind."

Qazai's face stiffened a little, but before he could respond a short, muted little cough announced that Senechal was still with them.

"Monsieur," he said, his tone deferential but firm. "We must be in Canary Wharf by noon."

Qazai glanced at his watch, a thin gold disc. "Surely not, Yves. We can be late." He turned to Webster. "Yves does his best to keep me on track, as you see."

Senechal shifted in his seat. "I must insist, monsieur."

"Yves, sometimes you can be a little too lawyerly. Never mind." He smiled a patronizing smile at Senechal, who didn't return it. "If it can't be helped."

"This won't take long," said Webster, feeling annoyance and relief at once. One part of him was happy to leave right now; the other wanted very much not to have to come back.

"I'm so sorry. Early next week?"

"I'll be in Dubai next week."

"Dubai? You should see Timur."

"Thank you. I'd like to."

"I'll have him make the arrangements. He'll be delighted." Qazai held out his hand for Webster to shake. "Thank you, Mr. Webster. I'm sorry to cut this short. Truly." His smile was frank and full. "I'll send Ava in. You may talk to her about anything you wish, but not the content of that report. If you wouldn't mind."

Webster had no idea what there was left to talk about, but little as he relished the prospect of wasting an hour talking to Qazai's daughter about heaven knows what, he realized that he was caught, and could do nothing but agree. Qazai shook his hand warmly, smiled one more of his big, bold smiles, and walked away.

Halfway to the door Senechal put his hand on Qazai's arm and whispered a few words that Webster couldn't make out. Qazai stooped to hear him, nodded and turned. "Yves has had a splendid thought. You must come to Como. The week after next. The whole family will be there, and we'll have time then. Bring your wife. My secretary will be in touch." And with that he left, Senechal dutifully following.

Elsa with a house full of Qazais by the lake. Webster smiled.

HE KNEW A LITTLE about Ava Qazai—a paragraph or two from Dieter in one of his many memos, drawn almost wholly from the society pages of the newspapers and the gossip columns of magazines. All he could remember was that she was the younger of the two children, didn't work in the family business and was of interest to journalists because she had found it difficult, despite much good work in that general direction, to find a husband. There were various accounts, relayed by Dieter in too much detail, of parties attended and engagements broken, and Webster wondered blackly whether he would be required to find some room for them in his final report. The one detail he had taken in, because it had prompted a grim chuckle, was that she was invariably described as "the billionaire's daughter, socialite and political activist, Ava Qazai." He could only assume that Qazai wanted him to hear about all the good works that he funded.

Webster had put aside his notebook and was leafing through one of the books on the coffee table when she came in. He was prepared for her to be powerfully dressed, probably in black, and to treat him as women too accustomed to money tended to treat people like him, as staff. But from the start she didn't conform to type. She wore black jeans, white tennis shoes and a gray silk blouse, and as he rose to shake her hand gave the impression not of superiority, exactly, but impatience.

"Mr. Webster. Ava Qazai. I feel like we've been told to play together."

Webster returned the slightly testy smile. Her eyes, almost level with his, were black, underscored against her olive skin with a thin line of mascara and but for a slight scroll at the side completely round. They were serious, not wholly certain; Webster felt himself being examined, as if she were trying to determine what sort of creature he was.

"Like good children," he wanted to say, but instead introduced himself, a little stiffly, and suddenly felt rather foolish. This wasn't the spoiled princess of his imagination, and the realization made him wonder how she must see him and his own strange, trivial mission.

"I see you've been looked after," she said, taking in the plates and cups on the table.

"Repeatedly."

"My father likes this house to be a little corner of Tehran. My oasis, he calls it."

"He has some beautiful things."

"Too many. One can only look at so much."

Webster simply smiled, resisting the temptation to agree.

"Please," she said, gesturing for him to sit down and putting her phone and her purse on the table. She had inherited her father's poise but not his self-consciousness about it, and when she sat as he had on the sofa opposite, dropping back elegantly and crossing her legs, she projected none of that air of carefully constructed ease. In other ways she was both like him and not like him—her nose was strong and straight, but finer, her skin the same healthy gold, her face rounder, her eyes somehow more honest.

She looked at her watch. "You wanted to ask me some questions?"

"Your father suggested we should talk."

"I don't have long."

"To be honest, I'm not sure what he wanted us to talk about."

Ava watched him closely for a moment, then shook her head and laughed drily.

"He likes to show me off. Does he realize you're married?" She nodded in the direction of the ring on Webster's hand.

Webster smiled. "I'm not sure he'd want the likes of me in the family."

Ava leaned forward and took a piece of nougat from one of the plates on the table. "I don't really understand what you are."

"I'm an investigator. I find things out."

"And what are you finding out for him?"

"Why his reputation is suffering."

"My God." She took a moment to chew. "We can't have that. Someone's been saying nasty things about him?"

"Is that rare?"

"He's a paragon. Hadn't you noticed?" She watched for Webster's reaction but he kept his expression clear. "So, what, you find out and then tell everyone it's all nonsense?"

"That's about it, yes." Webster wasn't expecting to have to defend himself. His conversation with Qazai had been odd and fruitless, and this was becoming as rewarding. It was time to leave the Qazai house.

"Then you're not an investigator. You're a PR man."

"Today, yes." He shifted toward the edge of the sofa. "I should go. If it's not convenient. Perhaps we could talk later."

Ava smiled, and for the first time it seemed sincere. "I'm sorry, Mr. Webster. I'm a bit wary of people in your profession." She paused. "Iranians don't trust spies. Tell me. Why do you think he wants us to meet?"

"I have no idea."

"I do. He wants you to know that he's a great man. You know he's a rich man already, and a clever one. But not great, not yet. That's what I'm for."

She went on. "How much do you know about what I do?"

"Not much, in truth."

"That's all right. We don't shout about it. He'd like me to, but it's not helpful. I run a small trust—a charity that helps other charities."

"In Iran?"

"From here, but yes, in Iran. It isn't like we see on the news. We see brave people dying in street battles and being sentenced to death for nothing. There are protests, and then there are crackdowns, and they arrest everybody. But all the time good things are happening. There are so many brave people there. And the bravest are the women. Protecting their children, challenging the government, educating each other. There are countless organizations in Iran—tiny, some of them, very local—run by women. The trust helps them. We give them money and advice. Here." She leaned forward and reached in her purse. "This is my card."

Webster thanked her. With the change of subject her shell had briefly fallen away.

"Do you go?" he said.

"I used to. But now they won't give me a visa."

"Because of what you're doing?"

"Because of my father. And the work. Others go."

There was a pause while Webster weighed an opportunity.

"Did you know Cyrus Mehr?" he said.

"Of course."

"Was he one of them?"

Ava frowned and her tone was cool when she spoke. "Is that what you're doing? Finding out how he died?"

Webster shook his head. "No."

"Wait. Is this job you're doing about him? Fuck." She looked away, working something out, then looked back. "Is he not telling me something? Has this got to do with the trust?"

"No," said Webster, raising his hand an inch and doing his best to sound reassuring. "Nothing at all." He paused to let her see that he was being honest. "If it was, I wouldn't have tried to get out of here earlier, would I?"

She thought about it. "Not unless you're exceptionally cunning."

"I'm not."

"And it's not about Mehr?"

"No."

"So why ask?"

"Public relations aren't my strong suit. I prefer investigating things."

Her eyes were still on his, still wary. "It needs investigating."

"You don't believe the official version?"

"I don't believe anything that comes out of there."

"So what happened?"

She thought for a moment, reaching up and slowly rubbing her ear.

"I don't know," she said, shaking her head. "I shouldn't think we ever will."

"Did people talk about it? In Iran?"

"Not in Iran, no. Not that I know of."

"Outside Iran?"

She gave him a searching look, deciding something.

"I don't think anyone talked about it enough." She looked at her watch. "I have to go. I'm sorry. It's been nice talking to you."

She stood, holding out her hand. Her eyes, which never left his, seemed to say that she was genuinely sorry: she had said too much, but he should not rule out the possibility that she would talk again. Webster watched her walk across the room and out of the door, graceful and composed, and before showing himself out took a last look at Qazai's cabinet. A piece he had not noticed before took his eye: a dull silver jug embossed with grapes and leaves curled around nightingales and a solitary, lurking jackal, its single eye picked out with a tiny bright green stone.

6.

CYRUS MEHR WAS BURIED IN RICHMOND, where he had lived with his wife and his sons in a house that looked out onto the green. Their number, Webster was almost sorry to discover, was in the telephone directory.

The articles published after his death had reported only that Mehr had been killed in Isfahan while on a buying trip. They hadn't mentioned how. His body had been found in his hotel room and local police were acting on the assumption that robbery had been the motive: the original reports, distributed by the Iranian state news agency, had mentioned that a number of receipts had been found in his possession, and that the most likely culprit was a "collaborator" in Mehr's "smuggling conspiracy." They had not identified the objects assumed to be missing, but speculated that they were "national treasures" stolen from museums and archeological digs. There had been a struggle, but neither Mehr's wallet nor his passport had been taken.

This account had been picked up by the international agencies and then by most British newspapers, who had added little more than some basic biographical information about the man himself. Mehr had had dual citizenship; he had left Iran as a teenager, moved to London, set up his business at the beginning of the 1980s, and married his wife, Jessica, in 1990. He was the head of the Qazai Foundation, and "a much-loved figure" in London's art world. The story had run for a day or two, padded out with the odd opinion piece about murder rates in Iran and the like, and within a week had faded to nothing.

Webster had read all the articles several times and wasn't satisfied. He wasn't sure, to begin with, whether Mehr would have stored his treasures, if that's what they were, in his hotel room, or that any smuggler would have insisted on receipts with every piece of contraband. Nor did it seem likely that someone who had come for a Safavid prayer rug would have taken the trouble to remove the passport from Mehr's jacket or the watch from his wrist. But most of all there was something in the tone of the Iranian articles that wasn't right—a sense that the matter had been instantly understood, concluded and dismissed. It reminded him of similar statements he had heard too often in Russia, about the sudden death of awkward people.

So Mehr's murder occupied Webster's mind, partly because it was a mystery, partly because he couldn't quite believe that Qazai being accused of smuggling and Mehr dying for it were not somehow connected. But a mystery it looked set to remain. He had spoken to the foreign journalists who had covered the story, and they had been unable to add anything to what had already been published. He had found sources at two Iranian opposition groups, one in London, one in Paris, and neither knew any more than he did. He had even tried the Foreign Office, who had brushed him off with a coldly polite referral to their previous statements on the affair.

In short his inquiry found nothing, not so much as a hint, until the only people left to call were the Mehrs themselves. His conscience baulked at the thought, but he found a justification: it was possible, after all, that Mrs. Mehr would welcome some interest in her husband's death—even possible that she would welcome some assistance. Her interests and Webster's were aligned, he should remember, because they both wanted to know why he had been killed, and by whom.

So he steeled himself, and feeling more or less ashamed despite all his rationalizing, made the call. At least only mild deception was necessary; the number was in the phone book, and he could be himself. The phone rang five times and he was close to hanging up when a woman answered.

"Hello."

"Mrs. Mehr?"

"Yes."

"My name is Ben Webster. I work for a company called Ikertu. Darius Qazai is my client."

He waited for her to say something in acknowledgment but there was only silence on the line.

"He's asked me to write a report about him. About his reputation. It's for his investors. I was wondering if I could ask you one or two questions about your husband's relationship with him. With Mr. Qazai."

There was a pause of a second or two before she spoke.

"He hasn't said anything to me."

"No. I've asked him not to call people. It prejudices the result. If you like I can show you a letter of introduction that he's signed."

Another pause. "I don't really understand, and I can't think what you'd ask me. Or why you'd think it was appropriate."

Then she hung up.

Webster took a deep breath, closed his eyes tight and sat for a moment, letting the shame wash through his body.

It was half past two, and the sun was shining. He should be leaving for an appointment at his daughter's school. He glanced at his watch and dialed one more number.

"Cantor Sassoon. Good afternoon. How may I direct your call?"

"David Brooks, please."

"Hold the line."

Sober music played in Webster's ear.

"David Brooks."

It was rare for a lawyer to take a call direct, and Webster realized that he hadn't expected to be put through at all. He began by giving Brooks the same account of himself he had given Mrs. Mehr, and the words sounded empty as they came out of his mouth.

"Your name was in some of the reporting. I wondered if I might ask you some questions."

"Ikertu, you say?"

"Yes."

Brooks gave a grunt, its meaning not clear; it could have been approval or contempt. "I'm not going to tell you anything without an instruction from my client." His voice was flat and all on one note, and he left the "g"s off the end of words. "Have you spoken to my client?"

"I have. She didn't want to talk."

"Then neither do I."

"Of course. Although it's not really about Mr. Mehr's affairs. I wondered if you knew anything about the investigation in Iran. Whether anything had been decided."

Brooks sniffed. "What has that got to do with Darius Qazai?"

I wish I knew, thought Webster. "Mehr was his employee, in a sense. There are rumors that Mehr was in Iran on Qazai's business."

For a second or two Brooks said nothing. "You have a very strange job."

"On occasion."

"Hm." Another sniff. "You're investigating Qazai."

"Yes and no. I'm . . . Look, this is more than I should say, but Qazai is doing a deal. He's hit a bump, and thinks someone somewhere is saying things about him that aren't true. I want to make sure that those things aren't connected to what happened to your client."

Brooks thought for a moment, grunted again. Webster could hear him tapping keys in the background.

"I'm not going to tell you anything. Obviously. But I will say—and I don't think this qualifies as privileged or surprising information—that the investigation in Iran, such as it is, is not being conducted to the standard expected by Her Majesty's justice system."

"Was he really robbed?"

Brooks seemed unable to answer without a substantial pause. Webster waited. "Mr. Webster," he said at last, "it is possible, one might suppose, on the balance of probabilities, that every now and then in Iran a normal antiques smuggling ring, during the normal course of its business, is called upon to murder an English art dealer. My own personal belief is that all this was far from normal. Thank you for your interest. Goodbye."

And before Webster could squeeze in another question, he too had gone.

. . .

THE BAKERLOO LINE WAS deadly slow and by the time he reached the school, five minutes late, Elsa and Miss Turnbull had already begun their meeting. Elsa gave him a severe look as he took a seat next to her on one of the tiny children's chairs.

It wasn't at all unusual, Miss Turnbull told them when they had explained the problem, for children of this age—especially girls—to have quite intense relationships with their friends. She had noticed that Phoebe and Nancy seemed to be spending a lot of time in each other's company, but hadn't realized that Nancy was feeling put-upon, still less upset, and if she was worrying about it at home and dreading school as a result then something would have to be done. What had worked in similar situations was to talk to all the boys and girls about the importance of having lots of different friends and playing together as a class, and to make sure that at playtime Phoebe wasn't allowed to keep Nancy to herself. Elsa, Webster could tell, wasn't wholly satisfied.

"Happy?" he said as they walked across the empty playground.

"We'll see."

"She seems to have the measure of it."

"I was hoping she might have a word with Phoebe's parents."

"If they're anything like their daughter they probably won't listen."

Elsa shrugged.

The school was half a mile from their house, and for a while they walked in silence, Elsa half a pace in front of Webster, her head down and full of thoughts.

"Why were you late?" she said at last.

"I'm sorry. The Tube was buggered. We were stopped at Paddington for five minutes."

"Then you should have left five minutes earlier."

"I'm sorry."

"You should have left enough time. I know you. You take it to the last minute and then you rush out and expect the world to fall into place for you."

There was a park opposite their house: a square of grass, a sandpit, a climbing frame and a seesaw, and this afternoon it was full of small children bouncing around each other like atoms in a jar. Webster saw Nancy first, hanging off the climbing frame by her legs, while Daniel carefully shoveled cupfuls of sand onto a growing pile on the grass.

As they reached the gate he touched Elsa's arm and she turned to him.

"I'm sorry," he said. "Really."

"It's OK."

"Do you fancy a couple of nights in Italy? The week after next. After Cornwall. I've been invited by my dodgy billionaire."

"To his house?"

"To his big house. On Lake Como. It has its own Wikipedia page."

She smiled. "Who would look after the kids?"

"The nanny? Your mom?"

"I'm not sure it's such a good idea. We've never been away in the week. I think I should stay here, for Nancy."

"I was hoping you could tell me what in heaven's name drives these people. I'm out of my depth."

"You'll be fine. They don't want a therapist."

"I'm not so sure."

Elsa collected the children from the friend who had picked them up after school, and together they walked back home. As they turned in to the short path leading to their house Webster reached up to hoist Daniel down from his shoulders and started feeling in his pockets for his key.

"Have you got yours?" he asked Elsa.

"You're hopeless. Yes."

As she reached for the lock, something caught his eye.

"When does the recycling go?"

"Wednesdays. Tomorrow."

"Did we put any out?"

"There was loads."

Webster looked at the empty box and wondered who had done the work, and on whose behalf.

. . .

TWO DAYS AFTER HIS calls to Mehr's widow and David Brooks, Webster received a package. It had come by mail—stamped, not franked—in an A4 manila envelope addressed with a printed label that bore no clue to its sender. Inside was a report, of sorts, printed on a single sheet of plain paper in plain, black type.

There was no title, and no introduction, but the moment Webster saw it he knew what it was. It was a private report into the death of Cyrus Mehr, and a very direct and unexpected document it was. Whoever had written it appeared to have seen the police file, and as he read Webster found himself wondering which of his competitors, if they were responsible, had such excellent sources in Iran.

Mehr, it said, had been invited by the Cultural Heritage Association of Iran to spend three weeks helping to catalog the treasures of the Golestan Palace in Tehran, a place so vast and run so inefficiently (some said corruptly) that the true extent of its largely chaotic collection was unknown. It was not unusual for foreigners to be asked to collaborate in this way, and Mehr, an expert above all else in carpets from the Safavid dynasty, whose kings had built the palace, was an entirely plausible candidate.

He had left London on the 15th of February, a Thursday, arrived in Tehran the next day and spent his first week working, staying at a hotel in the north of the city and calling his family at least once a day (the report didn't make clear whether the Iranians or the Mehrs had provided this piece of information). On the following Saturday he had flown to Isfahan, telling his colleagues that he was going to meet a dealer he knew who had called to offer him a particularly rare, fine prayer rug from the sixteenth century. At around noon he had checked into his hotel and then taken a taxi immediately to Joubareh in the north of the city, a journey of fifteen minutes.

He and the dealer had arranged to meet in an Internet cafe. It wasn't clear whether the dealer had ever turned up, but at a little after five o'clock, at some point between getting out of his taxi and reaching the door of the cafe, four men in balaclavas had grabbed Mehr and forced him, struggling, into a white van that had driven up at that moment, clearly after waiting a little distance away. The street was not busy, but there were a few passersby who would have seen the van leaving at great speed in the direction of the airport. Neither it nor the five men—assuming there was a driver as well—had been seen since.

This sparse little document, all of four paragraphs, contained two details that caused Webster to imagine Mehr's last hours more vividly than he would have wished. The first was that his body had not in fact been found in his hotel room. Shortly after daybreak the following day two women had discovered it by the side of the Zarrin Kamar canal, which ran through the middle of Isfahan. The canal wasn't lit, so it was entirely likely that the body had been there all night and that no one had passed. Mehr was dressed in the suit he had been wearing the day before, and everything on him had been taken, except for his passport (which, contrary to the version released to the press, had been found in his jacket pocket). When the police searched his room they discovered—or said they had—the receipts and other documents that were later reported extensively in the Iranian press.

And he had not been stabbed; at least not at first. There had been no postmortem, but someone in the Isfahan police department had noted that the three wounds in Mehr's stomach hadn't bled onto his clothes as one might expect, and that the marks on his neck, described in the report as livid, indicated that he had in fact been strangled. That was the most inspired moment of the investigation, it seemed: since then only three people had been interviewed, no evidence had been taken from the street where Mehr had been abducted, and the last sentence of the report merely stated that as far as anyone could tell, the policemen in charge showed no signs of wanting to make any progress.

Webster read the report three times, and when he was done he walked across the office and photocopied it, twice, before taking a copy to Hammer, who had been in for an hour but was still in his running clothes. The cap he always wore to run was on his desk by his newspapers.

Webster waited until Hammer had finished reading. "Do you think Qazai knows all this?"

"How'd you get it?"

"An anonymous benefactor. It came in the post."

"Who was it?"

"I've called a bunch of people. Journalists, Foreign Office. No one told me anything. It could have been the lawyer. Mehr's lawyer." He didn't mention his widow.

Hammer read it again, and when he looked up there was a challenge in his face. "I didn't realize this was a murder investigation."

"I thought it was worth following up. I'd say I was right."

Hammer settled himself with a long breath, his forearms on the desk. "You going to sit down?" Webster sat in one of the two chairs facing him. "Have you had breakfast?"

"Yes."

"Shame. I guess I'll have to do this on an empty stomach. So what's your theory? Qazai had him killed? He was mixed up in something big?"

Webster ignored the sarcasm. "I don't have a theory. But he's Qazai's man, and he died in Iran, which is already odd, and for whatever reason the Iranians lied about what happened. Isn't that enough?"

Hammer pushed out his lower lip and thought for a moment. "I'm finding it hard to imagine what the conspiracy theory is. This is Qazai's guy. Say he's doing something terrible in Iran. Say he's into drugs or arms or some shit. You think the Iranians aren't going to crow about that?" His eyes were on Webster, waiting for a response. "Look. This is interesting, no question. My money, what it's worth, is on some fucker in the government or the police milking this situation. The original articles, out of Iran, they said that not all the pieces had been recovered, right? Where do you think they might be? On their way to a collector, I bet. I think we can assume that at some point someone there is taking advantage of this situation. Either the Iranians had him killed or they made the most of it when someone else did."

Webster started to speak.

"Hold on." Hammer checked him. "That's part of it. The other part is, this isn't our job. It's too big. If I thought you could ever find out what really happened I might say go ahead. But we can't do work like this there.

It's too difficult. This is great," he picked up the piece of paper, "but what are you going to do next? Fly to Tehran? Get a bus to Isfahan? Ask a few questions? Can't be done. Even if you got a visa they'd arrest you at the airport as a spy. Which you sort of are. And our sources there are feeble. Fletcher's about as close as we get, through the Americans, and they don't know shit. So." He raised his hand. "Wait a second, I'm nearly done. With regret—and you know I'd always rather know things than not know them—we can't get into this. You need to concentrate on what we've been asked to do."

Webster hadn't been expecting this. From the start he had wanted to know what had happened to Mehr, and he had assumed everyone would share his interest—naively, of course, because it was like Ike to decide with cool logic which battles not to fight. A talent he would do well to acquire himself.

"All right," he said. "So you're happy if in a year's time we've written our report, Qazai's been waving it around, and it all comes out that his employee was up to no good on his behalf? You don't mind that?"

Hammer shook his head deliberately. "Not at all. Look. If you find that out, whatever it is, by doing the work we've agreed to do, great. I'll be delighted. But in a year's time I'll be quite happy to explain to whoever's listening that we don't do murder investigations. Not in Iran, anyway."

Webster nodded and suppressed a sigh. Ike, like Elsa, was impossible to argue with because he was usually right.

"You want that?"

Hammer put his palm on the document. "I'll hang on to it." He watched Webster get up to leave. "When are you flying out?"

"Sunday."

"Where you staying?"

"Timur's sending someone to pick me up from the airport. Fletcher offered but I opted for peace and quiet."

Hammer laughed. "Send the old bastard my love."

7.

THE HEAT IN DUBAI came in short, thick blocks: the walk from the arrivals hall to the car, from the car to the hotel. Webster, with his northern blood, felt it like a substance, a dense, invisible haze that offered a sly welcome and then held you in a burning grasp. Like the cold in Russia that could make your clothes as stiff as a board this deadly weather was exciting, somehow, but no one chose to endure it for long, not even the tourists, and the only people who did—the guest workers from India, Pakistan, Bangladesh, suspended against the sky on impossibly rickety scaffolding, so far up that they were almost lost in a cloud of heat, slowly building the shiny miracle of Dubai—had no choice. On the road to the city from the airport, crossing the bridge over the creek, there was a huge screen that gave the official temperature in square red figures. When it reached 50 degrees Celsius, all construction work, by law, had to stop; Webster remembered Constance telling him on his first visit here that during the summer it could spend weeks on an uncanny, unchanging 49, so that progress was never interrupted. Today, halfway through what must even here have counted as spring, it was a mere 41.

He was met at the airport by a young Indian man in a dark-gray suit and peaked cap holding a clipboard with his name on it. Webster let him take his luggage and followed him across the marble hall, through the slowly revolving doors and out into the dry heat of the evening. There was perhaps an hour before the sun disappeared. In his thin wool suit, a staple of trips to warm climates, he felt dehydrated, sweaty and decidedly unpressed.

A little way from the terminal his driver put his bag down and asked him to wait for a moment before disappearing into a concrete parking lot. Webster watched the cars driving past: a Ferrari, a Lamborghini, a Porsche. A lowly Mercedes taxi. He thought about calling Elsa, took his phone from his pocket and remembered that it was early afternoon in London and that she would still be at work. There were e-mails, though, and he started to go through them: one from Constance suggesting they meet for dinner the next day; several from Ike.

Something brilliantly white distracted his eye in the growing gloom, and when he glanced up he saw a Rolls-Royce, glisteningly new and looking like it had just arrived from the rich man's afterlife. It was obscenely massive, with great square headlights and a brutish expression, as if to say that this was Dubai and ostentation not merely normal but required. He moved back a couple of steps, giving it room, and then with a flush of real embarrassment saw the door open and his driver get out.

"Please, sir," he said, moving to the back of the car and opening the door for Webster, who for several moments simply stood, not quite knowing what to do. In the end, holding his phone at arm's length, he took a picture of his car and its driver and got in, sliding back into deep leather seats.

"I have arrived," he wrote to Elsa, and sent her the photograph.

THROUGH THE ROLLS-ROYCE'S TINTED GLASS Dubai was getting steadily darker, and as they approached Jumeirah the last glints of reflected sun on the skyscrapers were giving way to garish digital billboards and fluorescent office lights. In the three years since he had been here the buildings appeared to have doubled, in size and number. Now they crowded around each other in tight rows, straining ever higher, competing for air and sunlight, and Webster found himself wondering how many this dry desert earth could eventually support.

In twenty minutes they had reached Jumeirah Beach, where two hotels, one in the shape of a sail, the other a wave, both in pristine white, commanded the skyline and the shore.

Webster was staying in the sail. It rose up from its own artificial island and could only be reached by a private bridge, which curved gently toward the hotel so that guests could gaze up at it as they arrived. Webster did so now. He remembered reading that it had been designed to resemble the sail of a dhow, an Arabian fishing boat. A single mast of white steel rose a thousand feet out of the sea and from it a sheet of glass seemed to billow out toward land, as if it had just been caught by the wind and at any moment would run aground on the beach. As they approached, the top of the building drew back from sight under the bulge of the sail, and the Rolls-Royce slowed to a stop.

Webster pulled himself out of the car, thanked his driver and was shown into the hotel by two smiling staff, a man and a woman, both young, both from Southeast Asia—Malaysia, perhaps, or Singapore. His eyes automatically looked up as he entered the lobby, which rose to the full height of the sail, endless white landings narrowing slowly to a point above. Outside, the Burj Al Arab was modern, pristine, the only color the blue of the sky reflected in its glass; inside, the decorators had combined luxury cruise ship with the Arabian Nights. The carpet was thick and blue, the chairs green and red, and everything was edged and trimmed and patterned with gold. Columns carved as palm trees reached up four or five floors, their golden fronds forming arches around the giant room. Webster, entranced and horrified, was asked to take a seat on a sofa under a real palm tree. In moments two women in Arab dress had appeared with dates and coffee in a golden pot that gave off the scent of cardamom as it was poured, and then he was left alone to watch the well-heeled guests in their shorts and sports shirts and wonder what on earth he was doing in this demented place.

The coffee was good, sweet and thick. After five minutes, during which time, he assumed, he was meant to acclimate to the extraordinary atmosphere of the Burj, a new flunky appeared, introduced himself as Raj, and asked him whether he was ready to go to his room. Webster resisted the temptation to say that he had been ready for a little while, and was led into a twinkling glass elevator that shot them at stomach-lifting speed to the twenty-third floor.

The room was several rooms; four thousand square feet, Raj told him, with a king-size bed, two bathrooms, a dining area, a cocktail bar, and a living room on each of its two floors. Webster wasn't very good on areas, but he was fairly sure that his house in London was rather less. Beyond the curved double-height window that formed the outside wall was the flat sweep of Dubai, dark now but studded with lights that glared beside the unbroken black of the sea. Against the eastern horizon a thin band of purple and bronze mirrored the sunset he couldn't see.

"Would you care to join me in the office, sir?" said Raj, and Webster, beginning to tire of this elaborate induction, asked him why.

"We need to check you in, sir."

"Couldn't we have done that downstairs?"

"We think it is more private in your suite, sir." This was undoubtedly true, although even Webster, who might have had greater reason for discretion than most, had never found checking in to hotels particularly exposed before. "It won't take a moment."

Sitting at his desk—inlaid with gold-embossed leather—he was presented with two documents for signature. Neither made any reference to his name (the "client" in each case was Tabriz Asset Management Ltd.)— nor to the rate of the room.

"How much is this place?"

"Excuse me, sir?"

"How much does it cost to stay here? A night?"

"Tabriz have a special rate, sir."

"I'm sure they do. What's the standard rate?"

Raj hesitated.

"I could look it up on your website," said Webster.

"Sixteen thousand dirham, sir."

"About four thousand dollars."

"Yes, sir."

Webster thought for a moment.

"Raj, do you have a smaller room?"

"The hotel is full, sir."

"No doubt." Webster looked up at him, looked down at the papers, signed them with a gold hotel pen, and watched Raj leave.

AN HOUR LATER, in fresh clothes and feeling something like himself again, Webster found himself sitting by a wall of glass watching fish swim in an undersea playground of seaweed and rocks.

This was the Al Mahara restaurant, the Oyster, and was not to be confused with the Arab restaurant, or the Japanese restaurant, or any of the other dozen places to eat throughout the hotel. Guests reached it by way of a vestibule mocked-up as a submarine. They entered, had the door sealed behind them, and watched the old-fashioned portals slowly fill with water and various forms of sealife. Once on the sea floor, at the end of this phantom journey, Webster had been shown to a table beside the aquarium, a colossal drum of glowing blue at the center of a circular room whose chairs and walls and carpets were velvety and deeply red. He was the only single person there, and as he surveyed the menu realized that the food was simply too expensive to indulge in alone; at the other tables husbands and wives talked in softened tones, their tans fresh, enjoying the theater. A waitress came and brought him his whisky in a heavy tumbler filled with shaved ice. None of this seemed very Qazai, he thought. Perhaps Timur would turn out to be the gaudy playboy of the family.

Whatever he was, he was late. It was now twenty past nine. Webster read every last word of the menu and then watched the aquarium. Swimmer he might be, but he knew nothing about fish. That one, an intense orange with two bands of white, he had a good idea was a clown fish, and some deep vault in his memory told him that another, its shining yellow stripes drawn as if by hand on turquoise skin, was an angelfish. But the others were anonymous to him, and the thought that he could be so ignorant of something so beautiful shamed him. One, smaller than the rest, its black satin body flecked with tiny dashes of luminous blue, came and floated by, its steady eye appearing to ask a question of him through the thick glass: What are you doing here?

A beep from the table broke his reverie. A text message, from Timur: *Caught on NY call. Many apologies. Come to ours for dinner tomorrow night.*

Webster had been caught on New York calls himself; they happened. Looking around him he realized he had no desire to remain in this place; his friend the fish had gone, and he felt a sudden need for company, and air. He dialed a number.

"Webster, you fraud," Constance's voice rolled down the line, so loud that a man at the next table looked up in disapproval. "Are you here?"

"I'm not only here, I'm in the Burj."

"Ha!" Another look. "The Burj? Al Arab? What the fuck are you doing there, my friend? Prospecting for rich widows?"

"It seems the Qazais are keen to impress me."

"Jesus. That's no place to be. We have to get you out."

"We do. Are you free for dinner?"

"Fuck dinner. You must come and stay. If I'd known they were going to stick you in that upended gin palace . . . Jesus. Be outside in fifteen minutes."

And before Webster could say another word he had hung up.

Feeling relief and a sort of giddy mischief, as if he were sneaking away from a dreary party or a weekend in an unfriendly house, Webster left the restaurant, took the elevator to his room, collected his still-packed suitcase, and made his way through the lobby into the thick, dark heat outside, stopping only to tell a receptionist that room 2307 was now free.

WHAT A BEAUTIFUL NIGHT it was for a getaway. The last of the sun had disappeared from the west and at the edge of the sky he could see a dozen stars, their light impossibly fine above the dazzle of the city. He moved out from under the bulbous sail of the Burj to see the whole of the night, and by a conscious effort tried to picture this place just fifty years before, when the tallest buildings were the mosques and the planes landed on runways of sand. It wasn't so hard, to his surprise. With its artificial islands, its indoor ski slopes, Dubai was so much a work of the imagination that it wasn't hard to imagine it out of existence, to return it to a time when the desert ran without interruption into the sea.

The rasping pulse of an angry-sounding engine broke his train of thought and he looked down to see an old American convertible, low to the ground, the roof lowered, its paintwork black and so polished it was like looking into a pool of oil. Constance was at the wheel, in cream linen suit and bright-red cravat, and as he pulled it around in front of Webster he looked up and beamed through a thick tangle of graying beard.

"Quick!" he yelled, louder than was necessary. "Get in. Before they realize you're trying to escape."

Webster smiled, threw his bag onto the backseat and was still shutting his door as Constance edged the big car casually past a waiting Maserati and sped toward the hotel's bridge, the engine shrieking in low gear.

"I feel like fucking Lancelot!" he shouted over the noise.

"Delighted to be rescued," Webster said.

"They didn't want to let me in. But when I told them I was a close friend of Darius Qazai their mood changed."

Webster laughed. "This is quite a jalopy."

Constance looked over at him with indignation. "You Brits have no class. This, my ignorant friend, is a 1978 Cadillac Seville. Friend of mine took the roof off. I'm glad you like it. Do you want one?" He pulled a pack of cigarettes from a pocket, deftly flipped the top and pushed one out for Webster.

"No, thank you."

"I thought you did?"

"Not yet."

They drove for twenty minutes, Constance switching the Cadillac between lanes every thirty seconds to try in vain to get past the traffic. He explained that they were heading for Deira, Dubai's twin city across the creek, the only place he could stand to be for long, and that they'd eat before they went to his house. As he drove he gave Webster a distinctive tour of the city, mixing history with vivid summaries of corporate crime, prodigious debt and countless ludicrous schemes that had died during the financial crisis.

"You see that tower there? With the scaffolding on it?" he shouted at Webster, looking over at him every time he spoke, his long gray hair streaming behind him one minute and pasted across his face the next. "Headquarters of United Development Bank. They started building that in early o-eight. Not very sexy, is it? They've just started work again. The bank will take half the floors and the rest will stay empty for a long time. But they don't care. All they care about is it'll have more parking than any other building in Dubai. People here are obsessed with parking. Height and parking. Your skyscraper may be a mile high but mine can park ten thousand cars."

"Ten thousand?"

"I exaggerate a little." Constance laughed. "But they have a hard-on for this shit. They just love to build. There, that's the proof." He pointed excitedly across Webster at an immense silver needle transfixing the night. "That, my friend, is the other Burj. The Burj Khalifa. Tallest building in the world. Wasn't here when you came last. Amazing, isn't it? Looks like the biggest Biro refill you ever saw."

Webster watched it move across the horizon with a kind of wonder. It was a shining lance of light half a mile high—so tall that his brain struggled to place it in the landscape. Constance might be cynical about all this but it was difficult not to be awed by the fearlessness of Dubai, the extraordinary faith that underlay the whole project.

"So what is it about this place?" he said with a smile, glancing across at his guide. "Why do you love it?"

Constance looked back at him with real interest, as if he'd never considered nor been asked such a question before.

"Jesus. Dubai?" They were crossing the creek now and a smell of sea and fish and sulfur hung on the bridge. Constance stopped flitting from lane to lane, as if this deserved his concentration, and when he spoke again his voice was almost restrained. "The possibility. It's like building from scratch in the sand. A blank slate. Nobody told these crazy bastards what the rules

were. Nobody told 'em you can't ski in the fucking desert. Nobody told 'em
you can't have all this property without some sort of proper economy.
They don't care. And look what they've done," he gestured around him. "It's
unbelievable. It's fantastic. Literally. That's what I love. This is the most
entertaining place on earth."

They were now in Deira, he explained, once a town in its own right and
less inflated than its neighbor across the creek. Here fish and spices had
been sold in the souks for centuries, here dhows had docked with precious
cargoes for the Gulf and here, in dusty little pockets behind the main roads
and the office buildings (shabbier and shorter than their counterparts to
the east), between unlit parking lots and patches of waste ground, one could
find bits of what Constance called "old Dubai," where houses the color of
sand huddled together out of the way of progress.

"Do you know how difficult it is to find somewhere to live in this city
that's over ten years old?" he said, turning into an unlit street, weaving
the Cadillac between potholes. "Damned near impossible. This used to be
a beautiful place when I first came here. No building higher than a house.
You could see the minarets. Took me six months to find my place. Built
in 1936. You're going to love it. It's got more class in the fucking can than
in the whole of that beached liner they put you in. But first we eat. We
eat well."

Constance grinned at Webster and slowed the car to a stop by two low
buildings, each of two stories and built of coral stone and clay, that ran
parallel to each other into the darkness. In the wide passageway between
them, dark but for the yellow light cast from their small square windows,
two old men in Arab dress sat smoking and playing backgammon at a low
table. As Constance and Webster passed they looked up.

"Salaamu Alaykum," said Constance.

"Salaamu Alaykum," they replied, watching the two strangers as they
walked toward the darker end of the buildings and in through the only
doorway to bear any decoration: a small red awning and two fabric banners that framed the door itself. Webster hung back on the threshold of a
cramped, rug-lined vestibule, a tiny replica of Qazai's grand hall, while

Constance talked in Arabic to a small man with bright white hair who wore a jacket embroidered with silver thread. The man bowed and ushered them through one of three doors into a much larger room, where rugs again covered every surface and three or four groups of men, all in the long white dress of Dubai, some wearing gray suit jackets over the top, sat on the floor, eating and talking. The small man bowed again and gestured for them to sit. Constance bowed and sat on the floor; Webster did the same opposite him, his back to the wall.

Constance looked at him and winked, a huge smile on his face, his gray eyes shining with fun and pleasure. Where it showed through the coarse beard and flowing gray hair his tan was the color of maple, the skin around his eyes dry and flaking, his nose strong and straight. There was a simplicity about Constance, something foolish, something sage, and if it weren't for his Western dress and his paunch he might have been some man of ancient wisdom, newly returned from months in the desert seeking truth.

"You eaten Yemeni before?"

Webster smiled and shook his head.

"You're going to love it. We're in the men's section. The mixed is for tourists and we, after all, are men." He raised an eyebrow for effect. "Not that we'll be able to drink like them but there's plenty of time for that. You got clean hands?"

"Pretty clean."

"You'll be using them."

A waiter came and spread out a clear plastic sheet. A second weighted it down with a basket of bread, two glasses, a large bottle of mineral water and a huge platter covered in sliced cucumber, lettuce, shining green olives, long, curling peppers, bright pink radishes and bunches of parsley, tarragon and mint. Webster smiled.

"You like this?" said Constance.

"I do. It's like a dinner I had with Darius Qazai not long ago."

"You sat on the floor with Darius Qazai?"

"No. We had chairs."

"That bastard." Constance roared with laughter. "So fucking grand."

Constance ordered, without consulting Webster, and when two glasses of orange juice had been brought, he leaned in over the plastic sheet, preparing for confidences.

"So. How is the old fraud?"

"Qazai? Or Ike?"

Constance chuckled. "Qazai. I don't need to ask after Ike. He's always OK."

"Yes, he is. He is always OK."

"Must be infuriating."

"Never." Webster smiled and took an olive. "Qazai," he said, chewing and spitting out the stone, "is the same as he was. We've not found much."

Constance frowned, grunted and looked up from his food. "You think he's clean?"

Webster thought for a moment. "No. But I don't know why." He bit into a pepper and savored its heat. "I've checked out hundreds of people. Usually from afar. And you're never sure. You get little sniffs, bits and pieces, then you run out of money. The clients don't care because they want to do the deal anyway. But this is different. I can speak to the man. I get to ask him questions. I get to look him in the eye."

He paused, and Constance smiled. "He lets you look him in the eye?"

Webster gave a knowing laugh. "For now."

"Do you like what you see?"

Webster considered the question. "Anyone that polished has to be hiding something."

Constance rocked back and slapped his thigh. "That's it! That's it exactly. All that smoothness isn't right. People are only smooth when they've smoothed something out. That's a fact." He held up his glass. "A toast. To the roughing up of Darius Qazai." And giving Webster's glass a forceful chink he drank the orange juice down, wiping his mouth with the back of his hand when he was done. "You sure you don't want me to find out where his money comes from?"

"No. Unless you have something cast iron." There was something predictable about this line: it was the easiest thing in the world to call a man a money-launderer, and one of the most difficult to prove. Tiredness had seized him, and though he knew it was just the flight and the time difference—it was always worse coming east—he asked himself whether he really had the energy to scrape away the layers of Constance's vanity and enthusiasm to determine whether he actually knew anything that might help.

Constance looked a little put out. "You mean to tell me that you don't care if the whole Qazai palace is built on shit?"

"I do. If it's shit with evidence." He shifted his position, sitting up straighter and stretching his back. "What about Shokhor?"

"He can wait." Constance waved his hand. "This is from a good source, Ben. Very good." Webster knew what he meant by this; he was always dropping hints that he had a friend in the CIA, and Webster had sometimes suspected that this friend had a habit of playing on Constance's enthusiasms. This wouldn't be the first time that someone had planted a seed with him in the hope that it would grow in the repeated telling.

"If he can back it up, I'm all ears. Now. Shokhor."

Constance, a little deflated, like a schoolboy who has been told he must do his homework before he can go out and play, told Webster what he had found. Shokhor was a creature of the Gulf. If you wanted to move something from one place in the region to another and had reason to believe that law enforcement might raise an objection, he was your man. Money, guns, drugs, art, people: he didn't specialize. He operated from an office by the port in Jebel Ali and his sole asset, like all respectable businesses, was goodwill—the goodwill of the customs officers and dockworkers and policemen that he kept on his unofficial payroll.

"How well protected is he?"

"He's still in business. Flourishing. Pretty well, I'd say."

"Does anyone know him?"

"You mean, can I secure you a polite introduction?"

"Something like that."

"That needs a little thought."

"It's OK. I have some ideas," said Webster.

Constance glanced up and leaned back to allow two waiters to place three bowls of food on the floor in front of them: one with prawns, one chicken, one lamb, grilled golden and black and laid on top of steaming yellow rice. "This is mandi," he said reaching for a piece of chicken. "The best thing ever to come out of Yemen. Which is saying something."

He held the chicken between his fingers, ripped some flesh off with his teeth and gave a muffled groan of satisfaction. His nails were discolored and cracked. Webster took a prawn and prized the meat free of its shell.

"So," he said. "Did you like my fax? About Mehr's death?"

Constance grinned and carried on chewing. "I sure did," he said at last. "Quite an intriguing little document."

Webster watched him carefully. "You didn't write it, did you?"

Constance looked genuinely surprised, and struggled to get a mouthful down before he spoke. "Me? No. Not my handiwork. I write better than that."

"It did lack a certain verve. Any idea who did?"

Cupping his hand to scoop up some rice Constance shook his head. "None. Maybe it leaked from somewhere."

"Maybe. What did you think?"

"Well. Even for the Iranian police that's one slack investigation." Constance picked up a prawn and pinched its head off. "Put it this way," he said, pulling the shell away in one easy motion, "even the Iranians, even today, will pay lip service to the murder of a Westerner on their soil. They won't do anything, of course, but they'll make it look like they've done something. These fuckers sound like they're not even doing that." He was waving the prawn around in his hand, forgetting about it as he warmed up. "They haven't tried to trace the truck that took him, they're not interested in where these priceless treasures might appear for sale. No one's asking why the poor fucker had to get kidnapped when all they had to do is break into his hotel room. And he had his passport on him? In a country where a British passport would net you what, five hundred bucks? Those are some snooty criminals, my friend, that's for sure." He finally put the prawn in his mouth. "They haven't even interviewed the guy he was due to meet. Oh that's good. Damn that's good. And you know what?" He reached for another prawn. "They don't make decisions like that on their own. Not some terrified homicide cop in Isfahan. No way."

"Who does?"

"Someone with power. Could come from a couple of places."

Webster took a long drink of orange juice and thought.

"Can you find out?"

"I can try."

"Who would have done the work?" he said. "In Isfahan."

"What do you mean?"

"Well, there are five men, which is a lot, they have guns, and they know where Mehr is. Either they intercept his calls or they control the antiques dealer."

"I don't know. There's organized crime in Iran, like everywhere."

"What about the government?"

"Possibly. They're always up for an op. You have to give 'em that."

"If it was, who does the work?"

"The Revolutionary Guard. Most likely. Or VEVAK."

"What's the difference?"

"Well," Constance scratched his beard, "understand this. Every dictatorship needs terror. To keep going. But in Iran, it goes beyond necessity. They have a taste for it. It's not politics, it's cruelty. Viciousness. This is why they love executing people so much." He paused. "Do you know the story of the Shiraz martyrs?"

Webster didn't.

"No reason why you should. You would have been about ten, I guess. Jesus. So three or four years after the revolution, ten women were arrested for teaching religious classes. They were Bahai, and therefore supremely dangerous to the revolution." He raised an eyebrow and shook his head. "So dangerous that they had to be killed. All ten of them were driven out to a field near Shiraz and hanged, one by one. The older women went first, so that the younger ones might look on and recant. Convert to Islam. But they didn't. The youngest of them all was seventeen. She kissed the noose before she put it around her neck."

Webster felt the food in his mouth turn to clay.

"That, my friend," said Constance, with black cheerfulness, "is called protecting the revolution. The revolution must be protected from religious young girls, and dissidents, and anyone with an ounce of decency or brains or fire. Right now they're scared fucking witless that they're going to be the next sorry-ass tyranny to collapse and they'll have to hide out in Caracas for the rest of their lives with a bunch of mangy Arab dictators—who they despise, because they're Sunnis, but are in fact no different from them in any particular. That is if they make it out, which they probably won't. And if the Israelis don't nuke them to shit. But you know what? They're right to be vigilant. One day it'll be a seventeen-year-old that brings it all down. And until then, they're going to keep killing people."

Webster swallowed, waiting for Constance to finish.

"Grizzly, huh? They're organized, of course. You need structures to keep the killing efficient. So the Revolutionary Guard is the army. More powerful. More money. VEVAK is intelligence. They're both big on killing dissidents, sometimes with a noose around their neck, sometimes with a discreet little bullet in the head." He gestured with two fingers against his temple. "So you think your guy was political?"

"Not that I know."

"Everything's political in Iran." Constance grinned, took a shank of lamb and with theatrical delight took a hungry, wolfish bite. "Maybe he got sacrificed."

8.

If Zia Shokhor had thought to check up on the man who had called him up the next morning he would have found enough, Webster hoped, to accept a meeting. William Taylor was the managing director of Northwest Associates Limited, a London company that according to its nicely designed but rudimentary Web site sought "to maximize opportunities arising from disparities in finance and trade between developed and emerging economies." Whatever that meant, Northwest had a respectable address on Savile Row, its own domain name, and a telephone number that went through to a well-spoken receptionist who would offer to connect your call. Its accounts had been up to date since its incorporation in 1991 and its filings at Companies House in order. Taylor had become a director in 2004.

And if Shokhor was the diligent sort he would have found, among the hundreds of thousands of other William Taylors, a handful of hits for this one—enough to demonstrate that he existed, but not so many to alarm anyone who liked their business associates discreet. Taylor had spoken at a conference on Central Asian investment in 2007, and had published a handful of articles in more or less obscure trade magazines. To each was attached his biography: University of Bristol, a career in banking and trade, the specifics artfully elided.

Thorough investigation would find the cracks in the fiction, but for nearly twenty years, ever since Hammer had persuaded a friend of his to sign the documents in return for a small annual fee, it had held up. Taylor, Webster's double, had made several outings over the years, and had never been found out. For Shokhor he would do, Webster told himself. Just to get a meeting.

He had made the call on a cell phone he kept for these occasions and had had to concentrate hard on sounding more businesslike than he felt. Constance had finally stopped talking at two that morning, or thereabouts, a little while after the opening of a second bottle of whisky. Sitting on his roof, leaning back into a pile of oversized cushions, a half-spent, half-lit cigar in his teeth, he had been telling a long, snaking story about a German businessman who had been relieved of a large amount of money by a con-man masquerading as a sheikh. The ending hadn't seemed like much of an ending, but Webster had grunted his appreciation and tilted his head back to look at the stars, his own cigar short and glowing warmly between his fingers, until he realized, opaquely, that the story hadn't finished and that Constance was in fact asleep. Laughing to himself, he had staggered up and gone to bed, vainly trying to rouse his host and settling in the end for re-moving the dead cigar from his mouth and covering him with a rug.

After that it had not been a good night. He hadn't been able to sleep: with air conditioning it was airless and too cold, and without, instantly sweaty. Constance's kitchen had run to coffee but not to food, and as he sat on the roof in the early heat waiting for his host to wake and Shokhor to return his call, he felt like all the moisture had been drained from his sys-tem and replaced with sand. With luck Shokhor would set their meeting for tomorrow, if ever.

Webster had called the office number on Calyx's Web site, asked for Mr. Shokhor and told him that he had been given his name by a big collector of art in London, which was true, in a sense; that he was looking for someone to help with moving some large and delicate cargoes from Syria and Iran to Cyprus; and that he would like to meet, if possible, while he was in town for a few days. Shokhor had seemed wary but curious, and promised to call back once he had consulted his diary. That had been an hour ago.

Slow footsteps coming up the stairs to the terrace made Webster turn.

Constance was up. Wearing a plain white robe, his hair wiry and crazed, he looked more than ever like some wild prophet, but for the cup of coffee he was guarding carefully with both hands.

"You son of a bitch," he said, sitting down opposite Webster. Around them low roofs lay stepped like boxes, covered in white satellite dishes that shone blindingly in the sun. "What did you do to me last night?"

Webster squinted back at him. "Nothing untoward. You made it to bed then?"

"I woke up at six with the sun broiling my face."

Webster laughed. "I'm sorry. I tried to wake you."

Constance uttered something between a grunt and a groan and looked around him over the rooftops. "Another beautiful day. God, how they run together." He took a watchful sip of his coffee. "What's the plan?"

"Dinner with Timur Qazai. Until then, waiting for Shokhor to call me back."

"You called him? Before breakfast?"

"It's ten o'clock."

"Jesus, you're a machine." He stood up. "Come on. It's too hot out here. Let's go and eat."

SHOKHOR HAD CALLED BACK while Webster and Constance were eating eggs at an ersatz diner in Deira. He had suggested that they meet at the Hyatt Regency, explaining that it might prove more convenient for everyone since his office was so far away, and at ten to four, after a day of little more than sitting and eating, Constance had dropped Webster two blocks away. He had insisted on waiting nearby until the meeting was finished.

"I'm yours today. I'm certainly not myself. And you never know what this fucker's got in store."

Webster had told Shokhor that he would be wearing a light-gray suit and a plain dark-blue tie, but as he scanned the hotel lobby he could see that he was the first to arrive; everyone else was already in conversation. He found a pair of sofas by a window, sat down and ordered tea.

This was not the Burj. It could have been any hotel anywhere in the world: the marble floor, the low leather furniture, the absence of color, the bland courtesy of the uniformed staff; it was all of a piece. Outside, the pool had a lone swimmer in it, and the loungers surrounding it were empty.

"Mr. Taylor."

Webster looked around, experiencing that brief sense of disconnection that follows when someone calls you by the wrong name, quickly caught himself and stood up. Two men were standing by his table. One was small and plump, under his white kandura, with a thick black mustache; the other, standing a foot or so further back, with his hands clasped in front of him, was almost twice his height.

"Terribly sorry. I was miles away. Mr. Shokhor?" They were expecting an Englishman, and Webster would oblige. He held out his hand. "A great pleasure. Thank you so much for seeing me at such short notice."

"Please, have a card." Shokhor took a card from his breast pocket and passed it to Webster, who took the time to look at it for a moment, appreciatively.

"You are alone?" said Shokhor. The folds of his chin creased as he looked down at his watch.

"Quite alone. I've ordered tea. Will you join me?"

Shokhor nodded, sat down on the sofa opposite Webster, looked around comprehensively and nodded again, this time at his bodyguard, who started a slow patrol of the room. A waiter came, and left with an order for another pot of tea.

Shokhor was waiting for Webster to speak. His face was comfortable, well-fed, but his eyes were nervous; they flickered about.

"I know you don't have long, Mr. Shokhor, so I'll come straight to the point. Occasionally my company trades in goods that need to be transported with great care. They can get damaged when they cross borders, for instance. Sometimes when we take possession of them they are in places where . . . where discretion is required in dealing with the legal authorities."

Shokhor kept his face free of expression, and Webster, leaning forward, projecting an air of confidentiality, went on.

"Much of our work is in the former Soviet Union. Central Asia, mostly.

We have good relationships there. But we have some interesting opportunities now in this part of the world. That's why I'm here. That's why I wanted to talk."

Shokhor smoothed his mustache with his forefinger and thumb.

"How did you find my name?"

"I do business with a collector in London. He gets most of his pieces from this part of the world."

"What is his name?"

"He didn't want me to say."

Shokhor shook his head, made a frown with his lips. "That seems strange to me."

"I would imagine that he doesn't want you to know that I work with him. Perhaps I don't either."

"What does he collect?"

Webster smiled. "Well. If I tell you, you may know who he is. But at least I won't have given you his name." He pretended to hesitate. "He's a generalist. Islamic art. Pre-Islamic. He has a huge collection. But he has a special interest in Iran."

Shokhor frowned again, shaking his head. He shifted in his seat, so that he was no longer looking at Webster but out toward the pool. "Mr. Taylor. If we are to do business it has to be on an introduction. I am not saying we cannot, but you must first have someone vouch for you." He stood, and looked down at Webster. "You understand. This is business."

Webster rose, and they shook hands. "I understand completely. If you hear from me again you will hear from our mutual friend first."

Shokhor gave him one last look, inclined his head a quarter of an inch by way of a bow, and left, followed at a close but respectful distance by his man.

Webster watched them leave and called Constance.

"Jesus. You're done already? Did he blow you off?"

"Yes and no."

"Does he know Qazai?"

"I'd say he genuinely had no idea who I was talking about. But I have what I wanted. Come and get me." He hung up, and retrieving Shokhor's card from his pocket inspected it again. On it were two telephone numbers, one local, one Cyprus, either of which might be enough.

As he waited for Constance in the heat outside his phone rang.

"Mr. Webster?"

"Speaking."

"Timur Qazai. I need you to come now. Can you come now?"

Webster wondered whether he was about to have his plans changed again to accommodate a Qazai conference call. He gestured to Constance, arriving in the Cadillac, to wait for a moment.

"I need my papers."

"Forget the papers. Come right now. Find a cab." Timur sounded tense, with none of his father's smoothness. "To my house. My home address."

Webster suppressed a sigh. "Mr. Qazai, I'm here to interview you. I need my questions."

"Fuck the questions. I need your help." He paused, and Webster waited. "My son's been kidnapped."

CONSTANCE DROVE THROUGH the afternoon traffic like a man who had finally found a purpose in life, with one hand on the horn and the other gesturing at the mainly stationary cars to get out of his way, swearing robustly as he went. The Cadillac surged and stuttered and made slow progress until they left the main road.

The Qazais lived in the east of the city, in an area that like so many things in Dubai seemed to have been built just the day before. One aloof enclosure led to another on a lazily winding road whose tarmac was so fresh that it felt like a trespass to drive on it, but Constance seemed not to care as he swung the heavy car around corner after corner, past the security cameras perched on every wall. Webster caught glimpses of the villas through the wrought-iron gates: bricked driveways, black cars in the shade, arched verandas, young palm trees waiting to grow.

Timur's was no different. Not the largest, by any means, nor ostentatious for someone as wealthy as he must be, but new, and well built, and slightly bland. As the car pulled up on the verge Webster saw signs of life that had been missing from the others. Two children's bikes leaned against the porch; at the far end of the garden there was a small goal with a soccer ball in it; brightly colored towels lay scattered around the pool.

"Thanks, Fletcher. I'll make my own way back."

"Bullshit. I'm coming in."

"You want them to know we work together?"

Constance thought for a moment, pulling at the beard on his chin.

"Don't give them my name. Let's go." He had opened his door and was walking toward the intercom on the gatepost before Webster could respond.

The gates swung slowly open, and Timur came out from the porch to greet them, looking haggard and momentarily confused.

"Mr. Webster?" His eyes moved from one to the other.

"I'm Webster."

Timur offered his hand, looking at Constance. He had his father's eyes, almost, a clear blue but somehow dimmed, and the same proud brow, but his lips were fuller and his expression softer, less majestic. Thick black hair made him seem younger than he actually was, but he looked tired: the skin under his eyes was a livid gray and his hand was tacky with sweat.

"This is a friend of mine. Peter Fletcher. We were talking when you called." Constance beamed and held out a hand.

Timur shook it distractedly, looking at Webster. "I only want you."

"He might be able to help. And he won't say anything to anyone."

Timur considered it, and Constance did his best to appear respectable.

"Come," he said, and led the way into the cool interior of the house.

"This is Raisa, my wife. Raisa, this is Mr. Webster, and his friend."

Raisa took Webster's hand. Webster tried to place her; she was dark, but not Arabic, slight and pretty, her brown eyes quick and scared. "I'm so glad you're here."

"This way, please," said Timur, and they followed him into the kitchen, where they sat down around the table. He looked at Raisa briefly, with a mixture of reassurance and fear, and began. "We had a call from our driver forty minutes ago." He closed his eyes, collected himself and went on. "He takes our son Parviz to swimming every Wednesday. They were coming home when the car got a flat tire. A car pulled up, a man got out. With a gun. He took Parviz." There was a catch in his voice as he said it.

"Have you called the police?" said Webster.

"Straight away. They should be here." His hand tensed on the table.

"Where did it happen?"

"By the racecourse."

Webster looked at Constance, who understood. "About fifteen minutes away."

"How well do you know your driver?" said Webster.

"All his life. His father drove for mine."

"Did he get the number plate?"

"Yes."

"Where is he?"

"Looking."

"Tell him to come back. The police will want to speak to him."

As Timur typed a text into his phone Webster pressed on.

"Do they always take the same route?"

"Probably. I'm not sure."

"Who might have done it?"

"I have no idea."

Webster looked at him steadily.

"Really," said Timur. He glanced at his wife and shook his head. "None."

"We're rich," said Raisa, biting at the side of her thumb. "It happens."

"What sort of car was it?" said Webster.

"A BMW. A black BMW."

"New?"

Timur looked puzzled. "I think so. I don't know. Does it matter?"

Constance spoke, his deep voice full of authority. "It doesn't happen often. And they don't drive fancy cars when it does."

Timur shook his head, leaned forward in frustration. "Look. My son is out there. They might be at the airport by now. In half an hour they could be in Oman. You have to do something." His phone beeped and he looked at it distractedly.

"The police have the resources," said Webster. "All we can do is try to work out what's happening in the hope that will help."

"That's not a priority. It's not useful now."

Webster kept his expression neutral. "What did the police say?"

"That they'd put out an alert, and someone would be here soon."

"Do you think they will?"

"God. I don't know." He looked at Raisa in frustration. "Yes. They should. They know who we are."

The intercom chimed and Timur went to answer it.

"It's them."

He went outside, and Raisa followed. Webster and Constance looked at each other over the table.

Constance grunted. "What are you thinking?"

"That it's not about money. More of a feeling."

Timur returned with two men, both in khaki uniform, both wearing gray peaked caps, and introduced Webster to them as his lawyer. Constance he didn't mention. One of the officers, older, bearded, with a row of ribbon medals on his chest, offered his hand to Webster.

"Captain Faraj."

He shook Constance's hand and sat at the table, waiting for everyone to join him.

"Every police car in Dubai knows the number plate and model of the car. This is good. We are treating this as a top priority."

Timur thanked him, and the captain gave a bow of his head.

"Without a passport for your son they will not be able to leave the country. I will need a photograph of him that we can circulate." Timur nodded at Raisa, who got up and left. "Where is your driver?"

"On his way."

"I will need a full account. You trust him?"

"Completely."

"Have you heard from the kidnappers?"

"Nothing."

The captain gestured at his subordinate, who took a pad and a pen from the top pocket of his shirt.

"The basic details first. How old is your son?"

"Nine."

"Is he your only child?"

"No. We have another son. Farhad. He's five."

"Where is he?"

"Upstairs with his nanny."

"He doesn't swim?"

"Only here."

Timur's phone rang, the shrill tone like a shock. He looked at it, then at the captain, and shook his head, once, to indicate that he didn't know the number. Raisa came back into the room, a photograph in her hand, her face anxious. On the second ring he answered, glancing nervously between her and Webster.

"Yes . . . Yes . . . Yes I am." He turned from the table slightly, putting a hand to his free ear, as if he couldn't hear what was being said. "What, there? Oh, thank God. Thank God." He reached his hand up to Raisa and held hers tightly. "Where? I'm coming now. Right now. Let me speak to him . . . Parviz? Sweetheart? Everything's OK. I'm coming to get you. You're safe now. You're safe."

PARVIZ WAS A SKINNY, leggy boy, clearly bright, who held his mother's hand and answered the captain's questions with great composure. He was in shock, and his face looked drained, but he was a perfect witness, and by the time Raisa told the men that she was going to make him something to eat and that they should go and sit out of the way by the pool, he had described every last detail of his short abduction. The driver, Khalil, was if anything the more distraught, but what he said was consistent and plausible, if strange.

Khalil had taken Parviz to the pool as he always did. They had arrived a little before three, and at ten past four Parviz had come out with all the other boys. After half a mile one of the tires on the car, one of the Tabriz fleet, had run flat, and Khalil had been forced to pull over at the entrance to a construction site, telling Parviz to get out and stand a few meters back from the road while he changed the wheel. As he was fetching the spare from the boot, a black BMW with Dubai plates had driven up, and a man had got out of the passenger seat. He was in his thirties or forties, possibly Arabic, possibly Iranian or Iraqi, of compact build, and he wore sunglasses. Smiling, he had told Khalil that he was a friend of Timur's, that he'd recognized their car, and that he'd be happy to drive Parviz home rather than making him stand here at the side of the road. By this time he was standing by Parviz, ruffling his hair. Khalil had thanked him but declined, and at this the man had reached for his waistband and the silver pistol that lay concealed there. He had then taken Parviz's hand and led him to the BMW. Parviz had appealed to Khalil and tried to break free, but the man had merely dragged him to the waiting car, opened the rear door and shoved him in, sliding in after him as the car had driven off. Khalil, stalled at gunpoint, simply hadn't known how to react.

Parviz volunteered that the men in the car hadn't hurt him; they had just left him to cry. He hadn't been tied or blindfolded. There were two of them: the man who had put him in the car, and a driver. They hadn't said anything to each other. Not a word. For a long time they had just driven, Parviz wasn't sure where. Around and around, it had felt like. Then the car had gone into the parking lot of a big shopping center and stopped. The man in sunglasses had calmly taken Parviz by the hand into a supermarket and told him he was to wait by the fruit, count to three hundred, and let one of the cashiers know who he was and that he wanted to go home. Before walking away he had given Parviz a piece of paper with Timur's phone number printed on it.

Throughout, Webster and Constance said nothing. The captain was thorough, but no longer urgent, and though it was almost dark by the time he left and no question had gone unasked Webster sensed that this odd episode was no longer a priority.

Timur, though, continued to look both relieved and haunted. Webster liked him. He was less slick than his father, with a quiet sadness about him, as if this strange world had been forced upon him and he was dutifully living someone else's life. More than once he had said that such a thing wouldn't have happened if they had been able to remain in London, and nothing in his manner suggested that he relished the prospect of inheriting the Qazai empire. Webster was reminded of Ava's word for him: enslaved.

When the captain had gone, he offered his guests drinks, for form's sake, it seemed. Webster declined, and glared at Constance when he replied that a large whisky with lots of ice would go down very well.

"Do you have to?" he said, as Timur went inside.

"Hair of the dog, my friend. Better late than never."

It was so calm here. The pool water swirled, sprinklers swept the lawn, under the garden lights the grass was a pristine, uniform green, and for the first time Webster felt at one with the heat. Looking over his shoulder he could see Timur crouching down to say goodnight to Parviz, closing him in a tight hug.

A maid appeared with three tumblers full of whisky and ice. Constance took his, swallowed it in a draft, put the glass back on the tray and beamed up at her.

"Another would be lovely. Thank you so much."

Timur returned and raised his glass an inch to Webster before he drank, and for a while no one said anything.

"What do you think they wanted?" Webster said at last.

By the pale glow of the pool Webster saw Timur frown.

"Money. It must be."

"A ransom?"

"Yes. Of course."

"So why didn't they go through with it?"

"Because they got cold feet."

"But they said nothing in the car."

Timur frowned again. "I don't follow you."

"They stuck to their plan. They didn't panic."

"They don't sound like the panicking kind," said Constance, with meaning.

"Can you think," said Webster, watching Timur closely, "who might want to send you a message?"

Timur shook his head. "No." And after a pause, "That's ridiculous."

"Why? You're feeling vulnerable. Your family doesn't feel safe. Maybe that's all they wanted."

Timur held Webster's eye, and in that moment he seemed both resolute and scared.

"Is there anyone who might want you to leave Dubai? Run you out of town?" Constance asked, sipping at his new drink.

"All I want," Timur said, "is to know that my family is protected."

"That's difficult," said Webster. "Without knowing what the threat is."

Timur shook his head. His eyes seemed focused elsewhere, and in that moment Webster sensed that he was feeling acutely alone. But he rallied, and when he spoke again he was cool, businesslike.

"Do you have any advice for me?"

Webster waited for a moment before answering, his silence punctuating the change in tone. "Practically speaking, you should talk to a professional. I know a good man. His name's George Black. He'll call you tomorrow morning."

Timur nodded. "Thank you."

"But I'd have a good think about who it might have been. We should talk about it. When you have some idea."

Timur chewed his bottom lip and watched the eddying waters of the pool, his eyes full of quiet fear.

9.

WEBSTER'S PARENTS LIVED IN CORNWALL, on the Helford estuary, and at the end of the steep slope of their garden was a small cove, overhung by oaks, where at high tide a rowing boat could negotiate a course over the rocks to a mossy stone quay. In the early morning, whenever he was staying, Webster would walk through the garden down to the water's edge, the grass cold and alive under his bare feet, drape his towel over the same dead branch and swim. Today the water was high with a spring tide and he was able to dive, carefully leaping off the slippery stone, his body a straight line piercing the surface. The water here wasn't like other water; it was salty and fresh at once, of a green so dark it looked black, quickly deep and always, even in autumn after a good summer, icy. There was no place he liked to swim more.

In the drizzle and the early half-light the oaks' new leaves seemed lit up against the darkness on the banks. He swam to a buoy about thirty yards out and from there turned down sharply through new layers of cold and dark, tried with powerful strokes to reach the bottom, failed, and rising burst finally into the air again, taking as much breath into his lungs as he could, the fine rain soft on his face. The boats moored beside him hardly bobbed, it was so calm.

It was still enough to swim across the estuary but he wanted to be by the woods today, so turning back from the buoy he headed upriver past his parents' house toward Frenchman's Creek, keeping about five yards from the bank, his stroke a steady crawl. Here the oaks stood so close to the water that they seemed to grow out of it, their branches reaching down and brushing the surface, the roots exposed in the red earth where the land had fallen away, so that all the elements of the place—the river, the sea, the damp earth and the misty sky—seemed joined in an ancient, watery union. Webster was always revived here. Like a penitent to the confessional he would bring his doubts and his sins to the water and, addressing each in turn, find them washed away.

He had plenty today. Dubai had left him feeling dried out and restive. Three days switching between the solid heat and the air-conditioned cold, drinking too much with Fletcher: that would have been enough, even without the grim flight back that had left at three in the morning and dumped him in a gray, tired-looking London at six. But none of this was the cause. He had caught the train with Elsa and the children at noon, and though delighted to be with them had been tetchy throughout the journey, having to field e-mails and calls about the case, and beyond that preoccupied with something he couldn't clearly grasp. Part of it was having to deal with Dean Oliver, a private detective—for want of a better word—of Webster's faint acquaintance. There was nothing wrong with Dean. He was resourceful, slick, even charming in his own way, but his trade was grubby, and Webster would rather have kept his distance. As it was, he had called him with Shokhor's numbers that morning, and Oliver had said, in his most reassuring tones, that he would see what he could do, and suggested they meet in a week. Webster knew all too well what he could do, and what sort of trouble it might lead to—though on this case, he told himself, there was little risk.

No, there was something else. Elsa had given him a short period of grace and then let him know that he was going to have to rally, and for the rest of the trip he had done his best to give a convincing impression of cheer and disguise the fact that something continued to scratch at his nerves.

They were in Cornwall for his father's birthday, his sixty-fifth. Patrick Webster was not a man for grand celebrations, but the family would be

there, and one or two close friends. Webster's sister, a family lawyer, was flying down from her practice in Edinburgh. Tomorrow night they would all
have dinner and Webster was to give a speech, something he hadn't given
a moment's thought in the crush of everyday obligations, and now as he
moved through the water, twisting his head up to the air every fourth
stroke, he felt shame at the thought that he was devoting more time to a
man like Darius Qazai than he was to his own father.

What different men they were. Patrick Webster was a clinical psychiatrist who had devoted his career to the care of profoundly ill people: to the
schizophrenic, the irretrievably depressed, the bipolar, to those poor souls
whose minds had betrayed them.

As a boy he had found his father's job mysterious and, if he was frank, a
little frightening—not because he felt at risk but because the idea of a mind
failing seemed nightmarish, both terrifying and curiously real. His father,
though, he had found anything but. He was a quiet man, well-read, a stu-
dent of history, engaged in the world, a socialist by instinct but never a
member of any party, indefatigably kind. He was always trying to help
people: when Webster was eight one of the fathers in the street had left his
wife and small daughter, disappearing entirely with all the family's money,
and the Websters had put them up for four months while they recon-
structed their lives. A couple of years after that, a homeless man whom Patrick had befriended came one summer to dig over and replant the garden,
turning up every day in time for breakfast and after three weeks leaving
with the job, which was of course unnecessary, undone. If he had been born
in the eighteenth century, people would have called him a philanthropist,
and there was something classical too about his more caustic, satirical side,
which railed against entitlement and injustice. He was funny about these
things, but deeply angered by them, too, and if he dwelled on them for too
long could sink into a forceful gloom.

After ten minutes Webster had reached Frenchman's Creek, where the
trees swelling out over the water were in such health that he couldn't see the
bank on either side. He rested for a moment by a buoy at the entrance and
saw bass sliding past a foot below the surface of the water. Before Lock's
death, he wouldn't have taken this case so seriously. Now everything seemed

trivial, and corrosive: Qazai's vanity, Senechal's steely mania, his own determination to find his client guilty of something at all costs.

He set off again, up the creek now, swimming through the clustered leaves and twigs that the night's rain and wind had dislodged from the trees. At eye level water boatmen skittered around by the bank and bass broke the surface to snap at them.

Too much was wrong. The state of Shiraz Holdings, in particular, was beginning to intrigue him. A broker friend of his had asked around and found that it was widely assumed that Qazai's private fund was in trouble. Word was that in 2009, when Dubai looked as if would be cut loose with all its debts by Abu Dhabi, Qazai had decided that there was no way that the richer, more sober of the Emirates would let its brash younger brother default, and had bet heavily that the market was wrong. No one was sure how much he had lost, but it was known that he had placed not only a large amount of Shiraz's money but a larger sum he had borrowed from various banks, all of which he had of course had to pay back. There were some who were surprised to see Shiraz still functioning at all.

Then there was Mehr, whose death made little sense. It was no robbery, that was certain, and none of the other motives fitted unless Qazai was somehow involved. Webster had two theories, neither of which he particularly liked: that Mehr really had been smuggling treasures out of the country, perhaps on Qazai's instructions, and had been caught; or that he had been involved in a far deeper, darker game, perhaps for an intelligence agency somewhere—a game that for now he could only guess at.

No: even without Parviz's brief disappearance it was too much.

THAT AFTERNOON THE WEBSTERS rented a bass boat and took it out to the mouth of the estuary to fish for mackerel. The drizzle had cleared, scraps of blue showed through the white clouds and a breeze blew into their faces as they made for the headland, the faded pinks and oranges of their lifejackets vivid in the middle of the lead gray sea. The two-stroke outboard, flat out and managing three or four knots, strained away at a constant pitch behind them.

Half a mile short of open water Webster killed the engine and letting the boat dip up and down on the gentle swell unwound a mackerel line over the side, taking care not to let the shining sharp hooks catch his fingers. He passed the end to Nancy and started playing out another line while Daniel waited patiently. They both loved to fish. On land they weren't still for a minute, but out here they would happily sit for an hour jigging the lines and waiting for that moment when something unexpectedly powerful tried to tug them out of their hands.

"Move it up and down," Webster said to Daniel, taking his son's hands in his own. "Like this. You want the fish to think the bait's alive." Daniel gave the line a great jerk. "That's it. Gently. Do it again and again. That's it."

Elsa smiled at him, her dark hair falling in her face in the wind.

"You're such a countryman." She pointed at a grand stone house sitting in isolation on the headland to the north. "How about that one?"

"Too severe. And you'd get bored."

"I'd do something. Paint. Sculpt. Learn the violin."

"You'd still get bored. Although I'm sure you'd find plenty of patients down here."

"What would you do?"

"Fish."

She laughed. "These two have a better record."

"That's true."

Nancy turned to him. "Daddy, is this one?"

"Did you feel a tug? Let's see." He moved over to her side of the boat, which tipped a little with his weight, and pulled her line out of the water, looping the wet nylon in his left hand. There was nothing there. "False alarm. Do you want me to have a go?" Nancy shook her head and made to take the line back from him. He let it out again, passed it to her and moved back to sit by Elsa.

"What are you going to say then?" she said. "Tomorrow night."

"I don't know. I'm getting there. He's an easy man to say nice things about."

Elsa looked up at him and leaned against his shoulder. He put his arm around her. The breeze was beginning to gust a little and there was a trace of chill in it.

"You'll be fine," she said.

"I know. They're not a tough crowd. I've just never had the opportunity before. I want to make the most of it."

They all sat for a minute in silence, Nancy diligently tweaking her line, Daniel simply staring at his.

"You seem better for your swim," said Elsa.

"Much. This place never fails." He looked around him at the murmuring gray of the water, lighter and white-capped beyond the line between the two headlands; at the ragged tawny rocks on the shore and the secret sandy beaches that lay among them; at the hundreds of boats moored at Helford a mile or two behind. It was a complete world, the estuary. Maybe they *could* live here.

Nancy gave a little shriek and lifted the line above her head in her hands. "Daddy! Daddy! I think this is one!"

Webster moved forward and sat between her and Daniel, helping her reel it in. This time he could feel weight on the other end, and as he pulled he looked carefully into the water for the first silvery sign of a fish. There were a dozen or more hooks, and on the last were three plump mackerel, each about a foot long, whose shining backs squirmed in the light and dripped water as they struggled into the boat.

Webster let them drop and hugged Nancy while they thrashed at his feet.

"Well done, poppet. Three! We'll have these for tea."

The breeze was now a wind, and the swell beneath them choppy. They would have to go in soon. He took the first mackerel off its hook, held it firmly by the tail and raising his arm high beat its head sharply against the bench seat. The fish gave a final quiver and went still. As he bent to free the second his phone rang, an absurdly urban noise, and Elsa gave him a steady look. Distracted for a moment he let it ring out and set about his work again, killing the last two fish while Nancy and Daniel looked on with a childish lack of squeamishness.

The three mackerel lay beside him now, neatly in parallel and waiting to be gutted. As he reached into his jacket pocket for his penknife his phone rang again, its old-fashioned trill insistent.

"Just turn it off," said Elsa.

"It's a Friday," he said.

It was a U.S. cell phone number that he didn't recognize.

"Hello."

"Ben?"

"Yes."

"Lester. What's up?"

"Lester? Jesus. How are you?"

"I'm good, buddy, I'm good. We miss you. How's life with Ike?"

"It's all right. It's good, thanks. Listen, Lester, I'm on a boat, sitting next to three dead mackerel. Can I call you back in an hour?"

He turned to keep the phone out of the wind.

"Sure. Listen, all it was, I got a call from some guy, said he was a head-hunter, his client's thinking about giving you a job."

"Is he real?"

"He left his name and a number, his cell. No company. Jonathan Whitehouse. A Brit. I couldn't find any headhunter of that name. Not on this planet anyway."

Webster knew what that meant. "You'd think they'd bother to do it properly."

"I know. Don't they know who we are?" Lester chuckled.

"What did he want to know?"

"What kind of a guy you are. And why you left. He tried to squeeze that in. I told him I wasn't in the habit of talking to people I didn't know. So who's checking you out, Ben? You fighting someone you shouldn't be?"

"God, I don't know. Some Russian. Lester, I should go. But thanks. I appreciate it."

"No problem, man. Any time."

Webster switched his phone to silent and put it back in his pocket. "Sorry."

Elsa nodded, clearly annoyed. There had been enough Ikertu on this trip already.

"Right," he said with false cheerfulness. "Daniel. Let's see what you've got, shall we?"

Daniel had nothing, and when Webster told him that was fine, that he never caught anything either, he protested. He didn't want to go home now. That wasn't fair. He wanted to stay until he'd caught as many fish as Nancy. Webster tried to exchange a glance with Elsa but she was looking out to sea, more irritated by the call than he had realized, or by something unsaid. Her mood had changed.

In the last fifteen minutes the wind, squalling now and forceful, had blown them halfway across the estuary so that they were only two hundred yards from the northern shore, and over the headland to the south rain-clouds the color of wet rock were massing. The little boat danced erratically on the chop.

"Did you check the forecast?" said Elsa.

"There was nothing about this," said Webster, sitting in the stern and dropping the engine back into the water. Daniel started to cry and Elsa comforted him as Webster started it up, turning the boat back toward the village, suddenly feeling exposed and more vulnerable than he had thought possible here. Substantial waves crossed the estuary now and Webster took them on the perpendicular, the bow rising up and crashing down, sending thick arcs of spray over the boat. Everyone was quiet, the only sounds the blustering wind and the slap of the bow on the water, and Webster, adjusting their direction and concentrating hard, watched his family huddled together and found himself praying for their safe return.

"HE MAY NOT LOOK IT, but he's a daunting figure, my father." Webster had stood to speak, but there was no need. They were twelve in all, squeezed around a makeshift dining table that was really two tables artfully dressed, and in the candlelight each face was bright with expectation. He could have simply raised his glass and bid them all do the same, and they would have been happy—his father, perhaps, would have preferred it—but there were things he had never said before that needed to be said.

"When we were little, Friday night was discussion night. I think it started when I was ten or eleven." He glanced at his sister. "You must have been all of nine. After we'd eaten, Dad would ask us if there was anything we wanted to talk about that week. There never was. So he'd suggest something. Something from the papers, or something that was on his mind, or something he knew was on ours. The first one I can remember, there was a huge CND march in London, and you wanted to know," he turned to his father, "whether we thought it was right that these weapons existed. Or what we made of the miners' strike. Or hostages in Beirut. Or heart transplants. Or Chernobyl." He took a breath.

"Some of this scared me, to be honest. These were things I half heard on the radio or caught scraps of on the news when we were ushered off to bed, and I wanted to block them out. But you didn't let us do that. We had to know what the world was like, so that we wouldn't be scared.

"And it worked, more or less. I used to have the odd nightmare about nuclear winters, but that had more to do with my friend Peter Lennon gleefully showing me films about the likely aftermath. But generally the world was a less frightening place. It was still scary, but we didn't have to be scared by it."

Webster paused. "He did this for us. But more importantly he did it for countless others who were much more vulnerable than we ever were. We knew what he did at work, a little, because he'd explain it to us, like everything else. Not the details, of course, and in a sense I still don't know. But I can see the thousands of people he treated and begin to imagine how they were helped and changed and sometimes cured by his work. In thirty years of practicing, that's thousands and thousands of lives made better, sometimes in small ways, sometimes beyond all expectation. Thousands of people who because of him were less fearful. Became less scared."

He looked at his sister again. "It's quite an inheritance, not being scared of the dark. And Rachel, at least, uses her powers for good." He smiled. "But I don't think either of us can look at a thing we don't understand and not want to understand it. Dad showed us how to explore the world."

Webster stopped, took a sip of wine from one of the glasses in front of him, and looked down at his father, who was gazing at the tablecloth with a peaceful half-smile on his face. The little room was utterly quiet, and shadows thrown by the candles flickered on the walls.

"I'm going to stop, before this turns into a eulogy. I'm not going to go on about what a wonderful father he's been, or what a wonderful husband I think he's been—unless I've missed something. Or how he now has a new career as a local campaigner for truth and justice." His father laughed. "I'm very aware that this is not a funeral and that, like Mr. Jarndyce, the man on my right doesn't much like being praised. With any luck this little speech will have to last for a long, long time. But sixty-five isn't a bad time to take stock, and, well, there's a lot of stock to take. An awful lot. He couldn't have set a better example. That's why he's daunting. Just a little."

Webster took his champagne glass, specially filled, and raised it.

"To a courageous man."

Repeating the words everyone drank, and Patrick Webster, still smiling, turned to his son and gave a deep, humble nod.

10.

BECAUSE IT WAS SUCH A WARM DAY, Qazai told Webster as he greeted him, lunch would be served on the loggia overlooking the lake, if that sounded agreeable; quite often, even in late May, the breeze coming off the water could carry something of a chill, but today truly felt like the first day of summer, did it not? Timur and his family had arrived the previous evening and Ava was expected any minute.

Qazai motioned to a servant to take the bags from the taxi driver and putting his hand lightly on Webster's back ushered him into the house, inquiring after his journey and instructing Francesco, a neat man in his fifties standing by the huge double doors, to show their guest to the principal guest suite. Lunch would be at one.

The principal guest of the Villa Foresi, it turned out, received regal treatment. The room was in a corner of the building on the first floor, with Lake Como on one side and on the other a lawned terrace edged with towering cypresses. The walls, a refined light gray, were hung with fragments of textiles in frames, and a fine green silk rug covered half the tiled floor. These were the only touches of Qazai's taste; everything else, Webster suspected, had been designed fairly recently by a professional of enormous discretion.

French doors opened onto a balcony, and in the half an hour before he was due downstairs Webster sat outside, watching the boats on the lake and the servants making preparations for lunch and smoking what he was sure wouldn't be the last cigarette of the day.

He missed Elsa. She would have liked it here. The house occupied a small peninsula, heavily wooded with chestnuts and cypresses and jutting grandly into the lake, and looked in fact like three houses progressing in steps down the hill to the water. It must have been two hundred years old, perhaps three, and even though everything was spotlessly kept—the apricot walls and verdigris shutters freshly painted, the terraced gardens neatly clipped, the rhododendrons and azaleas and camellias freshly in bloom—it had the dignity and reserve of age, as if its current occupiers were fleeting tenants and not a matter of great concern. So yes, she would have liked it, and he would have liked her to be here, but at the same time he was relieved beyond measure that she hadn't come.

At five to one he made his way downstairs and found the Qazais sitting at a table under an open arcade. Only Ava was not yet there. Timur rose and coming to greet him shook his hand stiffly; Raisa was warmer, and remembered him to Farhad and to Parviz, who smiled shyly.

Webster sat opposite Ava's empty seat next to Qazai, who took the head. A waiter in a white jacket, white shirt and black tie poured him water, switched bottles deftly and before Webster could consider or object had poured him a glass of white wine.

"Your good health, Mr. Webster," said Qazai, raising his glass, "we are delighted to see you here."

Webster raised his and gently clinked the other glasses. "Thank you. It's a pleasure to be invited." It sounded stiff as he said it. "You have a very beautiful house." Behind Ava's empty seat the lake seemed to stretch across his entire vision, still and evenly blue, and from it on the far shore rose green forested mountains, the highest in the range beyond still tipped with snow.

"Thank you," said Qazai, with a little bow of his head. He wore an open-necked white shirt and seemed relaxed; but despite the casual air Webster thought his eyes looked tired, and the skin under them dry and dark. "This is probably where I am happiest. Right here. With my family." He raised his glass again, and drank a silent toast to them.

"Ava!" Farhad, Parviz's brother, had slid off his chair and was running across the lawn with his arms spread wide, clutching Ava's leg as he reached her. She ruffled his hair, squatting down and kissing him, then picked him up to swing him around in a low arc. Smiling and taking off her sunglasses, she crossed the grass to the table and went straight to Parviz, crouching down by him and giving him an enveloping hug. When she finally pulled away she held his face in her hands and looked at him for several seconds, her eyes full of intensity as if she were about to cry.

At last she let go of Parviz, gave him an earnest smile and went to Qazai, hugging him and Raisa and her brother in turn. Webster stood.

"You remember Mr. Webster," said Qazai.

"I do. Hello, Mr. Webster." She held out her hand, smiling, her eyes no longer intense but playful. "What do you make of our lakeside retreat? Not to be confused with the seaside retreat, or the mountain retreat, or all the other retreats."

"It's beautiful."

Ava sat, her eyes on Webster, and waited for her wine to be poured.

Now that everyone was here Qazai unfolded his napkin and placed it carefully in his lap. "I was just telling Mr. Webster, darling, that this is my favorite place. There is something about the lake and the mountains . . ."

"That reminds you of Iran. Yes, we know." Ava was smiling but there was a hint of needle in her voice.

Qazai also smiled, a little stiffly. "My daughter knows me too well," he said, to no one in particular. "But did you know," he leaned in to the table, pointing at the gardens, "that the cypress was planted in all the ancient gardens of Iran? They do not look quite like this—more bushy, less straight— but they have been in my country since history began."

Ava shook her head several times in mock surprise. "No. I honestly didn't know that." She turned to Timur. "Did you know that?"

Timur frowned a little, as if he couldn't quite understand what Ava was doing, and glanced at Raisa. "No, I didn't."

"The oldest tree in Asia," said Qazai, watching Ava closely as she turned back to him, "is an Iranian cypress."

Ava nodded briskly. "So. Mr. Webster. Have you ever been to Iran?"

"I haven't, no. I'm not sure that someone in my profession should try."

Ava raised her eyebrows, as if to ask him why not.

"They might decide I'm a spy."

"Which of course you're not."

Webster smiled.

"How old are you, Mr. Webster?" said Qazai.

"Thirty-eight."

"Then I hope you get the chance one day."

"Do you think I might?"

Qazai sat back, took a slow breath, and made a show of thinking. From the end of the table came the sound of Farhad clinking his knife and fork.

"I have high hopes. High hopes. Mixed with real fear."

Timur quietly took Farhad's cutlery from him, and they all waited for Qazai to go on, allowing the patriarch his moment. Ava looked down and tapped her fingers lightly on the tablecloth. Her nails were long and unpainted.

"It is not possible," said Qazai, "for such weak people to stifle a country that old, that . . . valiant for long. They are pariahs. They are desert dogs. Iran will wring their necks. But for now—for this year, for next—they will do what they have learned to do so well these past two decades. They will try to terrify their people." He was animated now, and he took a drink of wine before continuing. "But we are not as afraid as we were. It may not take much longer. What has happened in Egypt, in Tunisia—people see that it can be done. They sense the trick of power. The illusion."

Qazai leaned forward and put down his wine glass to signal that for now he was done; Ava sat back and crossed her arms, and Webster thought he heard her give a little sigh as she did so. No one spoke for a moment, and Qazai merely looked at his daughter calmly but pointedly, as if to say that he saw that she objected in some way but was not prepared to pursue it in company. Not meeting his eye she raised her eyebrows a fraction, glanced at Parviz and Raisa in turn, and reached forward for the bread that the waiter had just placed on her side plate with a pair of silver tongs. Timur and Raisa quietly tried to engage Farhad, who was growing restless.

"Do you do much work in Iran, Mr. Webster?" said Qazai at last, turning to him. He was smiling but his brow was tight and he was clearly angered by this small, public act of insubordination. Webster wondered whether he controlled every conversation with his family in the same way, and looked for neutral ground where the others might feel safe to follow.

"A little. It's not an easy place to do what we do. As you can imagine. Although it's not the worst."

Raisa gratefully took the bait. "Where is that, Mr. Webster?"

"Please—Ben." Raisa smiled and nodded. "It depends what you mean by worst. Poland is impossible to understand. The Germans hate to tell you anything. The Balkans are the most confusing place on earth."

Raisa smiled. "I should be flattered, I'm sure."

Webster looked puzzled.

"I'm from Slovenia," she said. "If that counts."

"Oh, I think so," said Webster.

"But the most dangerous?" Ava appeared to have recovered; she was contributing.

Webster thought for a moment. "Well, Iran would be up there. Iraq, certainly. Parts of Africa. Russia."

"I read about your difficulties there, Mr. Webster," said Qazai. "That can't have been an easy time."

This threw Webster. It was easy enough to find those articles but he was surprised that Qazai had taken the trouble, and more surprised that he should raise it here. "No, it wasn't an easy time."

"You have my sympathies," said Qazai. "To do something valuable it is sometimes necessary to accept misfortune. Everyone here has experience of this, I think."

Webster managed to nod, controlling an impulse to ask Qazai what on earth he meant, and was only distracted from his irritation by Ava laughing, a short hard laugh.

"Daddy, look around." She shook her head as if in wonder. "Look at all this. We are some of the most fortunate people who ever lived."

"Not all misfortune involves money, Ava."

"I thought everything was about money." Her eyes were wide in challenge, her head inclined slightly to one side.

For a full five seconds he looked at her, his features set.

"Ava, now is not the time." His mouth but not his eyes relented into a smile. "And this isn't like you. Please let us enjoy our lunch on this beautiful day."

"For Mr. Webster's sake."

"For all our sakes."

"I'm sorry, Mr. Webster," said Ava. "I didn't mean to embarrass you."

"You haven't." He and Ava exchanged a look; Webster thought he could see in her eyes a real fury that hadn't been there when they met in London.

Food came, the moment passed, and the rest of the lunch was spent in stiff but fluent enough conversation about children and education and holidays and other subjects deemed safe by some tacit mutual understanding. Qazai was in charge, distributing the conversation around the table with a diplomat's equilibrium. The only people he failed to engage were Parviz and Farhad, who sat dutifully enough and mourned the hot, bright day.

Occasionally he would set up a story for Timur or ask him to give his opinion on some matter but for the most part his son was withdrawn. Webster wondered whether he was always like this in his father's company, whether he didn't dare be himself, or whether he was merely preoccupied, or tired, or simply bored of some repeating pattern in the relationship between Ava and his father; wondered, too, why Qazai had invited him here to witness all this uneasiness, and concluded that he was as surprised by it as anyone.

As the coffees were cleared Qazai stood, thanked everyone for their company, and asked if they would mind leaving him alone with Mr. Webster and Timur because there were things they needed to discuss. Raisa and Ava did not delay and followed Parviz and Farhad as they ran, thin-legged and laughing, into the house. Webster watched them go with envy, and asked Qazai whether he might smoke a cigarette.

QAZAI, IT SEEMED, wanted Timur to sit in on their interview; it was important, was it not, that he knew exactly what had been found. Webster did his best not to show his irritation; the whole point of being in this secluded place was to get Qazai alone and see how he answered questions without an audience. He made cogent arguments, warned him that he would ask him things that he might not want Timur to hear, but Qazai insisted, and when your client insisted there was little that you could do. Not for the first time he cursed Ike for creating this impossible relationship.

He managed one small victory, however, which was to move inside the house; no one could ask or answer hard questions with the afternoon sun glimmering on the lake and the breeze soothing everything with its warmth. The three of them withdrew to Qazai's study, a modest room on the northwestern side of the house, cool as a result, lined with leather-bound books on mahogany shelves and looking out through a small grove of pear trees onto a terrace planted with roses and camellias. Qazai sat behind his desk, an elegant insubstantial thing that had never seen much work, and Webster took one of the half-comfortable chairs that faced it. Timur took the other.

Webster placed his recorder on the corner of the desk, set it going and began. His first dozen questions were about the sculpture, and Qazai's answers were predictable. No, he did not know a Mr. Shokhor; he had never bought anything at all from a Swiss dealer, to his knowledge; Mehr might have done but if he had he had never mentioned it. He was, in short, mystified by the whole business, and would be glad when Webster had finally settled it.

"Do you have anything to tell me?" he said, expectant.

"No. Not yet. We're making progress."

"How long, do you think?"

"It depends. Sometimes these things just give. Sometimes they can get tricky. Two or three weeks, I would say."

Qazai nodded briskly, as if to say that that wasn't quick enough but would have to do, and waited for the next question.

"Do you think," said Webster, picking his words carefully, "that there might be a connection between the death of Cyrus Mehr and this story?"

Qazai sat straighter in his chair, and when he spoke he was emphatic. "No. I don't."

Timur looked from his father to Webster and back again.

Webster went on. "I was wondering . . . perhaps there's something going on here we don't fully understand. Maybe someone thinks he was involved in smuggling for the same reason someone thinks you were."

Qazai shook his head. "No. No. I don't believe that's what happened."

"Of course, it's also possible that when he died, that somehow contributed to the story. Or triggered it."

"Mr. Webster, this is not a useful line of inquiry. We should move on." His jaw had moved forward slightly, as if he were clenching his teeth. Webster watched him, fascinated.

"But if he was smuggling, he'd be smuggling for you. People might make that assumption. Isn't it possible that's how the rumor about you started?"

Qazai leaned forward and pointed at Webster across the desk. His voice was level and hard. "All right. Enough. You're being paid to clear my name. Not to investigate the murder of my friend. Nor, for that matter, to phone up his widow and harass her."

That shouldn't have been a surprise, but it was. As it had been a mistake. But Webster persisted, only briefly thrown and encouraged by Qazai's vehemence.

"The story of his death doesn't make sense."

Qazai's face became set, stony. "Listen to me, Mr. Webster. You are an investigator. You want to know things. I understand this. But some things we cannot understand, sitting here, rational people, in this most beautiful place. The men who rule Iran are not like us. They deal in fear. And what they fear, they kill. That does not make sense. Not to us." He gave Webster a moment to absorb the words. "My best friend in Tehran was a doctor. He fled too, to Paris. He was political. A braver man than me. A better man than me." He paused. "His car blew up outside his apartment. In 1984. His wife and daughter saw it happen as they waved him to work that morning. At his funeral there were men we did not know, taking pictures at a distance." He left a space, but Webster knew better than to fill it. "Six months later, another friend, who had been there, paying his respects, was shot in Vienna. Twice, through the head." Another pause, his eyes not leaving Webster's. "My father's godson was shot in a restaurant in Hamburg. I knew two people who were killed in Istanbul. There are dozens more I didn't personally know, and none of them, not one of them, makes sense. These people do not know sense. Only fear."

Webster saw a new passion in his words, a rage that seemed to fill him.

"So do not look for sense. Cyrus died because they feared him. Heaven knows why." He had finished, and looking down he rearranged some papers on the desk. Then he was holding Webster's eye once more. "If I had wanted you to investigate his death, I would have asked."

Webster wondered if he should just let it go. Perhaps Hammer was right: perhaps there was nothing very much wrong with Darius Qazai, or at least nothing obvious, and to insist on taking him apart piece by piece until every last bone was found to be present, every vein and artery in place, was an exercise in vanity and not in diligence. It wasn't what they had been paid to do, and it didn't make anyone happier, or wiser, or better, least of all Webster himself. But he was too stubborn to stop, and too intrigued by the raw spot he had exposed.

"If there's a link, that's part of our job." He held Qazai's eye. "There's a lot going on. I'm wondering whether I should investigate what happened to Parviz last week."

Qazai looked at Timur, turned back to Webster, and closed his eyes. When he opened them again he had collected himself.

"I appreciate, Mr. Webster, that your job requires you to see the world as interconnected. Everything has a cause and an effect and you look for the cause. I understand that. But again, what happened last week is an unpleasant, personal matter and not your business."

Webster turned to Timur. "You told your father what happened? The whole thing?"

Timur nodded. He had his legs crossed away from them both and looked like he didn't want to be drawn in. "Of course."

"You still think the motive was money?"

"Yes," said Timur. "I do."

"Of course it was money," said Qazai. "Kidnappings happen every day in that place. That is what happens when you have billionaires and slaves living side by side. The sooner Timur can move to London, the better.

Which is why, Mr. Webster, we need you to finish your work. These are distractions."

Given another three or four questions along these lines Webster had the impression he might goad Qazai into becoming truly angry, but although this was tempting in its own right he saw that it served no one's purpose—not Ike's, not his own. He had learned something, and that was enough.

"All right. But if I were your adviser, and not your investigator, I'd say that you should have a good think about who your enemies might be."

An unconvinced smile flashed on Qazai's face. "Thank you, Mr. Webster. I will. We should all do that from time to time." He sat back, finding his composure. "Good. That was a useful session."

He stood, and came around from his side of the desk. To complete the reconstruction of his familiar, easy self, he put his hand on Timur's shoulder and smiled. In that moment of stiff contact Webster thought of his own relationship with Daniel: Had Qazai once been free to play with Timur, to whirl him around, to throw him in the air? Had they always been this reserved, or had they stiffened over the years? Curiously, the effect was to make Timur, eager for approval, desperate not to disappoint, seem more like a child, and despite his fine words about giving his son his chance this was exactly what Qazai wanted. All afternoon he had led, and Timur had merely watched.

BY ELEVEN, dinner had finished, the diners had gone their separate ways and Webster, relieved that the day was over, was walking on the lowest terrace and smoking a cigarette. The lake breeze was fresh, the sky free of cloud, the stars close, and from the newly watered flowerbeds rose the rich, cool smell of damp earth. He found a bench and watched the black stillness of the lake and the clustered lights beyond.

Dinner had been easier than lunch. Senechal had arrived from London just as they were sitting down, and his cold presence had made the situation somehow less intimate, as if Qazai was now protected again and not available for taunting—a corporate rather than a family gathering, throughout which Ava had been polite but spirited, Timur agreeable, Qazai quietly imperious.

Webster gave thanks for his own family's simplicity. His parents were still married, still seemed happy, had never filed vicious claims and accusations against each other. They had never directed him or been disappointed by the directions he had taken. His inheritance would be modest in financial terms but rich in love, wisdom, a certain clarity in thinking about priorities, the only burden a duty to live up to their example.

Perhaps Qazai had had no choice but to damage his son. Perhaps the anxieties that propelled him had inhibited the confidence that might have set Timur free. The Qazai project could not be seen to end with Qazai; his legacy was as important as his own achievements. That, more than mere riches or power, might explain why great men found it so difficult to pass on happiness to their children: that they could never stop to know it themselves. Webster smiled at the notion that he was unlikely to encounter this problem himself.

Deep in thought, he felt the cigarette grow hot in his fingers and flicked it over the low balustraded wall into the night.

Faint footsteps behind him on the grass made him turn and there was Ava walking toward him, almost silhouetted against the lights from the house. A shawl was pulled closely around her. She stopped in front of the bench and smiled as he made to get up.

"Don't be silly. Sit. Could you spare a cigarette?"

Webster pulled out his pack and tapped one free.

"May I?" she said, taking it.

"Please."

She sat beside him at an angle and he struck a match for her. Her face glowed as she bent over it.

For a moment or two they sat and Ava smoked.

"I'm sorry about lunch," she said at last. She held the cigarette delicately between the last joints of her fingers and turned her head away from him each time she exhaled.

"Don't be. It was much more interesting than dinner."

She turned to him and smiled. "God. I don't know which was worse."

"I can't say."

She nodded to herself. In the half-light her eyes were intensely on his. "Something bad?"

"Not obviously."

"So you think there's something?"

"I didn't say that. Do you?"

"No. Of course not." She shook her head, a tiny movement, and looked down at her hands in her lap. "It's just . . . He needs this work. He needs you."

"Are you sure?"

"He's not a vain man. He's not what you think. He's practical. Always practical. Everything he does is for profit or power. You're here because he needs you."

"Why?"

"I don't know. I thought you might have found out."

"And if I had?" Webster was finding it hard to tell whether Ava had come out here to grill him or warn him. Or to seek comfort.

"You wouldn't tell me."

"I shouldn't."

She nodded gently, sat up straight on the bench, collecting herself. He thought she was going to leave but instead she turned to him.

"My father is a very arrogant man. He thinks he's better than everyone else. At everything that matters to him. It's that simple. The best trader, the best businessman, the best collector. I've never seen him depend on someone before. First Yves. And now you, here." She shook her head. "He would never have had someone like you here before. This is his special place. It was never for business."

Her voice, which had been calm, was now uneven, and Webster thought he could sense unexplored anxieties there, close to the surface.

"I'm sorry," she said. "I didn't mean to be rude."

"Is there something else?"

"No. I'm just worried about him."

"Are you worried about Parviz?"

She bit her bottom lip but said nothing.

"Is Senechal often here?"

She shook her head and sighed, looking out at the lake. "Today was the first time in months I've seen them apart. It's not healthy."

Webster said nothing.

"The hold he has on my father. Since my mother ran off. I think that's when it started. It's getting worse. I don't know how it must make Timur feel."

Webster watched her profile as she drew on the cigarette.

"What do you mean?"

Ava sat up and back on the bench, crossing her legs. "My father treats Timur like one of his treasures. He's on display, to be admired. The most important piece in the collection. But he tells him nothing." She shivered. "But that freak knows the lot. I'm sure of it. Ever since . . . My mother didn't behave well. Since then my father has closed up. He was never easy, but no one's allowed in now. Except that man. Like he's the only person that can be trusted anymore. Because he's paid. He's a professional." She shook her head and looked past Webster out to the lake. "He's the one you should be interviewing."

"What is there to tell?"

She looked at him, raising her eyebrows and plucking a piece of tobacco from her lower lip with her thumb. The intensity he had seen earlier had returned to her eyes. "You tell me, Mr. Webster. You probably know more than me by now."

He smiled. "I wouldn't bank on it."

She took a long drag, coughing as the smoke filled her lungs. "God, these are strong."

"Sorry."

She dropped the cigarette half-smoked on the grass and trod it out with her toe. Behind them the lights in one of the downstairs rooms went out, casting the terrace into deeper darkness.

"Are you going to be able to give him what he wants?" She moved to the edge of the seat and turned to him as she said it.

"I don't know yet."

She hesitated. "What have you found?"

"Anything you tell me can stay with me. I'm not a policeman."

She shook her head, suddenly resolute, and stood. As she looked down at him her face was set again, the trust gone. "Nothing I know will be of any use to you. Goodnight, Mr. Webster. Tread carefully."

As he watched her walking back to the house through bands of floodlit grass Webster shook his head; how he wished Elsa could have heard this conversation. She might have understood it. She might have known whether Ava was desperate to say something or terrified to let it slip.

11.

To know that he was more or less an impostor in the house lent the rest of Webster's short stay a certain piquancy. He didn't know whether to be pleased or put out that the room he had been given, he had assumed on merit, had in fact been intended for grand acquaintances—diplomats, colorful entrepreneurs, heads of minor states, dignitaries of the Iranian diaspora—and not for English detectives, if that's what he was, who billed by the hour and spent their time rooting around in other people's affairs. But of all the hints and signs that Ava had given him the night before, by design or not, one thing was really striking: he had assumed since they had first met that Qazai found their work necessary, but not critical—serious, but not grave—and the growing realization that it was for some reason essential to him began to cast everything in a different light. Webster had gone to sleep feeling that the many and conflicting pieces of this project, not least his own feelings toward it, were beginning to align.

He slept well, in the vast white bed, and woke early to find the lake overcast with low cloud. As he came downstairs he was shown by one of the servants into a yellow breakfast room where eight settings had been laid on a long table, at one of which sat Senechal, neatly pressed in black suit, white shirt and gray tie, reading a document in a plastic binding and drinking a cup of black coffee. He didn't appear to have had anything to eat.

Webster wished him good morning and sat down opposite, cursing the fact that he hadn't brought his book. He ordered coffee and two poached eggs and taking his BlackBerry from his jacket pocket started looking at his e-mails, all of which he had already seen, while Senechal, for his part, returned the good morning without cheer and continued to read, every now and then raising his cup to his lips to take a tiny drink but never taking his eyes from his work. Webster did his best to decipher the document from across the table but managed only to work out that it was in French.

His coffee, when it came, was good. As he drank he watched the lawyer and tried to imagine the array of secrets stored up within him. Were they simply dry, legalistic, of little interest to anyone but himself and his client, the papery trappings of mortgages, incorporations, transactions and financings, impenetrable only by virtue of their complexity? Or in among them were there dark stories that explained Qazai and threatened to undo him?

Senechal closed his document and spoke, breaking Webster's sleepy reverie and making him start.

"I understand you had a useful session with Mr. Qazai."

Webster was amused by the lack of small talk, and grateful for it. "Yes, thank you. We're getting there."

Senechal paused for a second. He had an unsettling habit of leaving a short delay before he spoke, as if calculating precisely how to couch what he needed to say in the most efficient and anonymous terms, his gaze blank and always steady. "When do you think you will be finished?"

"Two weeks. Three. It depends how neatly everything stacks up."

The idiom seemed to puzzle Senechal; he frowned, then let it go.

"The first draft of the report—send it to me. I will respond."

"Of course."

"Mr. Webster, I think you understand how important it is that this case is successful."

Webster looked up. "I have some idea. But I don't decide whether it's successful or not."

Senechal frowned again, the merest movement of his brow.

"I can only report what I find," said Webster in response.

"I appreciate that," Senechal said, placing his cup on its saucer with great care and considering it for a moment before looking up and going on. "But the presentation is important too. The order of items. The level of detail. It is difficult for you to be completely neutral."

"Of course. You have to trust us."

Senechal smiled blankly. "And we do. We appreciate your work, Mr. Webster. If you complete the project to our satisfaction we would be happy to show that appreciation."

Webster frowned now. "What do you mean?"

"Only that we hope your good work will not go unrewarded."

"You're offering me a bribe?"

"Of course not."

"So when I write this conversation up in my report you won't mind?"

Senechal's expression didn't change. "I'm not sure what you think you heard, Mr. Webster. I was merely discussing our wishes for the project."

Webster held his gray, cold eye. He had never been offered a bribe before. He wondered how much he was worth.

If he played along, of course, he could find out, and a proven bribe would be enough to walk away from the case and leave this unhealthy pair to their problems. But he found himself too furious for games, and strangely riled by the prospect of his own corruption even while he knew it wasn't real and wouldn't happen. And besides, he had no desire to finish this now. Not when he was about to be proved right.

"I know what I heard," he said at last. "You hired us for our integrity. That's what you'll get."

If Senechal detected the trace of threat he didn't show it. He took the napkin from his lap, folded it neatly into two and then four, and placed it on the table.

"I am delighted to hear it." He stood. "Thank you, Mr. Webster. I look forward to the report." And with that, taking his document, he left, floating across the floor on his light, even steps.

AT LINATE WEBSTER WAITED in a single, snaking queue to take off his shoes and his belt and have his bag X-rayed, absently watching his fellow travelers with their refined traveling gear: suitcases obediently to heel, laptops held close, shoes ready to be slipped off in an easy motion. Like everyone else he checked his BlackBerry aimlessly, head bowed.

He should have taken the train. Overnight to Paris, the window open all the way, in his own cabin, on his own time; dinner in the dining car and a cigarette leaning out into the night somewhere around Lyon. A sentimental notion, attractive because it allowed him to indulge the fantasy that his life was his own.

As he untied his laces and unbuckled his belt he pondered the morning's conversation. Would Senechal have made the same suggestion, as subtle as a whisper, to anyone? Or was there something that made him seem a susceptible bribee? Something equivocal, biddable? Would Senechal, for instance, have made it to Hammer? Had he already?

He shook that thought from his mind. No one would try to bribe Ike. You'd have to be dimwitted to mistake that keen edge for greed. No, these were the wrong questions. The only one that mattered was whether to tell Ike what had happened. He would stop the case if he knew, and Webster could then wash his hands at last of these puzzling and unsavory people—and start looking for the next client, who might be better or who might be worse, but who was unlikely to have that noxious mixture of arrogance and threat that was shot through the Qazais.

He cleared security without a beep, collected his clothes and his bag, moved aside to put on his shoes and jacket and made his way to the passport queue. He would like to be rid of them, that was clear, but at the same time he wasn't ready to let them go. For the sake of Ava, and Timur, and most importantly Parviz, he told himself, he shouldn't stop until he had worked out what was at the dark center of Qazai.

From his glass booth an immigration officer signaled that he should step forward. Webster handed across his passport, old now and full of stamps, the gold lettering on the cover worn away, and watched the officer open it to the back page, tap at his keyboard, inspect the photograph, glance up at him and then study his computer screen. He always wondered what it said on his file, a universal curiosity perhaps: he had Russian clients who were forever asking him to find out why they were stopped for questioning when they came west, a hopeless task. The officer tapped some more, picked up his phone, leafed through the passport as he said a few words and then hung up.

"What are you doing in Milano?" he asked, still looking down.

"Business," said Webster. "I came to see a client."

The officer nodded slowly to himself and typed something into his computer, taking his time. Webster heard footsteps behind him and two men appeared at his shoulder, both in the uniform of the Polizia di Stato. One went to talk to his colleague in the booth, the other stayed back.

After a moment's grave conversation the first officer came out and nodded to his colleague, who took Webster by the elbow and told him that he would have to follow him and answer some questions.

The two men led Webster past shops and sandwich bars to an unmarked gray door set in a long gray wall. Behind it was a white room, well-lit from two fluorescent strips that hung from the ceiling, its floor tiled with worn carpet, its only furniture a glass table with a metal-framed chair either side of it. He was told that he should sit and that someone would be with him soon. One officer left and the other stayed, standing with his back to the wall by the door. Webster watched him for a moment and decided that his rigid bearing and serious gaze were there to suggest that he wouldn't answer questions if asked, so taking his phone from his coat he began to type a short message to Ike, letting him know where he was and why he might be late.

"No," said the officer. "No cell. Please switch off."

"Am I under arrest? Because otherwise I can make a call."

"Switch off the cell or I am going to arrest you."

He looked at his guard, saw that he was serious, cut his message to Ike short ("stopped at linate") and turned off his phone.

"Can you tell me what this is about?"

"Someone come," said the officer, and resumed his inspection of the opposite wall.

"If they don't come soon I'm going to miss my flight."

This was Italy. It could be hours. Resigned to being here for some time Webster took yesterday's newspaper from his bag. Forty minutes passed, and he began to be frustrated with the silence. His guard didn't move. Eventually the door opened a few inches and someone that Webster couldn't see beckoned to the officer to leave the room. After a moment or two he was replaced by two men in suits, one old and balding gray, short and tensed, the other younger and less compact, his black jacket scarcely covering his paunch.

They stood in front of the table and the younger man spoke; his partner merely cocked his head and looked at Webster with implacable gray eyes.

"Signore Webster. I am sorry that you are made to wait. Please, come with us."

Webster shook his head. "No. Either you tell me what is going on or I call my lawyer right now. And my embassy." He reached for his phone.

"Signore, we need you to answer questions about Giovanni Ruffino." Webster stopped and looked up. "Please, come with us."

Ruffino. Webster thought he had heard the last of him long ago.

"YOU HAVEN'T BEEN TO ITALY in a long time, Signore Webster," said the younger policeman. He had the high, sing-song voice of the Milanese, a little open trill on the end of any word that would take it.

"Not for a while."

"Not in seven years." He referred to a file that he had opened on the table in between them. "Is that a choice?"

"No. Just chance."

A little nod. "So we must not feel hurt." A quick, perfunctory smile at his joke and then a pause. "Why do you come here now? Chance?"

"No. I came to have a meeting. With a client."

"An Italian client?"

"A client with a house in Italy."

"Can you tell me the name?"

"Of the house?"

The detective smiled. He was being indulgent. "Mr. Webster, you will find it easier to be cooperative. We will all find it easier." He looked sideways to his colleague, who sat with his legs crossed, one elbow over the back of his chair, tending to his nails with what looked like a toothpick. "His name?"

"I might tell you when you tell me why you're wasting my day." They were now in a police station in the city, on via Malpensa. Webster didn't know enough about the complicated organization of the Italian police to know which branch was detaining him or what that might mean. All he knew was that it was eleven now, and the day was slipping into nothingness. He didn't know whether to feel concerned or simply angry. That Ruffino should come up now was strange: he hadn't given him a moment's thought in years and could hardly believe that he was of interest to anybody still. He watched the two detectives and tried to learn something from their carriage, from their body language. The younger officer was resting his arms on the table and his back was curved, his shoulders slumped. It was hot in the room and he had taken off his jacket to reveal dark-blue patches under his arms. But he wasn't anxious. He looked like a man with right on his side. His colleague continued to pick at his nails, unconcerned.

"*Bene.*" The younger detective ignored his question and looked down at the folder. "The last time you were here you came to Milano and saw a company of investigators. Investigazioni Indago. Yes?"

Webster merely returned the detective's look.

"You had a meeting with them at two o'clock on Thursday, March 8th, 2004. You attended, with Antonio Dorsa and Giuseppe Maltese, two detectives. Private detectives. At that meeting you ordered them to put a wiretap on the home and office telephone lines of Giovanni Ruffino, a lawyer, from Milano also."

"No, I didn't."

The detective looked at him for a moment with raised eyebrows before resuming.

"Also, you gave instructions to look in Signore Ruffino's bank accounts, here and in Switzerland, and in his medical history and his garbage."

Webster shook his head, partly in denial, partly in wonderment that this old, old story, which he had long presumed dead, had been merely dormant all this time. The interesting question was what had awakened it.

"No. I didn't. This is all nonsense. Old nonsense."

"Can you tell us what you discussed at that meeting?"

"Until you arrest me I'm not going to tell you anything. I have no idea why I'm here or why you're dragging up this crap again. If you're not going to charge me with anything you can open that door and drive me back to the airport."

The younger officer looked at the older, who gave the slightest nod.

"OK." The younger man shrugged. "That is fine. Benedict Webster, we are placing you under arrest on charges of illegal wiretapping, breaking of banking secrecy law, breaking of data protection law, commercial espionage and harassment. You have the right to speak to a lawyer. We can find one if you cannot."

Webster shook his head, dumbstruck. Alarm took hold of him. To be questioned was one thing: in Italy an investigation was a political plaything to be started, discredited, ditched and revived at will, and he had assumed until now that he had merely been dropped by accident into some game being played many levels above him whose purpose he might never guess. They were accusing him of things that happened in Italy every day and almost always went unpunished, so this had to be mere harassment. But if these two were prepared to arrest him, then the game was about him, and it was being played with intent. He said nothing, watching the two policemen watch him with the ease of those who have all the power on their side.

"Now would you like to talk?" said the younger, smiling a slick smile.

"Only to a lawyer." Webster sat back and crossed his arms.

At this the older man looked up from his nails and fixed a severe eye on him. There were dark hairs on his cheekbones and the skin on his cheeks was pockmarked and rigid with gray stubble. He didn't smile.

"Wiretap. Six years." He counted the charges out on his fingers as he spoke, his accent coarser and stronger than his colleague's, his voice a slow rasp. "Banks. Eight years. Other things. Five years." He leaned forward over the table until his face was a foot from Webster's. "Serious," he said, nodding slowly. "No game." He shook his head gently and sat back, resuming his former position, looking at Webster all the while. "No game. Your children grow old while you in Italy."

Webster felt his body tense and a powerless fury hold him. The

questions that had been crowding for attention left him and were replaced
by pure imaginings: interrogations, meetings with lawyers, spells in prison,
extradition requests, Elsa furious and scared.

These men across the table would once have had no power over him. He
had sat in rooms like this before, with worse men than this, answering their
questions and trying to work out what they really wanted, what part he
was playing in their careful fantasies. But he had never known a fear
like this. It wasn't fear of them, or what they could do; it was fear of what
he might once have done to destroy what he now held most precious.

He needed air, and time to consider, and for the first time that day it
dawned on him that he wasn't free. He couldn't walk out of the door, take a
stroll around Milan, call some people and return with the situation in
hand. He couldn't take the next flight home and pick up the children from
school. He was here, and here was all there was.

"I need my call."

"Signore Webster." The younger man pulled his chair up to the table
and rested his elbows on it, his hands clasped together, considering something grave. "I urge you to be cooperative. Easier for us, easier for you. There
are many outcomes possible. This is Italy."

Webster watched his pale doughy face and wondered whose bidding he
was doing.

"Give me my call."

"In a moment, Signore. We would like this to stay in Italy—a simple
local matter, under control. If you cooperate I give you my word that we
don't involve the British police. They know about the case, of course, but it
is, I think you say, dormant."

"My call. Nothing until then."

AFTER CAREFUL THOUGHT HE had phoned Elsa. She could tell Ike what had to
be done but it wasn't fair to ask him to give her the news. Being Elsa, she
was calm and practical—how serious was it, she had wanted to know, and
how long might he be—and he had been more reassuring than he yet had
reason to be. In truth, he simply didn't know.

His instructions for Ike had been simple: contact our best friends in Milan, ask them to recommend a good criminal defense lawyer who can find out what game the police were playing. In particular, have them discover who was making this happen. She had asked him if he was OK and he had answered, truthfully, that he was fine. Angry, frustrated, penitent about bringing this contaminant into their lives but otherwise fine.

The business of locating, instructing and sending a lawyer might take half a day, and in the meantime Webster, hungry now but calm again, had been shown to a cell, which mercifully he had to himself, and left alone. It was bare, well-lit, clean enough. From a high corner a camera watched him sitting on one of the bunks, staring at one wall, his back against the other.

This was the first time he had been in a cell since Kazakhstan over a decade before, where his friend Inessa, a journalist like him, had died beyond his reach four cells away. The memory, fresh at the best of times, steered him toward a more stable sense of proportion, and he began to take slow, careful stock. First, he hadn't done half the things he was charged with, and no wiretapping, certainly; in the Anglo-Saxon world that had been a no-no for decades. That was one source of comfort.

Another was that the Ruffino affair had been dead, politically speaking, for years, and the whole business completed: the Austrians had lost, the Russians had captured the company, and Ruffino himself, despite all his protestations that he wasn't their man, had no doubt been paid a handsome fee for the scheme's success. When Webster had come to Milan on that day all those years before, the fight had been in the press every day and his brief to Dorsa and his decidedly shady friend supremely delicate: demonstrate that this Italian lawyer, intimate of a dozen grubby billionaires, owned all those shares in the Austrian's company for the Russians and not on his own behalf. Delicate and grubby enough, in fact, that when Ruffino had filed a complaint against GIC, Webster's old company, for running a vicious campaign to destroy his reputation, Webster had been astonished that anyone would want to draw more attention to a situation that was already dangerously exposed.

He hadn't looked recently but he was sure that nothing had changed. The Russians were still in charge. Ruffino, so far as he knew, had moved on

to new acts of complex dishonesty. The stakes were no longer high; for
everyone but him, in fact, there were no stakes. Which meant that either
there had been news he hadn't heard, or he really was the center of all this
attention.

So his first questions for the lawyer would be simple: is this a real investigation or an exercise in manipulation? Has something happened to
prompt real interest in this ancient dead end of a case or is it being picked
over to unsettle someone close to it? Am I that someone and if so, why?

A client had once given him a single piece of advice for surviving spells
in prison: bring a book. Here he had nothing to fool time into speeding
up. His phone and bag had now been taken from him, and all he could do
was think, and overthink. An hour passed, and another.

At last the door to the cell opened and he was asked in Italian by a uniformed policeman to follow him. Who had Ike contacted, he wondered.
The first time around, GIC had found him an excellent lawyer, by repute,
a Signore Lucca, but before they could meet, or speak, Webster had been
sacked, his job the price of wild coverage in the Italian press and a nervous
legal department back in New York. This, then, would be his first meeting
with an Italian defense lawyer—or with a defense lawyer of any kind, for
that matter.

The cells were in the basement, the interrogation rooms upstairs. He
was shown into one of them and told to wait, for the first time that day
unguarded. He thought it was where he had been brought from the airport
but couldn't be sure. After only a minute the door opened and Senechal,
still as pressed and neat as he had been at breakfast, came lightly into the
room, closing the door silently behind him. Webster frowned involuntarily
and gave his head a shake. It was an apparition that made no sense.

Senechal set his briefcase carefully on the floor and sat down, his near-
black eyes on Webster the whole time. Neither said anything; neither
looked away.

At last Senechal smiled, even less convincingly than usual, the sides of
his mouth lifting perhaps an eighth of an inch.

"It was lucky for you that I am in Italy, Mr. Webster," he said, his reedy
voice high and cold.

"If it wasn't for you I wouldn't be in Italy at all."

Senechal nodded. "That is true. But when we set up the meeting we had no idea you had these problems."

"Neither did I."

Another curt nod. "And now of course the problem is ours."

Webster raised his eyebrows and cocked his head. "Yours?"

"Naturally. When we hired you we did not know that your reputation was compromised."

"My reputation is fine."

Senechal gave an awkward snorting laugh that was clearly not commonly part of his repertoire. "Mr. Webster, you have been charged with serious crimes. Very serious. I ask myself who would believe the Ikertu report if the man who wrote it was in an Italian prison."

"Then you should find someone else."

"It's too late for that." He smiled again, his eyes empty. "And it may not be necessary." He took a crisply folded white handkerchief from the top pocket of his jacket and dabbed at the corners of his mouth. "I hope not."

Webster waited for him to explain.

"I understand how things work in Italy, Mr. Webster. You, you know Russia. I am sure that you have done nothing wrong. The law in these places is not about justice. It is about power. We know this. Everyone knows this, even the British and the Americans. This does not make things any less grave for you, of course. But it does mean that perhaps I can help. On Mr. Qazai's behalf."

Webster studied his flat gray eyes like old coins and tried to divine their intention. They revealed nothing.

"I have only one question for you, Mr. Webster. Can I assume that the charges against you have no merit?"

How Webster wished he liked this man and his client, or felt that he could trust him at all. He began to understand what Senechal had in mind. "You can assume what you like." He paused. "How did you know I was here?"

Senechal, ignoring the question, made a last, brisk nod and stood up. "I shall be a moment only," he said, and left the room.

He was gone for ten minutes, no more, and in that time Webster tried to imagine what he was saying and to whom. His body registered his unease: for the first time that day the restlessness that he had been carefully controlling got the better of him, and as his leg jigged and his fingers tapped he had the strong urge simply to leave, to get out into the air and walk and walk until this strange production and its bizarre cast felt far away. But he needed to get home. And he needed Senechal's help. The realization sat unpalatably at the base of his throat.

The younger detective appeared first, followed by Senechal. The older colleague wasn't in sight.

"I have talked to your lawyer, Signore Webster," he said, standing with his hands behind his back, his belly out, and rocking slightly on his heels. "He assures me that you will return to Italy in three weeks. This is an informal arrangement. It is unusual but we are happy to do it because Mr. Qazai testifies to your character. You are fortunate to have friends like this."

Webster, still sitting, looked from the detective to Senechal and back again. He's not my lawyer, he wanted to say, and neither of them is my friend.

"Come, Mr. Webster," said Senechal. "Let me drive you to the airport. We should be able to get you on a flight back to London tonight."

Webster tried to imagine what had just passed between them. With a short sigh and a shake of his head he stood, stiff from a day's sitting, and as he followed Senechal, his uninvited savior, out of the room, he turned to the detective.

"Don't think I won't find out what happened here today."

The detective smiled, his full cheeks sweating and dimpled.

IN THE BACK OF Senechal's car on the way to the airport conversation was sparse. His host didn't seem to expect any thanks and Webster expressed none. He called Elsa and Hammer, but his mind was turning on the question that Senechal had left unanswered. It made no sense.

In the end he repeated it, his eyes straight ahead, watching the road past the driver's ear.

"How did you know where I was?"

"We had a call. From the police. They wanted to know if you were indeed working for us."

"I never mentioned Qazai."

"Well, they knew. It is good that they did."

As the car slowed onto the slip road to Linate Senechal turned to him.

"I do not believe you will hear from them again, Mr. Webster. They are interested in those private detectives, not you. Not for now. But it would be well for you to express your thanks to Mr. Qazai. In any way you believe appropriate. I do not need your gratitude but he is a man of honor and likes his acts of kindness to be recognized."

Webster blinked slowly. Now he understood. He turned his head to look at Senechal, frail but energized beside him, and found nothing to say.

"So," said Senechal, "I am not sure that the police will pursue the matter. But if they do I am quite certain that Mr. Qazai would be happy to offer the same assistance again. For the good of our project."

Our project. Now there really was no such thing.

12.

KENSAL GREEN, after a day in the cells, felt almost comically sheltered and still under its dull summer clouds. The first rain in weeks was falling and through the open window of the taxi came the stony smell of hot pavements being washed of their dust. Webster paid the driver early so that he could walk the last few streets to his house, turning his face up to the sky and stretching some of the stiffness from his neck, and as he turned off the Harrow Road the city noise dropped until all he could hear was the magpies chatting at each other across the rooftops.

In that brief interval he breathed deeply and tried to clear the day from his head, but it sat there, obstinately refusing to quiet down. He regretted phoning Elsa. It would have been better to have kept the whole incident from her, but of course he hadn't known at the time that it would be over so soon. As it was, the thing that he feared most—puncturing the perfect safety of their home—he had already half done, and he knew that no matter how much he made light of it and no matter how much she acquiesced, unease would now be sitting in the house like a canker.

If Elsa was downstairs that meant the children had gone to bed, and he found himself wishing keenly that bath time and stories had taken a little longer than usual so that he could properly wish them goodnight. He badly wanted to see them. With luck, he could slip into bed beside Nancy and read her one last story. But even as his key turned in the lock he could hear cooking noises coming from the kitchen and knew that he was too late. Putting his bag down in the hall he gave a matter-of-fact "hello" to the house, conscious that this was what normal people do when they get home from work and, threading his way past the bicycles and over the children's shoes, he joined Elsa, who was drying her hands on a tea towel and looking at him like a mother whose son has been in a fight.

"Come here," she said, setting the towel aside and drawing him into a close hug. Holding him around the waist she leaned back, looked at him and smiled. "You don't look too bad."

He snorted. "It was a bit like a day in the office. One big long meeting." But he knew she was being kind. Tiredness sat across his shoulders and he could sense the bags under his eyes.

"Do you want a drink?"

"God, yes."

She took a bottle of whisky from one cupboard and two tumblers from another and poured an inch into each.

"Water?"

He shook his head, took a glass and leaning back against the kitchen counter raised it to her and drank. Neither said anything for a moment.

"So you're free," said Elsa, a hesitant question in her voice.

"It's a good thing you didn't come." He tried a smile. "It was nothing in the end."

She took a drink. "It wasn't nothing earlier."

"No. I'm sorry. They were putting the wind up me."

She raised her eyebrows and looked at him.

"Some Italian policemen enjoy it," he said.

"Just a game?"

"Something like that."

She pushed her lips out and nodded. "What did they want from you?"

"I don't know." With his free hand he rubbed his brow from temple to temple. "They were fucking about. I got caught up in their latest project. You'd have to be an Italian to understand the rules."

A pause.

"Why drag it all up again?" Her eyes were guarded, screening off some pressing anxiety. GIC had sacked Webster three months before he and Elsa had been due to marry, and that unforeseen reverse, he knew, had played on her mind ever since as something that might one day be repeated; but despite this he felt a flash of resentment that his problems couldn't simply be his own.

"I don't know." He shrugged. "Really. Because they can, I suppose."

Elsa turned away and checked a pan on the stove, stirring its contents before replacing the lid.

"Can I do anything?" he said, watching her turn down the heat. She shook her head. "I might look in on the children."

"Don't, Ben." She turned to look at him. "They're asleep."

"I'm just going to look around the door."

"You'll wake them."

"I won't." He put down his drink and walked toward the kitchen door.

"Ben. Leave them. Please. It took an age to settle them. I know you've had a bad day but so have I. They're not a comfort blanket. They need their sleep."

He stopped short of the door, closed his eyes and took a deep breath, his fingers pinching the bridge of his nose.

"They'll be there in the morning," she said softly. "In the meantime you can tell me how worried I should be by all this. Because I just don't know."

He turned, relenting. He knew that she was right, and scared, but he couldn't answer her question. Perhaps it had all ended when he left the police station; perhaps it hadn't even begun. If it hadn't been for Senechal's parting threat—because that was surely what it was—he would have expected nothing more than to keep quiet for a few months and avoid traveling to Italy, but now? Now he simply couldn't say. He hadn't had time to think it through.

"As far as I know, it's fine. Really. Stupid charges, no evidence. They don't have anything."

"How good is your lawyer?"

"Good, apparently." The first real lie.

"And he thinks you'll be all right?"

"He thinks it'll just go away. If it doesn't, the Italians will have to extradite me, and their case is feeble. It won't happen." He paused, waiting for her to respond, then tried a smile. "We may have to holiday somewhere else for a while."

But Elsa wasn't ready for the mood to lighten. She continued to frown, her eyes lit with that light he knew so well.

"What did you do out there?" she said at last.

"I went to see Qazai."

She shook her head. "No. Back then. What did you do?"

"Are you asking me if I'm guilty?"

She didn't reply.

"Jesus. This isn't about what I did." He had a sudden, childish urge to smoke. And to get out.

Elsa watched him for a moment, unmoved. "That's good. That's all I wanted to know."

He shook his head. "Do you know what? Forget it. I've been interrogated enough for one day."

"Where are you going?" she said after him, as he left the kitchen and started wheeling his bicycle toward the door.

"Just out." But he knew. He was going to see Ike. "Why you can't just trust me I don't know." He looked over his shoulder at her, a righteous, fraudulent challenge.

"I want to. But if you were telling me everything you wouldn't be running away." Elsa's arms were crossed and her eyes steadily on his. When he couldn't look at them anymore, he left.

ABOUT HALF A MILE from his house Webster stopped pedaling, pulled over and reached down awkwardly to tuck the flapping trouser leg of his suit into his sock. The rain, which had been light, was now full and steady and as he bent over he could feel his thighs and shoulders cold with wet.

He should turn around, of course, apologize to Elsa, tell her everything—or more, at least. But he knew what her advice would be, saw its sense and had no intention of taking it, because it clashed with the plan lurking in his thoughts. So he cycled on, furious with himself, past Queen's Park, slowly climbing across the Finchley Road and then the last, sheer push straight up into Hampstead, the houses growing older and richer beside him all the while. It was cooler now. Water dripped from his forehead and his calves burned with the work. Through the clouds and the plane trees overhead the last light barely found its way, and in his dark suit, made darker by the rain, with no lights on his bike, he felt pleasantly invisible after a day of scrutiny. He didn't like attention, never had. The cold air and the exercise began gradually to sort his thoughts.

Hammer's house was over by the heath on the prow of Hampstead where it fell away down to Kentish Town and the city beyond. He had lived in it for twenty years and under his ownership it had taken on something of its original eighteenth-century air: he had reinstated its oak paneling throughout, kept his one television out of the way in an upstairs room and favored low light and log fires, so that on a night like this the only way of telling whether he was inside was by looking for a faint glow around the edges of the shutters. But for his housekeeper, who occupied the attic floor, Hammer lived alone.

He was at home tonight and that, Webster had the sense to realize, was a relief. Ike had a way of making the complicated and unpleasant seem manageable, and there was no one better to see when you were feeling disordered. I've fled from one therapist into the arms of another, Webster thought as he chained his bike to the railings, because I didn't like what the first was going to say.

He knocked briskly with the brass knocker. The door, when it opened, was on a chain; it jarred, somehow, that someone so pugnacious should consider such things as home security. Hammer pushed the door to, unhooked it and looked down on Webster with mild surprise in his eyes.

"My God. They waterboarded you. Come in, come in."

It was warm in the hall and Webster could see orange light flickering on the gray-green walls of the study on the left. Hammer was wearing his reading glasses, more delicate than the thick-framed tortoiseshell he wore in the office, and in the near-dark looked more delicate himself, and older.

"Did you walk?"

"I rode."

"Elsa has the car?"

Webster only smiled.

"You look like shit. Take that jacket off. I have no trousers that will fit but a sweater I can manage. Luckily we have a fire. Go on."

He started up the stairs. Webster took off his jacket, which was wet through, hung it on a coatrack in the corner and went into the study. On a table by Ike's chair, a high-backed affair with wings, stood a spotlight, an empty glass and a copy of Livy's *History of Rome*, open, pages downward, its spine cracked about halfway through. Webster stood over the fire for a moment, looking at the books on the shelves either side of the mantel.

"You caught me lighting fires in June. I'm ashamed. The truth is I wasn't feeling too good but the sight of you is enough to make anyone feel better. Here, try this." Hammer passed Webster a thick brown cardigan with a shawl collar, not unlike the one he was wearing himself. "No one'll see you. There. Now, do you want a drink?"

Webster shook his head. "I shouldn't, thanks."

"You should. I'm having beer."

Webster asked for whisky, put on the cardigan, which was tight and heavy, and sat down on the far side of the fire. He should have phoned Elsa before coming in. He looked at his watch and realized with a lingering sting of regret that by the time he got home she would be in bed, either asleep or pretending to be.

"Here. There's a drop of water in it."

"Thank you."

He watched Hammer pour his beer from a bottle into the long glass, failing to tilt it so that it ended up with a thick head of froth. They drank.

"So," said Hammer, licking foam off his top lip. "You owe your freedom to Mr. Senechal."

"I owe everything to him."

"What happened? I was expecting another call."

"I wanted to leave it to tomorrow. Let it settle. Which wasn't a great idea, as it happens." He took another drink; it was good whisky and he relished the burn in his throat. "They set me up. Or they took advantage of a gift-wrapped opportunity. I think they set me up."

"They had you arrested?"

"Why not? It's Italy. He's had that house for twenty years. Enough time to put down roots."

Hammer frowned. "They did a nice job. If it was them."

"They've been checking me out. I'm sure of it. The other morning all our rubbish had gone by six. Our recycling's gone missing. And I had a call last week from Lester at GIC after he had a call from a headhunter wanting to know why I'd left." He paused. "It's them."

Hammer took a deep breath in through his nose. "You think Darius Qazai is going through your bins?"

"Wouldn't you in his position?"

Hammer raised his eyebrows and nodded. His fingers thrummed on the arm of his chair as he continued to nod, a slow, gentle bobbing that meant he was really thinking.

"So," he said. "Their plan is to make you beholden to them. The carrot is they stop beating you with the stick."

"That's the second carrot."

Hammer looked quizzical.

"Senechal tried to offer me a bribe. He told me good work would not go unappreciated."

"You're sure?"

"If I'd looked greedy they'd have told the Italians to stand down. No question. It was a test. The whole Como trip."

Hammer sat thinking a little longer. "It seems a lot of effort. I had no idea he cared so much."

"Quite. His daughter thinks that we're more important to him than we might imagine."

"She was there?"

"Oh, they were all there. I suspect so that it wouldn't look like the visit was all about me."

Another deep breath. "If you're right, we stop the case."

Webster put his glass down and shook his head. "We can't stop until we know what he's scared of. What it is he thinks we'll find. Otherwise he'll carry on, and so will the Italians."

Hammer paused to take a long sip of beer. "What have they got on you?"

Webster blinked and tried to hold Hammer's look, but it was no use. "This and that."

"What, precisely?"

"The PIs I used were . . ." He sighed. "They were thorough."

"How thorough?"

Webster hesitated. "Some hacking."

"In 2004? Pioneering work. Is that it?"

Webster looked up at him and after a pause gave his answer. "All the usual stuff. Banks. Phone records. I think they paid someone in the Polizia for his file. And they broke into his office."

"Whose office?"

"Ruffino's. Photographed everything they could get their hands on. You could say they exceeded their brief."

Hammer's fingers thrummed and his head bobbed. "The police know about that?"

"From something they said yesterday, it could come out, yes."

"And you didn't know what these idiots were doing?"

"None of it. Not until they gave me their report. But I'd have a job proving that."

A pause. "When I hired you, you said all this was dead."

"It was."

Hammer took a drink and thought for a moment. "Why come here? If you don't want to stop the case?"

Webster hesitated. What he had wanted was a blessing to fight fire with fire, to do anything necessary to expose Qazai; but he had expected Ike to be as exercised by the day's events as he himself had been, and this coolness gave him pause.

"To talk it through. To get your support."

"For what?"

Ike, as ever, knew what he wanted. "Nothing. I thought you should know our client—the one you were so keen to sign up—is a crook. After all."

"You're sure?"

"Jesus. How much do you want? They're blackmailing me, for Christ's sake. And they wouldn't bother unless they saw me as a threat."

Hammer stopped tapping. In the firelight his eyes were serious now, emphatic. "If you're right, find something to nail him with. And if you can't, you need to let go. I haven't seen anything that convinces me either way. Did Senechal try to bribe you? I'm sure he did. He would. But set you up?" He paused. "Sounds to me like they may not have needed to." He let the words register. "Your job is to tell the world whether he's OK or not. But not on a hunch. You don't get to crush a man like that without something really good. Meanwhile, he's our client. He's paid us a lot of money, and we owe him more than suspicions in return."

Webster gulped his Scotch. He stood, peeled off Hammer's cardigan, laid it on the back of the chair and made to leave.

"The first time I saw him I knew he was wrong," he said. "I can't believe you don't see it."

"I'm letting you do the seeing."

Webster shook his head. "While you watch the fees? I understand."

He gave perfunctory thanks for the drink and left, taking his damp jacket from the stand.

THE NEXT DAY, after a cool morning at home, Webster took Nancy to school and Daniel to nursery and made his furtive way to the Caledonian Road to see Dean Oliver, stopping in Queen's Park to arrange for flowers to be sent to Elsa. They were a poor substitute for honesty but he couldn't afford that, not yet. Throughout his time at Ikertu he had told her almost everything almost all the time, only leaving out the details that he thought would

appall or bore her. This, though, would frighten her, and he persuaded himself, disingenuously, that he preferred to lie to her than see her scared. On
his way he left a message for Constance, telling him that things had become
more serious and asking him to call.

Webster had never been to Oliver's office before; their two or three
meetings had always been on neutral ground, where an illusion of distance
might be maintained. He was not someone to be seen with, if it could be
helped, and perhaps he understood this, because Oliver spent his days in a
single room on a light industrial estate in an anonymous part of north London, four hundred yards from the prison—which may or may not have
occupied his mind as he walked to work each morning.

Uniquely among that strange band of people who did occasional jobs
for him, Webster knew nothing about Dean Oliver: where he lived, who he
lived with, what he held dear; how he came to do the difficult and esoteric
work that made him useful. Still less about his trade secrets, which was
probably just as well. After every meeting Webster came away with the feeling that he had said rather too much, which left him at the same time
unsettled and reassured.

Even Oliver's face gave little away. It was tanned all year round to a
suspicious evenness, and otherwise smooth and so featureless that it was
hard to retain a strong impression of him without the original present. His
cheeks were tight and always clean-shaven, his lips a little too full. That was
all that was notable; all, in fact, that one could see. The rest of his face was
covered by a swipe of thin brown hair across his forehead and a pair of
metal-framed glasses whose tinted brown lenses were just dark enough to
obscure his eyes. Sitting with him, it was impossible to know whether he
was making some piercing survey of you or simply staring vacantly past
your ear.

It was his voice that bore all the distinction: it was rich, in a quiet way,
full of sympathy and invitation and gentle variations that irresistibly drew
you in. A good thing, then, and no surprise, that he did all his work on the
phone.

Oliver asked Webster whether he'd like coffee—"I wouldn't, it's not
good"—and excused himself while he finished an e-mail. There were five

phones in his office: two landlines and three mobiles, neatly laid out on a sixties wooden desk beside a laptop. Webster watched him type and found himself asking the same, unaired questions that always occurred to him when they met. Something about Oliver forbade inquiry: an aura of privateness, of a persona deliberately constructed to give nothing away. But Webster feared the answers more than the reaction. It was difficult to believe that this very particular man who performed such a very particular purpose had ever been a child, or cried to his mother, or worn shorts, or gone on holiday.

What was only too evident, though, was that Dean loved his work. From this anonymous bolt-hole he carried out silent raids on any organization foolish enough to think that it could keep its information secure. Banks, hospitals, councils, ministries, universities, the companies that sell us phones, power and credit: his job was to get inside them, take what he needed, and retreat without leaving a trace. He needed little more than cunning, and to every target he was someone else. To the local branch of Barclays, he was from the fraud department in London; to the person in the cell phone company call center who sent out copies of bills, he was the owner of that phone and that account; to the local tax office he was a colleague in another office looking to clarify an inconsistency. His work was a sequence of tiny masquerades. But despite his apparent hollowness, Oliver's great talent was not acting but eliciting; he didn't inhabit a role so much as simply create a space that others felt obliged to fill.

And they did. In his first meeting with Webster he had volunteered— unusually, it turned out, because he rarely offered information—that he had never been "compromised," in his word: never had a single call that had gone awry, never had a single mark suspect that they were being duped. Webster could believe it. For all his flatness there was something about Oliver that made you want to tell him things. Perhaps it was some hidden trickery; perhaps it was as simple as needing to banish a silence. Whatever it was, it hadn't changed, and Webster found himself once again giving too much away.

He had meant to leave the details vague: his purpose for looking,

what he was expecting to find. But in the end he told Oliver everything except the identity of his client: the looted sculpture, the death of
Mehr, the utter conviction he now had that the two were linked and that
the only way to find the connection was to go to the heart of it all, where
the money was.

When Webster had finished his brief, Oliver nodded several times to
show that they were now in harmony, part of a secret team.

"And what do you need, Ben?" His voice was warm, gently coaxing.

Webster took a last look at Oliver before committing. His calculation
was this: Qazai was blackmailing him, and in order to make him stop he
had to blackmail him back. That was the argument, and it was logical
enough. But logic wasn't what had brought him here.

Finding out who Shokhor phoned was one thing: he was a crook, without question, and in any case no one in Dubai or Cyprus cared much about
privacy laws. But this was London, and the targets were UK citizens, and
one of them was only recently dead. What was worse, it was conspicuous.
Ten years before, few journalists or investigators had stopped to think
about what they were doing; there had been safety in numbers and so little
interest in the activity that the crimes had barely seemed crimes. Then there
had been Dean Olivers everywhere, stealing secrets from celebrities, checking spouses' finances, tracing fleeing debtors; but now, as the world finally
objected to having its privacy ravaged, his kind was dying out, and it was
difficult to see how even Oliver himself, such a subtle, devious operator,
could avoid his fate. Hammer, early on, had outlawed any contact with him
or his kind.

Looking at him now, Webster felt a certain sadness—part of the man's
spell, possibly—that one day soon such people might simply not exist, and
that men like Qazai could relax a little more. Because occasionally, and
certainly now, what Oliver did, however unsavory, felt not merely necessary,
but right.

"I need you to look at Qazai. His calls. His credit cards. Don't worry
about the banks—they'll be too complicated. But I want to know what
he's spending, where and when. So credit cards. Any hotels he's stayed at,

I want to see the bills. Any calls made from the room. Flights. He has a jet. He keeps it at Farnborough. I want to know exactly where it's been for the last two years."

Oliver made some notes, and Webster went on.

"Have a look at Mehr, too. His company. His private accounts—any you can find. Money in and out. And his telephone calls. Everything you can think of. You have free rein."

"How long ago did he die?"

"Two months."

Oliver wrote it all down, and Webster had a sudden vision of his notebook in a barrister's hand being introduced as evidence. He would have a word about destroying it at the end of the case.

"And his lawyer." He went on. "What the hell. His name's Yves Senechal. It's a French cell phone. Just his calls." He paused. "How are you in France?"

"I have a good man in France."

Webster wondered whether he really had good men stationed across the world or whether they were all, in fact, just Dean himself, seducing unwitting bank clerks wherever they happened to pick up their phone. He wouldn't have been surprised.

"I think that's it."

"It's a lot. I have quite a lot of other work at the moment, Ben."

"I'll pay you a hundred percent bonus if you find something useful."

"How long have I got?"

"Two weeks."

"Are you serious?"

Webster ignored him, and Oliver, adjusting his glasses, went through his notes, ticking each item as he went. When he was done he looked up.

"Have you done his bins?"

"He's too savvy for bins. He's a shredder."

"It's worth doing. He may not realize what's important."

"Maybe. But the house is a nightmare. Right on Mount Street. Hundreds of eyes."

"I know all the binmen in W1. They'll do it for me."

Webster shrugged. It seemed silly to refuse, like refusing a brandy at the end of a rich dinner. "All right," he said. "Go ahead. Report to me. No one else at Ikertu. And only call me on my cell."

Oliver smiled. "You gone rogue, Ben?"

13.

THREE DAYS AFTER HIS MEETING WITH OLIVER, Webster received an e-mail from Ava Qazai.

> *Dear Mr. Webster,*
>
> *I fear that I ended our conversation by the lake too abruptly. If you think it worth continuing, I'd like to apologize in person. Can I buy you a drink one evening soon?*
>
> *With warm regards,*
> *Ava Qazai*

He wrote back suggesting they meet the following night at the bar of the Connaught, opposite her father's house, and she, as he had hoped, agreed the time but changed the venue—to the Mandarin Oriental in Knightsbridge, which was far enough away to be discreet. Clearly she preferred her father not to know.

That day and the next he speculated on her motives. He thought back to her fury at her father during lunch in Como and to their talk by the lake. What might she know? She knew Iran, she knew her father. She seemed exercised by what had happened to Parviz. Perhaps she knew something about that, or about Mehr, or about Shiraz's troubles. He hadn't heard anything from Qazai since Como; perhaps he had sent her to gauge his mood. It could be anything, Webster realized, and tried to concentrate on the other work that was making a feeble claim on his attention.

The next evening, a Wednesday, he finished at Ikertu, took the tube to Marble Arch and walked across the park. A strong wind was gusting from the west, churning dust into the air, and when the sun moved behind the clouds any summer warmth dropped suddenly to a chill. Webster buttoned his jacket, rubbed some grit from his eye and struck out for the hotel.

The bar—low leather seats, mirrored walls—was busy with expensive shoppers and the odd tourist, but a pair of stools were free. Webster took one, waited for a group of American businessmen in high spirits to be served and ordered a whisky. The businessmen were toasting a success with champagne, and Webster tried to pick out the subtle signs that told you at a glance they weren't English: the monogrammed shirts, the pleated trousers, the boxy jackets, the straightforward enthusiasm. To his left a young woman, dark, with thick eyebrows, Lebanese perhaps, listened patiently to the level monologue of an older, barrel-chested man wearing sunglasses and a bright yellow shirt under his blazer. Webster wondered at the possible connection between them and when Ava arrived he was so lost to his daydreams that she had to touch him on the arm before he noticed her.

"I'm sorry. I was miles away." He stood and shook her hand, and she smiled at him with her black eyes. The truth was that he was more startled by her appearance than by her arrival: she wore a plain, short black dress, black high heels and a wrap of some silvery-gray fabric that managed to be shiny and discreet at once. Her hair was up, but artfully loose, and a single diamond hung around her neck on a white gold chain. She might have been going to meet a president or accept an award, and Webster's first thought was that next to her he was a crumpled mess.

On his own, sitting at the bar, he had been an outsider, a wary observer of a different world; now, ordering a vodka martini for this beautiful woman, he was a part of it—incongruous, perhaps, but complicit.

"Are you going out?" he said.

Ava, straight-backed, sitting with a poise that seemed in an old-fashioned way to have been taught, swiveled toward him a few degrees and crossed her legs.

"I am out," she said, smiling and shaking her head. "What do you mean?"

"You look . . ." He hesitated, not knowing what to say that wouldn't sound like a compliment. "I rarely have meetings with anyone so well dressed."

She laughed. "You're worried that I've dressed up for you? Mr. Webster, I just like to dress up. It's not personal."

The barman finished shaking her drink, strained it into a frosted glass and carefully squeezed a spray of oil from a strip of lemon rind onto its surface. Webster smiled, feeling foolish, and raised his glass to her.

"To dressing up."

"To meetings," she said, took a sip, put the glass back on the counter and ran her finger back and forth across the base of its stem. "You left very abruptly last week."

That word again. "After what you told me I thought I should make myself scarce." She frowned, not knowing what he meant. "About the likes of me never normally staying there."

"You don't seem the sensitive type."

He returned her smile. "I'm not. I had to get back. In the event I could have taken my time."

She looked faintly puzzled by the remark but let it go. Either she didn't know what had happened to him in Milan or she had chosen not to refer to it, and by the look of her, making no effort to appear nonchalant, he'd have been prepared to swear that she had no idea. He didn't think it wise to explain.

For a while they talked about Qazai, about Timur and Parviz, about Dubai, which she believed was no place to raise children. About Iran, which was quiet after months of unrest. He asked her about her childhood, and she sidestepped his questions with deft jokes and subtle shifts of subject that seemed to mask a mild prickliness. Webster wondered where she'd got her sense of humor from, and for that matter her real charm. If he was solving the mystery of the Qazai family—and thank heaven he was not—he would have looked forward to the interview with her mother.

He was enjoying himself, he realized, warily and not a little guiltily. For the last six months he had rarely felt lighthearted, and feeling it now was unexpected, and the more refreshing for it. This, of course, was not why he was here. He had now finished his second drink, Ava's martini would soon be done, and after one more he would forget to ask half the questions that needed to be asked.

"That lunch in Como," he said, turning toward her a little. "What was all that about? With your father."

A lock of hair had fallen in front of her eye and she moved it out of the way, not smiling now. "Is this the part where you grill me?"

"You don't have to tell me."

She looked at him for a moment, then took her glass and emptied the last half-inch. "Are you going to get me another?"

Webster nodded and turning to get the barman's attention signaled that he wanted the same again. When he looked back she was watching him with her head slightly tilted to one side, not for the first time weighing him up.

"I think," she said at last, looking away, "that when your grandson has just been kidnapped it would be good not to pretend that everything is normal."

Webster didn't say anything.

Ava shook her head and flicked the lock of hair aside again. "Sometimes I wonder what goes on in his head." She took an olive. "Tell me something. What do you think of him? You must have a sense of him by now. Who do you think he is?"

That was an excellent question, and it took Webster a moment's thought to find something meaningful that was less than completely frank. "He strikes me as the sort of man who's built his own world so carefully that other people are an inconvenience. He expects them to come into line."

"That's it," she said, animated now, apparently surprised by Webster's acuity. "That's it. And what happens when your world starts to collapse? You prop it up. You can't change it, because you can't imagine another."

Their drinks arrived. Webster took a sip of his, waiting for her to continue, wondering what she meant by "collapse."

"Come on," she said, getting down from her stool. "Let's go."

"Go where?"

"Somewhere no one can hear us." And before he could object she was walking out of the bar, throwing the end of her wrap over her shoulder as she went. Webster fished his wallet out of his back pocket, put down some notes on the counter and left at a brisk walk. Out of the bar he turned right, expecting her to be heading for the hotel's main entrance, but there was no sign of her in the lobby or on the stairs that ran down to Knightsbridge. To his left was the restaurant and a private room with grand, tall French doors, one of which was open. He looked inside. The room was laid for a dinner, and beyond the long table running down its center more French doors gave out onto a wide terrace above the park. Ava was there, leaning against the balustrade, struggling to get a cigarette lit, her back hunched against the wind.

"Can I help?" Webster said as he approached.

"This fucking lighter is useless," she said without looking up. He moved around in front of her, took the lighter and cupping it closely in his spare hand struck the flint wheel as she leaned in. It was a cheap, plastic lighter, he noted with mild surprise. "Thank you," she said. "Do you want one?"

"No, thank you. I only smoke abroad."

"Seriously?"

"Seriously."

She inhaled deeply and smiled as she blew out the smoke, her poise restored.

He waited for her to speak again but for half a minute she simply smoked, looking out at the park and the runners and cyclists coursing around the sand track.

"I've thought a lot about this," she said at last, dropping her cigarette to the ground and twisting it out with her shoe. "When I saw you in Como . . .

when we had that lunch, I felt sure that something would change, but it hasn't. I think he's made his choice."

Webster did his best to look understanding, but what she said made little sense. After a pause she went on.

"You love your family, don't you?"

"Very much."

"How would you expect to be dealt with if you put them in danger?"

The words caused a brief flush in Webster's chest. "Harshly."

Ava said nothing but nodded twice, finally settling something.

"I don't know where to start." She paused, searching for the beginning. "OK. OK. I went to Paris, what, two months ago? To see a friend. I can't give you his name. Since I haven't been able to go to Iran he's become important to me. He's an exile, a politician." She felt in her handbag for her cigarettes, took one from the pack and passed the lighter to Webster, who lit it as before. "Thank you." She took a deep draw. "So I see this man every so often and ask him about what's going on in Iran. He has excellent sources. God, it's not warm, is it?" She shivered, drawing the shawl more closely around her. "This last time he called the meeting, which he's never done before, and when I got there he was odd. Cagey. He had something to say but it took him a long time to get there."

I could say the same about this evening, Webster thought, hoping that whatever she had to say would be good.

"Eventually he asks me if my father has been behaving strangely. How? I ask him. Since his friend died, he says, in Iran. Then he tells me that he knows, from a good source, that my father is in a lot of trouble. With some very nasty people."

"What kind of trouble?"

"He wouldn't tell me. He just told me that it had to do with money, that I should be careful, and I should talk to my father. Then he went."

"Did you believe him?"

"He's never lied to me. And he was agitated. Like someone who's said too much."

Ava blew cigarette smoke out into the wind.

"Have you talked to your father?"

"Not for a while. I figured his problems are his own. We talk less than we did. But after what happened to Parviz I had to. In Como, after you'd left."

"What did he say?"

"He was furious. He told me he had enough people prying into his affairs and he didn't need another." Her cigarette was only half smoked but she stubbed it out. "I told him that if he couldn't protect his family he wasn't the great man he thought he was." She smiled, but Webster could see that she was scared. "Do you think I'm right?"

FOR SEVERAL DAYS AFTERWARD Webster wandered from place to place like an outcast, waiting, comfortable nowhere. Elsa was cool, quiet, and unconvinced by his assurances, which felt both more plausible and more hollow each time he repeated them. His home, he realized, didn't tolerate dishonesty; it reflected it back at him, like some fairy-tale paradise that blessed the pure in heart and tormented the wicked. Had he been able, he would have taken himself off on his quest and returned, humbled, only when he had made everything right.

At least the contract was more practical at work. Hammer was being bright and businesslike, making it clear that while he hadn't enjoyed their last exchange he hadn't been offended by it, and that no harm would be done if the Qazai case could now progress efficiently to its conclusion. This was straightforward and reasonable. Concentrate on Shokhor, and finish the case. But Webster knew, somehow, that there was nothing there. He was sure that before Qazai had even thought of Ikertu, he had seen a copy of the allegations against him, and was confident they were nonsense; sure that he never expected some lowly detective to exceed his brief, not when he was being paid to do as he was told; equally sure that he was doing everything in his power to bend that lowly detective to his will.

In any case, Oliver had been through Shokhor's phone bills and found nothing of interest—or at least nothing of interest to this case. The police in several countries would no doubt have found them enthralling, but there were no calls to Qazai, Senechal, Mehr, or any Swiss art dealers, and even though the records only went back two years and didn't cover the period in question, Webster chose to see in them further support for what he knew already. Shokhor was not the story. The story lay somewhere else, and if he didn't find it soon Qazai would ensure that it was never told.

So when he had tired of sitting at his desk, trying and failing to start a report that he never wanted to see written, and long before it was time for him to return home, Webster would leave the office and walk, with no destination in mind, and try to resist the urge to ask Dean or Fletcher whether they had discovered anything more since his last call. Even in that short period he developed a routine: an early swim, breakfast with the children, Ikertu until a little after lunch, and then what was in effect a long walk home, in a broad arc around the top of the city or following the river before heading north. Every day, London was hot and close.

Serious concerns contended with grave ones. A formal letter had arrived from the Italians asking him to appear in Milan for further questioning, and the date they had set was four days after the Websters were due to leave for their summer holiday in Cornwall. He had not yet told Elsa. His Italian lawyer was trying to come to an agreement with the police that Webster would not be arrested if he did attend, but described his chances only as reasonable; and, on the other hand, if Webster refused to answer questions now it would count against him if the matter ever came to trial—a trial he could not avoid. Signore Lucca had no advice about the most difficult aspect of the whole business, which was whether Qazai had the power to stop the process that he had in all likelihood started.

It was on one of these walks that Oliver finally called.

HIS OFFICE FACED SOUTH and didn't run to air conditioning, or even a fan. A grubby cream blind was down over the window and Oliver, unusually, had taken off his jacket and rolled up the sleeves of his shirt. He was still wearing his tie.

"You don't want coffee, I take it?"

Webster shook his head, impatient to get on with it.

"I just had some luck with the banks."

"Mehr?"

"Mister Mehr. Correct. I'll be honest with you, Ben, it's a while since I've done a dead man's bank accounts. Got to think on your feet a bit."

Webster did his best not to think about what sort of agility was being employed on his behalf.

"So Mehr only had a couple of accounts. One here, one in Jersey. My man in Jersey—good man—found some interesting stuff a few days ago, but I wanted to see where it led before I bothered you. Truss it up nicely if I could."

Webster nodded.

"So." Oliver leaned forward against the desk and clasped his hands, pushing the thumbs together. "Mehr does all right for himself. Did all right for himself. Lots of business, most of it what you'd expect. He buys from the Middle East, and most of the money coming in is offshore. Smallest transactions are in the low thousands and they go up to millions. It's more or less random. And then every so often, you get a little flurry of big payments coming in. Last March, last May, July, October, there were millions in the space of two days. Round amounts, fairly regular. But nothing this year."

He looked at Webster to make sure he was keeping up, then carried on.

"OK. So that's not so odd. Maybe he's buying stuff for the Qazai Foundation or some other big client. But if he is, they're paying him in advance."

"What do you mean?"

"I mean the money comes in, then goes out. He gets paid first, then buys whatever he buys."

"So he's being financed."

"Perhaps. But it seems strange that he doesn't take a cut."

Webster looked at him, a faint, familiar thrill in his chest.

"The money goes straight through," said Oliver, leaning back in his chair and linking his hands on top of his head. "If two million comes in, two million goes out."

"Where does it go?"

Oliver smiled. "Deeper offshore. I'm working on it."

The sun still beat against the blind, and Webster could feel sweat standing on his skin. He looked at Oliver and shook his head. He had known it. He had always known that there would be something to find.

"Is it Qazai's money?"

"Give me time."

Along the frame of the window Webster could see a thin band of low rooftops and brilliant blue sky. He tried to work out what this meant. That money had been deliberately cleaned; if anyone looked, it would appear that Mehr had been going about his business, buying artifacts.

"What's he doing?"

"Nothing good," said Oliver, bright teeth showing in his grin.

CONSTANCE, MEANWHILE, HAD GONE QUIET. This was unlike him: his usual policy when he had found nothing useful was to proclaim the failure loudly and insistently until it felt like your fault, and his silence was bound to mean something interesting. Webster, who had left him a message on his return from Milan and another before his meeting with Ava, was beginning to think about asking common friends in Dubai whether he'd finally been thrown in jail or out of the country when early one morning came a call.

He stared at the number for a moment before answering, not recognizing it. Senechal had been bothering him every day since Milan and he had let each call go to voicemail. But this wasn't a French number, or an English one, and he decided to take the risk.

"Hello."

"Ben. Fletcher. You must have thought I'd died."

"That was the only thing that hadn't crossed my mind." It was impossible to imagine Constance dead: who or what would dare extinguish all that energy?

"I appreciate your confidence," he chuckled grimly. "Though I don't share it. My apologies, my friend. I have spent the last week fighting for my life, in Dubai at least."

Webster wasn't in the mood for a mystery, but knew he had to ask anyway, and Constance proceeded to explain.

"I had a visit—a visit, no less—at my office, last Monday. Nearly two weeks ago. From the General Directorate of Residency and Foreign Affairs, that august and valiant body of men. They wanted to know what my purpose was in remaining in Dubai. The betterment of my soul, I told them, but they weren't happy with that. Not plausible. No one would go to Dubai for the good of their soul, and they knew that, to their credit. So I gave them some of the usual guff about journalism and consultancy, etcetera, etcetera, and they asked to see my papers, and they pored over them for longer than it would take any dunce just to read the things, and then they told me that there were inconsistencies, whatever the fuck they might be, and that my visa was under review. Because I had been in Dubai a long time and had affairs that might need clearing up they would very generously not frogmarch me to the airport immediately but would expect to see me at their offices in exactly a week, for a hearing. Which was three days ago."

"And how did it go?"

"It went. Nothing was decided. I took my lawyer and he tangled them up a bit. I have to go back in two weeks."

"Who did you offend?"

"Ha! I have no idea. Take your pick. It's a miracle I lasted as long as I did. What I did not do, thankfully, was kiss anybody in public or bring in the wrong cough medicine. That would have been a whole lot worse. Anyway, I'm having a break from the place. Beirut is beautiful and sane. I was in the mountains yesterday. Maybe I'll stay. Finish the house. Ditch that harlot."

It would never happen, unless he was forced. Constance adored Dubai: it kept him alive. Without its absurdities and its intrigues he'd slowly wilt. Webster couldn't help thinking, obsessed as he was, that it was strange timing for him to be exiled now.

"Can I do anything?"

"That's sweet of you. Sweet of you. But no, thank you. I'm not sure there's anything to be done. And in any case I didn't call to moan at you. I called to tell you things."

"Tell me what?"

"Well, I have good news and bad news. And an invitation. The bad news is that my friend won't tell me anything more than he already has.

He seems to be regretting his earlier garrulousness. But. But. He is interested in what you know, and might like to get together to share. That's the invitation."

"Is this the sort of sharing where I tell him stuff and he thanks me for it?"

Constance grunted in amusement. "Only one way to find out."

"Can you tell me who he is?"

"Not until you agree to meet."

"When?"

"Next week."

"Fine. Set it up." Webster paused; on the other end of the line he could hear the click of a lighter and a long, extravagant exhaling of smoke. "What was the good news?"

"Ah, that. Your friend Cyrus Mehr. The case is closed. The order has been given to file that file."

"They have a murderer?"

Constance bellowed in contempt. "Of course not."

"That's good news?"

"Not unless you gave the order. But I happen to know who did."

14.

THREE DAYS LATER, Hammer came to Webster's office, the first time he had sought him out since events in Milan. He had just arrived from Hampstead and was still in his running things, all bone and sinewy health.

"Good morning," he said, in good spirits. "You look well."

"No I don't."

"Well, perhaps not." Hammer came and sat by Webster's desk. "I've been doing some investigating."

"That's meant to be my job."

"I thought it might be better for all of us, especially you, if I had a look myself."

Webster leaned back in his chair and gripped the armrests. "Go on then."

"The short story, which is very short, is that it's all garbage. Everything in the Americans' report." He looked for Webster's response but got none. "You remember we thought it might be from U.S. military? Part of their investigation? I made a few calls, and spoke to the Major in charge. Nice man."

"They wouldn't tell me anything."

"Well, maybe you weren't doing it right. If you'd come to me, maybe they would."

Webster thought better of reacting, and Hammer went on.

"It all came from them. The relief, Shokhor, the National Museum. And they thought it was true up until a month ago. Tell me, have you found your Swiss dealer yet?"

"No. That's going nowhere."

"I can tell you who he is. His name's Jacques Bovet, and he sells very expensive things to very expensive people out of Lausanne. Jacques has form. After the first Gulf War there was an amnesty on looted items and because he knew he was about to get caught, he returned something. Next time around he's stealing again, only this time they do catch him, and they make a deal. By the way, they have the sculpture, all in one piece."

"That's good."

"That is good. You should be pleased. It's a beautiful thing."

"I'm pleased. Believe me. It's the only innocent in the whole affair."

Hammer sniffed. "So they talk to Jacques: tell us who's in the chain. Well, he says, an Iraqi gentleman called Shokhor brought it to him and a Brit called Mehr took it off his hands. Mehr bought one or two things off Jacques in the past and Jacques thinks—says he thinks—he's acting for a wealthy London collector called Darius Qazai. Because Qazai is just the sort of person who would want this piece. Jacques is bargaining on my friends not doing a good job of investigating this . . ."

"Your friends?"

"They're my friends now. Never miss an opportunity to make a friend, Ben." Hammer gave him a look of amused rebuke. "But he's wrong. They do a great job, and three weeks ago they go to Jacques and tell him he's talking horseshit. And he can't squirm out. Turns out he wasn't telling the truth. Apparently you can't trust a Swiss antiques dealer like you used to."

Webster unfastened his watch and wound the pin. None of this was a surprise. "He knew there was nothing in it when he came here. Qazai. He'd seen a copy of the report, no question."

"Maybe. It makes no difference."

Neither said anything for a time, Hammer's unspoken challenge lying between them. Webster carried on winding his watch, looking at the second hand smoothly ticking around. He broke the silence.

"I can't write that report."

"You'll have to. But I'm not done."

"There's something else going on."

"Like what?"

Webster couldn't say. He couldn't reveal Oliver's work, because Ike would stop it. "He's in trouble. Shiraz has lost a fortune and he needs money."

"That doesn't make him a crook."

"Then why is he screwing me? Tell me that."

"Ben, he didn't invent what you did in Italy."

Webster shook his head and looked away. "I can't believe this."

"I said I'm not done."

But Webster wasn't ready to respond. Outside, far below, under a blue sky, people were hurrying home with determined walks, catching taxis, wandering away in groups to the bar. It would have been the most wonderful thing in the world to follow them: to write something bland, accept the compromise, hope Qazai did the same and resume his life. Go home.

"I need a week," he said.

"Would you listen to me?" said Hammer, his patience cracking.

Webster turned to him, his jaw set.

"You think I trust this guy?" said Hammer, irritated now. "I don't trust any client who badgers me as much as he does. He has his grim little side-kick call me every hour. He's a bully, at best. Did he set you up? I still don't know, and neither do you. But did he try to bribe you? I believe you. That's what his kind do. They buy people. They'd like to buy me."

Webster made to say something but Hammer raised his hand. "Would you wait? Jesus. OK. So he's in trouble. You're in trouble. I don't like to see you in trouble. It's bad for everyone. It's bad for business. I have no desire, believe me, to see your name in all the papers, because do you know what? Mine'll be there too. Again." He raised his eyebrows. "Understand? Good. So here's a guy, tried to pay off one of my people, and I don't want to give him what he wants. Part of me also thinks, if I'm going to hedge my bets, I should take you seriously about the business in Italy. If Qazai's not involved, then it'll make no difference, but if he is . . . Well, maybe it can help."

Webster had no idea where this was leading.

"But most of all," Hammer went on, "I don't know what he's going to do with my report. Heaven knows. He may not have lied to me about it but he sure as hell hasn't told me the whole truth. If we give him a glowing testimonial he can wave it around for the rest of time to whoever he likes, and he doesn't qualify for that. Do I want you to write a eulogy? No, I don't. So here's what we're going to do." He took a deep breath and pointed at Webster. "You . . . you are going to write a report—hear me out—that says yes, the sculpture story was a crock, but ultimately we can't say whether he's a good guy. We're going to put a story in there, about a reliable source—this is you, by the way—who witnessed him offering a bribe."

"That was Senechal."

"Same fucking thing." He shuddered. "He really is one of the weirdest sons of bitches . . . Anyway, we give Qazai that report, and tell him that if he doesn't like it, it will be quietly leaked that Ikertu actually had grave reservations about his ethics. That in the end we were pulled off the case before we could dig too deep. They've asked for a meeting. We'll tell them then."

Webster ran his hands through his hair, clasped them behind his neck and stared up at the ceiling. He shut his eyes against the fluorescent light. If only this would work. Like all Ike's plans it was simple, a little devious, and apparently sound. But he couldn't believe that Qazai would simply stand down, just as he knew he couldn't. They were racing against each other, and Ike was calling time. Neither would hear him. Neither would choose to.

"I don't think I can write that." He sat upright and looked Hammer in the eye.

"If you want to be shot of this mess, you will."

"We shouldn't write anything. Believe me. With what I know."

"Like what? Just tell me, for Christ's sake."

"Fletcher called yesterday. The investigation into Mehr's death has been officially closed."

"So what? I'm amazed it was ever opened."

"The order to shut it down came from someone inside the Quds force."

"Which is?"

"It's part of the Revolutionary Guard. Like the Iranian SS."

"Jesus. This is why I need to separate you two."

"And Mehr was laundering money."

Hammer's face became set. "How do you know that?"

"Give me a week. You'll thank me."

Hammer shook his head.

"Ben, you'll write it now." His voice was firm, but there was a softness in his eyes, a sadness. "This is not your company. If you can't do it, you should think seriously about whether you'd be happier somewhere else. Or on your own, where you can play out these romances of yours without interference." He gave Webster a last look, which seemed to say that he regretted his firmness but would be tested no further, and left the room, somehow older than he had entered it.

TWO AFTERNOONS A WEEK a young German woman called Silke picked up Daniel from nursery and Nancy from school, took them to the park for a while and then brought them home for their tea. Webster liked Silke, and so did the children, but a part of him wished that he could do her work himself.

Today he was later than he would have liked; he had spent the afternoon talking to Oliver, and now tea was finishing. Silke was washing up; Daniel was scraping around the inside of a clearly empty yogurt pot; Nancy had pushed hers aside and was bent over a notebook, writing something with a crayon, her face three inches from the page. When he opened the kitchen door she looked up, scrambled down from her chair and ran to him.

"Daddy!"

He crouched down, wrapped his arms around her and lifted her up in a tight hug, arching his back and kissing her face above his. She would be six in August but she was still so light, so finely built, so distinct from the mass and clamor of the world outside the door that her touch and her laugh pulled him from it instantly.

When Elsa returned home the children were in their pajamas watching television and Webster was cooking, slicing onions into thin half-rounds with a satisfyingly sharp knife. He turned from his work and kissed her.

"How was your day?"

"Fine," she said. "Good. How's Nancy?"

"She seems fine. No problems to report."

"Did you ask her about Phoebe?"

Webster looked over his shoulder at his wife. She was going through that day's mail; her hair was up and the skin on her neck golden from the sun, and her beauty, as it often did, gave him a shock of elation, or privilege, or something else that he couldn't wholly recognize. He hated it when there was distance between them, and this only served to heighten it.

"We just talked through her day. She didn't mention anything."

Elsa nodded, not looking up. "What are we having?"

"Chicken." Webster turned back to his cooking and a second later felt Elsa's hand on the back of his neck.

"How was yours?"

"Good. I had a chat with Ike. Or he had a chat with me." He slipped his arm around her waist and for a second they stood rather awkwardly together in front of the stove, like partners in a three-legged race, until he had to pull away to slide the onions into the pan.

Elsa let her hand linger on his back and then went to sit down at the table.

"Are you two OK now?" she said.

"So-so. Better."

"What did he say?"

"He's come up with a way out of the whole mess."

"Will it work?"

"It should all be over within a week."

He glanced at her, his face concertedly frank, expecting her to spot the evasion in his answer.

"What then?"

"What do you mean?"

"Will you stay?"

Webster stirred the onions, watching them bubble gently and turn translucent in the green oil.

"I'll see what happens. When this is over I'll know."

He glanced up to see Elsa looking at him closely. She knew he wasn't telling her everything. Whether by training or nature she could always tell.

"I called him." She paused. "Ike."

"You called him? When?"

"At the beginning of the week. I was worried about you."

He shook his head. "You should have talked to me first."

"You're not the easiest person to talk to at the moment."

He turned to her, running a hand through his hair and grasping the back of his neck. Suddenly he felt a great weight of tiredness. "I'm sorry, baby. I am. There isn't long now."

Elsa simply watched him for a moment. "What's his plan?"

"It's boring." Her look told him to go on. "It's very Ike."

"You're not going to do it, are you?"

He frowned, indignant. "I'm going to do my best."

Not strictly a lie; but Elsa knew precisely what it meant. "Jesus, Ben. You know what?" Her voice was steady and clear. "There is more to your life than the absurd"—she searched for the word—"vanity of your work. Do you think it matters to me whether this man is good or bad? Do you think it matters to Nancy, or Daniel? I was sorry about Lock. I still am. But his boss? The Russian who's quietly suffocated the last six months of our lives. I don't care. We don't."

Webster, his eyes on the ground, didn't answer.

"This is not a campaign. This is life. It's not some assault on, on what? What is it you're trying to destroy? Because I worry, I really fucking worry, that it's us. That you won't be happy until it is."

He shook his head. "I'm not doing this for me."

"Really? Who then? Mankind?"

He looked up at her, with all the candor—genuine now—that he could find.

"I'm not doing it for me. Not anymore."

He had never seen Elsa so intense, so adamant. She gave him one last, angry look and pushed out her chair to leave; and as she did so his phone, lying dormant on the side all this time, chimed once, a startling trill. His eyes went to it involuntarily.

"I tell you what," she said. "You deal with that. Save us all. I'm putting Daniel to bed."

Webster stood to one side to let her pass and watching her leave let out a deep, long sigh. The onions were beginning to brown at the edges; he stirred them, shook the pan once or twice and turned off the heat. Part of him wanted to throw his phone across the room, but a greater part had to know what it said.

It was Constance. The message was only five words. "Timur Qazai dead. Please advise."

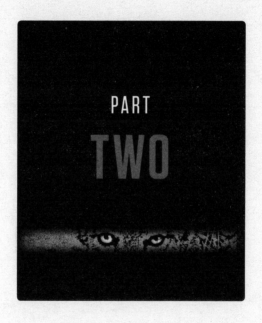

PART

TWO

15.

NO FUNERAL SHOULD TAKE PLACE in high summer. Even in Highgate, on the rising hills of north London, the city's heavy air had found its way through the oaks and sycamores to the mourners gathered around Timur's grave, bathing them in a waxy heat that seemed to drip onto the skin and stick there. Webster, sweating in his wool suit, could feel grime accumulating on the inside of his collar and ran a finger around it to loosen it from his neck. Ant-like bugs flew silently, drawn to the white shirts of the men; next to him Hammer swatted at one on his neck, caught it, discreetly flicked the remnants away.

Cool earth, that's what Timur deserved, but the ground looked heated today and seemed to offer no rest. Webster couldn't help but picture him in his coffin as it was borne in on the shoulders of the pallbearers, Qazai at the front. His body must have been badly broken. He had died, the Dubai police had said, when his car hit a wall at somewhere just under a hundred miles an hour. The collision had been side-on; at the last minute his car had swung around, flailing into the concrete and crushing him inside. Webster imagined the tremendous noise it had made and the greater silence that must have followed.

This was not a grand funeral—there was no splendor, no pomp—but there were many mourners. Webster could make out a wealthy Iranian set, some of whom he recognized from Mehr's memorial service: a handful of Tabriz staff, several friends of Timur and Raisa, less moneyed than the rest. And then there were the Qazais, in their black dresses and black suits, reduced, a flat outline of the people he had last seen in Como just two weeks before.

Timur's sons were both there, decked out in mourning, Raisa holding them close. Parviz stared quietly at the freshly dug black walls of the grave while Farhad hid his face in his mother's waist, nestling there, more shy than sad, occasionally glancing out as she stroked his hair. Raisa herself, the color in her face leached out, kept shaking her head, as if she was simply lost in the wrong place.

From the other side of the grave Webster saw all this. He saw Timur's mother, the former Mrs. Qazai, standing apart from the family with her new husband, her blonde hair piled up on her head and her eyes masked by sunglasses. He saw Senechal, in his usual uniform, looking like an agent of the afterlife come to take stock. Ava, with her head bowed and eyes shut. And he saw Qazai, pale, gaunt, erect and proper in his suit, working hard to counter the new look of fear and haunting in his eyes.

It was a quiet ceremony. The celebrant's soft voice was directed only to the family and Webster, standing far from the grave, couldn't hear the prayers that were said over the body as it was lowered into the ground. The words over, Raisa reached down, took a handful of damp soil from a neat pile at the edge of the grave, and threw it onto the coffin, where it landed with a gentle patter. As each of her sons did the same she squatted down and when they were done held them in a long, still embrace. Then she stood, smiled at both, wiped her tears and led them away down a dark avenue of oaks toward the waiting cars.

Timur's mother was next, then Ava, then Qazai, who stood for a long time—a full minute, perhaps two—staring at the coffin with the earth in his hand before letting it drop. His gaze was unblinking, intense, yet somehow absent. Webster wondered whether he was looking through the wood to send a last message, or making some inward search of his own soul. Behind and around him the other mourners started to disperse, and as the soil slipped from his hand an abrupt, silent sob shook him and he too moved away, making the procession back to the road on his own. Webster watched him go, sensing that he had just seen his first glimpse of an un-adorned Darius Qazai, the raw essence of the man that investors and grandees and private detectives didn't ordinarily meet. He could not com-prehend his pain. Even his tireless imagination baulked at the task.

By the grand gates of the cemetery people had stopped and were saying goodbye to each other. Senechal, bleached out in the full sun, had taken himself to one side and now stood waiting. Webster saw him ahead and waited for him to stroll lightly toward them.

"Mr. Hammer. Mr. Webster. It is good of you to come." He didn't offer his hand and spoke with greater than usual earnestness. "I felt sure that you would wish to have the opportunity to say your last respects."

"We're grateful to be invited," said Hammer. "It came as a terrible shock."

"To all of us, Mr. Hammer. To all of us." Senechal paused. He seemed at home here, almost relaxed. No smiling was required, no positivity. Just a meek, lawyerly deference to the likelihood that things will, after all, almost always go wrong.

"There is nothing worse," said Hammer, "than seeing someone die young."

Senechal inclined his head in a sort of bow.

"Our meeting tomorrow . . ."

"We will cancel," said Hammer. "Of course. Or rearrange."

"No, no. That will not be necessary. No, the meeting will proceed as before." Sensing their perplexity he went on. "I'm afraid that the death of Mr. Qazai does nothing to solve our problems. Indeed, it makes them more acute. When we see each other I shall want to know exactly where we are with the report, and when we can expect its release. In all honesty," he attempted a smile, "I think we have waited long enough."

Hammer checked Webster with a discreet motion of his hand. "I un-derstand. We'll see you tomorrow."

But Webster had stopped concentrating. He was looking over Senechal's shoulder at Ava, who had broken away from the people still mill-ing around the entrance to the cemetery and was now walking toward them with purpose in her stride. As she drew near, Senechal followed Webster's look and turned to find her already by him and fixing his eyes with her own, tired and red as they were. She glanced at Webster before addressing Senechal.

"Did you ask these two?" Senechal hesitated, apparently surprised, but not discomfited, by the question. "Did you?"

"Mr. Qazai asked me to invite them, miss."

Ava looked from one face to another, furious, shaking her head. Glancing behind her she leaned in slightly, lowering her voice. "This is not a business meeting. This is not a moneymaking exercise. Do you understand? For any of you. If he's invited you to the wake, do the decent thing and go home. And you," she turned to Senechal, jabbing a finger at him, "I don't want you there. I don't want you in my father's home. Sucking the life from him. Doing whatever it is that you do."

She glared at Senechal for a good two seconds, made to leave and then shook her head, as if remembering one last thing.

"Why did you come?" she said to Webster. "What is there to investigate here?"

"I came out of respect for your brother."

"You didn't know my brother."

"Sadly, no."

"I expected better from you."

Her eyes were trying to impart some meaning that he couldn't grasp; he felt baffled by her words, and awkward at having been singled out. Senechal, showing no signs of shock, looked intrigued, as if he had just heard something whose significance he couldn't judge but whose importance he did not doubt.

TWO DAYS EARLIER, when Webster had first heard the news of Timur's death, his response, after the shock, had been a strange, inappropriate lightness, almost peace: when he surveyed his thoughts the insistent muttering of his obsession had gone, and the switch was like moving from white noise to utter quiet. To continue his duel with Qazai now would be indecent and unnecessary. The man was already crushed, and though Webster wasn't proud of it, beside his sympathy for Raisa, and her boys, and Ava, sat something like relief.

His first call that evening, after he had spoken to an excited Constance, had been to Ike. They talked about Qazai, and what this would mean for his plan, and agreed that without Timur it would at best have to be completely rethought; about Timur himself, the misfortune of being born the son of a rich man; and, with a certain amount of professional detachment, the difficulties of staging a car crash so that it might look like an accident. Hammer was of the opinion that it was more or less impossible, certainly a great deal harder than anyone might imagine, and Webster, though he disagreed, said little. Even before he had spoken to Constance, who was convinced, as ever, of a conspiracy (the car had been tampered with, no question; a mysterious Range Rover had been seen racing it shortly before the crash; the Dubai police were saying, unconvincingly, that crucial CCTV footage was missing) he couldn't bring himself to believe that Timur's death wasn't the latest act in a sequence, a progression he could see but whose logic he couldn't make out.

One day, perhaps, that story might be told, but he no longer had to be the one to tell it. In any case, he had nothing. Some strange payments through a dead man's company and a hint of a conspiracy from, of all people, the Gulf's most energetic conspiracy theorist.

"I've seen the light," Webster said.

"Excuse me?"

"You're right. We should end this."

Hammer was quiet, waiting for more.

"As painlessly as possible. I've got no appetite left."

Webster heard Hammer take in a long breath. "Good. It's one thing you being ruled by your appetites. It's another when we all are. Welcome back."

His next call had been to Oliver, and just dialing the number had made him feel cleaner.

"Dean. It's Ben."

"This is late for you. Not for me, of course."

"We need to stop work. Send me your bill. Make it healthy."

There was a pause. "You're sure you want to do that, Ben?"

"I'm sure. Something's happened. The client's had enough."

"Well that's a shame. It's getting interesting."

"The money?"

"That's a long trail. Both ways. No. Something else."

Webster paused, knowing he had to hear it.

"We got the bins again on Tuesday. You should see some of the stuff that guy throws away. I could live off it. Anyway, not much of a haul, except two sheets of flight log for his jet. First quarter of this year, but I managed to get the rest. It's a Bombardier, super long range. Flies it to New York, Hong Kong, Dubai. Always those three places. And Milan. Once to St. Kitts for a week. But there are one or two odd ones in there. Caracas, for a day, back in November. Flies in in the morning, back overnight. Belgrade early last year. He spent the night there. And Tripoli, in January."

"OK. So what else?"

"Ben, you need to be a little more patient." Oliver paused, and Webster apologized. "I've also done his cell phone. Took a while because it's in the company name. He uses it a lot. Anyway, I couldn't see anything in there, but I fed it all into this program I've got that spots patterns in data, along with the flights, everything we know about transactions on Mehr's accounts, the lot."

"And?"

"And two or three days before each of those trips, he gets a call from the same number. A UK cell phone, pay-as-you-go. I checked with Vodafone. Set up with bogus details—false address, false name. But it only ever calls one number—Qazai's. That's it. It was set up two years ago, and in that time it's made just six calls. One before each of the trips, and three others. But in the last fortnight, it's made two more calls. Both to that number."

That was interesting. If Webster had wanted to establish a secure means of talking to a source, this is how he would have done it, and if he had wanted to meet him quietly—somewhere no one was looking, where discretion was assured—those might be the places he would choose. Interesting, but tenuous, and redundant.

"Thanks, Dean. But send me the bill."

"You're serious?"

"I am."

"What happened?"

"Qazai's son died."

"You have a very decent client," said Dean, after a pause.

"What do you mean?"

"Well, some people would say this is the time to press on."

"Some would," said Webster.

And that had appeared to be that. So convinced was he that the world had changed that when he and Hammer had received a call from Qazai's secretary asking them both to attend the funeral, Webster had seen it as confirmation, a formal offer of a truce.

WEBSTER'S GRANDFATHER HAD DIED when he was nine. For a year and a day his grandmother, a Catholic, had worn black: entirely at first, and slowly introducing muted colors as time passed. Fascinated by the process, he had asked her why she did it, and she had told him that his grandfather would want to know that she was missing him, and this was her way of showing that she did. He would see the black and know.

The day after the funeral, walking to Mount Street with Hammer at his side, unity restored, Webster thought this was no way to mourn, with meetings and negotiations and business. What it said about Qazai that he should persist in this way he didn't know. Was it heartlessness or doggedness? Or simple desperation? A week ago that would have been one of the questions that Webster would have liked answered above all, but now he couldn't bring himself to care. What he had seen yesterday had shown him that his client, proud and tricky and even poisonous as he might be, was still a human being and therefore worthy of some charity. And some humility: who was Webster, after all, to take it upon himself to judge this man?

It had rained overnight, enough to freshen the air a little but not enough to wash away the heat, and even at ten it was uncomfortably warm. Mayfair woke up later than other parts of London and was still quiet. So was Hammer, by his standards. He was letting Webster know that his mood hadn't softened nor his ultimatum changed just because Timur had died, and Webster felt a certain relief that for once he wasn't going to have to fight him.

At the Qazai house they were shown by the butler, with greater than usual solemnity, into the sitting room, whose many treasures were showing only dimly through the gloom. The curtains were drawn and the only light came from four large, fabric-shaded lamps stationed around the walls. The air was stale and warm and smelled of must.

Qazai and Senechal rose from their sofa, offered their hands to shake and then gestured that everybody should sit. No words were spoken. Webster kept his eyes on Qazai, who sat back with his hands neatly on his thighs, staring down at a fixed point ahead of him, the skin under his eyes purple and black like a bruise. Next to him, Senechal looked full of life. It was he who began.

"Gentlemen. I do not want to keep Mr. Qazai any longer than is necessary. So I will come straight to the point. You have had two months and hundreds of thousands of pounds. We need our report. Right now."

For once Webster didn't feel the urge to respond. He let Hammer reply.

"We understand. I have a proposal to make that I think will suit everybody." Senechal nodded that he should proceed; Qazai didn't lift his eyes. "We're in a position to write the report. I think you'll be happy with it. It may not be complete but it should serve your purpose."

"What do you mean, not complete?"

"Philosophically speaking, these things are never complete. We could go on looking forever."

"You've looked long enough."

"We feel the same way."

"What if we do not like your report?"

Hammer paused for a moment, his eyes on Senechal's. "Then I'm afraid you can lump it. We will only be writing one report on this case."

Senechal's expression didn't change but he stiffened. "That is not what we discussed."

"Mr. Senechal, you haven't been the easiest of clients. You haven't given us all the information we asked for. You offered one of my people a bribe. And some of what we've found smells off." He waited for Senechal's reaction but there was none. Either he had complete mastery of his emotions or he simply didn't have any. "For those reasons, you don't get full marks. The sculpture story we know is nonsense, and we'll say so. That'll be the focus. But we can't say you're saintly. Because you're not."

Senechal drew himself up still further but before he could reply Qazai raised a finger and spoke, and though his voice was cracked it had a cold authority that filled the room.

"When I hired you," his eyes were fixed on Hammer's, "I didn't know that the man you would assign to us—to a job of great delicacy—was a crude hack of low morals who thinks nothing of breaking into offices and bugging people's phones." Webster started to respond, but Hammer raised his hand and he kept himself in check. "But now I do, through good fortune, if you can call it that. So here is what I propose. You remove this man from the case. Then you yourself or some more reputable colleague writes a report to our specifications. If you do these things, I will not tell the world that Ikertu employs cheap crooks. And I will not encourage the Italian police to pursue their investigation."

Webster's vision seemed to cloud with red; he closed his eyes and tried to shake it away. When he opened them Qazai was staring at him in unblinking challenge, his tired eyes wide. Hammer was saying something but Webster was barely conscious of it and talked across him.

"So what's the going rate?" he said. "For an Italian policeman? More than you were going to give me? Or does he work it out for you? So that you don't have to think about it." He pointed at Senechal but kept his eyes on Qazai. "Tell me. How much was Timur worth? How much did you pay him to live in the desert sitting on your lies? I hope it was a lot. Because it strikes me he gave you his life twice over."

"Ben, that's enough." Hammer brought his arm up to restrain Webster, who was getting out of his seat.

But Qazai hadn't moved. He sat perfectly still, looking at Webster, his own rage contained. "What do you mean by that?"

"I mean that in one way or another, he died because of you."

Qazai pulled himself to the edge of the chair and pointed a finger at Webster, his words slow and filled with the certainty of the inspired.

"Mr. Webster, I have provided for my family for over thirty years. I am a constant man. But you, you have some resentment I do not understand. Perhaps you measure yourself against other men and find yourself wanting. So you do reckless things. You flirt with criminals, with prison. You are vain and weak. You even flirt with my daughter." The words hit Webster with the force of some shameful but indistinct recognition, like a drunken impropriety remembered the next day. He shook his head and started to speak. "No," said Qazai, "you will listen to me. Go back to your wife. Go back to your family. And when you have committed yourself to them, when you are a whole man, then we can talk about me. And my son."

Qazai stood up and looked at Hammer. "In the meantime, I want my report. Tomorrow."

Webster was standing too now, reaching for something to say or do that would settle this for good, but he was thrown, and nothing came. All he could do was listen impotently to Hammer.

"You'll have it in a week."

"Tomorrow. Or I go to the papers."

"In one week. Or on the front of tomorrow's *FT* will be a big fat story about how no one wants to buy your company because you might be an art thief. And whatever you've started in Italy needs to stop or I'll leak that too."

"I haven't started anything, Mr. Hammer."

"Well you can stop it anyway."

Qazai straightened himself. He was almost a head taller than Hammer and he did his best to look down on him from the greatest possible height.

"I'm beginning to understand the ethics of your industry, Mr. Hammer."

Hammer returned his gaze, a trace of a smile at the corners of his mouth. "And I yours."

OUTSIDE, Mount Street was reassuringly sane. The sun shone, taxis rolled past, people strolled about. Webster felt like he had been in some infernal show, a diabolical entertainment, and even though he had been released into the light his thoughts still whirled in confusion.

"Unbelievable," said Hammer, looking up the street. "Un-fucking-believable."

"I told you. He's a piece of work."

"Not him, you. We have it all neatly wrapped, ready to go, and you can't see it through. Can't just fucking take it."

He started walking toward Berkeley Square, one arm raised behind him telling Webster to stay where he was, not to talk to him. Then he turned, fury in his face.

"I don't know who's worse. You're a pair of babies. Do me a favor. Stop fucking squabbling, and finish this awful fucking case."

THE REPORT WAS HARDER WORK, not because Webster didn't know what to write but because each sentence was a provocation. Every phrase had to be forced from his fingers. The calm he had felt after Timur's funeral had gone, and above the words struggling onto the screen he could still hear Qazai's stinging condemnation of him, potent with both lies and truth.

His anger growing, his concentration lost, he let his mind wander over the facts of the case in the hope that he might finally find the design behind them, but it was still deeply buried, and try as he might he couldn't reach it. Mehr had been murdered, not by bandits but by someone who knew what he was really doing for Qazai. That was a fair assumption. His death had been organized, or at least condoned by someone within the Iranian government—the intelligence services, or the Revolutionary Guard. That was another. An unwelcome thought struck Webster. Perhaps the money that Mehr had been channeling had been destined to fund opposition groups in Iran. Perhaps Qazai's secret was a noble one, and the death of Timur the terrible price of some quiet heroism.

No. That might fit together, but it didn't explain why Qazai was so desperate to raise money that he had scarcely paused to mourn his son, or why he was summoned to clandestine meetings every six months, or why he had thought it necessary to threaten Webster's freedom.

What should have taken a day, then, was dragging into a second and evermore uncertainly into a third when, as Webster was trying to find some agile language for the summary, Oliver called. He looked at the number, let it ring four times, saw it go to voicemail and continued to watch the screen until an alert told him he had a new message.

"Ben, it's Dean. You never call anymore. Guess what I've found? Call me back."

Webster put his face in his hands and rubbed his eyes. He should let it go. He couldn't let it go.

"I knew you couldn't resist," said Oliver.

"I told you to stop."

"I had some inquiries outstanding. About Mehr's money. They came back." He paused. "Do you want the long version?"

"Just the highlights."

"I can do that. Last May, about seven million U.S. goes through Mehr's accounts, then on a tour of the world's most discreet little islands, before ending up with a company that finally spent some of it—on chartering a ship from Odessa to Dubai. With an interesting cargo. Customs got a tip-off, and when they had a look they found twelve containers full of machine guns and old Russian rockets."

Webster sat back in his chair. "You're serious."

"They denied all knowledge, of course, but no, it happened. I found two articles about it. Then nothing."

Christ. If only Oliver had found this a week earlier, or not at all.

"You're saying the money that went through Mehr was used to buy weapons?"

"Looks that way."

"Jesus. Where were they going? After Dubai?"

"Syria."

"Syria?"

"Correct. With an onward ticket to Lebanon, I dare say."

"Sorry. Qazai's money is buying rockets for Hizbollah?"

"We don't know for sure it's his money. I've found out where it ends up but not where it comes from." Oliver sniffed. "Are we on again?"

Webster considered it, and through his scrambling thoughts all he could see was Qazai's righteous face, full of pride and fury, taunting him with his weaknesses.

"What about the rest of it? Where does that go?"

"I don't know yet. Give me a chance. In all, I've found five groups of payments into Mehr's company. Forty-three million in total. This is the only batch I've traced to the end. But on the way they all go through the same place."

"Where?"

"Cyprus. A company called Kurus. Shareholders are obscure but one of them is a guy called Chiba. God knows what it does."

"Who is he?"

"Low-key. Very. According to the filings he's Lebanese, but there's nothing else on him anywhere. At all. He could be anything."

Webster thought for a minute, trying to make out the logic. Whatever was happening, it was serious, and sustained, and Qazai was involved. "Find out if the money really is his. Qazai's. I'll look at the shipment, see where it came from. Where it went."

"You could do that. Or you could see what he's up to in Marrakech."

"Excuse me?"

"Qazai's going on one of his little trips. Flight's due to leave on Friday. All logged in with the airfield."

Webster didn't say anything.

"That cell phone that keeps calling him? He got a call from it yesterday. Lasted forty-five seconds. Half an hour later he filed his flight plan with Farnborough."

Webster thanked Oliver and hung up. For a minute, perhaps two, he stared at the words on the screen in front of him until they were just black marks on the white. Then he picked up the phone.

16.

THREE HOURS TO AFRICA, that was all, but Webster wished it was longer. He would have liked to sleep. He had spent the night in the spare room, as he sometimes did before early flights, and with the short, terse argument he had had with Elsa still repeating in his head had passed a wakeful night.

He had to go, he had told her, and that much was true. Two days at most, the last act, the only way to finish it: all true. His lies were in the omissions. He hadn't mentioned that he was paying for everything himself, or that he hadn't told Ike he was going, or that he had little idea what he might find when he arrived. Had she known these things, she might have screamed at him, but as it was she did what Elsa did so well: let him spend time with his own faults.

In his tight, narrow seat, surrounded by holidaymakers and Moroccans heading home, Webster totted up what all this was costing, apart from his relationship with his wife. Seven hundred pounds for his ticket. Eighty pounds a night for his hotel, a little riad recommended to him by Constance. At least he hadn't brought George Black, as he would have liked. Black insisted on a team of five at least for surveillance, and they would all have flown out and stayed at Webster's expense; three days of that and he'd have been bankrupt.

No, George was unfortunately not a possibility, and in any case would have been hopeless for Marrakech, where five hulking ex-soldiers might have proved a little conspicuous, but Webster couldn't operate without someone to help him: he had never been to Morocco before, had no understanding of the place, spoke no Arabic, couldn't rely on his schoolboy French and would hardly blend in himself. So before he had left the office he had gone into Ikertu's files and found a handful of cases that had touched on Morocco. There weren't many, but all had used the services of the same woman, Kamila Nouri, who, judging by the correspondence, was an old friend of Hammer; some of her work dated back to the very first days of the company. Webster had called her, hoping to meet shortly after his arrival, but Kamila, insisting that any friend of Ike's was a dear friend of hers, had told him that she would meet him off his flight. Webster, who had told Hammer that he was taking a day or two off to write the report, hoped sincerely that she was such a good friend that she wouldn't think to check out his story.

Two days of her time, then, at whatever her rate was: probably another two thousand pounds altogether, or close to that. Say three thousand for the whole escapade, at least. That was money he should have been saving, or spending on the family's holiday. It was not money he had to throw away. The figures in his head, shifting up and down as he rebalanced his calculations, became a new and powerful symbol of his irresponsibility.

And all that expense was going to prove what, exactly? He wasn't convinced by any of the theories that coursed through his head. But from the scattered facts available two things were clear: that Qazai's money was being used for dark ends by some vicious people, and that whoever they were, and whatever their relationship with Qazai, something had gone wrong. The payments through Mehr had dried up in December, or shortly afterward, when the pattern would suggest that a payment had been due; Qazai had traveled to Belgrade early last year, Caracas in November and Tripoli in January; Mehr had died in February. And now Timur.

Webster toyed with the possibilities. Blackmail was one: some ugly secret was costing Qazai millions, and he hadn't been able to keep up the payments. Or, more plausible, having lost a vast amount in the Gulf and realizing that he had to sell his company, Qazai had decided to cut some old ties—to one of his original investors, say, who made his money in ways that might prove embarrassing.

Could that be this man Chiba, Dean's latest discovery? There was no way to tell. It was a long journey the money took, from the light to the dark, from the apparent shine of Darius Qazai through Cyrus Mehr and a dozen grubby little companies to crates full of guns and rockets in ships bound for Gaza. Chiba might be a money man, a mere processor along the way like the others, but he was near the end of the trail, and if he hadn't planned it all he would surely know who had. It was possible that he was the one phoning Qazai, summoning him to Marrakech. Webster allowed himself to imagine the perfect outcome of the next two days: a photograph of the two men together; a copy of Chiba's passport from the register at his hotel. That was all it would take.

The plane landed on time—no holding patterns, no detours, no delaying of the moment when he would have to put his rudimentary plan into action. Follow Qazai, was how it went: pick him up, in the jargon of surveillance, at the airport, and follow him until he had the meeting that he was surely coming here to have. After that, switch to the people he had met and find out who they were.

He met Kamila, as agreed, by the Hertz desk, but her description of herself had been so good he might have recognized her anywhere. "I am short, gray and one eye points wrong," she had said, and that indeed summed it up. Her head was uncovered, her hair thick waves of silver-gray cut shortish, and her left eye looked off to the left, just a little, making it hard at a first meeting to know which to focus on. A friendly face, open, but alert with it: the nose sharp, the eyes intense, taking in details.

"Welcome, Mr. Webster," she said, taking his hand and shaking it with a strong grip, beaming her greeting up at him: she was a head shorter at least. She wore a black canvas jacket and under it a long gray dress that did little to hide a neat paunch. "It is a great pleasure to see you here. My son, Driss."

Driss was tall, skinny, handsome, with a strong Arab nose and quiet eyes. He must have been twenty, no older, and smiled shyly at Webster as they shook hands. His hair was thick like his mother's, black and shining.

"How is Ike?" asked Kamila, leading them out of the airport building. Driss insisted on taking Webster's bag.

"In rude health."

"Still running?"

"Every day. Too much."

The glass doors slid back to let them out into Marrakech and the heat came rushing at them. It was more intense even than Dubai, more humid with it, and as they walked to the car Webster felt himself start to sweat. For once, thankfully, he wasn't wearing a suit.

On the drive into town Webster quizzed Kamila about her work for Ikertu and her relationship with Hammer. They had met in Paris fifteen years before, when he had been trying to find evidence that a Russian businessman was part of a growing scandal involving the illegal sale of arms to Africa. Kamila, then a young officer with the DGSE, the French intelligence agency, had met him and told him a number of highly diverting lies. Five years later, when she had left France with her new husband to return to Morocco, the land of her blood but not her birth, she had got in touch with Hammer and told him about her new business, a consultancy that aimed to help foreign companies understand the opaque politics of North Africa. Since then she had worked on half-a-dozen cases for Ikertu, not all of them distinguished: the last one had required her to locate the mistress of a Moroccan politician, which was not what she had imagined herself doing when she arrived here. But she was happy to do that sort of work for Ike—and few others—and when she did she called on the services of her sons, Driss and Youssef, who could do certain things that as a woman she could not. Not that there were many of those. Now: what did Webster have in mind?

He told her that he was interested in a man called Darius Qazai, who was coming here the following day. He wanted to know everything about the people Qazai met: who they were, where they had come from, where they went afterward, how they had paid for their trip. But in the first place all he wanted to know was where Qazai and his lawyer were staying.

"That shouldn't be too difficult," said Kamila, leaning over the front seat and grinning at Webster, who smiled back.

. . .

WEBSTER, COLD AND STIFF from the air conditioning in his room, was woken
by the call to prayer at dawn the next day. He pulled the sheets about him
and lay for a moment listening to the muezzin.

His first thought was Elsa. He had called her before dinner and she had
asked him to make a vow: that his return be the end of all this, no matter
what the result of his intemperate dash to Africa. He had promised, and
that had been the end of their short conversation. One more reason to make
the day count. He tried to imagine how it would play out, but only its
beginning was clear: it would start at the airport, him in Driss's car waiting
for Qazai, and Kamila with Youssef waiting for Senechal. Beyond that it
was an anxious blank.

Qazai's flight was due at noon; Oliver had established that Senechal
was coming from Paris, and would land at eleven fifteen. Webster, Kamila
and her sons had spent the afternoon and much of the evening trying to
find out where the two men would be staying, but with no luck. There were
over four hundred hotels in Marrakech and they must have called half of
them; the other half were not places someone like Qazai would consider.
Chances were they had booked an apartment or were using false names,
and while this wasn't a disaster it did make the whole operation especially
precarious, because if they lost Qazai he would almost certainly stay lost. At
nine, admitting defeat, Kamila had taken Webster to dinner.

It was now quarter past five, and still dark. Webster took the hotel's
handbook from his bedside table; they didn't start serving breakfast for two
hours. He reached for his book but put it down again without opening it,
far too restless to read.

So he got up, showered, neglected to shave, put on his jeans and a
light-gray shirt and left his room, stepping out into the cool morning shadows of the medina. The sun was taking its time to rise, and in the narrow
alleys the only light came from the occasional street lamp bracketed to a
coral pink wall. What a place this was for intrigue: every turning suggested
a surprise, every door a secret. For twenty minutes Webster saw no one, as

he threaded his way through the maze, and until the call to prayer began the only noise he heard was birdsong.

What was he expecting to find in Marrakech? The people who controlled Qazai, he hoped. The people he owed money, the people who were blackmailing him, the people he had perhaps betrayed. They were to be found somewhere along that trail of money that Oliver had been so patiently following, and in his imagination that's where they still lived, dry and theoretical, refusing to come alive. They could be one man or many, from anywhere on earth, with anything in mind.

Somehow, though, he knew that they were here in Marrakech, waking up for a day that meant as much to them as it did to him, waiting as he was for Qazai.

WEBSTER HATED SURVEILLANCE. For something so simple it required such huge quantities of thought and concentration.

Kamila, dressed today in a full length djellaba and headscarf—"because no one sees you in one of these"—came for him at nine and together they made their way to the airport, where Driss and Youssef were already in place. Webster had given everyone photographs of Qazai, taken from interviews and news stories, but had no image of Senechal, and although a five-word description would probably be enough—surely there was no one else in Marrakech who looked quite like that—he agreed with Kamila that he should wait inside the terminal and point him out as he appeared.

Both men would be coming through the same door, thankfully: passengers on private flights still had their passports checked in the main terminal in a separate queue. Senechal was due to land first, and would either take a taxi or have a car waiting for him; there was no railway station at the airport and he was hardly likely to take a bus. Kamila and Youssef would be waiting in her car, a decrepit Peugeot 205, at the far end of the concourse, ready for Webster to point out their target. When Qazai arrived, Webster would be waiting in the back of Driss's car at the same position on the concourse, ready to identify him. There was no reason why this shouldn't work, but similar plans, better resourced and more deeply thought through, had gone wrong before.

Air France flight 378 from Paris arrived exactly on time and Webster, wearing a cap and sunglasses that Driss had lent him for the purpose, took up his position by the rail and watched the taxi touts barracking the new arrivals. Some more sober drivers, most of them from the big hotels, waited patiently with signs bearing the names of their charges. None of them was waiting for a Mr. Senechal, but then that was no surprise.

A steady flow of people was passing through the arrivals gate, but there was no way of knowing when passengers from the French flight would start appearing. Senechal would in any case be one of the first through. Webster kept half an eye on the luggage tags, and at eleven forty the first Air France passengers emerged, wheeling their executive cases. There was no sign of him. A few minutes later the crew passed through, wheeling theirs. Maybe he'd had to bring some large piece of luggage. Documents, perhaps. But by five past twelve the stream of people had slowed and after another five minutes it stopped altogether.

This was why surveillance was so exasperating. So many impossible variables. Perhaps Senechal had been stopped by immigration or customs; perhaps he had some special arrangement that allowed him to bypass all the formalities and leave the airport from another exit; perhaps he simply hadn't come. But then if Webster had had the power to know any of these things he wouldn't have needed to follow the man in the first place: as Hammer was fond of saying, watching someone's back was a very crude way of finding out what was on his mind.

After a brief consultation with Driss, Webster called Kamila and told her that she could now switch her attention to Qazai; to be sure of picking him up, Webster would again endeavor to point him out. Then he called Oliver and asked him if he could think of some way to confirm that Qazai's flight had indeed left, and spent an anxious few minutes waiting for a response. It was possible, he now realized, that the whole thing had been a blind, and that in fact the two men were now in Beirut, or Belgrade, perfectly secure.

But before Oliver could respond, Qazai appeared. He was dressed in the clothes of a rich man at play—loafers, a jacket of light-blue linen—and at first glance looked fresh, comfortable. His hair had been cut and his beard was particularly trim. His gait, though, seemed slightly impeded, slightly heavy, as if he were walking on sand, and because he wore sunglasses Webster realized for the first time how much of his authority came from the clear imperious blue of his eyes.

He had a single case, of deep brown leather, which he carried. Ten yards into the hall he stopped and looked around at the two dozen or so drivers and their signs; not seeing what he wanted he paused, put his bag down, and made another survey. This time something seemed to click and shaking his head he made his way to a short man in a black suit, who took his bag and led him out of the hall. From his position Webster couldn't see the name on the driver's sign; he watched them go, and once they were level with him motioned to Driss to follow him outside. But as he did so, some movement in his peripheral vision registered as familiar, and focusing on it he realized that it was the strange floating walk of Yves Senechal, looking as he always did, pulling after him a metal case.

Webster turned around, walked away behind a thick column, took his phone from his pocket and found Kamila's number. He pressed the key, held the phone to his ear and waited. It took an age to connect.

Through the window he could see the driver holding open the door of a black Mercedes saloon for Qazai who, with a look around him, climbed in. The phone was still dead; cursing, Webster tried to cancel the call and at that moment a message from Oliver flashed onto his screen: "you are ok." A minute ago that would have been accurate. Driss appeared at his side.

"That's Senechal," said Webster. "Behind me now. In the gray suit with the metal suitcase. I can't get this fucking thing to work. That"—he pointed through the huge smoked glass window—"is Qazai. In the Mercedes. Get your mother to follow him, and then come back here."

He turned and watched as Driss ran to the exit, past Senechal and along the outside of the window. The Mercedes was indicating and waiting for another car to pass, and while it did so Webster made a note of the number on its plate. As it pulled away Driss was still running toward his mother's car, perhaps fifty yards away, so that by the time Webster himself made it out of the terminal she was just receiving the message. The little Peugeot turned into the road, was forced to wait for an endless moment while another car inched across its nose with extraordinary slowness into a small space, and then finally drove off. Webster looked for the Mercedes. It had disappeared from sight.

Trusting, or praying, that Kamila was good enough to make up the gap he looked around him for Senechal. He was no longer there. A moment before, he had been by a crowd of people, talking to a taxi tout, and now he had gone. He had to be in one of the dusty old yellow cabs that were queueing up yards away, but Webster couldn't risk peering in through the window—he was already nervous about Senechal peering out at him. Turning to face the airport building he waited for Driss to arrive, out of breath, by his side.

"Do you see the man in the gray suit in any of those taxis?" A half-dozen of them were pulling away, waiting for traffic to clear. "I'm going to text your mother that license plate number."

Driss looked, but saw nothing. He walked back, shrugging, as the cars rolled away, and stood for a moment looking anxiously at Webster, who had taken off his sunglasses and was pinching the bridge of his nose.

"What do you think?" said Webster, squinting in the sunlight.

"There are traffic lights at the bottom of the ramp. A hundred meters. If he was through before her . . ."

Webster nodded, and ran a hand slowly through his hair. Thirty seconds later his phone rang; it was Kamila, and he knew what she was going to say. He was reminded of the phrase George Black always used when reporting a cock-up of this kind. "We've had a loss, Ben." A loss was exactly how it felt.

He shook his head and answered it. "Meet us back here," he said, and hung up. "How long does it take to trace a number plate?"

"On Friday, a long time."

Of course. It was almost the weekend. And what better place to spend it, with time on your hands, than Marrakech?

"But I saw the name," said Driss.

"What name?"

"The passenger name on the sign. The driver's sign."

Webster felt his heart give a little kick.

THERE WERE TWO "MR. ROBINSONS" staying in the city's finer hotels, but only one of them had checked in that day. He was due to stay a single night in one of the private villas in the grounds, and a call from Kamila to the room to inquire after his comfort had confirmed that he was there.

It was Kamila who had found him, in the eleventh hotel they had tried. Webster thanked God for making Qazai too grand to slum it even for a single night, and checked out the hotel on its Web site. It had immense gardens, and dotted around them, away from the main building, where the only moderately rich were forced to stay, was a handful of secluded villas. Qazai was in the Sultan's Residence.

Despite their size, the hotel grounds had only one entrance. Outside, Webster and Driss sat in one Peugeot, Youssef in another, on opposite sides of the road, fifty yards away from the hotel gates, while Kamila, who had changed into a light summer suit, had lunch in the hotel lobby and waited to alert the team by phone the moment Qazai appeared.

Their vigil started at two, with the full heat of the sun pressing down on the roofs of the cars. The sky was a blue Webster hadn't seen before, pristine and deep, set off at its edges by the spiky green of the palm trees and the sandy pink of the brick.

By three Webster had finished his small bottle of water and was growing hungry. He quizzed Driss about his plans to finish his degree and move back to Paris as a postgraduate, about life in Morocco with such an unorthodox mother, about growing up in France and moving here when he was small. About Moroccan food and French food, which was a mistake. To dull his appetite Webster smoked the cigarettes he had bought the night before.

At four, just as Driss was offering to walk to buy food, his phone rang; he answered it, listened, and hung up.

"The same car," he said to Webster, starting his engine as the Mercedes pulled across one lane of traffic and drove away toward the center of the city. Driss followed at a distance, Youssef and Kamila twenty yards behind him.

After no more than a mile, at the entrance to the medina, where the streets narrowed to an arm span, the car stopped and Qazai got out. Webster turned his face away as Driss drove past and parked the car on the verge of road beyond some trees.

"We could follow in this," he said. "But not for long."

A moment later Kamila drew up in front of them and got out of her car. Through the back windscreen Webster saw Qazai look around him, a perfunctory check, and then move quickly through the broad gate into the old city. He was carrying a thin leather briefcase, and was alone.

Webster opened his door and was starting for the gate when he felt Kamila's hand on his arm.

"I go first. Keep as far behind me as you can. It's not easy in there." She set off with a quick walk.

Since his early morning walk the medina had filled with people, and as he walked through the gate he had to look hard to catch sight of Qazai, who was some twenty-five yards ahead trying to pass a slow-moving group of tourists. In among their khaki slacks and white sun hats Qazai looked elegant, patrician, aloof. An old man on a skinny old scooter snaked between them.

Qazai seemed to know where he was going—though how, Webster was at a loss to understand. Had he not had Kamila in his sights the whole time, he would have lost his bearings immediately: there were no landmarks. Some of the alleyways were so narrow that the only constant in view was the sky above, at its highest point still a fine cornflower blue, and the walls of the buildings all ran together in a continuous band of color, from rosy ochre to sandstone with now and then a clean block of white or blue as relief. Shops occupied the broader streets: tin buckets of yellow saffron and luminous red paprika set out on the ground, pastel gowns hanging from awnings, endless rows of pointed shoes, rugs strung across great expanses of wall in rough imitation of Qazai's house in London, and in the odd space in between a heavy studded door that opened into the private world of the city.

They were in quieter, closer passages now and Qazai was making a turn every ten yards; there were no crowds to hide behind and Webster, trying to keep only Kamila in view, was finding it harder and harder to stay in touch with her and at the same time keep out of sight. Shade now covered the ground, the buildings seemed taller, and he had the sense of going slowly down into ever darker, tighter circles. The walls around him were the color of redwood and the air thick and still.

He rounded one corner to find Kamila, all of six feet away, peering cautiously around another, her palm up behind her to tell him to stop. He stood as still as he could, hearing his own breathing in the silence. She continued to watch, her body tensed, and then, satisfied that she had seen enough, turned and pressed her back to the wall.

"He stopped at a house about five meters down there." She was whispering. "Knocked once, quietly. Then again. He's just gone in."

"What happens now?"

"Wait here."

She disappeared around the corner, and was gone for a minute.

"OK," she said. "It could be worse. There's one man on the door. When they come out they either have to come back around here, or the other way into a long alley with only one turning off it. Three people can cover it. You can't. Not like that."

She took her phone from her handbag, dialed, said a few words in French and hung up.

"They'll be with us in ten minutes. You shouldn't wait here. Go back the way we came: left, second right, left again. On your right you will see an entrance to a courtyard. A doorway. Hide in there."

Webster did as he was told, repeating her instructions as he went. He was feeling highly visible and not a little redundant, and found himself imagining what George Black and his people would have made of all this. Most of the time surveillance was carried out in a car on the wide streets of expansive cities, where it was possible to believe that it was a serious discipline; here it resembled nothing so much as a child's game, a scrappy version of hide and seek.

Hidden, then, he smoked a cigarette, breathing in the smell of raisins in the pack before he took one out and lit it. The smoke drifted around the courtyard, which was calm and clear of people and clutter, and from which three doors led into houses whose windows were all shuttered. When he arrived he could feel his heart beating in his throat, but it soon slowed, and for a time he felt strangely peaceful.

It was Driss who came to get him. He had a bag over his shoulder, and from it pulled a large piece of maroon fabric which he handed to Webster.

"Put this on. Over your clothes."

As Webster unfolded it he saw it was a robe, with a pointed hood. A djellaba, like Kamila's. The fabric was coarse in his hands.

"Pull the hood low and no one will know you. Forget your sunglasses."

It had been a long time since Webster had dressed up, and after a second's hesitation—more surprise than reluctance—he drew the robe over his head, his arms upright into the sleeves, a movement that he hadn't made since donning a surplice at school. It was lighter than he had expected and smelled of old books. He drew up the hood with both hands and instantly felt detached from the world, invisible; he might wander off through this endless warren of alleyways and never resume his old life again. The change complete, he followed his guide out of the courtyard.

Killing time is easier in a car, with company, than it is in a featureless passage on your own. For the first half-hour, Webster stood, until he realized that he might save his back and sit cross-legged on the ground, since that was an acceptable thing for a man in a djellaba to do. He tried as best he could to cover his shoes, leather and too English. Except for the call to prayer, which made him feel briefly conspicuous, there was no noise here, and hardly anyone passed: an old man pushing a bicycle, a tall man in a dusty black suit, several men and women dressed as he was. All he could do was watch the wall in front of him, stuccoed like coral, and wait for Kamila to walk past the entrance to his alleyway, which would mean that the meeting had broken up and he was to follow the next person he saw. Driss had brought him a bottle of water, and by sipping it slowly he made it last until six, when the heat was tailing off a little and the sky beginning to turn a cobalt blue. Under his robe his shirt was now wet and cool with sweat.

His phone sat shaming him in his back pocket: he should send Elsa a message. He had called the previous day and she hadn't answered. Wasn't he simply protecting his name and his family's future? And what would Elsa have thought of him if he had simply rolled over for Qazai? He wondered whether she really prized their security over his principles, and whether she would have been so happy to compromise her own.

He became so involved in this one-sided internal argument that when Kamila finally appeared he only noticed her when she whispered "now" at him as she passed. The passage behind her was clear but he could hear footsteps about to round the corner; he bent his head low and stayed still. Two pairs of feet came into view and passed, one in black leather lace-ups, the other in brown suede. Senechal and Qazai. Webster's heart skipped high in his chest. He and Driss would follow them; Kamila and Youssef would remain in place ready to shadow whoever else came out of that house. He waited for his quarry to round a corner, then moved off. Somewhere behind him, Driss fell into line.

Senechal had a map, and from time to time slowed to refer to it, Qazai, curiously slumped, giving him no assistance and appearing to take no interest. Webster hung back, expecting Driss to appear alongside him; but he never did, and as Senechal moved on he would resume his pursuit. Slowly the alleys grew into streets and the noise of traffic and shouting returned. Webster guessed they were on the edge of the medina now and began to ask himself what he would do if his prey were suddenly to hail a little Peugeot taxi and speed off. Pick them up again at Qazai's hotel, with any luck, and hope that Kamila and Youssef did better with their end of the job.

After five minutes walking Qazai and Senechal passed through a pointed arch into a broad square that jostled with life. Bicycles and cars zipped across it dodging carts and donkeys in their way, and around its sides the shops were beginning to close, taking their goods down and leaving blank walls behind them. The smell of wood and charcoal burning was in the air. Webster watched the two men head for the far corner, hung back for longer than he would have liked and then cautiously followed, now a good thirty yards behind and trying his best to keep them in sight while negotiating the traffic buzzing around him. Just short of the street that led out of the square Senechal stopped and got out his map. Qazai stood beside him and turned a quarter turn, looking over his shoulder in Webster's direction.

It was the last thing Webster saw that made any sense. A great weight struck him; he was conscious of feeling helplessly light, of skittering across the dusty ground, of coming to a stop with his face in the dirt. He could see a donkey's hoof up close, the horn gray and cracked, but he couldn't raise his head to see more. And then he couldn't see anything at all.

17.

THE FIRST THING HE was conscious of, before the pain and the utter dark, was the smell: an invasive mix of mold and urine and ammonia that sat inside his head and produced a sensation of intense nausea throughout his body. Pain coursed up and down his right side as if unable to find a place to settle. His mouth was dry as dust.

For a long time he lay on his side, the better one, trying to make out some trace of light. A sudden fear took him that he couldn't see, but after a while he knew that there was a different quality to the dark when his eyes were open: it had space, somehow; it gave a sense of extent. He had no desire to move into it but knew that he couldn't simply lie where he was and wait for the light to come, so by slow degrees he tried to sit up, pushing himself off the hard surface with his elbow bent under him. Immediately his ribs contracted in pain and a flood of sickness rose up through him. He tried again, prepared now for the worst of it, trying to roll forward to give his arm greater purchase and, with the exertion, finding that each breath caused a new release of pain. His right arm could do nothing.

After a minute's effort he was half up, supported by his good arm. He moved his legs forward carefully, pleased to find them working, and was wracked afresh as his feet slipped off into the blackness. So he was on a ledge, or a bed, and by working his legs off the edge he managed to swing the rest of his body upright and sat for several moments, hunched, exhausted, taking shallow breaths of the hot, bad air.

He patted his pockets, looking for his phone, and found that he was still wearing the robe. In the heat he longed to take it off but knew he could not. The phone had gone, but there was something else in there, and by leaning backward and straining, his stomach muscles in agony, he managed to force his hand through the opening in the djellaba and into the unobliging pocket of his jeans, where it finally discovered, next to a crushed pack of cigarettes, the smooth plastic casing of the cheap lighter he had bought the night before.

Lit up, the room was less encouraging than the pitiless dark. It was a cell, perhaps eight feet by eight feet, whose pitted gray walls, sweating in the heat, were broken only by a rusted metal door. But for the thin concrete slab he was sitting on, and another across from him that left a three-foot channel in between, the space was unbroken, and there was something pure about its single-minded commitment to its grim purpose. Nothing was scratched on the walls, and Webster wondered whether he could possibly be the first person to be brought here. Warily he checked his head and side for blood, but found nothing more than a long, deepish graze that ran from his forehead across his temple.

The wheel of the lighter had grown too hot to hold. Bending down in the dark, with effort, he untied his shoe and took it off before collecting himself and standing up in a single agonizing motion, his hand against the wall behind him for support. He shuffled forward and with the shoe in his left hand began to beat the iron door with its heel, hard and loud, with a slow, steady rhythm. He noticed that no light at all showed around the door frame.

The dull banging pounded in his head and made thinking difficult, but he tried to relax and imagine what could have happened to him. He had been hit by a car, or by a truck. That he knew, and he could remember knowing it the moment he landed on the ground. Then why wasn't he in hospital? People had seen that he was injured and would have called an ambulance, surely? He could hear the shouting, see them clustering around him, see someone pull a cell phone out and make the call.

Someone had arranged the accident, or someone had taken advantage of it, that much was certain. Call him Chiba. He needed a name. Perhaps Chiba's men had seen him following Qazai; perhaps they had seen him waiting in his djellaba for their meeting to finish. However it had happened, they had seen him, he was sure; sure, too, that soon he was about to meet the man he had been so blindly pursuing.

The clanging slowed a little as his arm began to tire, and he wondered how long he had been keeping it up. Ten minutes? Two? He clicked the lighter on again and looked at his watch, thankfully unbroken, which showed that it was half past ten, almost four hours since Qazai and Senechal had passed him in the passage. He continued for a minute or two, but his good arm now hurt almost as much as the rest of him, and he reluctantly conceded that he had to stop. Faint from standing, having had no water for several hours and no food for longer, he leaned his head against the door and finally gave in to the rushing stream of fear that this mindless activity, his one source of hope, had kept in check. How, he asked himself, had it come to this? Slowly, staggering a little and feeling profoundly sick, he dragged his feet over to the ledge where he had started, lay down, and fell at length into a shifting, churning half-sleep.

As he came in and out of consciousness he grasped at a series of jagged, fractured dreams. Children, not his own, played in unknown landscapes where the heat of the sun and its blinding light were so strong that they filled each scene with silent menace.

The grating of a key turning in the door brought him up from sleep, and a second later a flash of bluish white light woke him fully. A black figure was in the doorway, saying something he didn't understand. All he could do was blink at the brightness.

"Up," said the figure. "Now."

Webster pushed himself up on his elbow, but before he could sit he had been grabbed by his other arm and pulled erect. He could smell stale tobacco and old meat on the man's breath, and on the edges of his silhouette there was the fuzzy outline of a beard.

"Come."

The man's hand took strong hold of his upper arm and led him out of the cell, down a corridor whose bare cement walls were lit by a single fluorescent tube. There were no details, no features that might suggest the building's function. Nor was there any noise, but for their footsteps, harsh on the concrete floor. They passed three other doors—wooden, he noticed, with no locks—on the same side as the cell, before the man turned down a second corridor, knocked firmly at a door on the right and without waiting for a reply went in.

This room was whitewashed, unbearably bright under another single strip light, and smelled of heat and mildew. As Webster entered, hobbling and squinting, he could make out one man sitting behind a desk and another standing against the wall opposite the door, both wearing suits—one black, one gray—and white shirts with no tie. They were only superficially alike. One was lanky, all thin limbs improbably long, and he sat at the table like a crab trying to fit itself into too small a space. His suit was rumpled and in patches gray with dust, his face elongated and hollow.

The other man was shorter, taut with muscle, the skin on his face tight against the bone and his posture sprung, suggesting great energy barely contained and waiting impatiently for release. Black and gray hairs showed at the base of his neck, which was flexed and unyielding, like thick cable, and there was three days' beard on his face. He held his hands by his sides, tightening them slowly into fists and then releasing them, his knuckles white. Webster's body registered a fear of him at once, a physical knowledge of his viciousness. A pair of metal-framed sunglasses covered his eyes, and Webster knew from the moment he came into the room that he was the one in charge.

The guard shoved him onto a chair, and with a nod from the lanky man was dismissed. For a minute no one said anything. Against every message sent by the insistent aching in his head and the violent pain in his side Webster tried to breathe regularly, as deeply as he could, and to establish some sense of calm.

"Why are you in Morocco?" The thin man spoke. His accent was heavy but unplaceable, his voice languid, almost quiet, and while waiting for the answer he cocked his head on one side, staring at a point on the desk.

"I'm here on business."

There was a long pause. The thin man stared at his finger as it made an endless figure-of-eight over the wood. He hadn't yet looked Webster in the eye.

"What business?"

The best lie was as close as you could make it to the truth. "Research."

"Of what?"

"A businessman. In Marrakech."

"Name?"

"My name?"

"His name. You are Webster."

How did they know it? His passport was at his hotel, carefully hidden. He had no credit cards on him. They had his phone, but his phone was locked. Unless they had found Driss as well. That unpleasant thought had not struck him before.

"I can't tell you that."

The thin man's finger stopped circling. Out of the corner of his eye Webster sensed movement and turned stiffly, too slowly to see the flat of the other man's hand connect with the side of his head with improbable force. A rush of air broke into his ear with the noise of a thunderclap and he fell from the chair onto the floor.

He lay there for a moment, his cheek pressing into grit, dazed and shocked, the only stubborn thought in his head that he must be close to something devastating to be receiving this sort of treatment.

The man in sunglasses stood over him, his face silhouetted against the bluish fluorescent light.

"Up."

The word was hoarse, sudden; Webster felt the need to obey it, but could not. He lay still for a moment, processing the shock, before lifting his head off the floor, feeling the muscles in his neck straining with the work. This time he saw the man move. In one swift motion he drew his foot back and with great precision kicked Webster hard in the side, in the soft flesh between hip and ribs, filling his body with a great, vivid pain that seemed to swirl with color and brought nausea surging into his throat.

Webster rolled onto his side, curling up to protect himself, for the first time feeling real fear inside the pain. This man knew what he was doing. He had the discipline of the professional, the economy of effort, the singular focus. He had done this many times before. Shadow fell across Webster and he knew that the man was standing over him, calculating which piece of him to work on next.

But instead he took a step closer, bent down until his mouth was an inch from Webster's ear, and when he spoke his voice was a harsh, quiet rasp that Webster had to strain to hear through the ringing and the roar.

"Tell me why you are here."

Webster tried to speak, but had no words. The taste of acid was on his tongue and his mouth was clamped shut. It wouldn't open; his body was no longer taking commands.

"Up." The voice was still quiet, but it had power; Webster felt it occupy him. He made a weak effort to sit.

The man said something in his own language, and at his command his colleague came out from behind the desk, put a hand under Webster's arm and together they pulled him up, dumping him heavily onto the chair, where he sat slumped, conscious only of the pain and his own dead weight.

Again the voice in his ear, fierce but strangely delicate, and so close he could feel its breath. "Tell me who you are."

With effort he managed to shake his head. There was a pause, during which he sensed the man moving slowly away from him.

This time he was ready for it, almost, and managed through some instinct to bring his hand up to his head as the blow struck, the same as the first, an open palm aimed at his head. It was enough to send him over, but he grabbed the edge of the desk and righted himself, turning back with a defiant look at his attacker.

"The night will be long if you do not help us," said the thin man.

But the professional had finished talking. He put his arm around Webster's neck and pulled sharply, sending the chair crashing backward.

Webster felt his skull crack on the floor and looked up, stunned, to see the man pulling him upright again. He said something else to his underling, who took Webster, spun him around and held him tightly across his middle, clamping his arms and causing pain to rage through his side. Webster writhed against the grip but his strength had gone, and all he could do was push the man backward and try to unbalance him. They slammed into a wall, but his hold was still firm and Webster for a moment stopped struggling because the pain was too much, and at that moment he saw the smaller man bring his knee up with great force and precision into the middle of his thigh, once, twice and quickly again.

Everything stopped. Every thought, every sense. There was only the pain, sharp and raging, which began in his gut and spread out through his body until there was nothing else.

Webster reeled with the shock. The tall man let go of him and he retched, felt acid rise into his mouth. He hadn't been prepared. He hadn't thought it possible that so much pain could come at once. The tall man pushed him, just enough to send him back a pace, and he fell back onto the chair.

His torturer stood still for a moment, staring at Webster through the dark lenses of his glasses, giving him a simple message: if you persist, so will I, and in the end I will destroy you. After several seconds he clenched and released his fists once more, and stepped forward, stooping until their eyes were level.

"Pressure points. In your leg. I do it again, you pass out."

The pain was everywhere, but it had settled, become constant.

"After, I start with your eyes."

Webster felt any courage he had quail inside him, and blinked involuntarily.

"Are you Chiba?" he said, his lips numb, trying his best to look the man in the face.

The man stared at him, his gaze steady and black.

"If my friends don't hear from me twice a day," said Webster, hearing the words drop clumsily from his mouth as if someone else was saying them, "everything we know about your business with Qazai goes to the press."

The man looked up and smiled at his friend before turning back to Webster.

"Who is Qazai?"

"You know who he is."

At that, he took Webster's jaw in his hand and gripped it hard with strong fingers, holding it for a moment before he spoke. Webster could feel the flesh of his cheek being crushed against his teeth.

"You know nothing."

With two fingers of his other hand he closed Webster's eyelids, and pushed hard into the sockets.

"Nothing," he said, with a final stab, and left.

18.

WEBSTER PULLED HIMSELF SLOWLY to the wall and sat against it, his legs straight on the floor. Beyond the end of his robe his brown leather shoes stuck out, and he wondered vaguely whether it was they that had earlier betrayed his disguise. Something about their familiarity, their solid sense of the everyday, made him feel truly hopeless for the first time. Two men had died before him, and his mind was empty of any thought that might prevent him from becoming the third.

The relentless light was worse than the darkness that had come before because it left no space for evasion. This was real, it was happening now, and it would not end well.

He felt for his watch under the heavy brown sleeve. Two o'clock. An overwhelming tiredness took hold of him, but he knew that he could not sleep; not here, not while that man was somewhere close beyond that door. Fear, not resolution, kept him awake. Who was this man? Who had taught him? For he was no mere thug. He had learned his craft from others. It was a technique, and he was a technician.

Very probably he was even now preparing for more. What he had just done might only be a prelude to the real work, and for a terrified moment Webster let himself imagine what that might be; saw a bag full of rusting tools, and the torturer in his sunglasses calmly taking his pick. But there was a meager thread of comfort in that thought, because if they wanted information from him, they didn't yet want to kill him. The only moment of hope in his interrogation had been when he mentioned the name Chiba. That had registered; he knew it had. Why else tell him that he knew nothing?

Webster closed his eyes, fought the pain and tried to think. They were right: he seemed to know less now than before. The question that had brought him to Marrakech was no closer to being answered. He had met them, but he still had no idea who was persecuting Darius Qazai.

Instead, he tried to turn it around. Who did these people think he was, and what did they want from him? At some point they had spotted him in the city, and had followed him. He had been knocked down, and they had brought him here. But it was a stretch to think that they had merely taken advantage of an opportunity: they must have planned the accident. And in that case, he realized, with something like shame at his stupidity, it was entirely likely that they had known he was in Marrakech before he had started following Qazai. They had known he was coming and had made arrangements for him. That was how they knew his name.

With clarity more blinding than the light around him Webster all at once understood. They thought he was Qazai's man—his detective, his spy, his security person. If they had been monitoring Qazai's movements over the last month, or his phone, or his bank accounts, they would have seen Webster working, apparently doing his client's bidding. And why else would he have come to Marrakech—a day ahead, no less, to make his preparations—if not to make sure that Qazai was safe here, and to conspire against his enemies?

Safe in London, he might have laughed at the irony of it. Mehr had died, Timur had died, and now he would die as a Qazai loyalist, all to convince his master to pay up what he owed or honor his contract or return whatever wasn't his. Such was his bloody-mindedness that even now he resented meeting his end on Qazai business, bound for all eternity to his interests and never fully understanding how.

Surely that wasn't necessary. There had to be a way. Qazai's enemy may not be his friend, but if they knew, at least, that no purpose would be served by killing him—that Qazai might laugh sooner than mourn—perhaps they would think twice about making the effort. If effort it was.

Webster shook his head, scolded himself for being fanciful. He was alive because they wanted to know what he knew, that was all, and his only real hope was to offer, but not deliver, something that was valuable to them, something whose value was not yet apparent. That would be his slender strategy: explain his relationship with Qazai, try to find out what they wanted and think of something—create something if necessary—that he could offer them that required him to be freed from this room. It wasn't much, but briefly he felt better. He had a purpose, a feeble claim on hope.

Having addressed how he might survive, though, his thoughts turned to what would happen if he didn't. Webster was not a cowardly man. The notion of death didn't scare him. If there was meaning to it—if some part of him lived on beyond it—he retained just enough of his religious schooling to trust that the process would be benign; and if there was no meaning he wouldn't be around to miss it. No, the passing from one state to another didn't trouble him, but he found it hard to imagine an afterlife that wasn't consumed by a raging grief at what you had been forced to leave behind. At one with not existing he might be, but never again to watch his children sleep, or talk with Elsa in bed, or take their boat out to the mouth of the estuary in the rain—take those things away and he wasn't sure, in fact, how much of him would in any case remain.

But this, too, was indulgent. With a black laugh, thick with phlegm and blood, he acknowledged the only truth he could depend on, sobering and shaming: that despite these passions, for all that he might love his family and strive to be good, he had for months been inviting a living death, courting with a kind of grim glee an existence where everything he held dear might reject him without any help from Qazai or his enemies.

He tried the door, which was indeed locked. A single window the size of a shoebox showed through its four bars that it was still dark outside. For a minute or two he wondered how he might escape: find a way to get someone to open the door, overpower them, run. But previous experience showed that no one would answer his calls, and in any case he wouldn't be running anywhere. He could barely stand.

An hour passed. No noise reached him; the silence was as total as the light was unyielding. He had had no water for over eight hours, and even though it was now nighttime the room had lost none of its heat. Through a slow process of squirming and pulling he managed to bring the robe up to his waist and, after much pain, over his head. His shirt was dark all over with sweat, his mouth so dry it took effort to force his lips apart. He lay down on the floor, watched a beetle clicking along the far wall, and with the robe folded under his head tried to sleep; but every time he closed his eyes a jerking montage of the day's events played across them and wouldn't let him rest.

AT FOUR, OR JUST BEFORE, a key turned in the lock and the door opened. As Webster sat up the first thing he saw was a large bottle of mineral water being held by the cap in someone's hand; the second, as his eyes rose, was Senechal, perfectly pressed in a fresh suit, his skin translucent under the fluorescent bulb. As if from another world he looked down at Webster, closed the door behind him, sniffed in distaste, moved around to the far side of the desk and began to wipe the chair with a handkerchief that he pulled from his top pocket. Grudgingly satisfied, he sat. The door locked behind him.

"*Asseyez-vous.*"

It was the same thin rasp of a voice, but it was no longer ingratiating, no longer sly. Webster looked at him warily from the floor, trying to calculate why he was here and what in heaven's name it meant. All he knew was that the aversion he had once felt to him had become the most intense and disarming loathing, and if it hadn't been for the promise of water he would have stayed where he was. In that moment, his imagination wild, Webster saw Senechal as an administrator of death, a man whose talent was to bury things—problems, money, color, life—and who had now come to bury him. Somehow he knew it.

Using the wall to steady himself he stood, moved to the desk and took the bottle, uncapping it and bringing it up to his mouth in a single motion.

As he drank, feeling the water cooling his throat, he kept his eyes on Senechal, who stared right back at him.

"Sit," he said, when Webster was done, and watched him coldly as he sank, clutching the bottle, onto the chair. "You, Mr. Webster, are the most difficult consultant I have ever met. We all know that consultants do not do what you pay them to do, but you? With you it is ridiculous."

Webster didn't reply.

"We ask you to do a simple thing, but you are not a simple person and you will not do it. Well. Now you are in Marrakech, and it is not such a simple thing to leave."

Webster looked at him openmouthed; his side sang with pain. He shook his head in confusion and disbelief.

"So you're working for them."

Senechal adjusted himself on his chair so that he was upright and correct, and smiled a tight little smile.

"Truly you are the great detective. You have understood it all." He shook his head briskly. "No, Mr. Webster. I see you have no idea what is going on. Let me explain a little to you. You have put yourself in the way of an important transaction. Now, I am happy to say, the transaction can go ahead without you. This means that you are no longer necessary for what we want to do."

Webster closed his eyes tight, wishing Senechal away. But he went on.

"The men you met earlier are efficient people. They do not waste energy."

"I'd noticed."

"Confidentially, they do not see a reason to keep you alive. They say you threatened them, and that has not impressed them." He paused. "But I am efficient too, and it may be that it is less effort to keep you alive. I do not mind. To decide, I have to discover what is in your head. I have to tell them what you know. What you have to bargain with, in short." He smiled again. "I suspect it is not very much, in which case this will be the last room you see."

In the harsh light Senechal's face was inhuman; more than ever he looked like a clay figure granted some weak and temporary sort of life. Webster considered for a moment what might be gained from pushing the table over onto him, from knocking him off his chair, from taking his head and beating it against the wall.

"When London wakes up," he said, "my report will be going to the *Financial Times*, the *Wall Street Journal*, and the twenty largest investors in Tabriz. What did your master say? If he is your master. All he has is his reputation. In about five hours he won't be selling anything."

Senechal considered Webster for a moment, scanning his bloodied face for signs of a bluff.

"The thing is, Mr. Webster, you know nothing that could hurt Mr. Qazai."

"I know I'm here. Eventually others will know I was."

"You are in a police station. You caused an accident in the medina and the police brought you here. You had no papers and were dressed, ridiculously, as a local. They suspected you of planning some sort of atrocity. I came—for the second time—to see that you were freed and received proper medical treatment." He paused. "Unfortunately I was too late. Being here means nothing."

"Where's Qazai?"

"I have no idea. I am not his keeper."

"Tell him that I know all about Kurus, and Chiba, and where the money goes. What it buys. Tell him . . ."

"He is not here, Mr. Webster. You will deal with me."

Webster leaned forward and rested his forearms on the desk, never taking his eyes off Senechal. He lowered his voice. "I'm not talking to you. Tell him. He'll understand."

Senechal regarded him with cold disdain and just a trace, he thought, of concern. Certainly he had been made to think.

"This is nonsense. You have been missing for hours. Your report would already be on its way. If it exists."

Webster raised his eyebrows and shook his head. "You know, I've been trying to work out from the start who pulls whose strings. Looks like I'm about to find out. That's a big call for a lawyer to make on his own."

Senechal held his eye for a good ten seconds, stood up and left the room.

WEBSTER WATCHED THE DOOR close behind him, heard it lock, and thought that he might happily stay forever in this bleak little room if it meant he never had to see that man again. What could he be doing? Whose interests did he serve? A dozen scenarios suggested themselves, all preposterous, all colliding. Like a man suddenly realizing that he has been lost for miles, Webster looked back and tried to identify the turning that had led him astray.

He drank deeply from the water bottle, took a bent cigarette from the crumpled pack in his pocket, and lit it.

It made him feel no better. His head ached as it was, and the smoke tasted strange in his throat, acrid and stale. But he continued with it nevertheless, perhaps because it was the only action he could take, and soon the white cell hung with a soft haze and a tired, friendly smell. It was the smell of his life before Ikertu, before children—before Elsa, even, of a time when he was alone, as he was alone again now, just him and the smoke. He pictured his house, curtains and blinds drawn, everyone in their beds, a single light on outside the children's room, and for the first time felt anguish at the thought he might never be there again, and a greater anguish that he had chosen to desert them.

He was watching the smoke rise off the ember in a thin, twirling line when the lock turned and the door opened. Qazai was there. He stood in the doorway, and when his eyes had adjusted to the light simply studied Webster for what seemed a long time. It was a strange look: solemn, pained, even curious. Thoughtful, as if a long way behind it some delicate matter was being decided. Above all, though, it was not as it had been; the authority had gone from it. It made him appear old, and uncertain, and it suddenly struck Webster that it was meant to communicate something to him. But what it was, he couldn't catch.

Senechal was behind him, and as if only then becoming conscious of his presence Qazai glanced over his shoulder, raised an eyebrow wearily, and

walked slowly around the desk. There was a hint of resentment in the gesture that Webster noticed, and instinctively felt he might exploit.

"So you are here," said Webster, taking a last pull on the cigarette. "I
thought you might be."

Qazai didn't reply. He sat on the chair, Senechal standing by him, like
his nurse. He was exhausted; his shoulders slumped; that athletic energy
that had flowed through him at their first meeting seemed all spent. But he
held Webster's eye, and drew himself up as best he could before speaking.

"I understand that you're still trying to threaten me."

Webster dropped his cigarette on the floor and put it out with his foot.
"That's a bit rich, don't you think?"

"I'm not threatening you."

"Ten minutes ago your kept ghoul told me that he was terribly sorry
but I was about to be killed."

"That's not me."

"It's not you. Of course." Webster nodded. "It's just the company you
keep." He reached for his cigarettes and pulled another delicately from the
pack. "You keep very bad company. Starting with him. Tell him to go." He
looked up. "Leave the fucking room. Go." He stared hard at Senechal. "Go
on. I don't know which of you is the monkey anymore but I want to talk to
him. Alone." Neither man said anything. "I mean it."

"I will be staying with my client," Senechal said at last.

"Whatever he is to you, he's not your client. We all know that." He
looked at Qazai. "If I'm going to die I want to spend my last minutes with
the living. Tell him to go."

Qazai breathed in deeply through his nose, made a decision and let the
breath out. "Yves. Leave us."

Senechal frowned—it was the most emotion Webster had seen him
show—and with a stiff nod walked across the room and knocked on the
door, which was opened and locked behind him in a moment.

Webster lit the cigarette. Bits of tobacco stuck to his lip and he pinched
them off with his thumb. Qazai, across the desk, watched him charily.

"What did you mean?" he said. "That I'm not his client."

Webster smiled and shook his head, exhaling smoke. "I don't know. I wouldn't trust him with my home address, but you tell him everything. What does he do for you? Was it your idea to pick over my past, or his? Who talked to the Italians? Who suggested you buy me off? Why is he in here on their behalf? Whoever the fuck they are." He took another drag. "Who's in charge? That's the question. I've been trying to decide. Is he trying to help you out of this mess or is he out there right now selling what he knows? I would be. Christ knows."

Qazai looked at him steadily, but not with confidence, and for a minute neither said anything.

"So you have a buyer?" Webster broke the silence.

"I'm selling it all."

Webster raised an eyebrow.

"To the Americans," said Qazai. "I have no choice. It's the end."

Webster laughed, and his throat hurt as he did. He took another drink from the bottle and tried to understand. "So if it's all theirs they don't care about you. You won't be seen together. You'll be gone. That's why you don't need me." He shook his head. "Why the fuck didn't you just do that in the first place?"

Qazai pushed his chair back and made to stand up, looking at Webster with a strange sadness in his eyes.

"The thing is," said Webster, "when Ike sends my report out to the *Wall Street Journal* in about . . ." he checked his watch, "in about three hours, no one's going to be buying anything off you."

"There's no report. Hammer doesn't even know you're here."

"Of course he does."

"Then why did you book your flight yourself?"

To that Webster didn't have a response. So they had known he was coming.

Qazai watched him, enjoying his unease. "After all this time, Mr. Webster, you don't know anything. You have no idea who these people are."

"Tell me."

Qazai just shook his head.

"It doesn't matter," said Webster. "I know what they do." He turned his head to exhale. "Until a few hours ago, I really wanted to know what trouble you'd got yourself into. I really did. And now, I couldn't care less. Because I can't help but think that whatever happens to me, you're fucked too."

Qazai set his jaw. "I'm afraid only one of us is fucked." The word sounded odd on his lips.

Webster laughed, a dry cracked laugh.

"You're serious? No, I see. They can't break Darius Qazai. You're too big. You're a great man. Is that it?" Webster paused and the two looked at each other, Qazai's eyes dull and uncertain. Webster leaned forward. "Listen. You can't hold it together anymore. Killing Timur—they did kill Timur, didn't they?—that wasn't a threat, it was just the beginning. How much do you owe?"

Qazai said nothing.

"So it is money. And when you sell the company and you pay them off, you think they'll walk away? Given how much you know?"

"You don't know them."

"You're a dead man whatever happens."

Qazai scratched his jaw, his mind working. "You're not giving me much incentive to save you."

"You can do that? You're still in charge?" He laughed. The room was now hazy with smoke. "What's funny about this is that I'm the only hope you've got."

Qazai swallowed. "Go on."

"Get us back to England, and I'm in the same boat as you. A pair of loose ends. Your friends don't seem like the sort to forget." A pause. "I know how to neutralize them."

"Tell me."

"When we're in England."

Qazai held Webster's eye for a moment until an understanding had passed between them, then reached into the pocket of his jacket and brought out a lacquered black pen, an incongruously perfect thing, and a business card. "I'll tell my friends, as you call them, about the report." He uncapped the pen and wrote as he talked, bending over the desk. "They may choose to believe you. They may not."

He handed the card to Webster. *Darius Qazai*, it said, *Chairman and Chief Executive, Tabriz Asset Management*. On its reverse, in black capitals, were four words: "YOU HAVE A DEAL."

Webster looked at it for a moment, before slipping it into his back pocket. And with that Qazai walked to the door, knocked, and was let out.

19.

Ten minutes passed. When the door opened again, the tall man was there, and he had a gun in his hand. By his side was the man who had brought him from the cell earlier. Webster twisted around to look at them.

"Stand," the tall man said.

Webster stayed where he was.

"Stand." The man gestured with his gun. "You go home. Now."

Either this was true, or they were preparing to take him somewhere more final. In any event, his options were few.

With one hand on the desk he pushed himself upright and shuffled around to face his captors. The tall man kept the gun on him while his colleague wrapped a strip of dirty white material around Webster's head, adjusting it so that it covered his eyes and tying it tight. Then he pulled his arms behind him, tied them at the wrists, and putting his hand on Webster's shoulder started to lead him away. The tall man stopped him. Webster felt a hand go into the back pocket of his jeans and come back out again.

Then a hand between his shoulder blades was pushing him roughly forward, through the doorway, down a long bright corridor into a larger space. He put out his hands to feel his way but they found nothing, and after another shove from behind he heard Qazai's voice say something sharply in a language he didn't understand and felt a hand on his upper arm, guiding him forward. After half-a-dozen yards the hand brought him to a stop.

By tilting his head back he could see a yard or two of the floor around him. Qazai was there, next to him; Senechal was by his side; two other pairs of black shoes, dusty and scuffed, faced them.

Someone said something in Arabic, or Farsi, or whatever it was they were speaking, and Webster recognized the harsh croak of the man who had beaten him. A dozen words, no more, but in his chest there rose a shameful mix of fear and feeble rage. Then the same voice came closer and spoke in English.

"Now you go to airport. You go home. One week, I have my money. You say anything about me, about him, you die. Your family too. You are not safe. Understand?"

Webster understood.

"You think you know. Things about me. You don't." He reached down, put his hand around Webster's thigh and squeezed, hard, on the center of the bruise he had left. Pain sprang up, ending in a ball of nausea in Webster's throat. "I will watch you. Always." He stepped back. "We drive you to airport. Now. You two. Clear?"

No one said anything. Webster felt a hand on his back, but then Senechal spoke, and his voice after the other's sounded refined, thin, anxious.

"My baggage is at my hotel."

"We will get. You go now."

"I can get it myself. It is not a problem."

"You go now. Both of you. Qazai stays here. I talk to him more."

"This isn't . . ."

"You go. Now."

Senechal chose not to break the silence that followed, but Webster could sense his fear.

They climbed stairs, a single flight. Webster was being guided, as before, and ahead of him, as far as he could tell, were Senechal and another man. A door opened, and the change of air—the slightest breeze in the heat—let him know that they were now outside. It was still dark, and he could hear sporadic traffic some way off, the drone of a car, the thundering of a heavy truck. There was dusty tarmac underfoot, and after perhaps twenty yards the hand on his arm brought him to a stop. From under his blindfold he could see the wheel of a car and two pairs of shoes, Senechal's and one other. A car door opened and he felt a hand on his head pushing him down and onto a leather seat: he was in the back, on the left-hand side, behind the driver. The leather was cream and the car smelled new. That was all he could make out.

Two doors opened and shut again; Senechal was beside him; the engine engaged with a barely perceptible bass note and Webster felt fresh pain in his ribs as the car accelerated hard and his body was pushed back into the seat. Over the noise he heard another car start up a little distance away.

From what he could tell they were on a main road, almost completely straight, and no longer in Marrakech: there were no street lamps, and the only light came in flashes from passing cars. Occasionally they slowed for a moment before switching lanes and surging past slower traffic. No one spoke, but the car was so quiet, even at speed, that he could hear Senechal taking deep breaths, deliberately, as if calming or collecting himself, and in between them his own, rasping and tight. His ribs hurt so much that he struggled to take in enough air.

"*Ils vont nous tuer.*" The words came out in a hoarse whisper.

Senechal said nothing.

"*Ils nous suivent. Ils sont derrière nous.* See for yourself."

Senechal twisted in his seat to look out of the back windscreen.

"*Vous devez liberer les mains. Mes mains.*" Webster turned his back toward Senechal, pushing his hands toward him as best he could.

The driver said something sharp in Arabic, or Farsi, and Senechal replied in the same language, the words faltering, his tone ingratiating.

"*Ils ne sont pas vos amis.*" Webster tried again. "*Vraiment.* Do it now. Untie me, for fuck's sake."

"I will look after myself. Thank you."

Webster made a leap. "If that's what you've been doing, your usefulness may just have run out. Don't be sure it hasn't."

Senechal was silent for a moment, and then Webster felt a cold touch on his forearm in the dark as two hands began to work quietly at the coarse fabric around his wrists. The knot was tight, and the fingers pulling at it weak and unskilled. Webster willed him to hurry.

As Senechal continued to fumble, the car slowed sharply, pulled off the tarmac onto rougher ground and stopped. Webster heard the rumble of another car moving past and coming to a halt a short distance away, and felt the weight shift in the seat in front of him as their driver got out. For a moment the inside of the car was lit with a warm light; then the door shut behind him and with a beep and a clunk all the doors locked and the darkness returned.

"Hurry up, for fuck's sake. Use your teeth." Webster's face was pressed to the window, his arms out behind him; he had never felt so naked. He wondered whether they would be shot, or burned, or both. "What are you doing?"

The hands had stopped working and Senechal was trying his door.

"It is locked."

Webster didn't reply. Feeling the muscles in his shoulders tense and cramp, he pushed his wrists together and worked them hard against the fabric, looser now, until there was a space large enough for his hand to squeeze through. Senechal was still pulling in panic at the handle of his door.

In one movement Webster tore the blindfold off his eyes and leaned into the front seats, desperately looking for the switch that would release the doors. The car's alarm started wailing. A dim green glow from the dashboard was the only light; the car's headlamps had been cut and outside all was black. He ran his hands over the door, between the seats, pressing at everything, trying to keep his head. From the back he could hear Senechal quietly intoning *"Mon Dieu, mon Dieu"* over and over.

The window he had been sitting by burst with unimaginable noise, and Webster felt glass spray across his back. A second bullet smashed the driver's window, and he could feel the chassis of the car jar as a third hit his door.

He found the switch.

"Go! Fucking go!"

Sitting back he reached across Senechal, opened his door and shoved him out onto the sand, scrambling after him head first and over the howling alarm hearing the precise clunk of a bullet being pressed into the chamber of a rifle just before another shot cracked the air. He landed on his elbows in the dust.

There were two further shots, close together, as he shut the door and pulled himself against the body of the car. Senechal was to his left, his head leaning back against the other door, his eyes shut. After the brutal noise of the gun there was now silence: no cars, no wind. Webster, his breath quick and painful in his chest, thinking hard, leaned over to peer under the back of the car in the direction of the shots.

"One of us is going to have to . . ."

"Get up. It is you they want."

When he turned his head he found himself looking right into the black eyes of Senechal, set in a face of pale wax and darker than the night. He was kneeling and holding a small pistol in his right hand. His face was so close that Webster could smell his dead metallic breath as he half whispered, half hissed.

"*Allez.*" And then louder into the night, a thin screech. "Stop! Stop, I have him."

He gestured with the gun. A car sped by on the road, its headlights for a moment illuminating the scene. Senechal was still wearing his suit, his tie still immaculately in its collar, an apparition somewhere between nightmare and nonsense. Webster felt a bolt of repugnance and fury pass through him and with a cruel, childish certainty knew that this man was weak and brittle and no match for him. Ignoring his pain and a rush of sickness he brought the back of his fist across his body into Senechal's face, felt it connect with that sharp little nose, saw Senechal lose his balance and topple backward. A shot tore the silence but Webster ignored it and fell on Senechal as he tried to right himself, pinning him to the ground and trapping his right arm and beating his hand against the ground until the gun fell from it. Senechal's face twisted with shock and fear as he writhed vainly for a moment against Webster's weight; then he relaxed his muscles, composed his expression and looking right into Webster's eyes spat, venomously.

In the strange, silent interlude that followed Webster turned his head and wiped the spit away as best he could on his sleeve. Senechal leered up at him, his black teeth like beetles, and suddenly Webster couldn't bear to look at him anymore. He was filled with disgust. The desert and the pain and the bleak gunshots dropped away and all he knew was Senechal's gruesome image, hideous, staring up at him in petulant defiance. He released his hold and pulling Senechal's head up by his hair beat it against the ground, twice, hard. He moved to do it again but checked himself, his heart beating with force against his ribs, a strange giddiness in his throat. Senechal was unconscious, and his body had gone limp. Webster reached under his head and felt blood flowing thick and warm; felt the rock jutting out of the sand. From the darkness came another shot like a burst of light and the sound of another of the car's windows being blown out.

Webster ducked, involuntarily, and rolled off Senechal's prone body. On hands and knees Webster shuffled back against the car. He had to go now. There wouldn't be another chance. Feeling in the sand for the gun he pulled one knee up, set himself unsteadily, as if under starter's orders for a schoolboy race, took a deep breath and looked down at Senechal, wondering briefly what would happen to him, whether he should leave him here to his fate. He could do nothing else. With one last look at the ashen figure in the dirt he set off into the darkness, his leather soles slipping in the sand, adrenaline dulling the pain in his ribs and his head.

After perhaps fifteen yards he heard a hard crack behind him, a single shot, heard the tiny thin whine of the bullet as it passed, and kept running, changing direction a little, dodging rocks and doing his best to keep upright. Without turning he held his arm out behind him and fired shots into the night. He thought he heard voices shouting but paid them no heed. Two cars drove past along the road, and afterward another shot. This time he didn't hear the bullet in the air.

Running in almost total darkness now he stumbled up a shallow bank of sand and scrubby plants. At the top he lost his footing, rolled down the other side, and for a moment lay on his back looking up at the stars, panting. His body had had enough punishment. Somewhere behind him, a hundred yards away, perhaps a little more, a car engine started up; he heard it turning over slowly, moving forward into the desert toward him. Over the low ridge a bright light suddenly burst, scanning the night and casting Webster's refuge into even greater blackness. He lay still for a moment, then at a low crouch moved along the line of the ridge, parallel with the road, heading in the direction they had come. The lights tracked slowly across the sky and as they passed over him he dropped to the ground, the sand cool under his cheek. Ahead of him, ten yards away, was a little hollow, an indentation perhaps a foot deep, like the first workings of a grave. In the darkness behind the headlights he scuttled across the desert, keeping low, and pressed himself into the space.

The car reversed in an arc, and the lights swung back across the night. Webster felt them sweeping over him again, seeking him out, slowly moving away. A car door opened. He raised his head an inch to look. In the beams from the headlights a man in a suit—it looked like the guard from the prison—was standing by Senechal. Putting his foot on his shoulder he rocked the prone body back and forth, three times for good measure, before standing up and looking into the night, making a last search. Webster flattened himself out again. There was no noise but the idling of the engine until the car door slammed and the car crunched away, slowly over the dirt but once on the road accelerating hard.

Still he didn't dare move. He lay in the night and breathed in the hot air. In one corner of the sky he thought he could just make out the black yielding to midnight blue. Two cars passed together on the road, but otherwise all was silence. Putting his watch to his ear he counted the seconds, trying to settle into the calm rhythm of the ticking, but his head was thick with pain and new fears. He needed to know whether the man lying a hundred yards away on the sand was dead.

When he had counted five minutes he shifted onto his front and gradually eased up the bank on his elbows. By the light of a passing truck he could make out the car that had brought him here but nothing else.

He walked to it with the little gun in his hand, waiting for a shot or a burst of light, his heart refusing to slow. Senechal's body lay still, blood thickly covering his cheek, and for a few seconds Webster stood over him, not daring to know. Then he knelt, felt under the cuff for a pulse, and found one, faint and slow.

He searched the car but found nothing useful except the water—two small bottles. He drank one in one draft and kept the other.

A thought occurred to him. He had no money, no phone, no resources whatever. Dragging himself across the dust he patted Senechal's jacket, dipped his hand inside its pockets. There was a wallet, with euros, pounds and dirham in it. He took some dirham, a few notes. He left the French passport and a BlackBerry, which was in any case locked. But a second phone, a cheap Samsung, he put in his pocket.

For a moment he stood and looked at the gun, trying to decide how many shots he had fired and whether it was any use to him, before wiping it thoroughly on his shirt tails and leaving it by Senechal's side.

The phone had power but no signal. He looked through its recently dialed numbers, through its address book: there was only one number recorded there, a Dubai phone, probably a cell phone. Four calls made, seven received, every conversation with the same phone. Maybe Senechal had made his own arrangements after all.

Webster walked, east, toward the dawn, a bottle of water in one hand, the other ready to flag down the first car that passed.

KAMILA RINSED THE CLOTH once more in the water, now a dirty brown with Webster's blood, carefully wiped the wound, gently pulling the hair apart, and turned to Driss.

"Take this. Get me some clean water and a fresh cloth." She looked down at Webster, who was sitting on a stool with his shirt off. A dark purple bruise, lively with greens and yellows, had spread out from the ribs on his left side, up to his armpit and down to his waist; he expected to find another where he had been kneed in the thigh. His breathing was still tight and his head felt like it was wrapped with bands of spikes. Kamila had given him sweet mint tea and he sipped at it using his good arm.

"You provide a comprehensive service," he said, looking up at her and smiling, with effort.

"You need to go to the hospital."

"It's a cracked rib. I've had one before. Someone drove into the side of our car when I was twelve. There's nothing you can do about them. They just hurt."

Kamila snorted. "There could be internal bleeding."

Webster watched Driss return carrying the bowl of water and smiling a canny smile that seemed to say you don't know who you're dealing with.

"Sorry I woke you," he said.

"I'm always up at dawn," said Kamila. And then, pointedly, "How was Ike?"

"Awake. Not particularly happy." That hadn't been an easy call, not least because there was so much he hadn't said and so much he still simply didn't understand. By the time he had persuaded a car to stop, had reached the outskirts of the city and had found a phone signal, dawn had broken over Marrakech; in London the sun would have been up for at least an hour. He had expected a furious response, not at being roused but at being misled, or left uninformed—even, perhaps, at being wrong; but what he hadn't banked on was that Ike's love of a secret on the verge of being revealed was greater than everything else. In the end he had been stiff, but increasingly concerned, and when Webster had finished giving him the fractured outline of events had told him to call Kamila on her home number and to call him again when he had slept and eaten.

Kamila didn't reply, but her silence meant something. She put the cloth back in the bowl, took a large glass jar, opened it, and into the palm of her hand poured some white powder, which she began to sprinkle from her fingertips onto the wound. It stung keenly and Webster winced.

"He didn't know I was here." He looked up at her.

"Keep still. This is alum. It will keep the wound clean." She sprinkled more powder. "I did wonder." Inspecting his head closely she gave a small grunt of satisfaction and screwed the lid back on the jar. "There was something you weren't telling us. And you seemed alone somehow. There," she stepped back. "We'll leave that open to the air. I'll put a dressing on it later.

Now Driss will make us eggs and you can tell me what exactly you have got us involved in."

Throughout all this Webster hadn't really stopped to consider how his preoccupations might affect these people, and the realization that he had put them at risk made him feel ashamed.

"Sorry," he said. "It was thoughtless of me."

"Don't worry." She wasn't smiling but her eyes were lenient. "If I wanted security I would have become an accountant. But I want to know what to expect."

Webster was surprised by how hungry he was. While they sat in Kamila's kitchen, Driss brought them flatbread and fruit and eggs, and Webster told them everything he knew, and everything he didn't.

"But what I don't get," he concluded, "is why he's involved. He's not an arms dealer. The money he'd make is a pittance to him. I thought for a while he'd sold his soul to the wrong people, early on. Taken the devil's money. But he's in a different league now. He could have bought them out ten times over."

"Maybe they won't let him."

"Maybe. But why persecute him now?"

Kamila nodded, thinking. "Maybe he has always done it."

"What do you mean?"

"How a man makes his first million is always the most interesting story. Has he explained that to you?"

Webster thought back to those inadequate conversations in Mount Street and Como. "No. No, he hasn't."

"A lot of people got rich at that time. After the Shah went. Everybody wanted weapons. The diaspora. The revolutionaries. Maybe Darius Qazai was in the right place at the right time. Maybe he has just kept on doing it."

Webster considered this for a moment. "All I know," he said, "is that he owes them a lot, and they won't kill him until they get it. And then they will."

"They seem happy killing everyone else."

They sat in silence for a few seconds. Kamila spoke first.

"What are you going to do now?"

Webster rested his head on his hand and pinched his temples. He thought about the various components. Senechal would have been found: Kamila had called an ambulance for him as soon as Webster had contacted her. Qazai might already have left the country.

"You should sleep," said Kamila. "And then you should leave. Go back to England. Get rid of these people. You don't need them in your life."

Webster looked up at her and shook his head. "Sadly they're already in it. And I'm in theirs. I need to see that man again."

Kamila frowned. "Why?"

"So he stops trying to kill me. He thinks I know too much."

"You probably do."

"I do and I don't."

Webster picked up Senechal's phone from the table and looked at it for a moment. Now there were two numbers stored on it: Kamila's, and the anonymous number. He called it, and it rang twice.

"*Oui*." A quiet, harsh voice.

"This is Ben Webster."

"You have wrong number."

"We need to meet."

"I don't know you. Good-bye."

"If you don't meet me my friends in the CIA are going to learn all about Chiba, Kurus and your relationship with Mr. Qazai. That doesn't have to happen. I will be by the Air Maroc ticket office in the arrivals hall of Menara airport at ten o'clock. Come alone."

The line went dead. Kamila and Driss were looking at him across the table, their expressions somewhere between concern and incredulity.

"You should be going home," said Kamila.

"Never show a bully you're weak. And, besides, I don't have my passport."

20.

RISS AND WEBSTER DROVE to the airport together, Webster in one of Youssef's suits: dark gray, about half an inch too short in the limbs, tight under the armpits and around his waist. Kamila had put a discreet bandage on his head wound and after breakfast he had showered, inspecting his battered body in the mirror with a sense of curious detachment. On his thigh was a bright red patch of burst blood vessels and around them a growing storm of purple bruise. Dark bags hung under his eyes and when he walked it was with a heavy limp in his damaged leg.

They made one stop. Just short of his hotel, Webster ducked down in his seat, and a hundred yards further on Driss pulled over and turned to him for instructions.

"In the wardrobe there's a safe. My passport is taped under that. My credit cards are there too. You'll have to slide the whole thing out of its hole. If you can, get me a shirt." Youssef's was at least two sizes too small. "Here's the key. Room fourteen."

"How many rooms?"

"It's quite big. About thirty. Go straight up the stairs and turn left. No one will notice you."

In the wing mirror Webster watched Driss walk back up the street, cross and go into the hotel through its only entrance, a gate that opened onto a small garden and the studded front door. Webster's room was on the first floor, no more than a minute inside, and he calculated that Driss should be out in three minutes at most.

In the distance he could hear the lazy sawing drone of two sirens and thought at first it was the beginning of the call to prayer. He looked at his watch. Driss had been gone for two minutes.

Rounding a corner at the end of the street came two police cars with their green and red lights flashing. In the car's mirror Webster watched them drive at speed in his direction and stop abruptly outside the hotel. Two men got out of one of the cars and went inside; the others stayed where they were. A minute passed, and another, before Driss came out, maintaining a nonchalant pace all the way, a bundle of blue cloth in his hand.

"Are they for me?" said Webster as he got in.

"They won't find much."

"What do you mean?"

"Your room has already been searched." He handed Webster a crumpled shirt. "Your clothes are on the floor. Your suitcase has been cut open."

"My passport?"

"Not there."

"Fuck's sake. Did they say anything?"

"The police? No. They asked for room fourteen. They wanted to know about the Englishman staying there."

"Can you find out what they want?"

"I can call someone."

"Let's go."

"Doesn't this change things?"

"I have no idea."

Someone had called the police. His captors from last night didn't seem the sort, unless they wanted him in custody, where they could find him. Qazai hardly stood to gain. Perhaps Senechal. He tried to think it through. The ambulance would have come for him, and the police, at some point, would have become involved. Would he have told them who had beaten him? Surely not. There was too much at stake elsewhere, and no advantage to making himself more conspicuous than he already was. With a cold shock a further possibility struck him. Senechal had died.

A stifling dread took hold of him then, and as Driss drove through the widening streets, hot already under the morning sun, alive with color and motion, all he saw was Senechal's gray face, lifeless in the desert.

BY THE TIME THEY REACHED Menara airport the day was full, the sun high and blazing, and the car's air conditioning struggled against the heat. It would be hotter than yesterday, said Driss, and Webster found that hard to believe; hard, too, to register that in the twenty-four hours since he had last been here his life might have irrevocably changed.

Logic told him that Senechal was still alive. He hadn't hit him that hard and the wound had not seemed deep. Surely it took more than that to kill a man? Surely someone you had left breathing steadily, calmly almost, didn't simply die in the course of an hour lying peacefully enough in the desert? Logic, though, couldn't control Webster's memory of that moment, and each time it played out the blow seemed to grow in force and Senechal's otherworldly form became more frail and defenseless. An acid mix of fear and guilt rose in his throat. Perhaps that's all it took. A strong loathing and a second's loss of control.

They parked, Driss went ahead, and on the hot walk to the terminal Webster smoked a cigarette and tried to rid his mind of everything but the conversation he was about to have. What did he want from it? For this man to leave him alone: to make him understand that he was no threat now but might become one. That was all.

He was early: it was five to ten. He loitered to smoke the cigarette until it was tarry and hot in his fingers, exhaled the last drag, felt a strong urge to cross himself, and let the glass doors usher him into the arrivals hall, which was ice cool and humming busily—more busily, if anything, than the day before. Planeloads of tourists wandered in a gradual stream into the light, slowing their trolleys to read signs or locate drivers or reprimand children. Webster remembered his own holiday in a fortnight's time: two weeks in

Cornwall to try to repair the cracks he'd made in his family. How he wished, for a hundred reasons, he had never left them.

Resisting the urge to glance up or to check the voice recorder in his top pocket, he took up his position by the Royal Air Maroc office, leaning his back against the booth. Above him, in a gallery of shops over the main hall, Kamila and Youssef were already in position, their job to photograph Chiba—they had taken to calling him that for want of anything better—and to follow him once the meeting was done. Driss was on this level, somewhere nearby, watching Webster and making sure Chiba's people didn't try anything bold.

An unexpected sense of composure settled on Webster as he watched the crowds. He was working on the assumption that the man who had dealt him such pain the night before was the man he had called, but scanning the faces all around him he realized that needn't be the case. The real leader could be any one of these people: the bearded man who caught his eye, the sweaty one who didn't, the lanky one in sunglasses and a djellaba who loitered close by. By five past, he began to believe that none of these people was the man he wanted, that whoever he was he had been insufficiently troubled by Webster's phone call to think a meeting worth the effort, that he was confident this problem could be dealt with by other means.

And then he was there. The man from last night: short, vigorous, firmly set in front of Webster now with his hands clasped in front of him and his feet slightly apart, chewing something with his lips closed. Webster felt his body tighten, an involuntary response to the sense memories of the night before that caused a streak of pain to run right through him. The man was still in yesterday's suit, crumpled around the crotch, and his white shirt was grubby with sweat and dirt around its open collar. Tufts of graying hair poked out at the base of his powerful neck. As he had last night, he seemed ready to spring and to savage, like a dog bred for attack.

Another man was with him, someone Webster hadn't seen before: thickset, jowly, with drooping shoulders. He was carrying a laptop bag.

"I said alone." Webster stared as steadily as he could into Chiba's mirrored sunglasses and wondered what lay behind them.

The man cocked his head slightly on one side and said nothing.

"You need to take those off," said Webster. "I won't talk to you like this."

Rather to Webster's surprise, he reached up and slowly brought the glasses down his nose and away from his face, his eyes on Webster's all the time. They were almost sky blue, the irises flecked with light, the pupils sharp and bottomless, and they caught Webster off balance: he had expected them to be flat, thuggish, any intelligence to be found there base at best, but these were vividly alive and quick, and they seemed to look at him with utter confidence that they owned him outright.

Perfectly still, his expression blank, he continued to challenge Webster to begin.

"Do you know who I am?" Webster said at last.

Chiba remained silent.

"You seem to think I'm a friend of Darius Qazai. I'm not. He hired me to do a job. The job is over. That's all."

Again, nothing.

"So what I want to know is, why you think I'm worth killing."

Chiba looked down, scratched the back of his head, and looking up held Webster's eye again.

"I said to you. You know nothing. Not about me. Not about Qazai." He paused, his eyes fixed. "I want, you die. Understand. That is all."

Webster shook his head. "No. You understand. How much does Qazai owe you?"

He didn't expect a response, and he got none.

"Tens of millions? Hundreds? He has no money. Not until he sells his company. And when I send this to the CIA, MI6, and the editor of the *Wall Street Journal* in London, who happens to be a friend of mine, he won't be able to sell it." He reached inside his jacket and from a pocket pulled a thin sheaf of A4 paper, fifteen sheets perhaps, folded into three. "And then you don't get your money. Read it. It's yours."

The man took the paper and started to read. Oliver had e-mailed it that morning. It was rough, but it had substance, and more importantly, detail: every transaction they had found between Qazai and Kurus and along the chain in both directions; everything that could be found on Chiba, all the odd correspondences and coincidences; not quite proof but nearly proof, and in the right hands surely enough, Webster thought, to cause this man problems.

When he had finished reading he passed the pages to his friend and said, with a caustic smile, something unintelligible that contained the word "Chiba." The friend laughed, and made a show of leafing through the document.

The man chewed for a moment, watching Webster. He had something in his front teeth, in his incisors, and each time he bit on it a vein on his temple stood out. "It is bad you do not know me. Who I am. Bad for you. You are not scared." He paused. "You should be scared. If you knew."

It was Webster's turn not to reply. He tried to remember that this man was just a gangster, a modern-day hoodlum, a piece of nothing. He wasn't worthy of his fear. This was what he told himself.

The man turned his head and nodded to his friend, who unzipped his bag, put Webster's file inside it and took out a black, spiral-bound report. Webster felt a strange lightness in his chest, some new sense of foreboding that he couldn't explain.

"Please," he said, passing Webster the document. "Read."

The text was in Arabic, possibly Farsi. Webster turned to the back and found a full page of writing that he couldn't understand, bar his own name in Roman script at the bottom and other words dotted among the text: Ikertu, Isaac Hammer, Cursitor Street. He turned back a page and saw four photographs: one showed Ikertu's offices; another, grainy, taken from a distance with a zoom, showed him arriving at work one morning; the third was of him leaving Qazai's house; the last of him and Hammer leaving Timur's funeral. Webster, his heart pounding, glanced up and turned the page.

He took it in before he was fully conscious of what was there. A cold pulse of fear spread through him and a sharp pain drove into his temple. He forced himself to concentrate.

There were more pictures: one of the Websters' house on Hiley Road; one of Elsa leaving for work; two of Webster taking the children to school and nursery, their hands in his. On the next page, Silke coming out of school with Nancy and Daniel and alongside that a single shot of the three of them in the playground around the corner from their house. All the photographs were dated and timed.

Webster stared at them for a long time. He couldn't bring himself to look up because he didn't want to betray his terror.

"Same deal for you as Qazai," the man said. "One week, he pays me the money, I hurt only you. Longer, I hurt your family."

Webster raised his head and did his best to appear unmoved.

"I'm not with him."

"Here you were with him."

"No." Webster shook his head. "No. If anything happens to me, you will be exposed. Your name will be everywhere. When you get your money, it's over."

The man looked at him and smiled. "You say one word and your family is not safe."

For a moment Webster felt as he had last night in the desert with Senechal's head in his hand: he wanted to smash this man's skull until it crumbled. To strangle him until those blue eyes started from his head.

The man leaned in, his voice lowered and strangely intimate. "You do not know me. You do not even know my name. Do not try. It will be bad. For your family."

He took the report back from Webster.

"Qazai understand this. Do you understand?"

His eyes, adamantine, scoured Websters,' a search as brutal and invasive as the punishment he had administered the night before, and with that he turned, nodded to his goon and left, replacing his sunglasses and walking with a compact, muscular stride into the crowds. Webster, watching him go, felt like his body had been hollowed out.

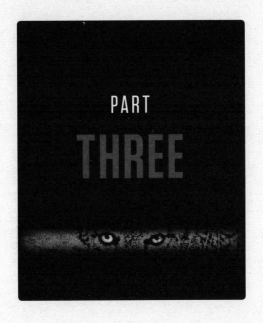

PART

THREE

21.

IN HAMMER'S OFFICE, hanging on the wall behind his desk among the
other trophies of his career, was a framed quotation in Chinese that he
had received from a Mexican client on successfully completing some particularly difficult job. The Mexican, to hear Hammer tell it, was somewhere
between eccentric and dangerous: he kept Samurai swords on the wall of
his office, tigers for pets at his country home, and a vast library of texts on
the nature of combat and war. *The Art of War* was his favorite, and the quotation, in just four characters, said that to know your enemy you must
become your enemy. Hammer, intellectually sympathetic to that sort of
thing, liked to refer to it often—not least, Webster knew from his own
experience, because it was true. But what Webster wanted to know was
what Sun Tzu would have to say when you had no idea who you were
fighting.

His thoughts were scattered. What he needed more than anything else
was to collect them, rank them, lock some away as dangerous or irrelevant,
but they tore around his head, ungovernable. But in among them, most
insistent of all, were those words: you do not even know my name. And that
made his enemy not only impossible to defeat, but impossible to defend
against.

Back in the car he played Driss the recording of the meeting and silently prayed that Kamila might track the man down; it seemed unimaginable, however, that he would leave any trace. Driss listened, but couldn't make out what the man had said to his friend on reading Webster's report. It wasn't Arabic, he was sure; it sounded like Farsi.

Webster lit a cigarette—four left now—closed his eyes and took a deep drag, letting the smoke hit the back of his throat like a small act of self-mortification. For a while he just sat in the heat, head back and one elbow out of the car's open window, keeping the smoke in his lungs a moment before letting it out, forcing himself to relax into its rhythm until slowly the storm in his head began to abate. When he finally opened his eyes he knew three things. One, that he should be at home to protect his family. Two, that this man had to get his money. Three, that Qazai was the key to both.

He took the pay-as-you-go phone that Kamila had given him that morning and dialed Qazai's cell. It was switched off, but his next call established that he had not yet checked out of his hotel, and he asked Driss to drive him there as fast as he could.

"Is that a good idea?" said Driss.

"Why?"

"The police."

"When will you hear from your friends?"

"I don't know."

"Could we ring the hospitals?"

"If the Frenchman is dead he will not be in hospital."

"But if he isn't he will."

Driss shrugged. "My mother and Youssef are following your man. I am here."

"I know. It's OK. Then I have no choice. Let's go."

There was every chance, of course, that the police would be wanting to speak to Qazai, or were speaking to him already, but he had to see him; there was no other way.

He and Driss made a plan. They would drive past the hotel, make sure there were no police cars in the area, and then Driss would go in to make his reconnaissance. If all was clear, Webster would find Qazai while Driss, having tea in the lobby, would call him the moment anything happened.

THERE WERE NO POLICE in the hotel, Driss called from the lobby to report, and as far as anyone knew Mr. Qazai was in his room—at least it had not yet been made up. Webster thanked him, locked the car, left the keys in the exhaust, and crossed the street to the hotel gates, looking about him at every car, every driver, every passerby. The heat was so strong he could feel it bouncing back off the sticky tarmac.

Feeling sweaty and thoroughly conspicuous, with his trouser legs flapping above his shoes, Webster limped through the lobby and tried to look like he belonged. A few people were sitting here, drinking tea, leaning forward to have quiet conversations. Despite the loud clack of his leather soles none of the receptionists looked up as he passed, and soon he was in the garden, walking through the shade of the cedars, barely noticing that the racket of the city had given way to the swish of sprinklers and the chattering whistles of unseen birds. To his right, fat orange fish played in the apple-green water of a shallow pond and for a moment Webster longed to join them, to feel the cold on his face and on his side.

He passed half-a-dozen villas before he reached Qazai's. He unlatched the low gate marked Sultan's Villa and followed a brick path bordered with flowers until he reached a large private lawn, and standing in it a modern stone structure that was at least three times the size of his house. A portico the width of the building jutted into its own swimming pool; palm trees and cypresses shaded the water and the entrance, which was by way of a tall glass double door. Curtains inside were drawn across it.

Webster paused for a moment, then knocked. Nothing. He knocked again. After half a minute he took off his jacket, draped it over one of the sunloungers, unbuttoned the cuff of Youssef's shirt and pulled his arm up the sleeve so that his hand was covered. Then he tried the door handle, and found it locked. Once upon a time his favorite private detective back in London had shown him how to open certain locks with a credit card, but he didn't have his cards anymore. He made a circuit of the building. All the windows were closed and the door he had tried was the only one. There were no small panes of glass to break, no way up to the roof, no obvious way in.

He knocked, harder this time, using the metal of his lighter against the glass, then the heel of his hand, banging as hard as he could.

"Open the door," he said, leaning in to the glass. "Open the fucking door." He banged again, and shouted now. "Darius, open this fucking door."

Behind the glass the curtains parted an inch. Webster couldn't see in. Then a hand reached through them, the lock turned, and the hand withdrew.

Webster opened the door and slipped through the curtains. It was like walking into a crypt: almost completely dark, its air stale and so cool he felt he must be hundreds of feet underground. He could just make out a low table surrounded by armchairs but otherwise all was in gloom, and as he shut the door behind him he opened the curtains, filling the room with sun.

The light showed Qazai sitting with his hands on his knees, staring straight ahead of him like a drunk in a station waiting room. In front of him was an empty bottle of brandy, a bottle of whisky nearly half gone, and an ashtray full of cigar ends and long ash trails that gave off a decaying, dead smell. He was still in yesterday's clothes, still wearing his shoes and his crumpled jacket, as if he had made it back here from the desert, sat down with his bottles and not moved since. Occasionally his eyelids drooped and his head lolled before jerking back into place. Christ, thought Webster. What a pair we make.

He looked around the room, at the freshly plastered walls distressed to look centuries old, and saw in one corner a cabinet with glasses arranged on it. Inside it was a fridge full of bottles. Webster took two of them, and a glass, and went to sit by Qazai, watching him for a moment before he spoke and wondering what, if anything, was going on in his head.

He opened one of the bottles and poured.

"Here. Drink this. You need water."

Qazai looked at him as if seeing him for the first time and reached for the glass, taking only a sip before putting it back on the table. As he sat back a shiver ran through him. His eyes were bloodshot and his forehead was creased in an expression of perpetual pain.

"Have you heard from Senechal?" Webster shook him, desperately hoping that he had. But Qazai simply looked blank. "From Yves? Have you heard from Yves?"

Qazai glanced at him, failing to meet his eye, then looked down at the ground as if considering something, and shook his head. Webster passed him the glass and he drank.

"Are you." Qazai paused and frowned, as if remembering. "Are you all right?"

"I'm fine."

Qazai nodded slowly and reaching up began to scratch his jawline, absently at first and then with more and more energy, like a dog finding a flea.

"And Yves? What did they do to Yves?"

"We need to leave," said Webster. "Marrakech. We need to go and make a plan. We've been given a week. Do you understand? One week. We have to move." Webster put his hand under Qazai's arm and started to pull. "And then you can tell me what the fuck you've done to my life."

Qazai turned to look at him, as if for the first time.

"He took my son." He shook his head again and tears started in his eyes. "He took my son." Qazai brought his hands up to cover his face, shaking his head harder and harder, pushing his palms into his eyes and clawing at his scalp. "My son," he moaned, and his voice was thick from crying.

Webster had to get him out of here. The police might turn up at any minute; might already be drawing up outside the hotel.

He reached out and put his hand on Qazai's shoulder, finding from somewhere a final reserve of patience. "Look at me. Please." Slowly Qazai took his hands away from his eyes, then drew his sleeve across his face to wipe them. "Very soon I won't be able to leave here. You need to fly me back to London, and together we need to deal with this. Do you understand? If we do, there's no reason for anyone else to get hurt. Not Ava. Not your grandchildren. But we have to go. Right now."

Qazai turned his head to look at him, glanced away and nodded. Under Webster's hand his shoulder twitched.

"How quickly can you get your plane ready?"

Qazai scratched his jaw. "When . . . when did you see Rad? Did you see him?"

"Is Rad his name?"

Qazai nodded.

"Who is he?" Qazai said nothing, and Webster felt his anger rise. "Who the fuck is he?"

"One of the worst of them. One of the worst." He looked up at Webster, and his eyes, for the very first time, showed humility. "I'm sorry. I'm so sorry."

WEBSTER BEGAN TO LOOK around for Qazai's things. A suitcase stood outside the bedroom door, clearly unopened since he had arrived.

"Come on," he said. "We're going. Do you have anything else? Do you have your passport?"

Qazai didn't hear; he was staring straight ahead and slowly shaking his head. Webster fitted his hand under his arm and helped him up.

"Do you have your passport?"

Qazai felt inside his jacket and nodded.

"How do we get the plane ready? Where's the pilot?"

"It's ready."

"What time were you due to fly?"

Qazai looked puzzled.

"When were you flying back to London? What time?"

"What . . . what time is it?"

Webster sighed sharply and checked his watch. "Eleven thirty. It's Saturday."

Qazai screwed his eyes up, rubbed them with the heel of his hand. "Today. Lunchtime. I was going to call."

"Do you have your phone?"

Qazai nodded.

"Then call."

Qazai fished around in his jacket pockets, searching for his phone, and as he did so it rang, an unfamiliar tone. It took Webster a moment to realize that in fact it was his own, the new one Kamila had given him.

"Yes."

"Two policeman are here." It was Driss, speaking just above a whisper. "Not in uniform."

"How can you tell?"

"I know. And they are asking for your friend."

Shit. Webster closed his eyes and thought. "Bring the car around to the front. Twenty meters to the left of the gates."

He carried the suitcase into the bedroom, opened it and as quickly as he could put the clothes in drawers and the suitcase, now empty, on a stand in the corner. The wash-bag he took into the bathroom, removing the toothbrush and the toothpaste and laying them out on the basin. Back in the bedroom he pulled back the covers on the bed and messed up the pillows. It would have to do.

Qazai was standing now, hardly steadily, and trying to negotiate his phone.

"Leave that," said Webster, and ushered him toward the door. "Later."

"My case."

"Some people are coming. You don't want to talk to them." He started pulling Qazai toward the door at a quick walk but he resisted, trying to go back for his suitcase.

"Leave it. I want them to think you haven't left. Come on," he moved behind Qazai and shepherded him through the door. "Out. We've got to hurry."

"What about Yves?"

"You don't need to worry about Yves."

He took the key from the lock as they left, put it in his pocket and shut the door quietly. With his finger to his lips he looked at Qazai. "Not a sound. We're going this way," and instead of going left down the path he led

Qazai to the right of the villa in among the shrubs and trees by the pool. Qazai followed meekly enough, but his tread was heavy and the dry needles from the cypresses crunched loudly under his feet.

Webster kept him close and moved as stealthily as he could away from the villa, checking over his shoulder for signs of the police and avoiding the patches of sunlight that cut through the canopy overhead. Over their own footsteps he heard a metallic clink—the latch, he thought, opening or closing on the gate—and he stopped, one finger on his lips, touching Qazai on the arm and gesturing for him to do the same. Looking back toward the light he saw two men in brown suits walking in no particular hurry along the path to the Sultan's Villa. Beside him Qazai tottered. As one of the policeman knocked on the door, Webster put his arm around Qazai, who was now leaning heavily against him, and started walking him carefully toward the next villa, which was coming into view between the trees. The policemen knocked again, stood back, looked up at the building's facade, tried the door handle, found it open, and went in.

"Come on," said Webster. "Quick."

Half pushing, half dragging Qazai, he came out by another swimming pool, thankfully empty, and noticed too late the middle-aged couple on their sunloungers in the shade of the villa's porch.

"Security," he said, reasoning that English was the language they were most likely to understand and praying that they didn't start talking to him in French. "We had report of an intruder. I'm afraid he's drunk. Forgive me."

Qazai was certainly that. Since standing and moving he had gone pale and was finding it hard to keep his head up. Webster fixed a smile on his face, pushed Qazai ahead of him and when they reached the path back to the hotel tried to adopt a casual gait, his arm still around his charge.

As ever, this all came down to timing. If the policemen spent a minute or two in Qazai's villa, inspected the spent bottles and the slept-in bed, there would be enough time to get to Driss.

But the bottles. He had forgotten the water bottles. If they were decent policemen they would notice that they were still cold and assume that Qazai couldn't be far away. He quickened their pace.

"Slow down," said Qazai. "I don't . . . I'm not feeling well."

Christ, thought Webster. We don't have time for him to be sick.

"It's not far. Twenty yards." It was at least a hundred. He held Qazai up as best he could, but he was increasingly a dead weight and the effort greater and greater. He didn't want to be lugging a body through reception. Behind them the Moroccans would surely have left the villa by now.

As he entered the cool of the hotel's main building he hitched Qazai up, tried, hopelessly, to arrange him to look as respectable as possible, and set off for the final stretch, keeping a low commentary going to help sustain him, as one might a toddler that needed coaxing.

"That's it. Just through the lobby. Only a few more yards."

God he was heavy. Webster was beginning to slow.

"Not far now. That's it."

He tried to keep his eyes straight ahead but couldn't help glancing at the receptionists, three of them in a row. One was busy with a guest, another had his head down on his computer screen, but the third was watching them, and as Webster looked away she made to pick up her phone. He could stop, reassure her, but there was no point. All they had to do was get to the car.

They were at the steps down to the driveway; Webster hadn't noticed them when he arrived, but now they seemed long and sheer. Watched by an intrigued doorman, and bent almost double, Qazai took them one by one, like a child.

This was hopeless. They'd never make the last fifty yards.

"Stay here," he said to Qazai, and to the doorman, "Hold him a second, would you? He's not well."

Qazai staggered a couple of steps, came to a halt, tried to straighten himself, then closed his eyes and brought a hand to his mouth. Hardly daring to look at him, Webster ran through the gates to the street and seeing the brown Peugeot started waving at it, beckoning it forward.

"Thank you," he said, returning to the doorman. "Come on. The car's here."

The car drew up at the gates, and Webster guided Qazai into the back-seat, pushing him across the worn fabric.

"Go. Drive. Get us to the airport."

"Is he going to vomit?"

"Almost certainly."

As the car moved off, waiting a second for traffic to pass and then accel-erating sharply, Webster saw through the back window two men appear at the top of the hotel steps and look swiftly around. He lost sight of them when Driss took a sharp right, but by then they were skipping down the steps, and the doorman was pointing in Webster's direction.

"How long to the airport?"

"Ten minutes," said Driss. "There's not so much traffic now." He looked in the rearview mirror. "What are you doing?"

"Finding his fucking phone. Christ. This man has caused me a lot of trouble."

"What will you do at the airport?"

"Get on his plane. God knows how."

"But your passport."

"I know, I know. I don't suppose you know anyone who works there?"

Driss merely shrugged.

The phone, when he finally found it and had Qazai, with clumsy fin-gers, unlock it for him, showed five missed calls from the same number, a UK cell phone that Webster didn't recognize, and a text:

Mr. Q. Trying to call. Will miss slot if not confirmed by 12:20. Paperwork filed. Please advise. Carl.

Webster called the number and told the pilot to prepare the plane for an unwell Mr. Qazai. Carl baulked at taking instructions from someone he didn't know, but Qazai managed to frame a sentence or two of reassurance, and in the end all was set: they had ten minutes to be at the airport, ten to clear security, and another ten to find and board the plane. It could be done—or at least, it could be done by someone leaving the country with a legitimate passport and unimpeded by police. Then it could be done.

While Webster was wondering whether the police would suspect that Qazai was going to the airport, and deciding that on balance there was no way of knowing one way or another no matter how carefully you tried to think it through, the heat and the jolting suspension were taking their toll on Qazai, who was awkwardly slumped against a door with his eyes tightly closed. A mile short of the airport Webster felt a hand on his arm and knew immediately what it meant.

"Driss. Stop the car. Now."

It was too late. Qazai leaned forward and a quick stream of watery vomit burst from his mouth, onto his trousers, the back of Driss's seat, Webster's shoes. Alcoholic fumes rose from it. As the car slowed at the side of the road Webster leaned across and opened Qazai's door, trying to prop it open.

"Do it that way. Outside." With his spare hand he pushed Qazai in the right direction as cars zipped past. "That's it. Christ. May as well get it all out." He had only ever done this for his children before.

Driss had swiveled in his seat and was watching with a look of pained regret.

"I'm sorry," said Webster. "I'll pay for it. Can you put it on my expenses?" Driss raised an eyebrow, sighed, and turned back to the road.

Webster patted Qazai on the back. "Are you done? You're done. Let's go. Let's go."

A little after twenty past, Driss pulled up onto the concourse of Menara and slowed to a stop by a door marked "Private Flights." Webster didn't really know what to expect inside. Nor, he imagined, would the airport staff: he and Qazai—bandaged, dusty, beaten, stinking—would have looked improbable catching a bus together, let alone their own jet.

"Driss," he said, "thank you. I owe you."

They shook hands.

"You do," said Driss.

"You never know," said Webster, "I may be calling you in half an hour from a cell downtown." Driss didn't know the word. "From jail. Thank your mother for me, and tell Youssef to buy himself some new clothes. He's paying." He nodded at Qazai, who had managed to get out of the car himself and was taking deep breaths by the curb.

Inside, all was cool and peaceful. There were no tourists, no baggage trolleys, no taxi touts: just a single check-in desk and two airport officials, a man and a woman, with little or nothing to do. Consciously standing tall, clearly trying to gather as much of his dignity as he could, Qazai told them in French who he was and presented his passport. The woman tapped at her keyboard, asked if there were any bags to check, and printed off a piece of paper that told him his plane was on stand twenty-three. She didn't so much as look them up and down, and Webster realized that in his pessimism he hadn't banked on the blanket entitlement conferred by money. If you had paid for your private jet you could fly in it naked for all anyone would care. She didn't ask to see his passport either, and for a moment his heart rose hopefully in his chest.

But even billionaires, and their guests, need to go through immigration, and as they made their way down corridors to their gate they found their way blocked by a security scanner, and beyond that a glass booth with a Moroccan border policeman sitting inside it. As he emptied his pockets Webster counted his money—Senechal's money, in fact—in preparation. Sixteen hundred dirham; a hundred and eighty dollars. That might do it.

Collecting his things he whispered to Qazai, "Let me go first," and taking him by the upper arm led him up to the yellow line, where they stood for a moment waiting for the policeman to look up. At his nod they approached. Webster's breathing quickened and he could feel his heart working harder. He couldn't bring himself to think what would happen if this didn't work.

"Passports."

Webster tried his best, laughably, to look respectable.

"Good morning, " he said, and got no response. "*Bonjour.* I am this man's doctor, and I need to make sure he is handed over to medical staff waiting on the plane. I do not have a passport but will not be flying."

The policeman, slouching on his chair, stuck out his lower lip and shook his head. He didn't seem to understand. Webster tried again, in his basic, unpracticed French.

"*Je suis un médecin. Cet homme est mon . . . Je suis avec cet homme. Il faut que je vais avec lui sur l'avion, parce-qu'il est très malade. Très malade, et il y a médecins sur l'avion qui lui attendent. Je n'ai pas de passeport mais je reste ici. Je ne vais pas voyager.*

Under heavy lids the policeman's eyes gave him a long, searching look. Slowly, he shook his head.

"No passport, no entry."

"*Mais c'est imperatif.*" Was *imperatif* a word? He had no idea. He could feel the situation slipping from him. "*Mon . . .*" God how he wished he knew the word for "patient." "*Il est très malade, et je suis son médecin.*"

The policeman raised his eyebrows and shook his head again, looking down at his desk.

"OK," said Webster. "*D'accord. Je voudrais . . . non, je suis heureux payer un, un,*" Christ, what was "fee"? *Droit*—that was it—"*Un droit médical, pour votre cooperation.*" God, that was horrible. It was a long time since he had tried to bribe an official, and somehow in Russian it had always felt easier. He produced Senechal's cash from his jacket pocket, and put it on the counter. "*Un droit médical.*"

The notes sat there for what seemed like an age while the policeman looked first at them and then at Webster, steadily in the eye. Whether he was making a moral or financial calculation wasn't clear, but at last he shook his head, said a few words in French that Webster couldn't make out, and reached for his phone.

Then Qazai spoke. In Arabic, with great authority and even greater seriousness, his voice clear and deep. The policeman straightened in his seat. Whatever Qazai had to say it was short, and when he had finished he waited grandly for a response. Without looking up the policeman reached up to the counter, took the money, and nodded them through.

Neither man said anything until they had reached the gate and were taking the stairs down to the tarmac.

"How did you do that?" said Webster.

Some color had returned to Qazai's face but he still looked pained. "I told him he should take the money. And that if he didn't I would tell the director of the airport police that he tried to solicit a bribe from us."

Webster nodded, grateful and not a little embarrassed.

"I didn't know you could speak Arabic."

"There's a lot you don't know."

Webster, still not entirely confident that they had outrun the police, took one last look around at the airport, buzzing with heat in the midday sun.

"That's about to change," he said, and let Qazai go first up the steps to the plane.

22.

I T HAD ALL BEEN the doing of a man called Nezam; in a sense, he had ordained all this thirty years ago from his office in Tehran. Dead for twenty, he had no doubt imagined this day, or one like it, and would have been saddened to see his careful arrangements finally coming undone. That was what Webster had to understand. It would be no exaggeration to say that Qazai had had no choice then, just as he seemed to have so few now.

People imagine that revolutions are clean-cut affairs: the emperor loses his head, his followers flee or are put to the sword, the state is transfused with fresh blood. No one from the old guard is meant to remain; there were no aristocrats on the Committee of Public Safety, no Whites on the Council of Public Commissars. In Iran, though, where politics is ancient and complicated, despite the reach and the viciousness of the revolution, despite the departure or death of almost everyone who had held a post of importance in the old regime, there was one place where one man somehow managed to stay on, darkly welcomed by his new masters, and that place was the secret police.

The odd junior officer from the ranks made the same jump—experience, after all, was hard to come by—but Kamal Nezam was a senior man, the deputy head of the service, in charge of monitoring sedition for the Shah, and to the Ayatollah no one should have been more deserving of

a swift and public death. But either because he was already a traitor, or because he knew too well how valuable he might be to a government desperate
to control the people it had just freed, he stayed on, smoothly making the
switch from the Shah's service to the service of the revolution, from SAVAK
to SAVAMA, from one sinister acronym to another.

Whatever path he had taken, Nezam was no idealist. He was a technician of the highest order who set about creating an efficient, brutal, nasty
little agency that mirrored many of the qualities of the revolution itself, and
one of his first, critical jobs was to help the new government find a place for
its money. In those days Iran wasn't rich but it wasn't poor, either: oil dollars were still coming in but it was soon spending most of them on its war
with Iraq. Nevertheless, it had enough to put some aside for its youthful but
ambitious foreign intelligence service, or for operations outside its borders,
or for lining its own pockets, perhaps. And it wanted its money to accumu-
late, of course, which it wasn't going to do sitting around in a recently
nationalized bank in Tehran. So Nezam had gone to Paris to meet an old
friend of his, and the old friend had suggested that he consider Parviz
Qazai, who had recently arrived in London and was setting up a little bank
that might be to purpose.

Here Qazai paused. He drained his glass of water, swirled the ice for a
moment, put it down and looked out of the window. It was clear below,
barely a cloud in sight, and Webster, facing forward, could see the west
coast of Morocco stretching in front of him and in the distance, just visible
through the haze, southern Spain and the points of the Strait of Gibraltar
pinching together. Qazai was looking a little better. He had showered and
changed into some loose gray pajamas that made him look as if he was
about to start meditating, and though he looked drawn—pale, somehow,
beneath the tan—he was lucid enough, and had been telling his story with
odd, pained attention, almost relish. Webster had expected to have to force
out the truth, but all he had done was ask what was really going on, and
after a pause and a deep, sorrowful breath Qazai had begun, tired but con-
structing his sentences with care, as if he were laying down a piece of history
that deserved total clarity.

But something had brought him to a stop, and for perhaps half a minute he closed his eyes before going on.

"For years I've wondered . . . I have tried not to blame my father for all this. He wasn't a bad man. He needed more brilliance, I think. If he'd been more brilliant there wouldn't have been so much room for his fears. And when he got to London I have to believe he was really afraid. About my future, for one thing." There was an ironic note in his clipped laugh. "But I think we can agree that he set me up very nicely."

Webster, not knowing whether the double meaning was intended, tried to keep his expression clear of sympathy or judgment and let Qazai go on.

Father and son had drawn up the first plans for their London bank during the summer of 1979, when Qazai was twenty-eight and a little lost; not a loafer, exactly, but wanting direction. In Paris, five years earlier, he had studied philosophy and economics at the Sorbonne and had done well enough, but his heart—no, his soul—was in art. When he was twelve, and committed to boyish notions of romance and adventure, he had read a novel by Stevenson that had seemed to capture precisely what he wanted his life to be. In it, the son of a stony, conservative, rich American goes to Paris to become a sculptor, before being led by an impetuous friend to chase after treasure lying in the wreck of a ship in the middle of the Pacific. That was living, the young Qazai had thought, and in a way, not that he had ever seen it in that light before, his progress since had indeed followed a similar track.

His sculpture was no better, in truth, than Stevenson's hero's had been, and when the revolution came about—or rather, when all the rich Iranians started leaving the country some months before it happened—he had been back from Paris for three years, in Tehran, working at this job or that but spending most of his energy planning (and delaying) a business that would export Persian art to London and New York. Life, in short, was too easy then. Too comfortable.

Exile was not. After they were forced to leave Iran he watched his father become fearful, prone to irrational alarms about the future, anxious about his reputation and his influence in this new city, which, while not hostile, was hardly friendly. That, rather than exile itself, was what had shocked

Qazai into changing: he was overcome by a powerful desire never to be cowed in the same way by life and its possible misfortunes. Money, he realized, was the key to fearlessness, and he had surprised his father with his enthusiasm for the idea that they set up in business together. Later he would surprise him with his talent for investing, which had turned out to be his real genius, but for a time the job they had before them was simple—to raise funds—and for a dreary six months their lives had been nothing but meetings, and the same meeting every time at that: they would explain their idea, answer questions, and be shown out, with varying degrees of politeness.

After a while Qazai began to wonder whether it was his father's profession, and not his character, that had caused his collapse. Finance was not like art. It had no soft edges. Either you had money, or you didn't; either you were making more, or you weren't. And if you weren't making anything, you were nothing. A bad sculptor keeps his sculptures and may think them good, but a banker who cannot raise money has nothing at all, and slowly Qazai came to understand the distinct atmosphere of exclusion that his father must have been forced to breathe since leaving Iran.

So when his father told him—some time in April 1980, it was—that he had secured a little funding, it had felt like a deliverance, and he remembered wondering why he was the only one who seemed to be relieved. They had fifteen million pounds to invest, from one investor, whose name was never mentioned; ten of it conservatively, the rest with some imagination, a commodity that Qazai possessed in larger quantity than his father. They divided it accordingly, and the following year Qazai made his first real investment: an apartment building in Swiss Cottage. Within a year he had made a return of thirty percent, and his other decisions were coming good. He began to realize that he was a natural. He could see value. He could look at a complicated, scattered set of facts and know exactly where one could make money, and at what risk. The heady power of that realization had never really left him. Not, at least, until the last two months.

Anyway. The unseen investor entrusted the Qazais with more funds; they took an office in Mayfair, hired a secretary and a property analyst, and began to do well. Then his father became ill. He was a smoker, and his lungs were shot. When he found out how bad it was, he became unusually concerned, even by his standards, about the future of the business—started talking about the "legacy," rather as if it was a curse and not an asset. All this seemed to worry him more than his illness, and one day, looking weak, he had flown to Paris to see their investor, whom Qazai had never met and whose name he still did not know.

Qazai was living in Kensington then, with Eleanor, and though they were not yet married she was pregnant with Timur. It was early on, and no one knew. It was a time of promise and excitement. That evening his father phoned to say that he had come back from Paris with the investor, and that they should all meet. Eleanor had been out with her sister, and Qazai suggested the meeting take place in his apartment. His father rather shakily agreed.

Nezam introduced himself that evening only as Kamal; it had taken Qazai another ten years to learn his full name. In a smooth, low voice like the drone of a wasp that unsettled Qazai straight away, he explained that the money they had in their care was more than usually precious. With it, great things would be done, all for the greater glory of Iran. At first Qazai thought that the money must be a fighting fund of some kind for the country's opposition, but as Kamal explained, his tone growing more threatening, that just as keeping the money was a sacred trust that would be well rewarded, so losing it or betraying its whereabouts was an act of heresy that would merit acute punishment, it began to be obvious that he spoke for the enemy. He didn't mention the revolution, or the Ayatollah, or the Revolutionary Guard, but he didn't have to. Throughout this speech, Qazai's father had looked down at the floor, stifling a cough from time to time and failing to meet his son's eye.

And that was that. It was made clear to them both that what had begun as a family business could never leave the family, and that the younger Qazai would abide by the same, stark rules as his father: no fraud, and not a word out of place. Failure to observe these two simple precepts would result in death, for them and those dear to them. From time to time they would receive more money; from time to time withdrawals would be made, when funds were required elsewhere. Qazai hadn't liked to ask his client how that money was spent.

So. Fifteen million had become twenty, thirty, sixty, a hundred. When the number was somewhere in the thirties Qazai's father had died. But on the strength of his skill and his record, after three years Qazai had gone looking for other investors and found, some without difficulty, wealthy families who wanted a decent return. That was Shiraz, and it made him his first fortune. The Iranian funds continued to grow but were no longer everything, and when he founded Tabriz and let the real money pour in—the pension money, the insurance money, more cautious but vast—there were times when he could forget the mixed, poisonous inheritance his father had left him. Never for long, mind: they were an odd client, undemanding and incurious generally, but hard work nevertheless. Funds always arrived from surprising directions and had to leave by the most meandering routes, usually through companies incorporated in bizarre places by Qazai himself—or by Senechal, his loyal lieutenant.

The mention of the name seemed to stop Qazai's flow, and for a moment he stared blankly ahead and said nothing. Throughout his monologue he had hardly once looked at Webster, and this was so unusual that Webster had no doubt of the truth of what he was saying. Nor was his tale incredible, for all that it was astonishing. Now that it was out, it made a grotesque sense; it fit.

IF YOU TOOK THE man Qazai wanted to be and inverted him, here he was. Not a great patriot but a paltry traitor, his weakness, after all, the same as his father's: love of money, and a greater fear of there not being enough. While Webster was letting the story settle, alternately feeling sympathy and repugnance, the one thought that grew stronger and stronger was that Timur need not have died.

"So why didn't you just sell the whole thing? I don't get it."

Qazai was silent.

"None of this need have happened."

Qazai scratched at his beard. "Perhaps."

"You know it."

"I wanted to leave it for Timur." He paused, stopped scratching. "I really did."

"I'm not sure he wanted it."

Qazai stared at Webster and in his eyes there was a suggestion of the old imperiousness. But it softened, in an instant, and he looked away, resting his forehead on his hand, pinching his brow.

"They never threatened him. They said they could destroy my life. I didn't know they meant by taking his."

"After what happened to Parviz?"

"I thought they were just trying to scare me."

"If only they had." Qazai glanced up and nodded, his eyes looking inward. "What about Mehr?"

"That was on their territory. I thought . . . I thought it was opportunist."

Webster snorted. "They invited him."

Qazai said nothing, and for a minute or two there was an exhausted silence between them.

"Who is Rad?" said Webster.

Qazai clasped his hands together and stared down at them.

"Does he have a first name?" said Webster.

"Not that I know."

"Who is he?"

"He's intelligence. I assume."

"No shit."

"That's all I know. I've only met him three times. When Ahmadinejad came to power everything changed. After Nezam I dealt with the same man for over fifteen years. Mutlaq, his name was. I would see him once a year, always somewhere different."

"How did you communicate?"

"We had a brass-plaque office in Mayfair. Just a letterbox. I checked it once a week."

"Do you still have it?"

"A different one."

"What if you wanted to talk to him?"

"We had emergency procedures. I never needed them."

"Go on."

"So. Two years ago I went to meet Mutlaq in Caracas and he wasn't there. Rad was in his place. He told me that things in Tehran had changed, that they were concerned about the money. What I was doing with it. Investing it in Sunni businesses, in American companies. It was strange, but before that no one seemed to care where their money went. He told me from now on I would need to consider my investments differently. I told him I would see what I could do but it might be difficult to change. He just looked at me from behind those glasses and told me that I had better remember who had made me." Qazai paused. "That was the first meeting."

"Then?"

"Then the world collapsed. Half of Shiraz was in the Gulf and half of that was in Dubai and property. We still haven't recovered."

"How much? How much did you lose?"

Qazai ran a hand through his hair. "Over half. Without what we owed the banks. And then Rad appeared again."

"Appeared?"

"There was a letter. Asking to meet. This time in Belgrade."

"Do you think they knew?"

"Probably."

"And they wanted their money?"

"All of it."

"How much?"

"Two point seven billion."

Webster raised an eyebrow. "That's enough. How much do you have?"

"Less." Qazai sighed. "Until I sell."

Astonishing though it was, Webster sensed that after everything Qazai was still reluctant to part with his empire. He fought his irritation.

"So. The Americans are ready?"

Qazai chewed his lip and sighed. "Yes. They're ready."

"Can it happen in a week?"

"At the price they're getting we could do it in a day. They're flying in on Wednesday. We'll sign the papers then."

Neither said anything for a moment.

"What happened to Yves?" Qazai asked finally.

That was an excellent question. Webster fielded it warily.

"They tried to shoot us. In the desert. Yves seemed keen to help them out."

Qazai looked blank.

"He had a gun. I think he wanted me to sacrifice myself."

"And?"

"I hit him. And left him there."

The revelation seemed to give Qazai pause. He watched Webster closely, as if reassessing him.

"So he was in on it?" Webster punctured his thoughts.

"Yves?"

"Yes. He knew about your dark little secret?"

"Someone had to."

"Was he blackmailing you?"

Qazai's expression went dark. "No. But I paid him well."

"So that was the hold he had over you."

Qazai didn't respond.

"Ava thought it had to do with your divorce but it wasn't, was it? He was milking you." He paused. "Did you know he was talking to them?"

"I'm sorry?"

"With this."

Webster fished Senechal's phone out of his pocket and chucked it into Qazai's lap. Qazai looked at it, puzzled, working out what it meant.

"You did know really, didn't you?" said Webster. "Deep down. He had two masters. And none."

"That doesn't make sense."

"Oh, it does. If I was Rad and I wanted someone to keep tabs on you he'd be my choice. I'd pay him well for it, too. Maybe he threw in extras for them. Like Timur's schedule. Like when your grandchildren swim."

Qazai continued to stare at the phone. "Why kill him?" he said at last.

"Because he outlived his usefulness. Because they thought you no longer trusted him. Or just because it's neat."

The stewardess came and asked them if they wanted more drinks or anything to eat. Qazai asked for water, and as he was waiting for his glass to be filled Webster watched him closely. After everything, he wasn't broken. A few minutes ago when he was telling his story he seemed to have given up on the notion of his greatness, and his unassailable sense of self seemed to have crumpled with the fiction that had supported it. But any shame he was feeling, Webster began to realize, was for the mistakes he had made, not for the lie he had spent his life telling. That deep, deep pride was showing signs of reviving.

Qazai sipped at his water. It was clear that something was exercising him, and Webster waited for it.

"If you'd just done what you were asked," he said at last, looking away from Webster, the words bitter.

Webster blinked, frowning. "Are you serious?"

"I'm completely serious."

"I did just that."

"Nonsense. It was a crusade. Some sort of . . . obsession. And for what? What were you hoping? To expose the truth?" Qazai shook his head. "No. I do not understand. Who benefited? Who won?"

"I wasn't prepared to lose."

"Not to me."

"No." Webster said it quietly. "Not to you."

"I thought for a while that you might stop for Ava's benefit. That she might have power over you where Yves and I had none."

There was a faint taunt in his eyes as he said it that made the blood rush to Webster's head. With effort he checked himself.

"Then you were wrong about that as well." He paused. "What will you tell her?"

Qazai closed his eyes, shook his head. As Webster had hoped, the thought clearly unsettled him.

"She can't know." He fixed his eye on Webster's. "She cannot know."

"Oh, I'm not so sure. If you tell her what you told me she might go for it. I wouldn't mention how much of the money you made went on arms. Or how much ended up as rocket launchers in the hands of terrorists. Or how many assassinations of her friends it's paid for over the years. If you leave all that out you might be all right. Until it dawns on her that you caused her brother's death."

Qazai's eyes flashed with pain and scorn, and for a moment he said nothing.

"I should have left you in that cell."

"You don't have to like me. But I do need you to understand. We have a week. You sell Tabriz. You pay the Iranians their money. If you do that, I won't tell everyone who you really are. Not even Ava. It will make me feel sick but I'll do it. And I'll work out how we stop them killing us afterward."

Qazai was quiet for a moment; his frame relaxed and he sat back in his seat. He examined his hand, pulled his fingers back until the knuckles cracked and then nodded his head, the faintest movement.

"What's your plan?"

"I don't have one," said Webster.

23.

IT WAS EVENING BY THE TIME Webster turned the corner into Hiley Road, still in Youssef's suit, bruised and grimy from his long journey, body and mind exhausted. Everything was as he had left it two days earlier. Fewer cars, because it was Saturday, but he glanced inside them all nevertheless, even walking twenty yards beyond his house to make sure that he was unobserved. He had never had to do this before, and it made him feel sick.

Automatically he patted his pockets for his keys, found none, walked up the short garden path and lifted the heavy wrought-iron knocker, trying to find a rhythm that was positive but not jaunty. Inside he could hear voices and light skidding steps and through the glass he saw Nancy's hand reaching up and struggling at full stretch to turn the Yale lock. The door opened and he crouched down to receive her and Daniel, who came at him so fast he struggled to keep his balance. Both were in their pajamas. Hugging them close, he looked up at Elsa, who was standing in the doorway, tried a smile, and watched her turn and walk down the long hall into the kitchen.

"Daddy," said Nancy. "Have your trousers shrunk?"

Webster looked down at himself. He looked ridiculous.

"I'm just going to the loo, sweetheart. Tell Mummy I'll be down in a minute."

Upstairs in the bathroom he checked himself in the mirror. One eye bruised and spreading black, one merely tired, both bloodshot, neither confident nor particularly honest. He took off Youssef's filthy shirt, stopping for a moment to examine the bruise that had settled on his side, struggled out of the trousers and put both in the laundry basket before taking a T-shirt and some shorts from the chest of drawers in his bedroom and hurriedly changing into them. In his own, clean clothes, the uniform of his weekends, he forgot for a short moment where he had been and what he had done.

Elsa had finished the washing up and had started wiping crumbs off the table.

"They watching something?" said Webster.

"Yes."

"Sorry I couldn't be home for dinner."

She looked up, then went back to her job. "We're just glad you could be here at all."

Webster wondered how he was going to say the things he needed to say.

"Did you eat with them?" he said at last.

"I didn't know when you'd be back."

The fridge was more or less empty: some rashers of bacon, children's yogurts, ends of cheese. Even though he hadn't eaten since that morning, he realized, he had no appetite.

"Do you want a drink?" he said.

"Not till they're in bed."

He found himself a glass and reaching up to the high shelf, took down a bottle of whisky, wincing at the pain in his side.

"You have one, though," said Elsa as he uncorked it.

"It's been a long day."

She didn't say anything straight away, but ran water over the cloth in her hands and wrung it out tight.

"I thought it was the weekend in Marrakech."

"Today is. They have the same weekends as us."

She had turned to him now, her arms crossed. Under the bright kitchen lights she looked tired, too.

"But a good meeting?"

"It wasn't exactly a meeting."

"It never is."

"I was there. I'm not lying to you."

"I know you were there. That's the problem. You go to these places and I have no idea what you're doing. Or what other people are doing to you. Most people who go away, they sit in rooms, they talk, they come back. They get bored. Perhaps they get drunk. Perhaps they get laid. Not you. Look at you. You're a mess. You bring your shit into our house, Ben. Every day. Every day you might as well come home looking like this. In a stranger's clothes. With a black eye, frightening the children."

"They're not frightened."

"No? Then why does Nancy want to know why you're hurt? Perhaps she's just curious. Perhaps they're used to you. That's good. But I'm not. I'm not used to you anymore. I can't stand it. If you call, you don't tell me anything. You're not going to tell me anything now. I know it. Well OK. That's fine. All I want to hear is that you've dealt with it, whatever it is, and that's it. It's over."

Webster hoped that this was their lowest point. There was fury in Elsa's eyes but what frightened him most was the disappointment he saw there, and the firmness, the resolution. Elsa's decisions were not undone lightly, and he sensed, with a terror greater than any he had yet known, that she was close to making one that she had long delayed.

But what to tell her? The truth hardly served. If he shared it, she might leave him for his idiocy; if he kept it from her, for his lack of trust.

He took a step toward her, made to put his arms around her. "It's nearly over."

"For fuck's sake." She pulled away. "What does that mean?" She stood, her hands on her hips, about a yard from him; he had never felt so alien in his own home. He took his drink from the side, moved past her, sat at the kitchen table and drank, the heat of the whisky harsh in his throat.

Trying to make his face as open as possible he looked her in the eye. "It's been bad. Nasty. But it will be finished. In a week. I have one more thing to do."

He watched her face for a response but she was distracted.

"Jesus Christ, Ben, what's that?" she said, pointing.

"What?"

"That. On your leg."

Looking down he saw an inch or two of purple-gray bruise showing on his thigh, just above the knee.

"Show me."

With a sigh he pulled up the leg of his shorts.

"My God. Who did it?"

"It was just a fight."

Elsa shook her head and crouched down to have a better look at it.

"Which you lost, I take it."

He didn't say anything.

"Is that it?"

Webster nodded and took another large sip of whisky.

"Lift up your shirt," said Elsa.

He hesitated, frowning at her.

"Go on."

She moved around the table as he lifted the T-shirt on his right side.

"My God. What did they do?"

Her eyes softened and she gently touched his cheekbone, at the edge of the bruise.

"God, baby. You need to go to hospital." She fetched her phone from the side and started dialing. "Silke might be free. I'll drive you."

"I'll be fine."

"Don't be silly."

"It's just a cracked rib."

"Ben."

"I don't need to go."

She put the phone down and looked up, her eyes shut and her neck tensed in frustration before she turned back to him.

"Because, what, you're really tough? You're a big man?" She paused. "They"—stressing the word and pointing toward the sitting room—"would rather you were less big. They don't care about big. Neither do I."

"It's a rib. There's nothing they can do."

"It's one thing being fearless. But this? This is pride. This is conceit." She held his eye. "I'm calling a taxi. You can go on your own." She stood up.

"Wait," he said. "We need to . . ." He didn't know how to say it. "I need you to go away for a few days."

Elsa simply looked at him.

"Start the holiday early."

She looked down at the floor, shaking her head, unable to say anything.

Webster went on. "The man who did this. We've made an arrangement. But I don't trust him to keep it. I think he will, but I don't want him coming here."

"He knows where we live."

"I have to assume so."

Elsa sighed. Her eyes were cold. "Tell me," she said, and her voice was clear and hard, "do you know how bad this is?"

He thought he did. He pictured Rad in their house, opening the door, his hand on the stair rail. He knew what he had sacrificed.

"I do."

"You've brought danger into our house. I can't have that here, Ben. Don't tell me you can make it go away because even if you can, that's not the point. You brought it in. It will never be the same." She paused. "We'll go to Cornwall. I can't be here with you."

WEBSTER WOKE IN THE spare room the next morning: four hours it had taken for a doctor to see him, a further two to be X-rayed and dismissed with a prescription for painkillers, and by the time he had returned home Elsa's light would have long been switched off. It was shameful, but that was a relief. He had slept heavily and couldn't recall his dreams, but he had a sense that they contained deserts, and unreachable oases, and low buildings in the sand.

For an hour after breakfast he helped Elsa pack, filling bags with games and books and films to watch, making a picnic, digging out the wetsuits and the fishing nets for the rock pools. This was what he did before a holiday. Elsa would pack the children's clothes and her own; he was responsible for fun. Every item sharpened the guilt.

They left at eleven, and as he saw them off, the children waving frenetically in the backseats, he felt as if it was he who was going away, he who was being excluded from the home. All morning Elsa had talked to him only to exchange practical information.

He watched the car reach the end of the street. As it rounded the corner a second car moved out from a parking space a few doors down from the Websters' house and set off in the same direction. Webster checked his watch and went inside.

At noon, Hammer arrived, in his running things, covered in fresh sweat, his face patchy red from the exertion.

"God. You look worse and worse," he said merrily as Webster opened the door. "So you're all on your own?"

Webster nodded, smelling Ike's sweat as he moved past him into the house.

"You call George?"

"I did," said Webster.

"What'd he say?"

"A discreet tail to Cornwall. Then counter-surveillance on the house."

"How many men?"

"Four. Two shifts of two."

"Hard work. Is that going on Qazai's bill?"

"Damn right."

Hammer laughed. "We making a turn on that?"

"Go into the kitchen. Do you want tea?"

"Water."

Webster had expected a cooler greeting than this; in truth, he was surprised that Hammer had even agreed to see him. But he appeared to be at his most energetic, and whether that was his recent run or the sheer exhilaration he felt when a situation became particularly intricate and unpleasant, it didn't matter. Perhaps he felt that Webster had suffered enough. Regardless, Webster felt a great relief at the sight of him, because he would help: see something Webster hadn't, turn the situation around, dream up some strategem. That was what he did. But more than that, it was good to be with someone who understood.

As Webster ran the tap Hammer shrugged a slim backpack off his shoulders, unzipped it and took from it a book which he passed to Webster.

"No better book about rediscovering your mojo."

It was a copy of *The Fight* by Norman Mailer, an old paperback. From the front cover Muhammad Ali stared out, bare-chested, his face full of mischief and defiance, his hand just curling into a fist; on the back a short account of what he was about to face in the ring: "Foreman's genius employed silence, serenity and cunning. He had never been defeated."

"Thank you."

Hammer took his water and nodded. "Read it. There was no way Ali was meant to win that fight. He was a mess."

Webster looked at the energy in Ali's eyes, the certainty that lived there, and found it hard to imagine he had ever felt quite this defeated. "I will. But at least he knew who he was fighting."

Hammer took a long drink of water. "Tell me exactly what you know about him."

"Let's go in the garden."

The sun was high in the sky and the garden table in full sun. Hammer sat down, stretched his legs out and held his face to the light, his eyes shut, and listened to Webster repeat much of what he had said on the phone the night before: the history of the debt, the extent of it, the very little that Qazai seemed to know about Rad.

"And Kamila?"

"She's found a bit. Actually she's done well. Rad lost them on the way back from the airport but she got the car. A rental, from a local firm. Paid for with an Amex in the name of Mohamed Ganem, who also provided a Dubai driving license. The same Amex was used to pay for two rooms at the Novotel in Marrakech. She has the names of the four men who stayed there. Or at least the names they were using."

"Passports?"

"Not yet."

"So is he Rad or Chiba or Ganem?"

"All of them. None of them. Rad is the name he gave Qazai. Ganem's an operational name, I'm guessing. Chiba's a red herring. Christ knows who he is." He paused. "I've spent the past hour searching every database we have. There's a company in Dubai registered to Mohamed Ganem, but it's not an uncommon name. Otherwise nothing. And then . . ."

"What?" said Hammer.

Webster hesitated. "Dean's working on it."

"Of course."

"You don't mind?"

"No. It's the lesser evil. It wasn't before." He shrugged. "You've given him the Amex? Checked the flights to London?"

Webster nodded.

"Who's checking the hotels?"

"Dieter."

"On a Sunday? Very loyal."

Hammer got up to get more water. He went inside, ran the tap for a few seconds and came back drinking from the long glass. "Does Fletcher know anything?"

"No, but he says his friends might."

"Ah," said Hammer. "His friends."

"They're real. I was going to meet one of them before . . . before Marrakech came up."

"Oh, they're real. It's just that what they know and what they want to tell us are two different things." He thought for a moment. "Any word on Senechal?"

Webster shook his head. "Nothing. No one of that name is in any hospital in Marrakech."

"That's not nothing."

"Maybe."

"What about the morgues?"

"Driss seems to think that no foreigners have been taken in since Friday."

"I don't understand you sometimes. That's good news."

"Perhaps. I'd prefer just to know. Every time I close my eyes I see his face."

Webster put his hands behind his head and stretched, forgetting for a moment the pain in his side. "So. What do we do?"

Hammer sighed. "Do you think they're here?"

"I'd be surprised if they weren't."

"OK. If we find them? We could call the police and tell them they have terrorists on their doorstep."

"Is that the best you can do?"

"Perhaps they have weapons with them."

"True. Perhaps they don't."

"True."

"So then what?"

"I don't know."

"We've got a week. Less than a week."

"I know," said Hammer. "Plenty of time."

24.

ON MONDAY MORNING WEBSTER woke long past dawn to hear planes softly droning overhead. Hammer had left him with his favorite painkillers, some American concoction that he swore would work better than any feeble London drugs, and after several hours of bullying Dean Oliver to work as fast as he could he had taken them early and fallen into a deep, dense sleep that didn't want to let him go.

The first thing he was conscious of was that empty space next to him; he sensed it without opening his eyes. Somehow he sensed, too, before he remembered it, that the house was empty. Lying there now, his head fogged from the drugs, Webster felt his world unbalanced around him, all its delicate symmetry wrecked, and saw himself sliding through it, giddy and out of control.

He opened his eyes and forced himself up, stiff from the pain. A faint nausea lay at the back of his throat; his head hurt; his eyelids barely wanted to open. It occurred to him that if someone was slowly poisoning him this is how it would feel.

No swimming for four weeks, the doctor had said, but he couldn't help but think that to immerse himself in the cold green waters of the pond—still better the sea—would heal him instantly of this sluggishness, this confusion that was in some ways the hardest thing of all to bear. Even without these painkillers, he had been slow ever since his return from Marrakech, as if his mind, just as it needed to be at its sharpest, had recoiled from the impossibility of its task. If he could just be in the water, the answers might come. Must surely come.

IN THE EAST THERE was a burst of sun over the city, but the heath was under clouds that were dark and laden with rain, and a strong northerly wind was ruffling the trees that hung heavily down to the edges of the pond. The air was sharp and for the first time in weeks, as he stepped out in his trunks, Webster felt cold. There were only three swimmers, each in their own world, swimming lengths. He watched them for a moment and then, instead of diving from the platform as he usually did, lowered himself slowly into the water from the ladder, the chill pinching its way up his body, and launched himself with great delicacy into a slow, stately breaststroke. This was how his parents swam, he thought, with dry hair.

Gently he dived under the surface, letting the cold find its way into his head and his thoughts, opening his eyes and seeing nothing but the murky dark green. All the pain washed away, and emptying his mind he hung in the water for as long as he could, floating toward the surface like a corpse.

As he came up the rain started, fat drops warmer than the pond water, and he turned onto his back to watch the sea-gray sky. It was like Cornwall here. Green and gray and wet, the earth and the sea and the sky at one. If he came through this he would never go to the desert again.

BY TEN HE WAS outside the Mount Street house and had made a number of resolutions. His head was clear, and he was no longer fearful. This might not end well, but at least he could make provisions.

A man he had never seen before answered the door. He was big, dark, his hair cropped short.

"Yes."

"I'm here to see Mr. Qazai."

"Your name?"

"Webster."

The man moved aside, scanning the street before shutting the door.

"I'll let Mr. Qazai know you're here."

Webster took off his raincoat and as he looked around for somewhere to hang it Ava came out of the sitting room. She was wearing a black sweater and black jeans, and she gave him a long, searching, uncomfortable look before she said anything.

"Come to plot, have you?"

"I've come to help," he said, running a hand through his wet hair.

She held his eye for a moment and seemed about to leave when something changed her mind. She turned back to him, biting her lower lip, her hands on her hips.

"I want you to explain what's going on. He won't tell me anything. I have no idea."

Webster took a deep breath and looked down. "I can't. He has to tell you himself."

She shook her head. "No. No. That won't do." Her voice was tight. "Everything's a fucking mystery. On Saturday he calls me and says that I have to leave London for a week. Out of nowhere. He asks me where Raisa and the children are, and can I find a number for them in Croatia. Then he sent someone to bring me here, but won't say a word. Except that I'm in danger." She crossed her arms. "I'm not a bystander. I'm involved. Do you understand?"

Her eyes were pained and bloodshot, and as she waited for his response Webster could see her biting the inside of her lip, trying to keep control. Hammer was right. She should know; not because she could be useful, although God knows he would rather deal with Qazai through her, but because she was right. She was as much a part of this as he was.

Behind her came the brief rap of footsteps on stone. Ava turned, and there was Qazai. He stood for a moment, taking in the scene, imagining what had just been said.

"Ava. This is between me and Mr. Webster. Leave us, please."

Ava looked at Webster meaningfully, as if she understood what he had been thinking, silently appealing to him to air it. But he couldn't do it. He couldn't throw Qazai off his fragile course.

"He needs to tell you," he said. "I'm sorry."

Staring at him, she gave a small, contemptuous shake of her head, turned, and walked away without so much as a glance at her father. Webster watched her climb the stairs and felt painfully mute.

"Let's go to my study," said Qazai.

BOOKS LINED THE SMALL ROOM on three of its walls from floor to ceiling; the fourth was all screens, all switched off. It was gloomy: a thin light came from a single sash window that looked out onto a brick wall six feet away, and a lamp on Qazai's desk was unlit. Webster could smell the sweet smell of whisky in the air.

Qazai gestured for him to sit, and moved around behind the desk. Physically, his change was complete. There was no spring about him now, and his movements were ponderous. He was an old man.

"Have you heard anything?"

Webster frowned. "From whom?"

"From . . . from the Iranians."

"No. Why would I?"

"No reason." In the half darkness Qazai's eyes were staring. He shook his head. "You never know. I just wanted to check."

Not for the first time Webster sensed that Qazai was veering off course.

"You're going to go through with this. You know you have no choice."

Qazai looked at him, raised his eyebrows in resignation, and nodded, just once.

"I have good news for you."

"I'm not in the mood for jokes."

"It's not remotely funny. Yves called me."

Webster scratched the back of his head, harder than was necessary. He felt the strain in his neck relax a notch. "What . . . When did he call?"

"Last night."

"What did he want?"

Looking down at his hands, Qazai thrummed his fingers on the top of the desk for several seconds. Eventually he spoke.

"Money."

"True to form."

"He wants fifty million dollars. A bonus at the end of the scheme, as he put it."

"Or he tells all."

Qazai let out a long, heavy breath. "You should have killed him."

"Perhaps you should. I'm glad I didn't."

Neither man said anything for a moment.

"Can you find him?" said Qazai.

"I have better things to do. I could try to speak to him."

"This is more than an irritant. He wants the money before the deal goes through."

"Do you have it?"

"Barely."

"You'd better find it."

"I want you to stop him."

"I'll do my best. But I want something in return."

Qazai leaned forward against the desk. "What?"

"For all my help. Two things. You tell the Italians to stop whatever it is you started."

Qazai raised an eyebrow a fraction. "I don't have anything to do with your problems in Italy."

"Bullshit. You make that stop or so help me I will do everything I can to make it easy for Rad to find you and fuck you up." Qazai, with an effort, held his eye. "I mean it."

Qazai ran his tongue around his teeth. "Yves looked after that. I don't know what he did."

"Yes you do."

"Not exactly. I don't know who he spoke to."

Webster laughed. "You know, I'm not sure I can rely on Yves. I'm not sure he likes me anymore. So you're going to have to make some calls. Call your Italian lawyer, or your politician friend, or whoever you need to call, and sort it out." He paused. "Do you understand?"

Qazai understood.

"The other thing will be easy for you. Provision for my family. If I don't come through this, whenever that happens, I want money to be paid to Ikertu."

"How much?"

"A million dollars. From your estate. Ike will add the interest to my life insurance payments as they go out. I don't want my wife to know."

"It's not much."

"It's enough. Any more and she might think it was from you."

Qazai nodded, thoughtful. "If you deal with Yves, yes."

"No. Regardless. In writing."

Qazai narrowed his eyes.

"It's a million," said Webster. "Even for a broken billionaire that's nothing."

THE REST OF THAT DAY Webster spent with Oliver, who was tired and becoming tetchy. The American Express card belonging to Rad's alter ego, Mohamed Ganem, was registered in Egypt, and after a morning of frustrating calls to Cairo and easier ones to head office in New York—conducted in a highly plausible East Coast accent—Oliver had eventually established that in the last forty-eight hours it had paid Royal Air Maroc some three thousand dollars for flights, and withdrawn cash from a machine at Heathrow. So Rad was in London, and while that was no surprise it made Webster realize that the threats made to him and Qazai were not empty—not that he had ever been in any doubt—and that while the Iranians were making their plans he was failing utterly to find one of his own.

Senechal's phone, meanwhile, remained switched off, and Oliver was able to see that no calls had been made on it since his call to Qazai the previous night. The last payment on his credit card had been for a hotel in Marrakech on Saturday night and a flight to Paris the next day. His office merely said that he was in meetings. It was impossible to know where he was.

In the evening Webster ate half a pizza, drank whisky and felt like a stranger in his empty house. The thought struck him, while he was listlessly watching television, that he might never see it full again. He considered calling Elsa, but decided against it; spoke to George Black, and heard that nothing of any interest was happening around his parents' house; tried Ava and got her voicemail. Then he phoned Qazai, and told him that he should send Senechal an e-mail letting him know that the money would be paid, and that they should meet at St. Pancras Station the following afternoon to agree how it would be exchanged. Qazai bristled, and Webster explained to him with greater patience than he deserved that this may be the only way to get Senechal to break cover.

That was all he could usefully do. In the end he called his parents' phone, deciding that if Elsa answered fate had meant them to talk. His father picked up.

"Hello."

"Hi, Dad."

"Ben. Hello. How are you?" His father's voice was gentle and rich. It was like Oliver's in one respect: it made you want to confess.

"I'm fine. Fine, thank you. I was just calling to see how you all were."

"We're all well. The children are having stories."

"Everyone happy?"

"Everyone's happy." A pause. "When do you think you might be able to join us?"

"I don't know, to be honest. Saturday, maybe. Let's see."

"And everything's OK?"

"It's all fine."

"Do you want to talk about it?"

Webster closed his eyes and shook his head. He longed to talk about it but it wouldn't do any good.

"Not now. Soon, maybe."

"I understand."

Both were silent for a moment.

"Always remember," said his father, "that you're not wholly responsible for everything. Others play their part. You have a tendency to forget that."

"Some of us are more to blame than others."

"Perhaps. But only because you bear all the weight you can. That's a good thing. Not everyone does."

Webster nodded. He couldn't speak.

"It will fall together again. You'll see."

Webster didn't respond.

"Hope to see you at the weekend."

"OK. Thanks, Dad."

He put the phone down, his head full of an unsettling sense of being young and old, his father's son and his children's father, fatigued and childish at once.

WEBSTER TOOK NO PAINKILLERS that night and when Constance called hadn't slept for longer than an hour.

"Ben. Fletcher. You sound unwell."

"What time is it?"

"Nine thirty here. A little earlier where you are."

"Jesus, Fletcher."

"I thought you'd want news when I got it."

"I do. I do." Reaching over to his bedside table, he fumbled in the half-light for his glass, drank water awkwardly through the side of his mouth and slumped back. "You in Beirut?"

"No. I'm back in paradise. They gave up when they saw what a pain in the ass I was about to be."

Webster grunted.

"I know a thing or two about your new friend," said Constance.

"About Rad?"

"About Mr. Zahak Rad." He paused. "Now you're awake."

"Go on."

Constance gave a low whistle. "You picked one evil bastard to fuck with, my friend."

"Tell me."

"Well. Up until a couple of years ago he was a big cheese in VEVAK, an intelligence guy all his life. Joined when he was a teenager, as far as anyone can tell, right at the beginning. There's a story that he was in prison when the revolution happened, a political. Been trying to blow up the Shah or some shit. Anyway, seems he blossomed. Spent the eighties and nineties in Europe assassinating dissidents. Or helping to. He crops up in the file of some poor fucker who got shot eating his breakfast in Paris. He's the go-to-guy for foreign ops, basically. Doesn't spend much time in Tehran, he's in such demand, until the last five years, when it looks like he's recalled to center and given some new, nasty job doing intelligence for the Revolutionary Guards. Keeping an eye on dissidents. Suppressing uprisings. Seems he's mainly in Dubai."

Webster was sitting up in bed, his head clear.

"Do we know what he's like?"

Constance laughed. "He's a regular charmer, Ben. Family man, head of the local Rotarians, gives to charity. What the fuck do you think he's like?"

"Come on."

"Sorry. You have to understand, there's not much on him. Most of it comes from one source. And it's patchy. But he's good. Obviously. He's been doing what he does for a very long time and that Paris job is the only time his fingerprints are on anything. And he's old school. He's an Ayatollah guy rather than an Ahmadinejad guy, apparently. The new regime isn't sure about his spending all that time abroad, prey to the thousand seductions of the West. Man might lose his revolutionary fervor. I get the impression they shouldn't worry."

"That it?"

"That's your lot, my friend. And it comes at a price."

"Go on."

"My friends would like to talk to you about Darius Qazai's pot of gold."

"With pleasure. But they'd better be quick. I may not be around."

Constance scoffed. "There's no percentage in killing you. They just want you scared."

"It's working."

Zahak Rad. Webster could see him clearly, a knot of energy and malice, making his murderous, unstoppable progress across thirty years.

25.

TUESDAY PASSED; WEDNESDAY CAME. The Americans were due to land early, and in something of a posse: a chief executive, a chief financial officer, a chief legal counsel and a large pack of lawyers just behind all the chiefs. Qazai would meet with his own lawyers at ten, with his conquerors, as he undoubtedly saw them, at midday, and at eight with Webster, who had insisted that they go to Tabriz together for no other reason than he didn't trust Qazai to go through with it all.

At Mount Street Webster pulled the bell and chimes sounded somewhere in the center of the house. The door opened immediately, and there was Qazai's new security guard; Webster made to go in, but the guard narrowed the gap and stood in it, filling the space with his bulk.

"Can I help you, sir?"

Webster paused a moment before answering, looking up an inch or two into the guard's steadfast eyes. "I'm here to see Qazai. He's expecting me."

"Mr. Qazai is not at home at present, sir. I'm afraid you'll have to come back when he is."

Webster shut his eyes and gave the slightest shake of his head.

"I have a meeting with him at eight. It's eight now. He'll be back any minute." A pause. "Now let me in. Please."

"I'm not authorized to admit anyone unless Mr. Qazai is on the premises, sir. That is my brief."

"When did he go out?"

"I'm not at liberty to say, sir."

"Did he take the car? Is his driver here?"

No response. Webster stared a little longer at the man's block of a face and did his best to control his irritation.

"I want to speak to Ava. Miss Qazai." The guard didn't react. "Can you call her for me, please?"

"I'm not authorized to admit people without an appointment, I'm afraid, sir."

"Then call her," Webster said, slowly, as if to a child, "and she can come downstairs, and we can make an appointment, and then you can let me in. How's that?"

The guard looked at him squarely before answering. "Miss Qazai is not here. Sir. It looks like you're on your own." He closed the door, with irritating composure.

Webster swore under his breath, took the phone from his pocket and rang Qazai's number. After a second the voice of Qazai's secretary was in his ear, telling him that this was the voicemail of Darius Qazai and asking him to leave a message.

It was possible, of course, that the old bastard had gone for a walk. Or to his office, to prepare. But somehow it seemed more likely that he was doing something that would throw their delicate plan into confusion: he was seeing the Americans on his own to talk up the price or tell them the whole deal was off; he had finally given in to the despair that Webster had seen growing in him and was now poised on a high bridge or wading slowly into the sea, inviting his doom. He had to be found.

Webster looked at his phone, searched for Ava's number, and called it. The line rang twice and then went dead; she had canceled the call. He redialed, and found himself talking to her voicemail.

Running a hand through his hair he looked up and down the street, and did his best to think. Qazai's phone sounded as if it was off. Even if he had the means it would take far too long to trace. No, that route was closed.

But Ava might know where her father was, and if she didn't, the answer might lie in the house, which only she could open for him. Regretting even more keenly that he hadn't treated her better, he wrote her a text message.

> If your father isn't at his office by noon he will be dead by the end of the week. Help me find him and I'll explain everything. I know I should have done so before. Ben.

He hit send, watched the message go, and sat down on the bottom step of the Qazai house to wait. It was warm again, the sun just showing through thick morning haze, and the air already felt slow with unreleased heat. Webster took off his jacket and draped it across his knees. He could find out where Ava lived, if he needed to, though what good that would do he wasn't sure.

His phone bleeped, and a message flashed onto his screen.

> No need to explain. Find him yourself.

Webster stared at the words and did his best to take them in. No need to explain. She knew. Did she know? He shook his head and took in a deep, worried breath before replying.

> You may be dead too. And others more dear to you. If you know anything, you should know that. Call me.

A butcher's van passed, and on the opposite side of the street an old man, incongruously unkempt, wheeled his bicycle along the pavement, muttering to himself and occasionally ringing the bell, tinny and clear against the low hum of traffic from surrounding streets. Webster watched him make his progress. Surely she would call.

But she didn't. Not straight away. After a full two minutes, just as he was making plans to find her house and somehow force her from it, his phone rang in his hand.

"Where are you?"

"Mount Street."

Ava hung up as the old man rounded the corner out of sight.

In three minutes a small, understated Mercedes, black, with black windows, drew up in front of the house, and after a nervous moment, just long enough for Webster to begin to worry that she had changed her mind and was about to drive away again, Ava got out. She walked briskly toward him, with such purpose that for a moment Webster thought she was going to hit him; and he wished, when she stopped in front of him and started speaking, that she had.

"You don't need to explain. I found out." She was wearing no makeup and her face was drawn, the skin around her eyes thin and bruised, the eyes themselves bloodshot and black and raging, as if all the life in her was concentrated there.

Webster didn't know where to start. "I'm sorry." He meant it, but it sounded redundant. "Did he tell you?" It began to dawn on him that perhaps Qazai had disappeared to escape the fury of his daughter.

She shook her head, her arms tightly crossed. "No. I found out. I went to Paris." Each word was hard and distinct. Webster looked blank. "To see my friend. He told me what he couldn't bring himself to tell me before. What you thought you should keep to yourself."

"I'm sorry."

"Why? Because my father's a traitor? Or because you lied to me?" There were tears in her eyes.

"I never lied to you."

"You never told me the truth."

He nodded. He could tell her that it had been necessary, and that would have been true, but she was still right.

"Does he know?"

Ava drew the back of her hand across her eyes, sniffed, collected herself. "When I think of all the good people his money has had killed. All the guns his money has bought. He disgusts me." She looked up at Webster. "He knows. He was still up when I got back. I told him . . . I told him I was leaving. I told him he wasn't my father. That he never had a daughter."

"Do you know where he is?"

"I don't care where he is. I won't ever care where he is. He tried to get me to stay. Told me if I did anything stupid, that Raisa, and . . ." She trailed off.

"That's all true," said Webster.

She shook her head. "It's bullshit. He's lying, all the time, to everyone. He's sick with it."

"Not now. If he doesn't pay them back, in four days, you and your family are at risk. Mine, too."

Ava looked away down the street, watched a car drive too fast toward and past them.

"They're dangerous," he said. "I think they killed Mehr."

"So did they . . ." The words caught in her throat. She turned and looked at him, her eyes courageous and fearful at once. "What happened in Dubai?"

He hesitated. He knew what had happened in Dubai. "I don't know. Really."

"Did they kill Timur?"

With effort, he held her eye. "We don't know."

"Oh God," she said, clutching herself, shaking her head, her hands scratching at her upper arms. "Oh God. Tell me that wasn't because of my father. Tell me. I couldn't . . ."

Webster moved toward her and put his hand on her shoulder, felt her body gently rocking.

"We might never know. Ava. Look at me. Look at me. This is real. If your father doesn't pay back what he owes something bad will happen. They will make it happen. It's their job. It doesn't matter where we go, how many guards we have, they'll keep coming. Ava, look at me. I know that you don't want to save him. I don't either. But if we don't . . ." He couldn't finish the thought. "I have to find out where he is."

Her eyes, endlessly sad now, held his for a moment, and so intense was the pain there that he felt sure he had lost her, that all she could hear was her grief. But then she spoke, sniffing and wiping her eyes.

"Your family?"

"Yes, my family. And yours."

She nodded, as if considering something for the first time.

"Your children?"

"My children, yes. A girl and a boy."

"Where are they?"

"Somewhere safe. Fairly safe."

She turned away from him and for perhaps a full minute stood staring down the street, her head gently shaking.

"What do you need?" she said at last.

"I need to get into the house. And I may need you to go a meeting."

Blankly, she nodded, and he guided her up the steps.

"LEAVE US," Ava said to the guard once they were inside. He hesitated for a moment, clearly wondering whether Webster posed a threat. "It's all right," she said. And then with irritation as he continued to stand there, conspicuously upright and in protective mode, "Go. Please. I'll call you if I need you." Webster watched him leave without satisfaction.

"He's good," he said, once he had disappeared down the corridor that led out of the hall at the back of the house.

"No doubt. I just don't want him in my world." She looked at Webster meaningfully.

"I won't be around for long."

"You're here now. Do what you need to do."

"I need to ask you some things."

A pause. "When do I get to ask you something?" He held her eye, and she sighed. "Go on."

"What did you say to him?"

"Everything. Not enough."

"What did he say?"

"It's not important what he said."

"It's all important. What did he say?"

"I don't know . . . Excuses? Justifications? I couldn't stand to look at him."

"He didn't mention any plans? Any meetings?"

"Nothing. Just that he had to pay the money back and was selling everything. I think he wanted my sympathy for that." She sounded more astonished than disgusted.

Webster nodded and walked across the hall toward Qazai's study, turning as he reached it at the sound of Ava's voice.

"He keeps it locked."

Webster tried the handle.

"Who has a key?"

"He does."

"What about the housekeeper?"

"Not to this room. He keeps it with him. We were never allowed in here. He used to tell us when we were children that everything in his study was electrified."

Webster stood back a pace, set himself and kicked at the door just below the handle, startling the muted house with a shock of noise. He balanced himself, and kicked again, harder, finding satisfaction in the sudden burst of energy. At the third kick, the wood around the lock began to splinter and shear; at the fourth it gave way, and the door swung powerlessly open. Ava, her face empty, didn't say a word throughout. As they went in, the security guard came bounding into the hall with heavy steps, his face professionally alert.

"I'm still fine," said Ava, "please go," and left him looking thrown.

There were papers on the desk, neatly arranged in piles: sale documents, hard copies of Tabriz e-mails, general correspondence. Nothing of interest. A cordless phone stood on its own small table to the right of Qazai's chair: Webster picked it up and made a note of the last numbers dialed, all of them UK, the most recent a cell phone. He called Oliver.

"I've got a number for you. It's urgent."

"Morning, Ben. How are you?"

"I mean it, Dean. This is important."

"Ben, where do I put it? Is it more important than all the other important things you'd like me to do?"

"Dean. I'm sorry. But I need it right now. Who it belongs to. That's all. Take you five minutes."

"Ten." Dean's voice was resigned.

"Thank you. Call me."

"Does anyone like you at the moment?" said Ava.

Webster looked up and managed a grim smile. "My father," he said, and immediately regretted his lack of tact. "Sorry." Ava just looked away.

The desk was delicate and had two shallow drawers. He tried one, then the other, found both locked, and after inspecting the keyhole for a moment reached for a brass letter opener that lay beside some unopened letters and slid it into the thin gap at the top of the drawer, near the lock.

Ava was frowning at him. "What are you doing?"

"I'm going to see how strong this lock is," said Webster, standing up and levering the drawer away from the desk, at first with constant force and then jerking it as hard as he could, crouching down and gripping the letter opener in his fist.

"Don't they teach you how to do this sort of thing?" said Ava, as the wood holding the bolt of the lock gave way with a snap. Inside were two cardboard folders, each full of Tabriz correspondence that meant nothing. Webster tried the next and it gave way more easily. Lying on top of a neat jumble of pens and stationery was a large envelope of coarse brown paper.

There was no address, no stamp—only the name "D. Qazai" printed in thick black marker pen on the front. He lifted the flap, which had been sealed and already opened, and from inside drew two photographs the size of holiday snaps. At first they appeared to be in black and white, but there was some color in the stark chiaroscuro of the flash-lit scene, some dusky red about the temple, matted in the hair, running down the cheek; a flick of brighter red on the plain bright white of the shirt. It was Senechal, lying curled up on his side like a child, clearly dead.

Webster closed his eyes. A burst of fear ran through him. The image matched so perfectly his memory of that same body prone in the desert that he could only believe that he had killed the man after all, and that soon afterward someone had photographed the evidence. He forced himself to look again. The blood was scarlet, fresh, still liquid, and at its source so red it was nearly black; the body was lying on tarmac, not sand, and in the top right-hand corner of the picture there was something like a car tire. He took the next photograph. Senechal stared at the camera in close-up, one eye open, the other a dark hole in his face where he had been shot.

Acid rose in Webster's throat; he fought the urge to be sick. One fear took the place of the other, and as he closed his eyes he saw Rad standing over the body, getting down on his haunches and holding the camera close to the ground so that he could capture the horror whole, like a butcher saving the blood.

"What is it?"

"It's nothing," said Webster, putting the photographs back inside the envelope and reacting too slowly as it was snatched away from him. He watched Ava's face and saw it pinch with disgust, then dread.

"What . . . was this them?"

Webster nodded.

"Why?"

"At a guess?" said Webster, taking the pictures from her and putting them back in the drawer. "Because he wanted some of their money. He was blackmailing your father."

"How did they know?"

"Perhaps he told them."

Ava looked at him, closed her eyes and shuddered.

"Or they were eavesdropping . . ." Webster broke off as his phone rang; it was Oliver. He listened for a moment. "OK. When was it registered?" He listened some more. "Thanks. I'll see you later." He hung up and looked at Ava. "The last number he dialed from this phone was a pay-as-you-go cell phone. It was registered on Sunday to a name and address that don't exist. In London."

She looked at him, not understanding.

"They're here. And he's still talking to them."

Both were silent for a while. Ava leaned back against a bookcase and stared through the window at the brick wall opposite, her expression lost.

"Should we call the police?"

"With what?" said Webster. "It's a picture of a dead man. We don't know where it happened. Where the body is."

"We need to tell someone."

Webster shook his head. "No. This can't come out before the money has been transferred." He paused, watching her reaction. "He doesn't have a family. He doesn't have friends."

"How do you know?"

"I know."

For a minute neither said anything.

"What if my father doesn't show up?" she said at last.

"I'll find him. And you stall."

26.

I CAN'T SIT IN THERE," said Ava. "There are too many of them."

She stepped back, and Webster looked around the door. At the grand black table, arranged along one side with their backs to the mismatched towers of the City standing stark in the midday sun, sat five men, all in suits, each with a notepad set purposefully in front of him. Webster wondered whether they had sat on that side to keep their faces in shadow or to allow their visitors to enjoy the view.

"You're right," he said. "That's far too many lawyers. Come on."

He led the way down a wood-lined corridor and through a glass door into the lobby of Tabriz, marbled and bright.

"Do you want some water?"

Ava shook her head and sat down in one of the armchairs. She had changed, into a suit, put on makeup, and was on the surface composed, but in her eyes—unfocused, intense but unseeing—lay signs of the discord within. Even now she appeared not to hear Webster, and he had to ask her again before she looked up at him, smiled a quick, tight smile and said no, thank you, she was fine.

Webster sat on the edge of the chair opposite and started thrumming his fingers on his thigh, watching the room and waiting for one of the elevators to open and produce the Americans. Tabriz staff wandered through alone or in pairs, studying documents or in hushed conversation; a motor-cycle courier arrived, his helmet under his arm, and gave an envelope to one of the receptionists, who talked in low voices about things that Webster just failed to catch. Ava glanced down at his hand and he stopped tapping, his fingers continuing to fidget in his clasped hands.

"I don't see what you're nervous about," she said, shifting around in her chair at the sound of lift doors sliding open.

"I'm not nervous. I'm tense."

"No word?"

Webster reached inside his jacket pocket and pulled out his Black-Berry, even though there would be nothing new there. "No word," he said, pressing the buttons anyway, checking his e-mails, his texts, his missed calls. Yuri in Antwerp had told him that he would try to locate the phone, but that it would probably take a few hours, and had bristled a little when Webster had told him that it seemed a little pointless to offer a service that could tell you with reasonable accuracy where someone had been a while ago but not where they were right now. No one at Tabriz knew where Qazai was, and nor did the lawyers. His passport was missing, as far as they could tell, but he didn't appear to have booked any flights or, for that matter, bought anything at all. The chauffeur was still in Mount Street, and his employer's phone was still very much switched off.

"I'm nervous," said Ava.

"Don't be. You'll be fine."

"What if they know I'm lying?"

"You're not lying. Your father wasn't feeling himself this morning. He's having a brief rest and will be here shortly. That's all true."

Ava raised her eyebrows and let them fall.

"Listen," said Webster. "They're here to buy something they really want to buy at a price they probably can't believe. They're as keen as we are. A delay won't matter to them. It matters to us, but not to them. They'll talk to the lawyers, the lawyers will talk among themselves . . . it'll be fine."

"If it matters so little why can't those men in there do it? Tell them he's not here."

"Your father's sent you as a mark of respect. It's the sort of thing he'd do."

Ava stroked the back of her hand, smoothing it out, staring at her skin as it tightened and released.

"What if he stays away?"

"Then we get you somewhere safe. I've made arrangements."

"Forever?"

Webster gave her his frankest look and tried to sound confident. "I'm working on that."

Out of the corner of his eye Webster saw the nearest set of elevator doors part and heard the distinctive sound of genial professional conversation, buoyant small talk made by people who know each other and move in the same world. He glanced at Ava, and shifted in his seat. One voice was louder than the rest, richer, full of bonhomie, and as the huddle of suited men stepped out its owner moved into view, ushering his guests into his world as if he had never left it.

Webster watched Qazai cross the lobby, a head taller than the rest, crisp in a silver-gray suit, his white beard neatly trimmed, and doubted that anyone else would see the strain that showed in his tired eyes. As he passed, talking to the Americans, he glanced once at Ava and appeared thrown for the shortest moment, before guiding the group through the glass door toward their meeting.

Ava and Webster looked at each other without saying anything, like people who cannot trust what they have just seen.

EVERY HOUR THAT PASSED made the outcome more certain, Webster calculated, but that was no reason to relax, just as Qazai's apparent composure was no guarantee that when the moment arrived he would take his pen from his pocket, uncap it, look around one last time at the business he had created and put that grand, sweeping signature on the necessary line. People would do strange things before parting with what they loved, and Webster was beginning to understand, finally, that while Qazai's professional genius might lie in a kind of relentless reasoning about the workings of the world, in his life he applied no such logic. He was as bold as he was spineless; as loving of his children as he had been neglectful of their upbringing; as principled in speaking out against the government in Tehran as he was dissolute in sustaining it. But behind all these contradictions, Webster had come to suspect, was a simple fear: that Darius Qazai was not, after all, a great man, but a simple coward whose craven fealty to money he had inherited whole from his father and had failed to subdue. No one understood better than he how money worked, and still it controlled him.

Who could know, then, how this fear was operating on him today? In that room he had bought companies, seduced investors, fired staff, rebuked traders, entertained statesmen. Tabriz was his court, and now he was being asked, in the stateroom no less, to sign it over as he might one of the thousands of assets he had bought and sold in the previous thirty years.

As Webster glanced up at Ava, he saw her attention switch to something happening behind him, and twisting around he saw through a glass screen the Americans walking their way, jackets draped over shoulders, ties loosened, fastening the catches on their briefcases. They looked, as far as one could tell, like people who had achieved something. The most senior of Qazai's lawyers was seeing them out, and after a minute of goodbyes they were in an elevator and gone.

"Where's my father?" Ava stopped the lawyer as he passed.

"I'm sorry?"

"Never mind," she said, and asking the receptionist to open it marched through the glass door. Webster followed, and the lawyer followed him.

Empty glasses, empty cups, half-eaten plates of biscuits and half-a-dozen chrome coffee pots covered the table, where Qazai sat, his back to the window, watching his lawyers tidy up their papers and appearing not to hear their words of congratulation. Behind him the sun was still high in the sky.

"Leave us, please," said Ava as she walked in.

To a man, the lawyers stopped what they were doing and stared at her; none offered a reply.

"I need to speak to my father." There was no doubting her seriousness. "All of you. Go."

Behind her the senior lawyer nodded at his colleagues, who hurried themselves and left, glancing at Ava as she moved swiftly past them toward her father, giving Webster and his black eye a longer look. The door shut behind them.

Qazai, who had stood up as the lawyers left, was now looking out at the city, contemplating his old domain.

"What the fuck did you do?" Ava was by him now, and as he turned to her she pushed him, hard, so that he lost his balance and stepped back. "What the fuck did you do?"

He looked at her in surprise and incomprehension. "I sold it. The company. For you. For us."

Ava shook her head, her face cold and set. "Not that. You're incredible. Not that." Her eyes were locked on his. "I know now. I know. You didn't lose a son. You sacrificed him." Qazai did his best to meet her stare, but could not. "You sacrificed him for this. This shining fraud."

Qazai rested his head on his hand and shut his eyes. He didn't see Ava turn and go, and when he looked up, she was halfway across the room.

"Ava. Ava, I didn't know. Come back."

"Never," said Ava, her back to him still, and left.

Qazai pulled a chair toward him and slumped onto it, shaking his head in tiny movements back and forth.

"I've lost her, too," he said at last, addressing no one.

Webster watched him, feeling contempt for his self-absorption and the first traces of pity.

"What happened to Senechal?"

Qazai looked up, his face blank.

"What?"

"Yves. Your faithful retainer. We found the photographs. What happened?"

"I don't know." Webster looked hard at him. "I don't know how it happened."

"Did you tell them? About the blackmail?"

"Who? No. No, of course not." Qazai seemed honestly surprised. "You think I would do that?"

"Where did you go?"

"When?"

Webster's patience was gone. "Stop fucking about. Please. Just tell me where you went this morning."

Qazai adjusted his tie, out of kilter since Ava pushed him. "I had a meeting."

"With Rad?"

There was a long pause before he replied.

"With Rad."

"Why?"

"Everyone has his price."

"I didn't." Webster stared hard at Qazai. "You mean to say that you were going to pay off Rad? To try to avoid this? What, you thought the rest of them would just forget their billions and let you swan around into your old age?" He paused. "Was it a long meeting?"

"That's not how it was. I offered him a hundred million dollars to leave us alone after the money was paid back. You and me."

Webster hadn't been expecting that.

"I wasn't sure I believed him," said Qazai. "That it was just bluff. I thought, once they had their money, that would be that. Why draw attention to themselves by killing me? And then . . . This morning, I came down, and that envelope was on the mat. I knew it was from them. It was early. Before six. And when I opened it . . . What it said to me was, this is what we do to people when they're no longer useful to us. This is a spent asset." His voice became a degree louder. "And in two days, when the money goes through, I will be spent." He looked up to Webster. "And so will you."

Webster hadn't forgotten. He felt a lightness at the base of his throat. "What did Rad say?"

"He laughed, and said he would rather be poor and alive."

And in that moment Webster knew what he had to do.

27.

THERE WAS VERY LITTLE POINT, as Hammer had explained, in having such a simple, treacherous little plan if no one knew you had made it.

By Friday everything had been done. A Mauritian company, suitably exotic, had been taken from Qazai's emergency store and injected with twenty million dollars, a figure large enough to be convincing but still within Qazai's reduced means.

After that, there had been two obstacles: finding Rad's signature, and securing the services of a lawyer who wouldn't mind notarizing false documents. Hammer had argued with Webster about the need for the first. If—and this was the great beauty of the idea—the set-up needed only to be plausible, not perfect, surely it didn't matter whether the signature was accurate or not? The point wasn't whether the whole fiction would stand up to real investigation, but whether Rad believed it would be investigated at all; and he would assume, as they themselves had, that internal investigations carried out by his superiors in Tehran were unlikely to be thorough and stood no chance of being fair. Justice was vicious in Iran. Rad had administered it for thirty years, and he more than anyone knew how it worked.

For Webster, though, this was flirting with abstractions. The more real the fiction, the less likely Rad was to see opportunities to discredit it. He wanted those documents to bear the signature of Mohamed Ganem, and for Rad to know when he saw it that he was well caught.

The trouble was that Ganem's signature wasn't easy to find. Kamila had been back to the hotel where the Iranians had stayed and despite bribing every desk clerk and chambermaid in view had found no credit card slips, no room service bills, nothing. An imprint of the American Express card they had used to pay was in the file, but that was all, and somehow each of the three had managed to check in without having a copy of their passport taken. She had been to the car rental firm as well, but no written contract existed.

So Webster turned to Oliver. Bills for the Amex card went to an address in Dubai: an apartment in a complex built two years before and rented on a short-term lease by a local company, Abbas Real Estate. The incorporation papers for this company were missing, and the letting agency refused, much to Oliver's irritation, to answer its phone. Much as Webster might harry him, there was little more he could do.

Meanwhile, a much larger amount, from the sale of Tabriz, was making its way east across the world: from the Americans, through Qazai's account and on, through an intermediary or two, to a bank in Indonesia, all according to Rad's instructions. It would reach Indonesia on Friday, all being well, and at that point Qazai's contract with his masters would be void, and a new kind of contract would take its place.

The lawyer proved easy, in the end. A Mr. Holmes, partner at a firm in Mayfair that had once benefited from some penetrating and effective personal advice from Hammer, was happy to oblige, having received reassurances that the chances of his honesty ever being called in to question were extremely remote. Hammer scheduled a meeting for Thursday afternoon to sign all the papers, and halfway through the day the acuteness of the deadline spurred Webster to the breakthrough he needed. Five calls to hotels in Caracas later, Hammer, whose Spanish was still good, had been faxed copies of a passport for one Mohamed Ganem, who had stayed there in November—dictatorships, as Hammer had observed, being sticklers for documentation. There was Rad's face, just discernible, looking almost vulnerable for the first time.

Mr. Holmes had kept his word, and by four o'clock on Thursday Webster and Hammer had left his office with a set of dependable documents, utterly false and wholly genuine at the same time, showing that Mohamed Ganem, of Dubai, had just become the owner of Burnett Holdings Ltd., which, if one happened to check, was currently holding twenty million dollars in an account in Singapore.

Now all they needed to do was tell Rad what they had done, and what they proposed to do if he started having murderous thoughts. The trouble was, he wasn't answering his phone; the number he had given Qazai, which had worked just three days earlier, was now dead. He had no intention of communicating, because his job no longer required it. Webster could think of no way to contact him, but Hammer, contrary as ever, had told him not to worry: if you couldn't tell someone to come to you, you merely had to entice them.

THAT NIGHT, PAST NINE, having laid the last pieces of his plan, Webster called his parents' house, and after a short talk with his mother asked to speak to Elsa. He heard footsteps fading down the long corridor that led to the sitting room, and during the silence that followed pictured the house he knew so well: the old phone sitting on the counter in the kitchen with its cord hanging down from the wall; the children's bedroom above, just dark, both windows open behind the striped curtains, and Daniel and Nancy asleep there under thick striped duvets; the living room where Elsa would be sitting with his father, watching television or reading the papers, a warm light reflecting off the deep red walls. He imagined her getting up, and wondered whether she shared that strange mix of hope and fear that he felt when they had these distant conversations.

He heard her footsteps, and then her voice, flat. "Hi."

"Hi." He paused, not knowing where to start. "You OK?"

"I'm fine."

"The children?"

"Fine. Asleep." He could see her clearly. She would be standing with the phone in her left hand, looking down, with her right hand clasping the back of her neck. He could see her lips slightly pursed, holding in the words.

"What have they been up to?"

Elsa was silent for a moment, and he knew he had asked the wrong thing. This wasn't a normal conversation. "This and that. What we always do."

Through the scratched glass of the phone box he looked around him. The sun had just gone down behind the black trees of the park, and the sky was a sprawling pink. It would be beautiful again tomorrow. "I miss you," he said.

"I imagine you do."

He sighed, moving the receiver from his mouth so that she wouldn't hear him. How he wanted her to thaw. He would have given Rad's phantom payoff ten times over to know that he would one day get his family back. But Elsa wasn't the sort to give reassurance, and he hadn't done anything to deserve it. And what he was about to say wouldn't change that.

"Tomorrow . . ." He hesitated. Closed his eyes tight and opened them. "Tomorrow, I need you to move. Just for two days . . ."

"What do you mean, move?"

"Some friends of mine are going to come . . ."

"What the fuck do you mean? What have you done?"

"Nothing. It's just . . . For a day or two things are going to be difficult. Then they won't be. For two days, I need you to go somewhere else."

Silence. He could see her shaking her head. "Christ. Christ, Ben. How can we not be safe here? I thought we weren't safe in our own home. Because of you. I didn't realize we were on the fucking run."

"You're not . . ."

"Wait. I'm talking. Do you mean to say that there are people who might come here and hurt us? Hurt our children? Is that it?" His silence told her that it was. "What the fuck have you done? To put them in danger. What the . . ." Her voice trailed off in anger and sorrow.

Webster rested his elbow on the phone and cradled his forehead in his free hand, scratching at his scalp so hard that he could feel the nails digging in. He had nothing to say. Just instructions to give.

"Listen to me," he said at last. "Wait. Listen. I have fucked up. I know that. You know I know. But right now, I am making it better. I've dealt with the Italian thing. That's over. And I'm making it so that in three days' time, we won't have to worry about anything. At all. Do you understand? But in the meantime I need you to be somewhere completely safe. Not probably safe. Completely safe. After that, there will be no risk to any of us. And definitely not to you."

"What does that mean?"

"Just that."

"Sorry—are you planning some heroic gesture to save us all? Because I'm already wondering how to explain to the children that their father's work is more important than they are. I don't think I'm ready to tell them that he sacrificed himself in the line of duty, or whatever it is that drives you on."

"I'm going to be fine. I'll be fine."

Elsa paused, challenging him to say more. "You're not going to tell me what you're doing?"

"No. I'm not. I can't."

"Right. OK. Obviously we can't be trusted. So you know what? I don't want to be part of your plan. We're not going anywhere. If it makes you feel better, send in the troops. Surround the fucking house."

The line went dead in Webster's ear. Outside the phone booth Kensal Rise was still and quiet: no cars, no people in sight. On the other side of the little park Webster could see his house, a dark gap in the middle of its terrace, the windows either side shining warmly in the twilight. He took another handful of coins from his pocket and slotted them deliberately into the phone, waiting for each to drop, watching his credit rack up, his head full of noise. He closed his eyes and collected himself; reached into his jacket and pulled out a pack of Camel. Fletcher first. Then George.

The phone rang six or seven times while he lit a cigarette, a long lazy tone, and then rang out. He dialed again, and on the fourth ring Constance's voice, low and irritable, came on the line.

"Bit fucking late for a personal call."

"I did say."

"Yes, yes. You said. You said a lot. Although not why it couldn't wait till morning."

Webster blew out a lungful of smoke and opened the door of the phone box to let it out into the dusk. "Sorry. Thanks for the e-mails. That should do it."

"I still think you're crazy." He paused. "How can you be sure they'll see them?"

"I forwarded them to Qazai."

"Oh good. So now the traitor of Tehran has my name as well."

"Your name won't be on them. You're just my friend. Your friends are your friends, who have agreed to debrief me and Qazai in Dubai and see about some sort of protection."

Constance grunted. "I wish I had your confidence."

"It'll be fine. All they're going to see is e-mails from me to a Google account that if they check originated in Dubai. There's no trace to you."

Constance gave another grunt and Webster heard the click of his lighter. "I am too fucking old"—he drew on his cigarette—"to be fucking about in Internet cafes. Do you know how many bearded sixty-year-olds there are in those places? You call that tradecraft?"

"Fletcher, Christ. Since when were you so timid?"

There was silence on the line. After a full five seconds Constance spoke. "How did you dream up this master plan, anyway? Was it Ike?"

"For once, no. Qazai gave me the idea, if you can believe that. In Marrakech. He showed me you can bribe a man against his will."

"Is that what he calls it?" He paused. "If you say so. OK, Captain Marvel. What do you need me to do?"

"Find a good spot to pick me up."

"Jesus, Ben. I don't need a whole day to pick a fucking spot." He paused to let his pique register. "We could use a parking lot. Where are you staying?"

"I don't know that we are. There are rooms booked at the Burj."

"He fucking loves it there, doesn't he?"

"He seems to think it's safe."

"Oh it's a regular fortress. He just feels safe because the place is made of money."

"No doubt."

"Let's do it there. That'll work. They'll never come over the bridge. You drop your bags, then our favorite money-launderer leaves and I'll be there to take you the back way to our little rendezvous. At that distance they'll never see who's getting in and out of cars."

"That," said Webster, "is quite neat."

"Thank you. What time?"

"Be there by six forty-five."

"In the morning?"

"In the evening."

"Jesus. Why so late?"

"I need to give Rad time to get there. I don't want him sending a stooge."

Fletcher sighed, and Webster heard him drawing deeply on his cigarette.

"What if they haven't been watching Qazai's mail?" he said at last.

"Then it's a long trip for nothing."

BEFORE THE LONG TRIP, there was a long day's wait. Webster sent his e-mail to Qazai a little after eight on Friday morning, and at much the same time the next day the two men climbed the steps to the Bombardier, glaringly white in the full sunshine of the morning, and set off for Dubai. In between, Qazai stayed in Mount Street, with double the guard, and Webster took an overnight bag to Hammer's house, watching his back from time to time along the way.

Hammer was sure that there was enough in the message to have Rad leaving on the next plane—forwarding the brief correspondence with Constance, it had named the time and place of the proposed meeting in Dubai and, to make sure he took care of it personally, had mentioned Rad by name—but even he could see that for once caution was prudent. "If you're going to Dubai there's no way he'll try anything in London," he had said as he and Webster had drawn up the plan in the first place, "because the British have an irritating habit of investigating murders. Our friends in the Gulf are not similarly encumbered. But he is one unpredictable fucker and you'd better keep out of the way until we're sure." For the same reason

Ava, who wasn't speaking to her father and only reluctantly took a call from Webster, was eventually persuaded to have two guards outside her apartment, and a small army of former SAS men had been dispatched the previous night to Cornwall. Webster could picture them stationed at the beginning of the only lane that led to the house, with perhaps a man or two on the path from the woods and another, if they were being thorough, on the jetty by the sea. His mother would be making them tea, and Elsa would be doing her best to pretend they weren't there.

For much of the journey neither Webster nor Qazai spoke. Quite simply, Webster thought, each had had enough of the other, and was waiting for the moment when they could finally separate. Each reminded the other of the faults in himself that he least wanted to contemplate: each depended on the other for some sort of redemption. No, redemption was not being offered. Seen in the best possible light, they were trying to ensure the safety of their families; in the worst, they were indulging in a grubby piece of blackmail to save their own lives.

Sitting in his leather seat, watching the clouds and occasionally reading a paragraph of Norman Mailer, Webster studied his client, studied himself and found it difficult to conclude that either life was worth saving. Qazai was vain, slippery, callously self-assured; a man who had no idea where his center was, and who had filled that hole with money; a bully, a sham and ultimately a coward. Webster liked to think he was none of these things, but wondered now whether the qualities they shared were as repugnant: a weakness in the face of temptation, a distorted notion of responsibility, an easy way of manipulating people when the cause seemed sufficiently important—or when it suited them. Neither was as distant as the other liked to believe. They had become a pair.

PAST THE BLACK SEA the cloud that had covered most of Europe cleared and below them desert stretched ahead, a haze of heat blurring the horizon. For an hour all he saw was sand, sometimes criss-crossed with roads, and every now and then a city like a smudge in the distance. The sun had reached its peak and was beginning to hang lower in the sky as they approached the

Persian Gulf, abruptly hard and black. Qazai, who had read a *Financial Times* and a *Wall Street Journal* with great concentration, and was now scribbling in a notebook on his knee (which Webster took to be a sign of undue confidence in their mission), happened to glance up to check on their progress, but instead of going back to his work as he had before, continued to stare out of the window, his expression suddenly rueful and detached. Webster watched him, guessing at the reason for this sudden change and wondering, not for the first time, whether it was sentimentality, or performance, or some real sense of his betrayal.

"That's Iran," said Qazai, without looking at Webster.

"I know."

Qazai said nothing for a full minute, his face close to the glass.

"I haven't served my country well."

Webster didn't reply.

28.

B Y THE TIME THEY TOUCHED DOWN the sun was beginning to set behind the tallest of Dubai's mirrored towers, glinting like gold in the yellow light, and the desert around the airport was turning a deep, dead ochre. As they stood by the door waiting for steps to be wheeled to the plane Qazai gave Webster a long, meaningful look, and then nodded, as if to say that after all this time, at the end of it all, he finally considered him to be a worthy cohort.

They breezed through the terminal—open only to private flights, and so obliging that even Webster's spare passport, reserved for occasional trips to Israel, caused no delay—and found in a line of shiny cars outside a discreet black Mercedes that Webster had last seen parked at Timur's house. While Qazai greeted the driver, Webster took off his jacket, draped it over his shoulder, where it hung heavy in the heat, scanned the road and wondered whether Rad was there to greet them.

Almost certainly not. He had one chance to stop the meeting taking place, and he had to kill two people to make sure. If he chose to intercept them on their way from the airport, he had all manner of unknowns to consider: their route, whether they would travel in one car or two, whether they would stop along the way, whether he would ever have the perfect opportunity to act. Given enough men he might follow them from the airport, just to make sure they went where they were meant to go, but otherwise he would surely do what he was being encouraged to do, which was ambush them at the meeting place, specially chosen to tempt a practiced assassin. They were returning to the restaurant where Constance had taken Webster, which was perfect for Rad's purposes: a quiet, ill-lit road ran past it, and a gunman in a parked car or on one of the low roofs would have all the time in the world to take his shot. It would be dark, and it would be more or less deserted. Webster was certain that Rad had taken one look at it and known exactly what he was going to do.

Among the sports cars and the Bentleys he saw no obvious tail, and as Qazai's driver pulled away he carefully checked the road behind them through the black glass. At first he could see nothing, but as they turned onto the main road that linked the terminals he saw a dark-gray Audi move out from the queue of cars and head in their direction.

"Anything?" said Qazai, twisting around in the seat next to him.

"Possibly. It doesn't matter. We know what to do."

Qazai was trying to look calm but his forehead was spotted with sweat, and more than once since getting in the car he had scratched absentmindedly at his beard.

"Do you think it's him?"

"I don't know. If I was him I'd want to be there waiting for us." He shook his head.

"Why don't we just lose him?"

Webster pinched his eyes closed. They had been through this. "Because whoever that is, if it's anybody, we want them to think we don't know they're there."

It took them half an hour to reach the Burj, and for all that time, with apparent skill, the gray Audi stayed six or seven cars behind. Webster couldn't be sure, but nevertheless he knew, and he felt his heart quicken and his breathing grow shallow in his chest. All week he had been so taken up with planning and arranging that he hadn't stopped to imagine—hadn't dared imagine—how it might actually feel to be here, like this, driving slowly into a trap of his own making. He sat as calmly as he could, one hand on the documents beside him.

The bridge to the hotel was four hundred meters long; he had measured it from the satellite picture. At the end of its sweeping curve the great steel sail—still pristinely white, still unlikely—rose up into the blue-black sky. As they waited for the guard on the gate to talk to their driver, Webster watched the tourists coming and going in the faded sunshine. Through the open window came the sound of chatter and fleeting screams from the water park that overlooked the sea.

The guard nodded, the gate rose, the steel barrier sunk down into the tarmac and they moved off, driving over the water at a stately pace. Webster checked behind them. While they had been stationary the Audi had been out of sight, but halfway across the bridge he looked back to see it round a corner from the main road and draw into a parking lot opposite the guard's hut.

"Is it there?" said Qazai.

Webster nodded, but as he glanced across at the strain in Qazai's face he wished he hadn't. It was important for this next stage that they both remain composed.

The car slowed to a halt under the canopy of the hotel, and as he got out Webster looked back along the bridge. He couldn't see the other car, and at this distance in this light no one from the shore could be sure of seeing him, but they had to be quick. Chances were the Audi would stay where it was until it saw them leave, but one of them might try his luck at convincing the guard to let him cross the bridge.

Qazai's driver was handing the bags to a porter; Qazai was looking about him with the lost air of someone who was used to buying hotels like this and who couldn't quite believe that he was now reduced to playing such tawdry games in them. Beyond their car, its hood down and pointing toward them, positively rakish amidst all the glitz, was Constance's Cadillac.

Webster found a young woman in a suit with a name badge and told her that they would be back to check in later and would she please put these bags in Mr. Qazai's suite. Qazai looked troubled.

"We have to go now," said Webster. "You have to go now."

"I need to freshen up."

"You're perfectly fresh. I can't have them see we're not both in your car. Go now," he addressed this half to Qazai, half to his driver, "and drive to Timur's house. Like we agreed. Stay there for ten minutes, then leave for this address." He handed the driver a slip of paper. "Do you know it?" The driver nodded. "Good."

Over Qazai's shoulder he saw Constance's face, beaming. How he wanted a cigarette.

"Have you got that?" Qazai nodded. He looked scared. "Don't worry. They're not about to try anything. And if they do you're sitting in an armored car. They can't shoot you and they can't blow you up. You're going to be fine. If they do something, just drive at a reasonable speed to a busy place. But they're not going to." Qazai took a deep breath, looked Webster in the eye and turned toward the car. "You'll only have to come all the way if I need to flush them out. Chances are I'll have found Rad before you get there and shown him what we've done. Then this will all be over."

Without looking up Qazai nodded, opened the door of the car, nodded again and got in. Webster turned and watched the Mercedes drive in a loop around the concourse and then slowly out into the dusk, its rear lights glowing red. He tried to will the future into being. The Audi would follow Qazai, first to Timur's and then to the rendezvous, where Rad and his men were surely already waiting. There were three places they might be: on the roof of the restaurant or the building next door; in a car on the road outside; or hidden in the darkness of the wasteland opposite, keeping low. All Webster had to do was find Rad, and talk to him before Qazai arrived.

A hand clapped him on the shoulder but he barely glanced around.

"Evening, my scheming little British friend. All going to plan?"

Webster took his cigarettes from his pocket and offered one to Constance, who took it and, producing a lighter, lit Webster's and then his own, his gray beard illuminated by the flame.

"Such as it is," said Webster.

The Mercedes was now in the middle of the bridge, two hundred yards away, gliding slowly behind two other cars. Then its rear lights shone brighter and it came to a stop. For a moment it sat still in the middle of the road.

"Fuck," Webster said, as he saw the rear door open and Qazai get out, looking down at the palm of his hand. "What's he doing?"

"His e-mail, by the look of it," said Constance.

Qazai looked back toward the hotel, frozen, in shock. He ran his hand through his hair, turned to look along the bridge toward the shore, and started walking away, fast and with purpose.

"Oh fuck." Webster flicked away his cigarette and began running, past the taxis and the limousines and the guests, out from under the canopy of the Burj and across the bridge, clutching his envelope, hardly noticing the curious faces passing him and not taking his eyes from Qazai, who was now a hundred yards from the guard's hut and still marching, arms swinging, like a man who has finally had enough.

"Darius!" Webster shouted, his shirt instantly patched with sweat, gaining but too slowly. The word sounded strange on his lips. "Darius! Stop!"

Webster was over the bridge now; the guard by his hut looked for a moment as if he was going to try to stop him but in the end just watched, more puzzled than anything else, as he ran by. Ahead, Qazai was turning into the parking lot, just yards in front now, ignoring his shouts.

"Darius, would you fucking stop? What is it? What are you doing?"

In the near corner of the parking lot, facing them and the road, its lights off, was the Audi, its black windows impenetrable. Webster drew level with Qazai and put his hand on his shoulder.

"Stop."

Qazai glanced around at Webster, handed him something, and carried on walking toward the car. It was his phone. Webster looked down at it, and saw on its screen an image that at first made no sense: a photograph, all dark colors and indistinct forms. He blinked, took it in again and it became clear. It was Ava. She appeared to be lying down; her hands were behind her back, and black tape was wound tightly around her mouth.

For a moment the grainy horror of it held him, until a sharp noise brought him around. Qazai was banging on the window of the Audi, first with his knuckles, then with his fist. He began to shout in Farsi.

Webster ran to him and grabbed his arm.

"Wait."

"Enough waiting." Qazai shrugged his arm free and hammered once more on the glass. "Enough fucking waiting."

Webster looked around him. The hotel guard had appeared at the entrance to the parking lot and was watching with professional interest.

"Darius." Webster stopped his arm again, speaking in a low voice now and leaning in to Qazai. "Darius, stop. People are watching. This is Dubai. In a minute we won't be able to do anything."

Qazai's arm fell by his side and he looked up, his eyes burning with a passion and a noble fear that Webster had not seen there before.

"What do I do?" he said. "Tell me what to do."

Webster checked on the guard, who was standing with his arms crossed waiting for the next development. A colleague had joined him.

"Tell them," said Webster, thinking hard. "Tell them to take us to Rad, or I'll tell that guard that they're armed. Tell them that before their boss kills anybody we have something that he will want to see."

Qazai bent down to the driver's window and said some words in Farsi, just loud enough to get through the black glass. He repeated them, but got no response. As he straightened up, looking to Webster for the next idea, the car's engine started and the central locking clicked.

Webster tried the door, and held it open for Qazai.

THERE WERE TWO MEN in the car, both young, both bearded, both silent. As they drove through the evening traffic neither responded to Qazai's questions, which he repeated in Farsi over and over, obstinately refusing to give up.

How in God's name had they taken Ava? He told himself that when Rad saw how the game had changed he would quickly understand that he was beaten, as perhaps he was; but all along they had been gambling that he understood logic, and with a cold sinking fear Webster saw with great clarity now what the price would be if they had miscalculated.

"Darius," he said, putting his hand on Qazai's arm. Qazai turned to him, and in the yellow light from the street lamp Webster could see that his face was tight with fear. "It's OK. We're still in charge." He tried to look convinced.

They headed toward Deira along Sheikh Zayed Road, and Webster guessed that they were being taken to the original meeting place. Why change a perfect plan? Now that the circumstances had changed he cursed himself for choosing somewhere so perfect for Rad's purposes.

Soon they were crossing the bridge over the creek. Webster watched the other Burj, the immense tower, rise up above the water and resisted the temptation to turn in his seat and look for Constance. Either he was following or he wasn't, and in any case there was little he could do.

Away from the edges of the sky the stars were coming out, weakly reflecting the glitter down below, and as they drove into Deira the roads began to narrow and to clear. Webster remembered the route from his time here with Constance, and he watched the buildings shrink and grow dusty with a sense of inevitability that was nothing like calm. Finally they pulled off the main road and within a hundred yards they were in darkness, sparse street lamps casting only narrow white pools of light.

On the street ahead Webster could see four or five cars parked; he scanned the area for signs of people or movement but could see nothing. To his left were the two low brick buildings, the further hung with the red banners that marked the entrance to the restaurant. On the other side of the road there were two hundred yards of sand and gravel before the bright line of the main road. There could be anybody out there. The driver said a few words to his colleague that Webster couldn't understand and pulled in at the back of the row of cars.

"Wait here," he said, in English, and both men got out, shutting their doors behind them.

Webster watched them walk casually away, not looking at each other, their jackets creased and identical.

Why had they both gone? Did they know they wouldn't run or were they clearing a space? "Get out," he said to Qazai, who looked at him blankly. "We're better out. Come on."

The driver glanced behind him at the sound of the car door shutting, returned Webster's defiant look without expression, and carried on walking. Webster waited for that familiar crack, for that flat, dead sound, but none came; just the sound of traffic way off and an engine being killed somewhere in the dark behind them. He looked at Qazai across the top of the car, and in that moment they were the same: taut, every muscle fixed, afraid. Qazai was shaking his head.

"They won't let her go."

The men had stopped by the last of the parked cars and the driver was bending down to talk through the window. For an age he stood like that, dimly silhouetted against some distant light; then he straightened, the car doors opened, and two men got out, one tall, one short.

The short man closed his door without looking behind him and started walking, ahead of the other three, toward Webster, who moved around to the front of the car, beckoning Qazai to follow him.

He knew it was Rad, but as he drew closer, he realized how accurate his recollection of him had been, in his dreams, in every waking moment: the small, solid frame; the unshaven jaw jutting slightly; the widow's peak of slick black hair. And the sunglasses, which he was wearing even now, making his way surely toward them with a boxer's quiet strut. As he drew close Webster felt his body tense, felt pain—a memory, but real—shear through his thigh, and only with concentration resisted the urge to back away.

Rad stopped a yard away, took off his glasses and stared up into Webster's face, his head cocked ever so slightly on one side. He didn't look at Qazai. In the darkness his eyes glowed pale gray and cold, and Webster again felt possessed by them.

He heard Qazai's voice, sensed that he had stepped toward Rad. "Where is she?"

One of Rad's men moved forward; Rad held Webster's gaze for a last moment and turned to Qazai, taking him in before answering.

"Where I want." He let the words hang in the dark, then looked back at Webster. "Show me."

Webster collected himself. He was now in charge.

"Get in the car," he said.

"No. Here."

Webster shook his head. "You need to see these. And they don't." He looked over Rad's shoulder at his henchmen.

Perfectly still, Rad thought. Then he held his hand up, and without looking around said something in Farsi. The three men hesitated a moment, turned and walked back the way they had come. When they were twenty yards away Rad held his arm in the air, clicked his fingers and they stopped.

"Show me here." He took a phone from his pocket, and lit up its screen.

Webster handed him the documents, watched as Rad took them from the envelope, got them steady in his hand and moved the phone over them. In the greenish light his eyes flitted quickly across each page, scanning them; understanding them.

When he reached the last he put it to the back of the pile and looked up, his lips pressed together. His head turned from Webster to Qazai, then back.

"I am rich." He had lowered his voice; it sounded clear and scratchy in the night air.

"If you want."

"No one will believe."

"They'll believe. The next thing is we start spending it. There'll be a house in the Caribbean with your name on it. Works of art. A very unrevolutionary Ferrari."

Rad's forehead creased but somehow Webster knew that he understood.

"The thing is," he went on, quietly, leaning forward, "that's real money. Sitting there. Everybody believes money. Even your superiors. His clients." He nodded at Qazai. "They all understand how it works. You made a rational decision. You chose to sell what's yours. That's what we all do, surely? Your power over his life. Over my life." He paused. "But they won't like it, will they? No one likes to see a fellow revolutionary making the most of his opportunities. How do you think they'll do it?" Rad's eyes were fast on his. "Hang you from a bridge? Drive you up with some other enemies of the revolution and leave you dangling in space? Or shoot you while you're having a coffee in Paris? Is there anyone else who does that sort of thing? Or is that just you?"

He was talking loudly now, and he felt Qazai's hand on his arm.

Rad snorted, a sort of laugh. He looked off into the darkness, shook his head, and turned back to Webster, rubbing his chin with his hand, squeezing the skin hard as if it wasn't his own.

"I need him." He glanced at Qazai.

Webster shook his head. "No. You let Ava go, we walk away, and you get to keep the money. It's yours. This is a good day for all of us."

Rad's thin lips tightened into a smile. "Understand. He is ours. If not me, someone else take him. If he lives, I die anyway. And someone will come for him."

In the meager light Qazai's face was ghostly.

"I need him," said Rad.

"No," said Webster, his chest tight. "That isn't the deal. You don't negotiate."

Rad breathed a deep, satisfied breath, filling his lungs. He handed the documents to Webster, and spoke to Qazai with the air of someone who isn't about to say more.

"You. Or her."

Qazai turned his head to Webster, not in appeal but simply to confirm that there was nowhere left to go. Webster had never felt so helpless. He thought of Lock, just after he had been shot, lying in the snow on his back, a clean black hole in his coat over his heart. He had no ideas. No schemes. But Qazai's eyes told him he didn't need any; that this was the end.

Qazai took a step forward.

"I need to know she's safe."

Rad looked at him for a moment, then took his phone from his pocket and dialed a number; in the quiet Webster could hear it ring once. After a few words in Farsi, Rad passed it to Qazai.

"Hello? Hello?" He held the phone away from his ear and was about to say something to Rad when a voice, thin and distorted, sounded on the line. "Hello? Ava. Ava. Where are you? Are you OK?" Webster watched Qazai listening to his daughter, his spare hand pressed against his ear to hear better. He looked old, drawn, dignified. "Where are you? . . . Oh, thank God. Thank God . . . Find a taxi. Get home . . . No, I'm in Dubai . . . I don't know, my angel. I don't know."

Rad took the phone from him and ended the call. Qazai was a head taller than him, upright now, braced.

Rad gave Webster a final look. "Leave the money where it is," he said, and making sure that they understood each other, turned and walked toward his men.

Qazai watched him go, and Webster watched Qazai.

"I'm sorry," he said.

"No need," said Qazai, and held out his hand.

"I'll do what I can," said Webster as they shook.

"There's no need," said Qazai, and with a single, deliberate nod followed Rad. Car doors opened and closed; headlights flared on; and Webster watched the blacked-out windows pass him into the night.

Footsteps crunched on gravel behind him, and he realized with a sting of fear that he wasn't alone: the two men who had driven him here were walking toward him. There was no one else in sight. As he watched them approach he could hear far off the sound of a car's engine revving deeply in a low gear.

He moved away from them, backing toward the buildings and the restaurant. But the men didn't look at him. They reached their car, opened the doors and climbed in; the engine started, and they pulled out, turning at him quickly. Webster, dazed, stepped clumsily backward, waiting to be hit, and took a moment to recognize the shining chrome and black of Constance's car, which had driven up at speed and was now shielding him from the Iranians. For a second or two the two cars simply sat there, Constance with his arm on the sill staring down the Audi, all of a yard away from him, until it reversed a little and with a burst of acceleration that made the gravel spit under its tires, sped away.

"Good thing they didn't touch the car." Constance was looking behind him with his arm across the passenger seat.

Webster ignored him and got in. "Go. Turn around." Constance didn't respond. "Let's go."

Constance slowly shook his head.

"Qazai was in the first car."

"You want to give them another chance to kill you?" Constance turned to him, his eyes grave.

"They weren't going to."

"Sure."

"Turn the car around. Fletcher, I mean it."

"Uh-uh. No. You can't save that man from his sins. This is his share."

"They'll kill him."

"Maybe that's what he needs," said Constance, his arms crossed, his head like marble in the gray light.

29.

THE MOMENT WEBSTER HEARD that Qazai had died, he sent everything he knew to Constance, with instructions to pass it on immediately to his friends; and because he didn't wholly trust that it would reach them, he sent a second copy through Hammer to Virginia.

It had been quick, at least; so quick that Webster couldn't help but believe that the plan had already been in place. Perhaps, perhaps not. He was done with overthinking things.

If the news agencies were right, Qazai's plane had flown from Dubai to Syria, landing in Damascus some time around midnight. It was thought that he was alone, but no journalist had yet checked the passenger manifest. What was known was that he had booked a suite at the Four Seasons, eaten breakfast there alone on Sunday morning, and then taken a taxi to Bab Touma, in the east of the city. At a little after ten, according to the state news agency, shots were heard inside a carpet shop near the Church of Saint Francis, and when police arrived they had found Qazai in an armchair, shot twice through the head, three cups of tea still warm on the table. The owner of the shop was discovered hiding upstairs, though whether from the gunmen or the police was not clear.

Webster had received the news on the train to Truro: a call from Hammer that he let go to voicemail, and then an e-mail with links to the first agency articles. He read them once, asked Hammer to send the file, switched off his phone and sat with his eyes closed, imagining the strange, late courage required for Qazai to walk knowingly to his death; seeing him being poured his tea as he waited for Rad to arrive, still beautifully dressed, still outwardly the great man. And his mind? Was it full of fear? Contrition? Or some growing sense of peace?

He thought of Ava. If she hadn't heard, she would soon; there was no need for him to call again. He had tried to speak to her from Constance's house as he waited for his flight, but had only reached her voicemail, and for an hour or two had worried that Rad had betrayed them, taking another Qazai as his prize. But just before midnight she had rung him, anxious but composed, and wanting to know why he, and not her father, had called so many times. She had known the answer—had feared, in fact, from the moment she was taken, that she was part of an exchange—and had said little in response, reconciled to the news but still not equal to it.

So the sacrifice had been made. He found himself considering the hundred practical questions that Ava would now have to answer. Where to bury the body, if she was given that choice. How to tackle the journalists when they started calling, and how much, eventually, to tell the world. What to do with the money that remained. He would have liked to have helped her, but could not. He was not responsible in the end: not for Qazai, or his daughter.

BY THE TIME HE REACHED Helford it was late. He told George Black to stand down, watched the four anonymous saloon cars leaving up the track until their lights had stopped glowing red in the gloom, and walked through the quiet and the darkening trees down to his parents' house. The sky was clear, and the light from the moon shone bright and gray on the estuary.

Only Elsa was still up. What he wanted her to understand more than anything else was that he had never meant to bring danger into their lives, but that once it was there his only choice had been to drive it out again. It had been vanity, he told her, and he was finished with it. Elsa listened with professional detachment, coolly pointing out the inconsistencies in his account, making him feel the weight of his recklessness. But behind her anger she was as relieved to see him as he was to see her; he knew it, and it gave him hope.

After a time their words ran out, and while the house slept they walked through the garden down to the little stone quay where the air was warm and still and the tide high enough for them to bathe their feet in the water, and there they sat in silence, not reconciled but together, until the sky began to lighten in the east.

AVAILABLE FROM PENGUIN

The Silent Oligarch

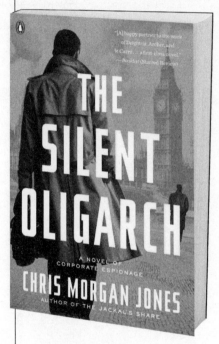

ISBN 978-0-14-312298-2

This **bone-chilling** first novel introduces Benjamin Webster, a London intelligence agent hired to pursue a money launderer and to expose the dealings of a shadowy Russian oligarch. Racing between London and Moscow, Kazakstan and the Caymans, this beautifully written thriller explores a threatening world where private spy agencies battle for dominance, governments eagerly defer to the highest bidder, and colossal wealth is collected through shadowy networks of companies. *The Silent Oligarch* is a heart-pounding and unforgettable novel of our time.

"A happy partner to the work of Deighton, Archer, and le Carré . . . carried on craftily understated prose that approaches cold poetry . . . a first-class novel." —Booklist *(starred review)*

PENGUIN BOOKS

FICTION MORGANJONES

Morgan Jones, Chris.
The Jackal's share

                                NWEST
R4000885167

NORTHWEST
Atlanta-Fulton Public Library